CAROLE NELSON DOUGLAS

"You never know what madness and mayhem you'll find in Douglas's mysteries, but you can be sure it will be wild, witty, and utterly irresistible."
—*The San Francisco Chronicle*

"A saucy style and a delicious sense of humor."
—*The New York Times*

Raves for all the richly witty Delilah Street novels

Dancing With Werewolves

"A wonderfully written story with a unique take on the paranormal."
—*New York Times* bestselling author Kelley Armstrong

"Douglas spices the action with fabulous characters. . . . Readers will eagerly await the sequel."
—*Publishers Weekly* (starred review)

"Captivating . . . some of the most unique supporting characters around."
—Darque Reviews

"An entertaining urban fantasy that rivals that of Kim Harrison and Kelley Armstrong. The protagonist jumps from the frying pan into the fire as she tries to stay one step ahead of her enemies and those who want to use her. . . ."
—Alternative Worlds

"An amazingly rich world of shadows come to life. . . ."

—Award-winning author Nancy Pickard

"A creepy and dangerous new world, where telling friend from foe is not so easy. A wild new ride!"

—*RT Book Reviews* (4 stars)

Brimstone Kiss

"Filled with kisses and kick-ass action. . . . Douglas's dishy style complements the twisty plot."

—*Publishers Weekly* (starred review)

"The most outrageous and outlandish cast of supporting characters this side of the Wizard of Oz. . . ."

—SciFiGuy

"The plot thickens and the tension builds and you find yourself carried along for the ride. . . . Douglas has a way of drawing you in and keeping you entertained."

—SF Revu

"Another masterpiece."

—Romance Junkies

Vampire Sunrise

"Douglas tells one heck of a good story."

—SF Revu

"Delilah's street smarts, intelligence, and self-assurance make her a female heroine that you're sure to love."

—Best Fantasy Stories

"With plenty of twists, *Vampire Sunrise* is a roller coaster doing loops with each spin accelerating the ride."

—Alternative Worlds

Silver Zombie

Don't miss any of Delilah Street's adventures!

Dancing with Werewolves
Brimstone Kiss
Vampire Sunrise
Silver Zombie

Available now from Pocket Juno Books

CAROLE NELSON DOUGLAS

VIRTUAL VIRGIN

POCKET BOOKS

New York London Toronto Sydney New Delhi

Pocket Books
A Division of Simon & Schuster, Inc.
1230 Avenue of the Americas
New York, NY 10020

This book is a work of fiction. Names, characters, places, and incidents either are products of the author's imagination or are used fictitiously. Any resemblance to actual events or locales or persons, living or dead, is entirely coincidental.

Copyright © 2011 by Carole Nelson Douglas

First Juno Books/Pocket Books paperback edition December 2011

JUNO BOOKS and colophon are trademarks of Wildside Press LLC used under license by Simon & Schuster, Inc., the publisher of this work.

POCKET and colophon are registered trademarks of Simon & Schuster, Inc.

For information about special discounts for bulk purchases, please contact Simon & Schuster Special Sales at 1-866-506-1949 or business@simonandschuster.com.

The Simon & Schuster Speakers Bureau can bring authors to your live event. For more information or to book an event contact the Simon & Schuster Speakers Bureau at 1-866-248-3049 or visit our website at www.simonspeakers.com.

Cover illustration by Gordon Crabb

Manufactured in the United States of America

10   9   8   7   6   5   4   3   2   1

ISBN: 978-1-4391-6779-3
ISBN: 978-1-4391-6780-9 (ebook)

For Marisela Escobedo Ortiz,
heroine and martyr of Juarez

VIRTUAL
VIRGIN

Meet Me, Delilah Street

EVERYONE HAS FAMILY issues, but my issues are that I don't *have* any family. My new business card reads "Delilah Street, Paranormal Investigator," but my old personal card could have read "Delilah Street, Unadoptable Orphan."

I was supposedly named after the street where I was found abandoned as an infant in Wichita, Kansas. (I guess I should just thank God and DC Comics it wasn't Lois Lane.) I've googled and groggled (the drinking person's search engine) the World Wide Web for Delilah Streets and not a single bloody one of them shows up in Wichita.

Whoever my forebears, they gave me the Black Irish, Snow White coloring that is catnip to vampires: corpse-pale skin and dead-of-night black hair. By age twelve I was fighting off aspiring juvie rapists with retractable fangs and body odor that mixed blood, sweat, and semen. Really made me enjoy being a girl.

My growing-up years of group homes are history now that I'm twenty-four and on my own. I had a good job reporting the paranormal beat for Wichita's WTCH-TV— until the station's jealous weather witch forecaster forced me out.

Now I'm a freelance investigator in wicked, mysterious post–Millennium Revelation Las Vegas. Vegas was wicked, of course, long before the turn of the twenty-first century brought all the bogeymen and women of myth and legends out of the closet and into human lives and society. Now, in 2013, Vegas is crawling with vamps and half-weres and all-werewolf mobs and celebrity zombies and who knows what else.

My ambitions on hitting town were simple.

One, staying alive. (Being turned into an immortal vampire doesn't count.)

Two, being able to make love in the missionary position without having panic attacks. (Whoever thought someone would *aim* for the missionary position?) Position hadn't been an issue until recently and neither had sex, until I finally found a man I *want* to make love with, ex-FBI guy Ricardo Montoya—aka the Cadaver Kid. He's tall, dark, handsome, Hispanic, and my twenty-four-hour partner. Scratch this one off the list. Phobia solved. I am now fully adjustable and ready to rock and roll.

And, three, tracking down Lilith Quince—my spitting image—to find out if she is a twin, double, clone, or simulacrum. Or if she is even alive. Seeing her/me being autopsied on *Crime Scene Instincts V: Las Vegas* one rerun-TV night in Wichita brought me to Sin City in the first place.

Lucky me, Lilith became the most desirable corpse ever featured on the internationally franchised show. When that *CSI* episode made Lilith Quince into a macabre international sex symbol, it inadvertently made me, Delilah Street, a wanted woman. And not necessarily wanted alive, but as the naked and dead image of another woman. So not me.

The *CSI* cameras showed a discreet maggot camping out in a nostril that held a tiny blue topaz stud like my very own, so Lilith's corpse, dubbed "Maggie," became the It Girl of 2013: Maggie dolls and merchandise are hot and so are bootleg Maggie still pictures, outtakes, and my hide, if anyone could snag it—dead or alive. One werewolf mobster almost did already.

At least ambition number four is now also a done deal: Identifying the embracing skeletons Ric and I discovered in Vegas's Sunset Park just after I hit town and just before the town hit me back, hard.

I discovered more than Ric and corpses in Sunset Park. I found an ally who has heavenly blue eyes and is seriously gray and hairy. That's my dog, Quicksilver. He's a wolfhound-wolf cross I saved from death at the pound. He returns the favor with fang, claw, and warm, paranormally talented tongue.

(I have a soft spot for dogs—especially since Achilles, my valiant little white dust-mop Lhasa apso in Wichita, died from blood poisoning after biting a vampire anchorman who was trying to bite me. Achilles's ashes rest in a dragon-decorated jar on my mantel. Lhasa apsos are a Tibetan breed, Grasshopper, so I haven't given up the ghost on him.)

Oh, where that mantel is might be of interest. It's in the Enchanted Cottage on the Hector Nightwine estate. Hector rents the place to me cheap because, as producer of the many worldwide *CSI* franchises, he's presumably guilty of offing my possible twin on national TV. Hector doesn't really have a conscience, just a profit motive. He's banking on my finding Lilith or becoming her for his enduring financial benefit.

The only thing Hector and I have in common is loving old black-and-white films. The Enchanted Cottage is a setting from a 1945 movie of that name and I suspect it's supplied with the wicked stepmother's mirror from *Snow White*. Although it's been mum about my degree of "fairness" so far, I do see things in it besides me.

The most complex beings in my brave new world are the CinSims. Cinema Simulacrums are created by blending fresh zombie bodies illegally imported from Mexico with classic black-and-white film characters. The resulting "live" personas are wholly owned entertainment entities leased to various Vegas enterprises.

Hector and Ric blame the mysterious Immortality Mob for the brisk business in zombie CinSims, but can't prove it even exists. Hector wants to wrest the CinSims from the mob's control into his. Ric aches to stop the traffic in illegally imported zombies. It's personal—he was forced to work in the trade as a child.

I'd like to help them both out, and not just because I'm a former investigative TV reporter used to crusading against human and unhuman exploitation. My own freedom is threatened by various merciless and sometimes downright repellent factions bent on making life after the Millennium Revelation literal Hell.

Luckily, I have some new, off-the-chart abilities simmering myself, most involving silver—from the silver nitrate in black-and-white film strips to sterling silver to mirrors and reflective surfaces in general.

Which reminds me of one more sorta sidekick: a freaky shape-changing lock of hair from the albino rock star who owns the Inferno Hotel. The guy goes by three names: "Christophe" for business; "Cocaine" when fronting his Seven Deadly Sins band in the persona of Pride, and "Snow" to his intimates. He seems to consider me one of them, but no way do I want to be.

While thinking of my lost Achilles, I made the mistake of touching a long white lock of Snow's hair he'd sent as a mocking gift. The damn thing became a sterling silver familiar no jeweler's saw or torch can remove from my body. Since it transforms into different pieces of often-protective jewelry, it's undeniably handy at times. I consider it a talisman-cum-leech.

That attitude sums up my issues with the rock star-hotelier, who habitually enslaved groupies with a onetime mosh pit Brimstone Kiss.

Then I discovered *why* those post-concert kisses are so bloody irresistible . . . and Snow forced me to submit to his soul-stealing smooch in exchange for his help in saving Ric from being vamped to death. This kiss-off standoff between us is *not* over.

Now Snow owns a prized new CinSim, another gal famous for being confined in a glass coffin like Snow White, only she's a silent film hottie who's part virgin saint, part sexy silver robot, and part Babylonian love goddess. Wouldn't you know my partner, Ric, is responsible for raising this *Three Faces of Eve* babe who will endanger all our lives.

Not to worry. I'm on the case. I've been called a "silver medium," but I won't let anyone define me or my world, or stop me from exposing every dirty supernatural secret in Las Vegas, if necessary, to find out who I really am, and who's being bad and who's being good in my new Millennium Revelation neighborhood.

Chapter One

THE CADAVER KID isn't such a kid anymore and he isn't in the FBI anymore either.

Yet here he stands in Quantico, Virginia, a guest lecturer with an attentive audience.

And there's still a cadaver on tap. And it's horny.

Death and sex, that's where it's always at in criminal matters.

Behind the Kid, an eight-foot-wide screen displays a decomposed human corpse that would make any *CSI* TV show producer proud.

Its muted gray, black, and beige tones don't offer the graphic punch of color. The photo was obviously shot at night. Still, the grinning skull shows a pair of small, ram-like horns, two ribbed ridges growing back from where the hairline would start.

Welcome to post–Millennium Revelation crime scene issues. It's not just *who* the corpse du jour is, but *what*.

I'm sitting at the back of the room, the Cadaver Kid's anonymous but proud significant other. I'd been introduced as a "consulting partner" when the senior agent in charge had escorted us in. He'd found us quite the "dramatic pair."

This is my partner's solo show, though, and I'm happy to play wallpaper. I'm wearing my dullest TV reporter navy-blue suit, chosen to blend in here, but when we're a duo my Snow White looks are the cream in Ric's rich, Latino coffee-bar coloring.

Besides, he looks so great in the foreground.

Ricardo Montoya left the FBI in his midtwenties for freelance consulting work and landed a reunion lecturer spot before he's even pushing thirty, but he's cool with not being part of the dark-suit-and-tie crowd anymore.

No monotone façade that reads "FBI Agent" for him. His usual pale tropical-weight suit would look good on Brad Pitt. It also proclaims he's from a hot climate and a hot crime town, Las Vegas, Nevada,

So do the Lucchese cowboy boots whose pointy roach-stomping toes peek discreetly from his pant legs. They warn he might have a switchblade or two on him to handle a motorcycle gang on instant notice.

He's been introduced today as a former agent "phenomenally gifted" at finding buried corpses. Hence the nickname.

The Cadaver Kid surveys the large conference room converted to a mini-auditorium in his honor.

Once the Kid had to keep his methods secret from his FBI colleagues. Now the agency has lightened up and smartened up. Ric's been invited here to confess just how "phenomenally gifted" the FBI's legendary Cadaver Kid was. I get to watch.

"We all know the Three D's of Finding Bodies 101," Ric begins. "Directions, Dogs, Digging."

A knowing chuckle shivers through the audience, all models of the modern FBI agent, serious, dark-suited people in their early twenties. They're relaxed enough to show a sense of humor. Good. He's going to take them into the horror side soon enough.

He paces like an attorney in court, keeping eye contact with the most people possible. "The perpetrator or a witness or the investigation team itself supplies Directions to where the body might be."

Ric picks a remote control off the desk. A dark, woodsy site fills the screen. "If the area is large and success isn't forthcoming, we bring in the cadaver Dog teams." Another slide of dogs at work, oddly resembling truffle-hunting pigs in France. "And then we Dig."

In the next image Ric clicks to the screen to focus on a body freshly pulled from an excavated hole.

The audience has been nodding along with Ric, not nodding off. He's showing procedure as usual but each body and every "dig" is different and fascinating for different reasons. I can hear the unspoken question. "When will we see a close-up of those weird horns?"

Ric steps around the tabletop lectern. "To find bodies when I worked with the FBI, I used a fourth D." He holds up an odd object, a fallen branch from the thick brush that so often surrounds body dumping grounds.

"A *Dowsing* rod," Ric announces, being definitely dramatic in his own right.

I study the audience as their murmuring profiles turn to one another. Polite frowns indicate attention but not full understanding. Yet.

"This fork of willow wood," Ric says with a smile, "was the Cadaver Kid's secret weapon for all those remarkable body finds I made while with the Bureau. Even though it was long after the Millennium Revelation, my superiors called it 'gifted profiling.' This small forked stick is my trade secret. It was all I used and absolutely free for the taking."

Now they laugh softly.

"Let's see if there are any buried bodies beneath this conference room."

"Ooooh," the audience coos in spooky unison. Somebody hums the iconic *Twilight Zone* theme music. "The truth is out there, Mulder," someone else shouts.

Ric grins. "This just a demonstration. I promise no corpses will be harmed."

His wrists twist, forcing his hands and the Y end of the implement downward.

"Here I'm obviously moving the dowsing or divining rod myself. In the wild, I use my strength to hold it level until some possibly chemical-magnetic force rotates the wood in my hands so forcibly I can't keep it from spinning until the end stem points due *Down*. One last *D*."

Everyone chuckles. Are they solid *D* students now?

"I'll paraphrase an infamous politician, ladies and gentlemen. I am not a water witch. That's what dowsers are sometimes called. My family was adept at finding water. I dowsed up dead lizards instead, not a valued gift in the desert."

Murmurs stir the crowd as people consult one another on how much of this to believe.

"The force is really undeniable," Ric continues, now sounding like Luke Skywalker from *Star Wars*. "Perhaps we can hold a future talk at the Body Farm so you all can get some hands-on experience. I can work through anyone, true believer or skeptic.

"The Millennium Revelation, as you know and are now allowed to admit and use in your profession, intensified any borderline paranormal abilities ordinary humans had. Its major effect was bringing *un*humans out of their protective shadows and into our twenty-first-century lives in many roles . . . unsuspected neighbor, possible ally, victim of hate crimes or violator of the law, enemy of the state, and perpetrator of crimes against humanity undreamed of."

Ric leans against the front of the desk, the object in his hands now the focus of every eye. The rod reminds me of the chopped-off forked tongue of a giant snake. He's holding a branch of the fork in each fist with the stem of the Y aimed at the audience like a gun barrel.

"I call on Miss Delilah Street to stand and testify. She knows I only needed to touch the backs of her hands on a dowsing rod to dredge up the dead."

I stand.

A wolf whistle shrieks from somewhere and another anonymous guy calls, "The pretty shill in the audience, Montoya. Cheap trick."

I can see Ric smolder from fifty feet away at someone inadvertently calling me a "cheap trick," but I can speak for myself.

"Can you argue with his FBI record?" I ask. "I'm a former award-winning TV reporter, no shill and no patsy, and I don't believe in water dowsing."

That gets the group mumbling again, bewildered that I'm not supporting the speaker who'd introduced me.

"But I do believe in dead dowsing," I go on, "because the Vegas police dug up the seventy-five-year-old bones of an embracing couple on the park site where"—How am I going to put this delicately for a mostly male crowd? Not possible—"where I saw and felt the dowsing rod act as if it had a twenty-mule team pulling it."

The mental picture of the mules distracts attention from how I saw and felt the dowsing rod perform, which is just too, too phallic for bureaucrats. The audience quiets as I sit back down.

"Most authorities," Ric reminds them, "most *people* don't believe anyone can water dowse, or dowse for precious ores and stones, much less the dead. Traditionally dowsers favor certain tree woods, like willow, but most can also use bent metal rods, glass, or improvise with a coat hanger if necessary. I've even dowsed with barbed wire."

A mass intake of breath makes the room seem to sigh. The audience has made the leap to realizing how painful that would be . . . barbed wire spinning in your palms so hard and fast the point of the Y aims down.

Ric nods. "Tore my hands up on that occasion, ladies and gentlemen, but the blood is necessary for stage two of my facility. When my blood drops to the ground where the dowsing rod has indicated it harbors a body, the dead will rise."

Actual gasps fill the room.

Ric clicks a 3-D night scene into life on the screen behind him. At first glance, to me, it looks like a still from the first great zombie movie, the black-and-white *Night of the Living Dead*.

"This is a night shot of a desert ranch I call the Lazy Z," he explains. "I'm not presenting a day scene because I don't want any landmarks to betray its location. These are zombies I've reclaimed from the traffic in unhumans across the Mexican border."

A horse ambles through the corral, led by a poky cow-poke.

"Is the horse a zombie?" a smart-ass voice calls from the audience.

"No. Horses calm feral zombies. Consider the ranch a rehab facility for the supernaturally abused. Here's one reason I've come here today. I know how skeptical people who haven't fought in the trenches of the border wars the US and Mexican governments are waging on drug cartels gone demonic can be. Still, you might have seen traces of a new and hidden force on the crime front, the Immortality Mob at work in your own cases."

Now the murmurs are serious, questioning.

"Some of you might have borderline abilities of your

own that will aid in your work. I've come before you, risking ridicule, to ask you to merely open your minds. It starts with inhuman traffickers smuggling zombies like those I showed you into the US from Mexico. Next comes a secret process to combine them with figures from black-and-white film. Only the silver nitrate in vintage film can animate zombies and that may be a scientific lead. Las Vegas is the nexus of this latest illegal trade."

"Isn't it always?" someone yelled. "Viva Las Vegas."

Ric clicks again. The screen switches from still images to moving ones. "Here's some of the Immortality Mob's handiwork. You may recognize a few favorite movie sleuths."

I sure do, and settle back in my seat with a nostalgic sigh as the luminous black-and-white scene plays onscreen.

Nick Charles, in his white tie and dark dinner jacket, is leaning on the Inferno Hotel bar, handing a martini to his sophisticated wife, Nora, whose plunging neckline draws a lot more wolf whistles from this crowd than my buttoned-up navy-blue career blazer.

"I deduced where the body is buried, darling," Nicky drawls, "but I need Asta to dig it up."

"I am not having Eau de Corpse on Asta and all over our apartment." Nora is her delightfully feisty self. "You'll have to take Asta to the groomer after the dog does its dirty work for you, and *you'll* need to visit the groomer too, or there'll be no treats for the both of you."

Even as chuckles echo through the room, a white blur passing in front of the bar obscures the famous film couple.

"Pay no attention to the man in the white suit," Ric says quickly. "He wasn't supposed to be in the film clip."

Snow? The Inferno Hotel owner and albino rock star had been caught on film, like a ghost? What is that about?

Why is Snow showing up in a conference room in Quantico, Virginia?

Ric turns to face the screen. "And, by the way, in real life that horned skull you saw first off belonged to a half-demon CPA. Okay. This is . . . an example of how the Immortality Mob manipulates illusion and reality for its own profit." The film jerks, breaks, resumes.

More wolf whistles. The robot from the silent film *Metropolis* stands front and center, a curvaceous silver metal woman robot out of a *Playboy* centerfold.

Ric hasn't revealed the truly fantastic side of his dead-dowsing gifts . . . not just raising the dead but raising a dead actress off the movie screen in her robot likeness.

I want to stand up and explain how it's all done through mirrors and the power of silver, the silver that can vanquish werewolves and even vampires sometimes and can now walk characters off the silver screen.

Once again I watch Ric raise Brigitte Helm, a dead silent-screen actress in the form of the robot costume that had been molded to her body.

People are used to 3-D movies, but seeing this blend of human and machine walking off the screen into their midst without the aid of the usual eye devices is even too much for FBI agents. They run screaming, overturning chairs in their fever to escape the room. My hands lift to block the painful light from the huge screen, from the sight of the Second Coming of the Silver Zombie.

I guess the Cadaver Kid has more than made his point.

"Ow!" RIC SAID beside me, suddenly.

At least he recognized my existence again.

"Delilah! Your flailing elbow almost put my eye out."

A small lamp clicked on from the direction of his voice.

I stared at his at his naked chest, at his eyes blinking in the light—one espresso-brown, one silver if not disguised by a brown contact lens, as it wasn't at night—and looked around.

Oh. We're not in Quantico anymore, unless an FBI conference room has a double bed.

What's new? Irma, my in-board invisible friend, has kicked into On in my head again.

"This isn't Quantico," I said slowly.

"I hope not." Ric's pupils widened as they got used to the light. "You had a major dream?" he asked.

"Yeah."

"Bad?"

"No. Good, I guess. At least at first."

He braced his head on his hand to turn to me and block the harshest rays of the bedside lamplight. "We're in a motel in Cold Creek, Colorado, Del, one that's a teeny bit more upscale than the one we stayed at on our way out to Kansas from Vegas. We'll be home late tomorrow. Everything okay?"

"Yeah. Maybe I get different dreams now that I can lie on my back."

"I gotta say that's nice. We can finally sleep and, ah, do other things any which way we want. You've pretty much ditched that phobia against lying on your back now that you know what caused it."

"Ye-es. Except having Family Services implant an unnecessary intrauterine device that morphed to coat my pelvic bones and organs in sterling silver makes me feel like an unnatural woman. Like the semiBionic Woman."

I don't mention "like a dime-store Silver Zombie."

His hand burrowed under the covers to find my left

hip bone and swiped across like you would on a computer screen, smooth and fast, to the opposite hip bone.

Umm, amorous, Irma moaned.

He got the reaction he wanted. I felt the silver familiar's thin hip chain writhing in anticipation and my fingers found a new charm tickling my temporary belly-button ring . . . in the Y-shaped form of a dowsing rod.

"You feel like *my* woman in the middle of the night," Ric said. "Maybe that imported metal only makes your pelvis stronger, makes your, uh, reactions more intense, especially in this new flat-on-your-back position. We should test that theory."

Even the silver familiar had been won over by our sexy FBI lecturer. Unfortunately, we'd be back to unfinished business all too soon in Las Vegas.

"We have a lot to do when we get back tomorrow," I fretted.

"Such as?" Ric was totally awake now.

"You need to find out more about that silver she-devil you waltzed off the movie screen into our lives. Snow grabbed her and the film she came in on and flew out of Wichita, leaving us to make the three-day drive back to Vegas."

"She's his property."

"But your responsibility. I don't get why you're eager to wash your hands of her."

"They'd rather be on you."

Seriously amorous, Irma noted.

"I've got issues of my own to follow up on when we get home," I pointed out.

"Such as?"

"I can't let a werewolf mobster's daughter keep me out of mirror-world just because I tried to stop her from doing harm and she escaped."

"You can't escape Loretta Cicereau and I can't escape the Silver Zombie, is that what you're saying?"

"Right."

"I don't see any trace of either of them here and now."

He hadn't had my nightmare either. Loretta had been one of the embracing skeletons we found on the day we'd met.

"So," Ric said, "I see no reason not to take advantage of the fact that you woke me up."

"Quicksilver?" I asked.

"Out and about. Your dog likes night patrols, you know that. So do I."

And I did too.

He nuzzled my neck under my hair, a green light to foreplay that would implant a red-hot and blue hickey on my pale skin. We'd be back home tending to far less interesting unfinished business all too soon.

So I gave up worrying about robot dreams and vengeful ghosts.

But I knew I'd have to look myself in the mirror as soon as I got back to Vegas.

Chapter Two

SOME PEOPLE HAVE trouble facing themselves in the mirror, but just seeing my own image looking back would be a treat, even if I looked like hell.

Trouble is, I'm as likely to view a kleptomaniac doppelganger named Lilith as my own face and body.

The differences between me, Delilah Street, and Lilith Quince are . . . not visible to the naked eye. Not even mine. I've often wondered if even Ric would be able to tell between me and my shadow twin.

Really, I don't ever want to have to find that out.

Meanwhile, here I am, the morning after that harrowing but liberating road trip to my hometown, back in Vegas and mirror-gazing again. There's lots of unfinished business between me and my mirror. Lucky me. I've made enemies in two dimensions.

Right now, though, I'm seeing only my own face for a change.

What I see is what you get. I stand five eight barefoot, pushing six feet in my sling-back heels, the vintage shoe I'm wearing at the moment. What I weigh is not anybody's business, especially Lilith's. My India ink-black shoulder-brushing hair is just long enough to put up for wet work. My skin is so white I don't tan *or* singe in the sunshine; I sear.

No, I'm not a vampire. So let me inter that idea and slam the final nail in that coffin.

My eyes are the electric-blue color that halos an acetylene torch flame, always a dead giveaway to my identity, so I sometimes use gray contact lenses.

I used to loathe my pallid Black Irish skin, partly because tans were hot in the Wichita farm country where I grew up; mainly because I thought dead-white skin attracted vampires. Being an ex-TV reporter of the paranormal, I've tried that airbrush foundation all the newscasters switched to when HDTV came in, but I look even more made-up, laid out, and corpse-ish with that fake instant tan on my face.

During that recent road trip home to Kansas, I was finally convinced my coloring is pretty cool, after all. Now that I call Las Vegas home–where talking, moving Cinema Simulacrums from old black-and-white films are celebrity tourist attractions—hey, I'm three-quarters of the way there if I simply rock my gray contact lenses and add black lipstick.

My guy likes my lips glossed red and cherry-flavored, though, and loves to put it on me and lick it off, which makes for inventive nights. At the memory, I ran a fingertip over my top lip, feeling so Marilyn Monroe. If I could only lose my obsession with this phantom skank, Lilith, in my mirror, life might be almost perfect. I closed my eyes, rerunning the top five horizontal moments of the past week's getaway, leaving out the rotting zombies on speed and the weather witches riding lightning bolts.

"Do we feel pretty?" a snarky voice asked.

I had to decide whether I was hearing my internal secret pal since grade school, Irma, or if I was talking back to myself in the mirror again.

Sure enough, my reflected lips were moving.

"Great to be here in Vegas again," Lilith said, stretching her bare arms overhead to show off a clingy tank top with silver studs spelling "Vegas Sucks" above a large skull-and-crossbones strategically placed to frame our boobs.

"Goth is so over," I told her.

Lilith loves to flaunt her Bad Girl tastes when she isn't dolling herself up in exactly what I'm wearing at the moment, which is low-rise seventies bell-bottom jeans and a midriff-baring top with ruffled sleeves to the elbow. *Ay caramba*. *Olé*. I'm a vintage girl.

"You must be meeting Ric later," she said. "He goes for the belly-dancer exposure."

"Vegas is hot," I answered demurely.

"So is Ric," Lilith answered. "I should pay his mirror a visit."

"Can you? Without me there?"

"*Argh*. You there? No way. I'm a doer, not a viewer."

"Then, what are you doing here?"

"Checking out the old wardrobe to see if you're wearing anything worth stealing. It's my favorite hobby."

The feeling was not mutual. I was tiring of these two-way mirror conversations with myself, of always seeing Lilith on the other side of something. She's haunted me in mirrors since I saw her being autopsied on *CSI V* one TV night last spring.

I did come to Las Vegas to find her, but I'd expected a physical being or a tombstone, not a will-o'-the-wisp on silvered glass.

"Lilah . . . Ric *does* know about me, right?" she asked.

"Yes." I made my answer short and sharp.

Ric had only found out about my secret mirror-shadow days ago. With all the follow-up on the literal fallout before we left Wichita, we hadn't discussed several revelations that could affect our separate lives, and maybe our love life. I particularly was carrying my usual invisible knapsack of guilt.

"Where is Wonder Rod-boy?" Lilith prodded.

I debated whether or not to tell her I'd sent him off to see the wizard, Christophe, aka Snow, the Inferno Hotel's albino rock-star owner, to view a movie. That would be hard to explain. You had to have been there.

WE'D MADE IT back from Wichita and I was dropping Ric off at his house for the night before ferrying Quicksilver and me back to the Enchanted Cottage on the Hector Nightwine estate.

"You should call on Snow first thing tomorrow," I told Ric, "and get him to show you the *Metropolis* film that features your new virtual girlfriend."

"You're not jealous of an old-time movie CinSim that's more a metal costume than flesh?"

"No. Might as well be jealous of Robby the Robot."

"Tomorrow morning? Christophe's Inferno Hotel penthouse? Without you to referee?" Ric had asked.

"Right," I'd said. "He owes us, and besides, Snow's such a film nut he'll gladly sit through all almost-three hours of the restored version with you. *Metropolis* is his prize acquisition. I'd be excess baggage."

Irma had hastened to jump in. *And "baggage" is exactly what Snow would call you after your latest joint adventure—or should I say "assignation"?—in one of his domains in Wichita.*

"What will you do?" Ric asked before I could forget myself and tell Irma aloud that it was an accident, not an assignation.

"I, ah, have some unfinished business from Wichita to settle."

"Yeah?"

"Yeah. I'm taking your shrink foster-mama's advice and facing some of my own demons without even having to leave the Enchanted Cottage."

"So, after a night without you, tomorrow morning I'm indentured to view an almost-three-hour-long silent film from 1927." Ric sighed.

"There's a stirring, newly recorded symphonic sound track."

"Watching it with Christophe is not my idea of a film date." He never used the nickname I did: Snow.

"I know, but Snow's the only one in the world who owns the long-lost, utterly complete version of the film. You'll be amazed by how scary-relevant that Holy Grail of filmdom called *Metropolis* is to our lives and times," I said in farewell.

"I hope there's popcorn," Ric grumbled.

"And you'll see the Silver Zombie again, offscreen and in person."

"Not a draw, Delilah. She freaks me out. I'm not the Immortality Mob or a CinSim collector like Christophe and Hector Nightwine. I don't want the responsibility for any being that can be commanded by anyone else, including me."

"Admirable. The film will do an even better job at freaking you out than its iconic *va-va-va-vroom* automaton."

"I still think you're jealous. She's *mucho* curvy for a robot, but cold metal is not my turn-on."

"That shiny silver exterior is plastic wood molded onto the body cast of the actress, so she's not as cold as you think."

"She's still born of silver nitrate film," he pointed out, "on which the robot body was almost a solid image beyond what any human actor could convey, other than Joan of Arc in battle armor. I can see how powerful that could be in the wrong hands." He hesitated. "I've had some . . . disturbing dreams since I called that thing off the film reel and into real life."

"Me too. We need to discuss all this, *after* you've seen the movie."

"Just go and be mysterious about your next steps, Del. I might be mysterious about how I get on with Christophe and *Metropolis*."

By then we were at his house, so I'd bribed him with a quick good-night kiss. As soon as he'd exited Dolly, my prize '56 Eldorado convertible, Quicksilver leaped from the backseat into the vacant front passenger seat while it was still warm.

Ric shook his head. "If anybody is jealous of anything, it would be me of that dog."

"You've never had a pet?" I asked as Quicksilver growled. "I mean animal companion."

"Just goats. I get hooved herd animals more."

I remembered his south-of-the-border childhood captors had called him goat-boy. *Grrr.* I wish we had fully wiped out El Demonio during the perfect storm of a showdown at the Emerald City Hotel and Casino in Wichita.

Next time.

Given the battle of wills Ric had going on with his former boyhood captor, now a major drug lord, I knew another, maybe even final, confrontation was inevitable. Neither demon nor Ric Montoya ever gave up.

REVISITING LAST NIGHT'S memories of the serious enemies Ric and I had made in Vegas made my head start to ache.

I put a hand to my hot-skinned forehead without remembering I was gazing at my double in the mirror, that I was showing weakness to my sister image, my enemy.

"Poor Delilah," Lilith cooed in that irritating way of schoolgirls who lay on the "jealous" as thick as strawberry jam on English muffins . . . or toes.

She ran her still-upraised hands down and then up her opposite elbows to her shoulders, and then down again over her breasts and behind her back. The motion clothed her in the twin of my red top like a paint tool in Photoshop.

"What an obvious stripper move," I complained, "just to filch this old thing I'm wearing. Your wiles are wasted on me. Get your own wardrobe witch."

There are real advantages to living in a Las Vegas version of an animated Disney fairy tale. I have a wardrobe witch and a kitchen witch and a yard troll. I almost expected Lilith to ask who was the fairest of all.

Lilith didn't. She did laugh until the red of "our" top went fluorescent for an instant before she vanished. I was looking at myself for real, truly alone again. Sort of.

Wicked witch, Irma ground out in my ear.

"She may well be," I agreed. "And you are truly the last secret about me Ric isn't in on. He now knows I can see my identical self in the mirror, what his shrink foster mother called a shadow sister. He doesn't know I also hear voices."

But you do, *Joan of Arc,* Irma replied. *Only it's voice, singular.*

"Look, I am no longer a warrior maid. My virgin issue was resolved three months ago, thanks to Ric."

At twenty-four, Irma jibed.

"I had my reasons, as we found out in Wichita."

Lilith didn't have those issues. Can't you get her on the

wrong side of the mirror yourself? What's keeping you from following her?

Good questions.

"You're right. I'm being a wuss," I muttered. "Just because I've sorta done a vengeful murderess wrong is no reason not to use my mirror-walking talents."

Right. And what's with the silver familiar? Where is it?

I closed my eyes to take inventory in a body-sensing moment. "Oh. It's hiding out as an ankle bracelet under my right wide-legged pant bottom."

Skin-tight leggings are in and you're doing wide-legged retro sailor suits. Figures.

"The familiar must duck for cover when Lilith is occupying the mirror because she doesn't have one herself."

The familiar is envy-worthy. It's on my bucket list.

"You're disembodied, Irma. You can't have a bucket list. And being locked into a shape-changing hunk of sterling silver is like wearing a pair of mobile steel handcuffs, trust me."

Even now I could feel a cold, feathery shiver as the familiar slunk up my leg into its default position as a dental-floss-fine hip chain. I eyed my image in the mirror.

I'd faced some seriously dark, subconsciously buried news about myself back in Wichita and survived. Now it was time to confront what was keeping me from using and expanding my ability to walk into and through mirrors.

Maybe I could drag Lilith back out with me this trip, screaming and kicking in physical form. My gut felt a satisfying melted-caramel glow. Try to deal with real life like I do, Shadow Me.

So I walked forward to meet my reflected grin, feeling a breath, a sigh, a supersheer curtain of cool liquid silver clinging to my body like ectoplasmic Saran wrap. Then I was on the other side of myself, seemingly alone in a dark, bare place, a vacant soundstage built for psychic phenomena, an empty mirror viewed from the opposite dimension, a place of eternal twilight.

My world and welcome to it. I walked farther forward, poised for whatever would come, for what, or whoever, I would encounter. Bring it on.

Chapter Three

YOU CAN'T GO anywhere eerie in the post–Millennium Revelation's many underworlds, I'd learned the hard way, without sensing overbearing powers.

The fey remained an ancient presence everywhere, leaving traces in the form of mercurial paths, just as pre-Christian civilizations leave buried cities and fallen monuments and statues of forgotten gods.

That's what I sense when I walk in mirror-world, and what I encountered during my one expedition to the nomadic pestilence called the Sinkhole, under Las Vegas.

No sooner had these thoughts crossed my mind than a forest of skeletal, frosted trees materialized around me. Palm-sized, faceted jewels dangled like glittering fruit from their stunted limbs. You'd think I was shopping for red-carpet trinkets at Fred Leighton's vintage jewels joint in the Bellagio. I could easily reach up to pluck them from the branches.

Except . . . the silver familiar was weighing heavy around my wrists, a thick chain swaying between my sudden new pair of manacles.

"Off," I commanded, as I would a dog, but not mine. Quicksilver doesn't take commands.

I knew enough not to grab for fey fruit, but I'd never tried a verbal order on the familiar, which had come to me via someone I didn't trust. It didn't move a molecule.

Then I heard a sinister rustle among the leafless,

unmoving branches, like whispers in a language of shifting forest sounds. No wind brushed my skin, but some ghostly animation was stirring the trees on either side. I walked the open path between them, bound like a prisoner en route to a scaffold.

What a hateful setup! I'd visited mirror-world before without encountering this fanciful toll booth before I even got forty feet into the journey.

As I walked, a piece of glittering black against the surrounding dark became clearer.

Something tall and narrow and worse . . . winged— think demon or dragon or gargoyle or a supernatural unknown—barred my way. The closer I got, the bigger *it* got, though I could glimpse only the come-and-go sparkle of its skin, or was that a . . . hide?

Bogey incoming at high noon, Irma caroled in my brain.

Bogey*man* was the better word. The glimpsed musculature was male, broad at the shoulder and narrow at the hip, but lithe and fast, its glamorous surface a midnight sky all starry and depthless.

I had a feeling if I had seen its actual outline, every pore or scale or horny joint or thorny appendage, I'd run screaming back to the Enchanted Cottage.

Too late. No going back. In mirror-world you pushed forward to come out another mirror. Another exit. Or not.

My pace never slowed, although my heartbeat quickened. I wanted to curse the familiar for hampering my hands, but I knew it was only posing as a bond and was really a weapon that hadn't decided its necessary form yet.

Not for nothing had I scaled twenty-foot-high pillars and looming statues of animal-headed gods in the subterranean underbelly of the Karnak Hotel's vampire empire.

I'd freed an ancient chained god. I was going to let a Black Hole of Feydom stop me?

Taking in the probable shape of the negative image, I took a running jump at it and felt my shoes sink into solid sinew as I leaped up and up, my nostrils burning with a two-edged scent as sharp as ammonia or as addictive as absinthe. Just like the fey to be either corrosive . . . or cloying. I might as well have been climbing some museum reconstruction of a lost dinosaur. Unseen claws ripped at my sleeves and flared pant bottoms, and I felt the sickening wrench of cloth only millimeters from skin and bone.

At last I was at the summit, far above the fruit trees. I looped my manacle chain around any part of darkness I could lasso. I tightened and wrenched my makeshift garrote, using my entire body, and was shaken off like an errant dandelion head.

I went flying . . . forward, at least, not back. I hit the unseen path hard and curled into a defensive ball, blinking my eyes open. I saw nothing but the dark, so rolled over onto my side and looked again.

More undifferentiated darkness stretched ahead, but through it—as if caught in a follow spotlight—strode a muscled brown giant of a man, sporting shoulder-length locks like some circus Samson.

I breathed a sigh of relief. A woman named Delilah could deal with a long-haired muscleman.

Besides, we'd met before.

Chapter Four

"WHERE IN THE Nine Circles of Hell under the Inferno Hotel have you been for the past week?" he greeted me when we were still forty feet apart.

"Oz," I said, not exactly lying.

The details of the man's figure came into focus, lit by his own faint golden aura. His gladiator boots were the real thing—leather straps and heavy metal everywhere—and therefore the envy of any runway model. He wore a hip-hung item that was part loincloth, part Roman soldier kilt. His shoulder-blade-brushing mane of bronze hair was about as long as his kilt, so he was altogether a tasty sight for the females in his audiences.

Not my type, though.

"Since when," I wanted to know, "does the Gehenna Hotel house magician want to see me? Your werewolf boss hates my guts, except as appetizers for his pack. You itch to escape his indenture, but don't want to rile him. And since when do you mirror-walk, Madrigal?"

"Magic fingers," he said as we closed to conversational distance, waggling his own. "Once you'd used my front-surface glass mirror as a fey prison for Cicereau's crazy daughter's ghost I was forced to improvise other equipment for my stage illusions. During that process the girls helped me find a fey path through another mirror."

I looked up, nervously. The familiar was now an innocuous wrist bangle with a Hello Kitty face.

"The girls," his two feral fey assistants, were aerial creatures. Visitors to Vegas might see the magic show and take them for pretty little sparkling fairies, but both were venomous. They were also jealous of any females coming near their giant rescuer and now possession, Madrigal.

Luckily Madrigal and I had minimal chemistry, even when Cesar Cicereau had forced me into performing a sexy stage illusion with him. The werewolf mob boss had hoped the media frenzy spawned by my double Lilith's nude autopsy appearance on *CSI V* would turn me a ready-made media star.

I declined to stand in for anyone and had opted out via the hotel's industrial laundry chute at the earliest opportunity.

"I've come to lay Loretta Cicereau's ghost to rest," I told Madrigal. "She's just a kid, not even twenty. Maybe she's had time to cool down after trying to take over the computer and electrical systems in her father's hotel. He did have Loretta and her vampire lover murdered decades ago, after all, in a brutally nasty way."

"Mobsters are like that, Delilah. So are mobster's daughters. Loretta has been out for blood ever since some strong demonic presence has been paying court to her in my mirror."

"I sensed, even glimpsed, a looming evil influence as soon as I passed through the mirror on my end. Any guesses what it is?

"No idea. During my magic act I've detected a black miasma hanging over the hotel, nothing Loretta could summon, which makes it even more disturbing."

"Would Loretta really consort with a demon to take revenge on dear old Dad?"

"In a skipped heartbeat. And she wants revenge on

more than Cesar Cicereau. You're not exactly a model citizen now that you've taken down Loretta's resurrected lover—gruesome revenant that he was—all the way down forty stories to smash his immortal bones to bits on the Las Vegas Strip. I wasn't there, thank the Dread Queen, but Sansouci is still talking about that trick."

Knowing Sansouci, Cicereau's security guy, he probably approved the way I'd separated the dead lovers once again. Like a lot of perfectly ordinary people who've been horribly wronged, even ghostly mob princess Loretta and her Polish prince charming had hungered for restitution and revenge. They could accomplish it paranormally now that the Millennium Revelation had exposed all the dark powers and beasties among us . . . besides us.

"They were originally innocent victims," I reminded Madrigal, and myself. "Maybe Loretta can go to some rehab house for ghosts if she's seeing things more clearly now. Her resurrected lover was a new Frankenstein's monster. Tourists are not meant to be collateral damage. I hope to talk some sense into her. Dead bones don't dance, not even in today's really wicked Vegas."

"Things have changed, all right." Madrigal's expression showed the dark side of grim.

Or should I say Grimm?

That's when two dive-bombing mini-comets came at me out of the black nowhere, screaming like nest-defending blue jays. Sylphia was tangling in my hair while shooting pale, glittering webs of spider goo around my wrists and ankles. Madrigal once had called it "spit and fairy dust." Meanwhile, Phasia's dark, sinuous snaky limbs and iridescent locks of hair came twining around my neck.

Now I was getting a taste of the means Madrigal and I had used to bind Loretta in his magic-act mirror. The only difference: I was alive, not a ghost. Their lethal clinging-vine act was halfway to strangling me.

"Sylphia! Phasia!" Madrigal commanded, coming to untwine them. No dice. Their sticky and creepy extrusions kept moving to another spot, burning where they touched.

I could feel the silver familiar on the move, ringing my fingers with metal knuckles. A chill gloved my fingers as claw-long nail sheaths like Fu Manchu wore sprouted from all eight fingers. Nothing on the thumbs, so I didn't scratch myself.

Good familiar. *Smart* familiar. Now I had to figure out how to use these instant weapons.

I ignored the twining horror-movie appendages and went straight for the violet gleam of the sisters' slanted predatory eyes. The pupils thinned to an X-shape on each iris. My new artificial-nail job could make those Xes into asterisks.

Sylphia was mute but Phasia's cries became shrieks as they both recoiled from my silver claws. The entrapping net they'd spit at me broke from their dainty little bodies and spattered the dark floor of mirror-world, splashing tiny galaxies of glitter at my feet.

They still hovered twenty feet above Madrigal and me, hissing like mini-Medusas. They couldn't fly but they could attach and climb, which made me shudder to wonder what structures might loom unseen above our heads.

"What's with your fey assistants?" I demanded of Madrigal. "I thought you had them under control."

He was staring at my taloned fingers, which made me examine them in the light of the magical halo that surrounded him. The three-inch curved silver scimitars bore etched decorations I'd have liked to study, but I wanted full use of my hands even more.

Instead of nail-gazing, I flicked my fingers and the claws vanished. Even the magician blinked and frowned at the effect. Only I'd felt cool silver rivulets eeling under my palms and up my forearms to vanish under my clothing faster than the eye could see.

"Visible claws are a hot girly fad on the Strip," I told Madrigal, keeping my eyes watching upward.

"My girls have been volatile lately." He shook his glam locks.

I'm not saying his fey friends didn't have reason to be possessive of a half-dressed hunk like Madrigal.

"I don't know what's gotten into them, Delilah. They seem to regret teaching me to enter the spaces behind mirrors, but it's really amped up my act. What's most unsettling is what's happened to Loretta Cicereau while you were gone."

"What could happen? Her ghost was trapped in your front-surface mirror and wound with the same immobilizing web the fey sisters just tried to use on me."

I gazed up. "Mortal but mobile, girls," I announced. "Mess with me and I have the teeth to bite back." I raised my hands and fluttered my naked fingers. The dimly seen pair retreated into almost total darkness.

"They were always possessive," I said, "but now they're downright hostile."

"That's what I came to tell you. You may think they've changed, but it's Loretta who really has. Trapping her in fey lockdown may have backfired."

"How?"

"Using the bonds of feral fey may have put her into the Dread Queen's power. I didn't notice at first, but Loretta's ghostly form has been solidifying in the mirror. Now she's looking as lively as a well-fed vampire corpse in its coffin."

"Maybe the fey girls are jealous of *her*."

I barely got the words out of my mouth before another screaming Mimi was heading right for me—us. She came barreling out of the darkness like a berserk ship's figure-head, all head and shoulders and trailing body and clothes. Images of ancient Greek harpies, Viking Valkyries, and other mythic female monsters fast-forwarded through my brain.

I raised my naked arms and hands before the familiar could make its move, but so did Madrigal.

"Robaceous trilobelius," he bellowed a spell.

A thorny bell jar of brambles sprang up around and over us and burst into eerily silent beating orange flames.

The colors lit up the hovering forms of Loretta and her two petite former jailers.

Loretta's eternally pretty seventeen-year-old face screwed into a cartoon snarl of hatred. "My father ruined my life," she screamed like an overemotional teen, "and your interference on his behalf ruined my death and resurrection, and Krzysztof's too."

Her tirade reminded me that Loretta's vampire medieval Polish prince bore a name not that unlike Snow's French form of it. Could there be a connection? It might be a clue that Snow really was a vampire, despite his denials.

Loretta's furious gaze transferred to the man by my side. "Madrigal, you and Sansouci have always been my father's toadies. You now walk the old fey paths, as this meddler does. Your feeble magics can't protect you from the fey powers that soaked into my spirit while immobilized in your trap."

"Loretta," I warned. "Revenge will hurt you more than anyone."

"Drop the pious clichés, Delilah. I can smell a taste

for revenge on your own soul. See what you think about revenge after I finish with the one who revived me from death. You will know what it is to lose your lover as horribly as you took mine."

She fled into the dark like a falling star, swift and then . . . gone.

"Ric," I breathed. I turned on the puzzled magician. "Madrigal! She's gone after Ric. Banish the barrier." He frowned. "Don't argue with me. I can hold off your fey without hurting them, although they won't return the courtesy."

"It's not that I won't, Delilah." He stretched his hands into the flames of his ensorcelled wall of thorns. "The girls can't pass through my illusion, but I can't unmake it without their aid."

"You mean . . . we're protected but also trapped?"

He nodded. Grim again. "Very much like Loretta was in my mirror."

Impetuous by fear for Ric, I charged the fiery nettles in a fury, already what Loretta had predicted of me, wanting to tear her down to bones and bury her again. The thorn tips were so sharp my arms and hands sprouted bloody pore-sized bites all over that burned like fire ants.

I fell back. Madrigal's magic wouldn't hurt him, but it would tear and burn anybody, maybe anything, else.

Ric and I hadn't checked in that morning by phone yet. I had no idea where he was, en route to the Inferno Hotel or already there. I hoped to hell Loretta didn't either but I doubted a woman betrayed and then turned fey-tainted ghost could be stopped by much.

I leaped again for the thicket of thorns despite Madrigal's shouting, "No!"

Again I rocked back and forth on the floor, tormented

by an agony of flaming thorn bites that echoed my inner fear for Ric. I'd stopped Loretta's resurrected lover from a mass-murder tear through the Gehenna Hotel, but I couldn't do a thing now to protect the one person who meant everything to me.

If only I'd opted for a film date at the Inferno Hotel with Ric and Snow.

Chapter Five

R IC LOOKED SIXTY stories down to admire the fountains of cavorting flames that enveloped the Inferno Hotel's towering exterior night and day.

They flaunted every color of a high-Fahrenheit rainbow, azure to orange, gold and red blending with the blue into teal and bright absinthe green.

On the top floor the flame tips formed a dancing set of spearpoints outside the glass walls, but the penthouse temperature was as cool as its ice-white albino master, the Vegas mogul that Delilah called Snow.

Ric tried to see through the fire-shrouded stories but failed to glimpse the Las Vegas Strip. Only the crowding new towers under construction were visible at this level. These were brown-gray skeletons of concrete and iron, ugly and crude at this stage. They reminded him of the architectural equivalent of giant zombies gnawed down to their bare bones.

He felt a shiver despite the exterior flames and forced away a sudden eerie stab of foreboding. He had safe passage here now, despite being one of the few people in Vegas, besides Delilah, who dared to argue, hard, with Christophe. He wasn't going to stop now.

"I don't like the first part of your proposal," he told the long, pale figure lounging in an ivory leather conversation pit built into a ghost-pale plush carpet. "I do agree the *Metropolis* robot is 'extremely valuable,' but she's not a 'commodity' to me. She's a responsibility. I called her off the silver screen into being. I won't let her become a fancy new CinSim in your hotel's extensive collection of hapless celebrity zombies. I'm not even sure she is one."

"'Commodity' was a poor choice of words with you," Christophe admitted, his lanky frame stirring. "You're a man of admirable if tiresome responsibility. Unfortunately, post–Millennium Revelation Las Vegas is not much populated by individuals with scruples. Do you realize how much concentrated silver nitrate was on those film frames showing a solid metal robot? The mother lode. You must suspect that silver-power wielders are a new force on the paranormal scene. Hell, you're sleeping with one."

"Outta my private life. And I know where that silver familiar Delilah's locked into came from, Christophe." Ric eyed the mogul–rock star's long, almost luminous white hair.

Christophe shrugged. "Powers can rub off like fleas in a place teeming with them as much as Vegas is nowadays."

"You sent Delilah a lock of your damn hair like some lovesick Cavalier poet."

"She wasn't your girl then. And I didn't know the 'damn hair' had a life of its own that would transfer to her. More likely her own latent powers animated it." Christophe's body shifted again.

Was he uneasy? Lying? Or telling an inconvenient truth? Ric didn't know how to read it, but he sensed the Inferno kingpin was hiding a deeply personal reaction.

"Delilah has a wild talent," Christophe said. "Better watch out. You've caught her silver powers, so your dead-dowsing abilities might rub off on her some night, Montoya. Imagine Delilah free, willing and able to raise her favorite vintage film idols. Errol Flynn, say."

Now *that* Ric recognized as a guy-to-guy taunt designed to distract him. From what?

"Anyway, back to our *real* silver girl," Christophe said. "Every power in town will be after . . . her, as you call the robot. And, you forget, I now own the film you filched her from and every frame in it."

"It wasn't deliberate, my raising her."

"Exactly, not deliberate. Not planned, just like the case of the silver familiar. We're both victims of undiagnosed powers." Christophe's smile was mocking. "Yet this unexpected new angle to your post–Millennium Revelation talent did put you a step beyond your usual bounds of dowsing for the in-ground dead. That was a focused but useful talent when you worked in law enforcement. You realize what you've just done to raise the so-called Silver Zombie from a movie screen? That makes *you* an 'invaluable commodity' in post–Millennium Revelation Las Vegas."

"I can live with it."

The albino's perpetual inky-black sunglasses lifted to reflect the flames outside, not the sophisticated surroundings. "So you think," he said idly.

Ric sensed Christophe was taking his comment in a way he hadn't intended. That made him glad he hadn't bothered to correct one misconception. Ric had been born into a family of poor rural Mexican water-dowsers, a boy only able to raise dead things, long before the Millennium Revelation had brought supernaturals out into the open and had exposed weird abilities in ordinary people.

"Sit." Christophe's guitar-riffing right hand gestured to a spot three feet away on the sprawling couch. On top of having untold money, influence, and probably unknown powers, he was a freaking rock star.

"Sit down, Montoya. Relax. You're among friends.

Who gave you shelter and protection after the Karnak vamps tried to eat you for brunch?"

Ric sat. "I didn't ask for sanctuary here, with you, Christophe."

"Call me Snow. Someone had to provide you with secure R and R time, so the Inferno Hotel stepped up. Now you've probably brought a demon drug lord down on us all. Why didn't you kill your old tormentor when you had the chance in Wichita? You deserved to take your revenge on El Demonio and law enforcement would have loved you for it."

"As you say, not long ago I *was* law enforcement. We'd want the bastard alive and in custody so we could break his organization."

"You might have the power to do that solo now. *Something* enabled you to raise a CinSim directly without going through the Immortality Mob. That's another ugly coalition that'll be wanting you dead or on its payroll."

"Is that why you're making an offer you think I can't refuse? That I live at your hotel from now on? To give you leverage with all these bad guys supposedly wanting my hide?"

Christophe kept silent, sipping from the martini glass set on a built-in Lalique glass table, savoring the drink Delilah had created to annoy him, an Albino Vampire. Christophe violently denied he was any such thing, but the jury that could rule on that issue hadn't even been picked yet.

Ric could see why the man infuriated Delilah. He was unflappable.

"It's the ideal solution to my prize CinSim's security and your own safety," he was saying. "It *is* an offer you can't afford to refuse."

As Christophe's head had lifted to speak, Ric spotted a

bruise as dark as cherry amber underneath the pink-ruby-studded black leather collar he wore onstage, and now, apparently, off.

Pink albino eyes were ultrasensitive to light. That would explain the constant sunglasses and symbolic hot-pink jewels. It didn't explain why a flagrantly sexy rock star wanted to conceal a passion bruise . . . or a bite?

Ric didn't want to speculate about Christophe's sexuality any more than he needed to know what brand of supernatural he was. Sorcerer, it looked like, but looks were especially deceiving in a Vegas teeming with paranormal creatures and effects. The nickname "Snow" came from his onstage identity as Cocaine, the lead singer of the Seven Deadly Sins band. His stage persona reeked of sex, drugs, and rock 'n' roll.

Ric bet Delilah would have a fit to know he was seriously powwowing with the guy instead of just watching a movie, but Ric had learned long ago as a small boy in Mexico that sometimes you have to deal directly with the Devil.

"Moving in here would be . . . awkward . . . Snow." Ric sipped his own cocktail.

The pale lips smiled at this first step toward possible concession.

"I'll give you a whole floor," he said, folding his arms over his chest, now attired instead of bared for the stage. "A private elevator for Miss Street to come and go discreetly on her errands of surveillance and . . . other matters."

"I like my house."

"A suburban ranch-style equipped with a smart-ass computer? It has a certain earthy charm, like you, maybe. But it's not secure enough now, Montoya. You were in the FBI. You know that."

"Perhaps not safe enough for . . . her."

Christophe leaned forward, his long white hair brushing the lapels of his silk designer blazer. White, of course. The nickname literally suited him. "You can't keep the most valuable CinSim in the world at home in a closet, like a vacuum cleaner."

Ric sipped the Bloody Mary he'd accepted, silent and forcing the other man to speak.

"I'm building a new Metropolis for it . . . her," the mogul went on. "A modern Tower of Babel for the first silver-screen robot. Once it's done, I'll have the best normal and paranormal security in Vegas or the world for it. Her. But you still won't be free to return to your modest, middle-class house and play bait for whomever you like."

"Why don't we ask her?" Ric said.

"Really? That would be like boosting C-3PO from the *Star Wars* film strip and taking his scripted words for . . . well, scripture. That golden futuristic robot is her cinematic descendant."

"I can see that without being a damn movie buff. Where is she?"

"In the home theater, of course."

Ric stood, waiting to be shown.

He wasn't surprised to be led through a pair of double doors, but the semicircular 3-D surround screen that confronted them could match any installed at major national monuments. A curved single row of six lavish reclining theater seats seemed lost in the massive carpeted space.

"Lonely at the top, huh, Christophe?" Ric commented.

Then the lights came up and he saw her again. At one end seat, the Silver Zombie stood like an unused usher.

His . . . protégé? Creature? What was it . . . she, really? His responsibility, certainly.

"We need a name for her." Ric spoke softly, as if she might hear.

"Don't ask me. I was content with It."

"Delilah is right. You *are* a heartless bastard."

"The last individual I heard of who was hankering after a heart was a Tin Woodman not unlike my mute guest there."

The robot was evidently voice-activated, though, because the motionless metal figure had turned to home in on Ric. She moved stiffly at first.

Ric remembered Delilah saying that the actress had to wear the clumsy plastic-wood suit of silver-bronze painted "armor" to play the robot version of her character, even when it scraped her skin and a double could have taken her place. Poor . . . what was her name? Ric wondered.

"Brigitte," Snow mused as if answering a spoken query. "Sexy name. Pretty little Brigitte Helm. The actress was only nineteen. Just eight years later she was considered for the title role in *Bride of Frankenstein*. Fitting, that was, since that 1935 American film drew on Fritz Lang's *Metropolis*, with its invention of a mad scientist and 'machinery' of bubbling vials and neon. A vial shaped like a giant martini glass formed the centerpiece of the laboratory set. I imagine Delilah really enjoyed that part."

So, Ric wondered, the Silver Zombie cocktail Delilah had concocted in Wichita was an idea whose time had finally come?

"I don't know all these movie references," Ric said aloud, "but I know how to put two and two together. You're beginning to sound like Delilah, a film history buff."

"Always was, a bit, but no. Now I'm most interested in the film's futuristic cityscape, the gliding biplanes and bullet trains shooting along on tracks up among the skyscrapers with the Tower of Babel squatting like a gigantic horned god over the slick modern towers Las Vegas hotels have become famous for. I've been aching to pattern an addition to the Inferno on this film for . . . a very long time. You really must see *Metropolis*. Study it. Another reason you should move in here."

"To see a movie? I don't think so."

Ric glanced at the gleaming metal figure beside him, standing as still as a life-size female Oscar award. Her metal carapace was anatomically correct on superheroine terms. She was a powerful female figure, far curvier than a Victoria's Secret model in a Wonderbra but not at all caress-able.

"You'll probably use her as the centerpiece of a re-created mad scientist's resurrection laboratory," Ric said. "What a waste."

"She's not the most scintillating conversationalist," Christophe said with a smile, "but she *was* in a silent movie."

"She spoke in your Emerald City Hotel penthouse in Wichita," Ric reminded him.

The mogul's pale white eyebrows lifted over the rims of his aviator sunglasses. They both knew what she'd said; apparently Ric's reference had recalled that word to her as well.

Perfectly oval blank silver eyes seemed to bore deep into Ric's.

"Master," she said.

Again.

That one word gave him the creeps and drove Delilah crazy.

Christophe just smiled.

"Isn't that . . . useful? She's transferred her allegiance

from the film's evil genius who created her, Rotwang, to the do-gooder who re-created her in physical form in our own time. You, Montoya. At least you have a better-sounding surname. And, who knows? That one little word from her cold metal lips to your ears may save all our necks in the coming second Vegas apocalypse."

"A ROBOT CINSIM," Ric mused after they'd left the creature dormant again in the empty theater.

He'd returned to his seat, feeling as zombielike as . . . Brigitte . . . had acted.

"As you'll soon see in the movie," Christophe said, lounging in his white leather conversation pit again, "the robot was able to assume human likeness. I suspect the version you called off the screen is more of a cyborg, half machine, half human. You had to raise the dead body of the actress inside to draw the exterior likeness into being. Brigitte Helm died in 1996."

"That recently?" Ric asked, trying to imagine a wizened, bent shell of a woman imprisoned in that eternally erect and superheroine-curvaceous body. If it didn't mimic hard shiny metal, Ric would call it lush.

"Life expectancies have been climbing in recent decades," Christophe noted, "especially now that vampires have joined the human race . . . or at least live side by side with humans."

"Like you?"

"I'll deny that false charge until the day I die."

Christophe's smiles, Ric observed, always seemed eerie because you could never see the expression of his eyes. The idea of Delilah accepting a kiss from those colorless lips, so like a corpse's, and doing it on his behalf, made his skin crawl.

Some women might find that Ice King image hot, and obviously did by the legions, but not Delilah. She'd worked to free Christophe's Brimstone Kiss–addicted groupies from their obsession. Odd what women would fall for, as odd as the absurd idea of him falling for the Silver Zombie. Time to get back on topic . . . squeezing Snow for information.

"Isn't a cyborg a blend of human and machine," Ric asked, "more than the mechanized body parts doctors can install now? That's in steampunk films. Isn't true cybernetics blending the brain and the circulatory system with machines?"

"The head and the heart. Quite a theme in *Metropolis*, as you'll see."

"I don't need to view the film to know that the robot exterior is just an especially elaborate costume, and that the actress who wore it was an independent being."

"But it was shaped from her body cast."

"Still a shell. She has to be the sum of her parts, a CinSim raised inside one of her costumes for the movie, like a deep-sea diver brought to the surface."

"Interesting point. Perhaps you should try to call the character of Maria in her human form off the screen."

"No." Ric stood and backed away from the lounging figure before he knew his impulses had willed him to move. "I'm not going to be responsible for multiple incarnations of that poor actress."

"If not you, perhaps someone far worse than you."

"*You?* I suppose now that you own the film you could order any image on it revived as a CinSim. Why would you even need me?"

"I want *this* incarnation."

"Why did El Demonio Torbellino say there was a demon inside her that only he knew how to raise, Christophe?"

"Perhaps because it's true? For God's sake, toss out your anti-unhuman prejudices and call me Snow. Even Delilah does, and she hates my lily-white guts."

"Why?"

"I'm sure she can enumerate my sins better than I can or want to. Ask her. Unlike Brigitte, she talks, fluently and frequently."

Ric was done discussing his girlfriend with Christophe. "Why would the *Metropolis* robot be so powerful to a demon drug lord? Wasn't the robot destroyed in the film, burned at the stake?"

"By then the character was both monster and martyr. The monster part was wrapped around the heroic Maria in that robot's pseudo-metal skin. Perhaps your role is to draw out benign parts of her being: the role of Maria, the idealistic enslaved workers' advocate, or Brigitte, the nubile young film star. You seem to have a gift for bringing out unsuspected depths in naive young women."

Ric paused with the rim of the tall Bloody Mary glass at his lips. "You just want to use me and the Silver Zombie against your Vegas Strip rivals and Torbellino . . . and the Immortality Mob, I'm thinking."

"Of course. But they'll all want to enslave you for even more distasteful ends. Your life is in grave danger if you don't gain the protection of a major force in Vegas."

"My life has been in danger since I was four years old. No risk, no gain," Ric said.

He drained the Bloody Mary before setting it down on a table.

"Your commercial instincts are second to none," he told Christophe, "but there may be more seriously heavy players at work in Vegas than even you suspect."

Christophe stood too. He was taller than Ric, but not by

much. Ric suspected some lost Cuban blood in the water-dowsing peasant Montoyas.

The rock-star mogul's eyes, and therefore expression, remained concealed by dark glasses, but a hand went to his throat as if touching a talisman. The neck collar's vibrant pink rubies? Were they more than gemstones, as the vivid bruise might be something more?

Ric knew his hint had shaken the usually controlled stage performer. He also figured the babe who'd given 'Snow' that royal purple hickey must have been showgirl-tall, or wearing spike heels. An ex-FBI guy observes the little things.

"I'll think about your offer," he told Christophe.

"What does that mean?"

"What I said."

Chapter Six

RIC KNEW HE had to figure out what was best for . . . a robot. She was even more zombielike than the walking dead he'd raised since a small child.

After the penthouse elevator deposited him on the main casino floor, Ric headed for the Inferno Bar in search of a dapper fellow in white tie and formal black morning coat, whose face and hands were as black-and-white all over as his nineteen-thirties' monkey suit.

It was a fine point whether Nick Charles, the lush detective, held up the bar or it held him up.

Built like a giant aquarium with glass sides, the bar had a long top of polished wood carved into demonic faces. The scene below the bar top was a Hell in miniature, with tiny capering demons leaping within the same corona of colored flames that circled the hotel's exterior.

Nick Charles had leaned a hip on a red enameled steel stool and rested his crooked right elbow on the bar. He was rapt at the moment, gazing into a martini glass holding something liquid and bright blue.

Ric had stopped in front of him, himself a wall of well-tailored pale linen suit. As a respected private consultant on finding suspected murder victims, he dressed the part.

"Well," Nick Charles blessed him with an approving sideways look. "If it isn't Cesar Romero back from working a case with Charlie Chan in tropical climes. What may I do for you, young man?"

Ric shot his suit sleeves to reveal Day of the Dead grinning-skull cuff links, then leaned a hip on the adjoining barstool. "They had a Chinese detective in the old movies, and a soused one. Why not a Latino one? Why not Cesar Romero or Ricardo Montalban as a private eye?"

"Because they had Zorro, who was far more interesting." Nick Charles's forefinger stabbed a drunken *Z* into the air. "I do like your style," he said, looking down his pencil-thin mustache and not quite focusing. "But you're missing something."

"What?" Ric demanded, surprised.

"Bartender." Nick Charles raised his free forefinger and gestured to Ric. "A Blue Coast martini for my new friend."

Ric stifled a smile and a sigh. The famous film detective was just a shill for selling drinks these days, now that the Immortality Mob had merged his onscreen image with a 3-D zombie body.

Ric accepted the gaudy drink, and eyed it before sipping. "Is this a Delilah Street Special?"

"Lord, no, my lad. Her Silver Zombie is a marvel of delicate blue hue with a noose of electric Blue Curaçao at the bottom and top. The Inferno Bar doesn't have rights to that recipe. She didn't invent it here, just the Albino Vampire and the Vampire Sunrise. So the management is trying to push this abomination, a *vodka* martini, on the public. Martinis are always made with gin, preferably Boodles."

"Any *port* in a storm for Christophe, huh?" Ric suggested. It was hard to not get quippy with the founding father of screwball mystery films.

"A common saying . . . oh, you mean port as in *wine*." Nicky gave him a broad wink and sipped his Blue Coast martini. "And do you have a right to t-t-take . . . my second favorite wife's name in vain?"

"Naughty Nicky," said the willowy brunette CinSim who draped a manicured hand and winsome face over his shoulder. "What's this about your 'second favorite wife'? Are you aching for a second favorite *life*?"

Nick left his glass on the bar and put his hands up. "I've got a second life here and now, you audacious woman. That was just a figure of speech, wifey dear."

"I know Delilah's figure very well," Nora purred, curving her nails into his well-padded jacket shoulder. "*You'd* better not, or I'll divorce you and take Asta. And the key to the liquor cabinet."

Before Nick could defend himself, Ric said, "Delilah's my *amiga*."

"Well said, *amigo*." Nick Charles gulped the rest of his cocktail. "Bartender, another for me and a nice, fresh one for the lady."

Ric eyed the couple, back and forth. They liked to spar and probably "spark" too, in the old-fashioned way of public snuggling and private whoopee.

"I need to know something," Ric began.

"Nicky is the best man for the job in every bar in Manhattan or Vegas," Nora said, using her long forefinger nail as a swizzle stick. She offered her bluish finger to Nicky, who dutifully tasted it, then nodded thoughtfully. "Needs curing another ten minutes."

Ric shook his head at the byplay. "*I* need to know if you know who and what you are."

"The ball and chain just told you," Nick said. "I'm the smartest sloshed detective in the business and she's the sassiest siren on the planet. And rich too."

"What you're saying now sounds similar, but you've never said these lines onscreen," Ric said.

"*Oooh*, Nicky," Nora's lips looked rouged in black as

she cooed into her husband's pale gray ear, "the darling boy watches our home movies."

"Hardly home movies," Ric said. "You two were box office magic eighty years ago. You must remember that. Does your CinSim life allow you to improvise? Do you like that? Or do you hate being stuck in this one bar scene, on this one set, glad-handing every starry-eyed tourist who wanders by?"

"Nicky," Nora said. "The man is deeply troubled. We must help him."

"Of course." Nick's hands lifted, martini-less, and patted the air like a conductor's.

Looked damn like one in that formal suit, Ric thought.

"Have you ever heard of the fourth wall, my boy?" Nick asked.

"Sure. The part of a stage set that faces the audience. No wall at all. And I'm closer to thirty than to twenty, so I'm nobody's boy."

"Yes, you are," Nora said, as if cooing to Asta. She also made a kissy face at him that was too damn attractive even if she was technically a hundred and ten years old. "Don't call the man a boy, Nicky. If you want to call someone that, we'll be forced to have children and you know what will happen to the key to the liquor cabinet, then."

Nicky contained a shudder. "I believe we're being subjected to a serious interrogation, my love. What a novel experience."

"I *was* in the FBI," Ric pointed out.

"Did we have that in our day, dear?" Nora asked her husband.

"They were out there, but all about low dives and criminal vices and not in our elevated social circles at all."

"Apparently they've improved," Nora said, eyeing

Ric's suit and, he'd swear, speculating on what was under it.

Nick mock-slapped her hand on his suit shoulder. "Drink your drink."

"Yes, dear." She sipped provocatively, her eyelids half-closed under the thin sweep of eyebrow arches plucked to within an eighth-inch of their lives.

Ric remembered then. Delilah said Myrna Loy had been stuck playing pulp fiction Asian dragon ladies before she snagged the part of Nora. Holy *Excess Hollywood*! He was beginning to think like a film buff. All these CinSims hanging out at local hotels and casinos and watering holes made that likelier.

"Don't you miss playing other roles?" he tried to ask the actors that underlay the personas before him.

"Mr. . . . ?" Nick began.

"Montoya."

"Montoya," Nora echoed in a naughty tone.

"Mr. Montoya, I can see you are the sincere sort," Nick Charles declared with an air of sober dignity. "Rather dull for our Delilah, I fear, but we certainly regard her as one of our rare, real friends. If you are asking how we like our current lives, I can only reply that our careers were dead. We were almost forgotten, except on those interminable nostalgia documentaries. Gin was going undrunk. Our dog, Asta, was only a name in thousands of dreary crossword puzzles. 'Myrna' and 'Loy' got in them, but 'William' and 'Powell' almost never."

"Not my fault," Nora caroled, "if you were born with a stuffy offstage name."

"The producers did give you the 'Loy,' love. Shorter on a marquee than Williams. Your actual surname was a tribute to me, if you think about it."

Nora made a face at him. Nick frowned and sipped.

"In addition," he told Ric, "if you were to ask your Miss Street, she would tell you that I have been of some small service as an investigative advisor and that she derives any style sense she may have from my lovely and patient wife, with whom she helped to reunite me. As well as with the dog."

Nick Charles took a pause in his speech to sigh. "Where is the dog, dear?"

"Asta is on the other side of the bar, enjoying a dish of tourist pant legs, with discreet growls. No one can hear in this crazy, jingling jazzy casino."

Now Ric was patting the air, a conductor trying to hush his massive winds section.

"I think I get it," he told Nick. "You can't break character, but you've got more options than any of the Inferno Hotel brass might suspect."

Nora's observant eyes nailed her husband's. "Maybe not *all* of the Inferno Hotel brass. Nicky, you might want to direct the young man to the naughtier levels on the Nine Circles of Hell."

Nick edged along the bar, forcing Ric to retreat. It wasn't that Nicky used any muscle, more that Ric wanted to avoid direct CinSim contact. Who knows what they were made of besides zombie bodies and cinema silver nitrate and dreams?

In a few seconds, he saw how foolish that recoil was.

"We Darkside bar habitués," Nick Charles said, "work the civilized side of the Strip. I personally am glad that Nora and I are more known for our repartee and taste in booze than any intimate hijinks.

"Not that we didn't get up to them, my lad, but the scripts stopped to discreetly draw the curtains. You'll find the more 'personal' CinSims below. I had my share of lady fans, but I was valued for my mind and inimitable style, rather than my physique. We all acted the scripts we were given. How someone like Jean Harlow or Errol Flynn feels about a new life as the ultimate undead objects of desire, I am thankful to say I haven't the slightest notion. And if I ever do, I can sip away all that is so casually crass and modern these days. Cheers!"

Ric thanked the family Charles and looked down to see a quizzical white-and-gray wire-haired terrier eyeing his pant leg with intent to water.

"Asta, no!" Nora ordered, but Nicky merely bent to pick him up and install him on the barstool Ric had vacated.

Ric left them there, a family portrait in dramatic black-and-white against the vividly colored liquors above and the dancing demons below, both under glass.

Chapter Seven

I STOOD BECALMED and frantic in a mirror-world turned into a thorny trap.

Where was Ric now? Who would warn him he was under attack if I was confined to fey stir?

Loretta Cicereau had used my curiosity and my guilt at imprisoning her to reverse our roles. Her boyfriend was not only dead and unrevivable, but mine might soon be in the same state by her hands.

"Any magic you can use to help me overcome this wall you created?" I asked Madrigal.

His broad bare shoulders shrugged. "Phasia and Sylphia supplement my powers, but they've gone off to sulk now that I've put a wall between us. I'm in the doghouse with them as much as your clever canine Quicksilver ever was, but they won't abandon me here forever. They're just miffed you and I reconnected through mirrors. Where's the wolfbane of Cicereau's pack now?"

"Not where I could really use him." I couldn't help sounding brusque. "I've never taken Quicksilver into mirror-world. It's not like I need a bodyguard every minute."

"Allow me to disagree." Madrigal looked around. "I called up a protective wall, but this overgrown cage is like Sleeping Beauty's thorn forest, and she was stuck behind the briars for . . . what? Decades?"

"Who's counting? This thorn-spiked jungle transformed from those leaf-bare trees that were so petite and frosty and pretty when I entered the mirror, kinda like your fey assistants when I first met them and their claws were in." I looked around and up. "The entwined branches lock us in on three sides, even on the Black Beyond above us."

"Mirror backings are painted black," Madrigal pointed out. "No wonder the edges of everything inside the mirror are dark and look impassable."

I paced and tried not to grind my teeth. "I hope Loretta can't travel with the speed of the disembodied now that she's physical again. I've got to get out and get to Ric fast. I've got to get there before her."

Madrigal again shrugged brawny shoulders. "I'm a novice at mirror magic, compared to you, but I believe even if you managed to retrace your steps, you'd be back to wherever you entered the mirror."

"That would be my residence," I said absently. "The hall mirror there is a prop used for the Wicked Queen's talking mirror in *Snow White*."

"Really! Any magician would chop off his left hand to get ahold of a mirror with that provenance for illusions."

"What good is it doing me now?"

"If that's the mirror I've come toward from my own stage mirrors, it might amplify my magic, at least some. I don't know how, though. I can quench the fire." His theatrical gesture did just that, but the thick tangled wall remained.

"I haven't time to wait for your apprenticeship to take hold." I looked around desperately.

There was still no "back." Madrigal was right. The towering thorn trees hemmed us in and the floor was black stone. I stamped my heel on it, which only sent an impact tremor up my foot and leg. Well, I was no dormant Sleeping Beauty waiting for my prince to come rescue me. I needed to go rescue him, so this Jill had better start climbing the beanstalk.

"What are you doing?" Madrigal asked as I leaped up three feet onto the nearest thick branch. "There's nothing up there but matted limbs."

"And homicidal thorns," I said, discovering ten-inch-long spears hidden among the twisted, almost tortured black branches.

It was like climbing wrought iron with an ice storm slick on it. The surface now was numbingly cold, and slippery. And me wearing my midriff-baring salsa dancing top. Soon the red knit would be dyed a deeper shade of scarlet, if I didn't watch it.

I'd always had a knack for climbing. I remembered unsanctioned solo adventures along the river cliffs, clutching fistfuls of leaf-stripped, whip-thin branches to pull myself over eroding roots and fallen tree trunks. River cliffs? In Wichita? Those memories must be from that summer camp I didn't remember much.

I stayed close to the tangle's interior. That meant the higher I went, the more the growth turned into an arch. Soon I was clinging upside down like . . . Sylphia. My palms were reddened and sweaty. I looked down over my shoulder. *Yikes!* It would be a two-story fall to solid stone.

Madrigal looked small and wee, like an elf, not a muscleman.

If only these were the short graceful tree limbs I'd seen when I first crossed into the mirror, the frost forest dangling glittering gemstones out of a fairy tale.

I looked up through the twisted mass of limbs and

thorns and spied a flash of light just as I heard a tree limb crack. Now that I was hanging from the nasty growths, my weight had become too much for individual branches.

I climbed yet higher into the spiked nest. *Yes*.

This was a giant, thawed version of the frost forest. Huge pendants of faceted gemstones dangled above me, glimmering stars in a midnight-black sky. A clear glassy one was nearest.

If I broke the supporting limb and leaped into the plunging teardrop of rock crystal or zircon or even diamond, I could catch my reflection and jump through to . . . somewhere else.

That would require split-second timing and phenomenal luck.

And . . . those facets were another kind of thorn. The mirror of the dangling gemstone had already been shattered in a sense, to magnify the play of light. It would be like leaping through jagged plate glass into a network of deadly security lasers shooting back and forth inside. I'd be creamed corn.

Okay. I needed to woman up.

Marilyn Monroe had crooned that "diamonds are a girl's best friend," but they aren't if you're contemplating a leap of faith into the infinite hall of mirrors and angles inside a faceted jewel about four feet high.

Looking below, I saw the impressive figure of Madrigal still foreshortened to dwarf size.

Looking around the thorny hedge forming the wide archway, I spotted Sylphia and Phasia hanging upside down like bats, dainty, glittering bats preparing to loosen their unnatural holds and swing down to cocoon me as they once had imprisoned Loretta.

"Madrigal!" I shouted down. "Do you see it? The glimmer through the forest of branches."

"Barely," he shouted back.

"It's cut like a diamond."

"A diamond. That size? It would be invaluable."

"It *is* invaluable. It's my way out. I want you to melt it into a cabochon, a smooth rounded oval. Can you do that?"

"Alter an object? That large and distant? Transformation is a magician's basic illusion. I possess some real talent beyond tricks, but, Delilah, I can't guarantee anything. Even if I smoothed the stone, it might be acid inside, or boiling water. I'd have to melt it through a process similar to nature."

I eyed the one slim chance I had. "Don't worry, Madrigal. I have to break a limb, hopefully not one of mine, to get this piece of hard cold stone to drop. The chances of me connecting with it as it falls are a hundred to one. Just jump out of the way so no pieces of it contact you."

"I can see it well enough to concentrate my illusion over its surface. If my power is enough to make illusion real, you'll have your free-falling smooth mirror. For now, hang back."

I scurried down a long branch, puncturing a thigh. Luckily, the proven power of sailcloth was hard for even mirror-world thorns to pierce deeply. I got a rip and a scratch instead of a stab wound.

After checking my injury, I looked up.

The faceted giant gemstone was changing, its edges and brilliancy softening. It elongated into a melting marshmallow of a surface, so I bent my knees, pushed back my arms like a skier heading down a steep snowy mountain, and sprung off my thorny perch.

The familiar had stretched into heavy loops of climbing

rope on my right wrist. I grabbed one cool coil, lifted my arm, and started big circling gestures until it was a looping silver blur.

I wasn't wearing my ruby red slippers from the Emerald City Hotel and casino today, so I had no magic heels to click together. Instead, I thought of losing myself in Ric's one silver iris. And added his arms. My mirror mojo might respond to a kinder, gentler emotion than desperation.

There's no place like home, there's no place like home, I heard Irma whispering hopefully in my mind. Like we'd ever had one. A home, not a mind.

I'd have to count on the familiar being able to extend or shrink so I hit the diamond's rounded central plane dead on. When I launched into what I hoped was a trapeze-style swing into and through the dangling gemstone mirror above me, I felt the dang sling-back shoes slip off my heels, and then off entirely.

I had a second to hope they didn't brain Madrigal as they fell, then everything around me exploded into an icy nova of light and cold. Hunched in an upright protective fetal position I felt the familiar release from the limb as it wrapped and coiled around my forearm again, its job done.

For an instant my body hung in space before my stomach tightened as I passed through a smooth cool barrier like plunging through a swirl of soft ice cream.

Yummy! Irma chortled. *Home free with hot fudge on it.*

Madrigal's magic eased my way for only an instant. Then I was breaking through transparent layers of spun-sugar-thin ice, my breath sucked out of my body by a plunge into coldness beyond arctic. I landed with a sickeningly audible *crack* on one side and hip.

I had crashed into hard metal, stunned, and slid down a slick surface to an even harder floor. Looking around, I saw myself reflected in stainless steel. Was I up against the mirror backing of a giant rhinestone?

Loretta would love to trap me in a cage as I had immobilized her, a bug in a blender.

And I had done it to myself.

Ric was still on his own against the vengeful ghost at large, thanks to me.

Chapter Eight

Iᴛ ᴄᴏsᴛ Rɪᴄ a hundred bucks just to take an elevator down to the Seven Deadly Sins Dream-theme Park on the Nine Circles of Hell Limbo level.

He was the only passenger at this late-morning hangover hour. The reflective stainless steel walls of the bullet-shaped car hosted silhouettes of writhing nude women, which made him feel he was starring in the opening credits to a James Bond movie. He even had the concealed weapon.

A sudden turn, and he thought he saw . . . Delilah, like a swimmer viewed through a giant aquarium window, floating, brushing against the smeary glass, her lips almost touching the cold steel sides of the elevator capsule . . . car.

Ric shook off the hallucinogenic vision. Who knew what delusions modern technology could hurl at suggestible tourists in Vegas these days . . . ?

His forefinger hovered over seven different destination buttons, one for every deadly sin. Ric was crazy-curious how anyone could make Sloth entertaining, much less sinful, but pressed "Lust."

That was the most personal of sins. Employing chipped CinSims as exotic sex trade workers was as degrading as anything Ric could imagine, and he'd seen the worst results of human trafficking in women and children during his work in the Mexican-US Border Wars.

Here, he imagined the reality of involuntary prostitution would be prettied up.

Ironic that he was down here to settle a question of morality.

The doors sliced open without sound, framing a shapely woman with long brunet hair wearing a really short sarong. Flowers bedecked her neck, hair, and the print of the sarong. Everything was in shades of gray accented by black, with a luminous brightness putting the, uh, subtleties of her figure into sharp focus.

"Welcome, Ric" she crooned, lifting a lei over his head and picking up his left hand to lay her right-hand fingers on his. Her eyes closed. "The elevator scans reveal that I am your favored gender and physical type, but you need not choose me."

"How do you know my name?" he demanded. A credit card would record it but . . . he'd paid cash, not wanting to leave a record.

She pressed his palm to her fulsome cleavage. "My heart tells me you find me comely."

Her skin felt warm, soft, moisturized. He jerked his hand away. He'd never touched a CinSim before.

People tended not to, even in Las Vegas casinos, but he was in touchy-feely land now, a place of costly carnal knowledge, and it felt . . . creepy, not sexy. That probably was only because he knew a zombie underlay the Hollywood beauty queen's likeness. She was the sarong film queen of the thirties and forties, Dorothy Lamour, who turned to lust object and comedy with Bob Hope and Bing Crosby on their popular "Road" pictures. Ric had seen enough old TV to glimpse those.

"Come with me," she said, turning and swaying away. "You can tell me your preferences while we approach our private getaway. Lagoon?" she asked, gazing over her naked shoulder.

He didn't know whether she meant an assignation site or another new blue cocktail.

When she'd turned back he recognized a different face, more like Mexico, like home. Maria Montez, the name came to him. Must be a mental prod program active down here, so the customer knew what he was getting.

Ric swallowed. Both CinSims were about Delilah's height and build, curvier than today's gaunt movie queens. How had the . . . program running this black-and-white bordello sucked his personal preferences out of him during the elevator ride? Maybe those shadowy female figures in the wall had been succubae gauging his subconscious sexual reaction to their various types.

The woman's figure walking before him lost her sarong. A millisecond of total nudity was covered by a slinky long silver gown with back bared to her waist, a favorite Delilah dress-up look. This outfit coyly offered long sleeves and wide, sequined shoulder pads. An elaborate updo bared her neck, definitely a personal turn-on of his. When she turned her head to look over that glittering shoulder she had the face of Gene Tierney from *Laura*.

"Penthouse?" she asked.

Ric felt like the infatuated detective in that classic film, who fell in love with the portrait of a dead woman. He almost stumbled over his feet in confusion. He'd have to be brain dead not to react to this parade of beautiful women changing over and over again before his eyes into everything his teen self had fixated on. "Laura" led him on a few steps, then stopped and turned to face him.

"Will it be just us?" she asked.

She had become Hedy Lamarr, the most exotic brunet beauty of all. He recognized her from late-night films because she was a favorite of Delilah's for a bunch of reasons.

First, she was the rare woman who'd rejected Howard Hughes. Delilah took glee in that. Second, she was the rare Hollywood glamour queen with mathematical gifts. She'd helped invent an early version of frequency hopping with a piano roll to change between eighty-eight frequencies. That musical-mathematical duet had helped crack codes in WWII and had led to Wi-Fi, among other modern marvels. Delilah loved her digital-everything. It didn't hurt that Lamarr's title role in the sexy Biblical epic made *Samson and Delilah* the biggest-grossing film of its year.

Brains and beauty, just like his Delilah.

"Just us?" Hedy repeated. The most beautiful woman in the world in her day was even more exquisite in person.

"Dios, sí." He was feeling confused and . . . unfaithful. "Nothing kinky," he added hoarsely, as if he was actually contemplating . . .

She had stopped walking. Gliding, you'd really describe it. "A one-woman man. How refreshing for level L. My hair is caught in my necklace clasp." She lifted it to bare her neck.

He reached to touch it, experimentally. Warm. He fumbled with the clasp, tantalized by a virgin neck as white as Delilah's, or was hers as white as the Hedy Lamarr CinSim's? He wanted . . . needed to press a kiss on it, more than a kiss. He reached for the gown's shimmering side . . . and it changed into black satin brocade in his palm, a slightly raised pattern over a shape a blind man would lust for.

Ric stumbled back. Had the elevator pumped an aphrodisiac or drug invisibly into the air? This woman's black hair was coiled like a satin snake into a luxuriant sort of bun, her figure as willowy as the long narrow satin gown she wore, which was slit to the top of a white thigh.

That's what Chinese dragon ladies had worn for decades up to now. Ric recognized the gown, called a cheongsam. Law enforcement nowadays was attuned to global customs, but Delilah would know style . . . and Delilah would kill him if she knew what he'd walked into like any horny postadolescent guy.

"Don't stop now," the CinSim whispered, her head turning over her shoulder. Her eyebrows and eye makeup were dark winged slashes on her white face. "Opium bed?"

Ric's dazed enchantment ended as he recognized the nose, chin, and cheekbones under the cinematic makeup.

He stepped back, horrified.

This was Myrna Loy in one of her Asian femme fatale roles.

He'd been programmed to lust after Nick Charles's film wife, Nora.

That felt even creepier. No way could he tell himself she was Delilah in some other guise. He wasn't a homebreaker, not even a CinSim home-breaker.

"I . . . know you," he said. "You're about as Asian as I am."

Recognizing her seemed to disrupt the programming.

The Myrna Loy CinSim blinked. "You haven't been here before."

"No."

"It wasn't anything I said or did?"

"I found 'opium bed' highly inciting. Trust me."

"And you don't want to . . . ?"

"I won't," he answered honestly.

"I've never had to entertain a . . . won't."

"I'm . . . unentertainable."

Her original poise and film person were returning like gangbusters.

"You look perfectly functional. In fact, you look perfect. A tasty Anglo adventurer in a world of opium, yellow peril, and sin."

"You're charming, but politically incorrect down to your . . . metal fingernails."

"You'd be surprised what these can do in an opium bed."

"No, I wouldn't be. Delilah would know who you're playing—"

"I am not 'playing' you. I deliver."

"Isn't there something inside you that longs for a . . . kinder, gentler life than 'entertaining' any man who happens along?"

The black lipsticked CinSim lips paused, then pursed. "Fu Manchu is something of a bore."

"He is . . . ?"

"My . . . enforcer, I suppose you'd say. I have been schooled in current expressions."

"That's ugly to hear. Do you have any choice about what you do here?"

"Of course not. It's a role."

"Don't you long for a different one?"

She considered. "I do it very well. It doesn't seem out of the ordinary. I don't often get customers who ask questions, as you do."

"Wouldn't you give anything to escape this artificial atmosphere? To be a witty and devoted wife, for example?"

"I am Fa Lo See, I take much personal . . . satisfaction in tormenting the helpless white man."

"I'm Latino."

She shrugged. "I do not care what language you scream in." Her long metal nails extended toward his chest.

Ric caught her wrists in an imprisoning grip. Delilah would know what breed of movie villainess this was, Myrna Loy underneath it or not.

"Is this an S&M level? Why on earth would I end up here?" He looked around, encountering the same vague fog that had greeted him outside the elevator. "Why am I here?"

"Perhaps merely because I require . . . customers."

Her exotic features had turned satanic. Did customers get what they wanted, or did they "serve" the CinSim characters? That was not what he'd come here to find out.

One thing he'd learned: There was no Myrna/Nora here to save. Only his own skin.

If he'd stuck with the other women's images, he'd have been channeled into an island-girl or city-sophisticate setting. Recognizing and "picking" the Loy CinSim from a cheesy racist bent–sex film manifestation was going to get him pulp-fiction treatment. He knew what he should do, where he should be next.

Outta here.

Nick Charles wouldn't put up with playing pin cushion for a sexual sadist, even if she was enacted by the same actress who was his smart and sexy wife. Celebrity Cin-Sims were a more morally confusing construction than he'd ever guessed.

Chapter Nine

A DRY MIST curled up from my body, like steam rising. Breath came back with a cough. I scrambled upright, my barefoot soles burning. Support. I needed something to grab onto. My searching hands found slick cool walls circling me along with a multitude of my reflections.

I turned in a slow circle. My image turned with me, not Lilith this time, but distorted Easter Island heads of myself, familiar but . . . different.

This glassy cool chamber felt like the inside of a bullet. Recognition made me forget my burning feet and freezing fingertips. Was this was some . . . upright cryogenic preservation chamber?

No seam in the surface betrayed a door. I hadn't "gone" anywhere. I was trapped in the slick steel heart of the mirror-world diamond pendant. And, for sure, I hadn't reached my heart's desire and wherever Ric was a target for the wrath of whatever Loretta Cicereau had become.

I was more of a prisoner than ever.

At first I just threw myself against every curved slick reflective surface.

Reflective surfaces had been my friend since I'd come to Las Vegas in search of my roots. If it shone, glittered, and reflected, I'd always been able to pass through, even if I'd reach the other side bleary and confused. And Vegas had been built on shine, glitter, and glitz.

I'd grabbed my new talent and run with it, expecting it always to be there, like my shadow.

Not now.

Now my efforts to escape stainless-steel custody were just bruising my pale skin until my blurred reflection looked like King Kong had impressed his fingerprints all over me. I wasn't used to being simply human. I thought of Loretta Cicereau first sensing the fey twins' webs all over her ghostly image.

Someone . . . something . . . had made Loretta take physical form again.

Someone . . . something . . . had wanted to undo my clever method to freeze a girl gone wild. That same force was bottling me on the inside of a giant . . . bullet.

I would not go gently into that shining metal night, like *Metropolis*'s human heroine Maria went from lying comatose in a glass coffin in a mad scientist's laboratory into the instant mummy case of a robot suit, no matter how glamorous. I pounded my fists against their distorted fuzzy reflections.

I stopped, feeling like Superman confronting Kryptonite for the first time.

Stainless steel was somewhat reflective and had a reflective chrome component, but contained not a bit of sterling silver or silver nitrate. It was not a friend of mine, and it had been chosen to entomb me, to torture me with what might be happening to Ric beyond my power to prevent it.

Panting, I pushed my face and body tight against the curved side of my personal mummy case. I'd have to rely on Ric to save himself, and maybe me.

Oops. I was kissing myself. I was so close to my blurry reflection that I couldn't focus. My palms felt the metal warming against my touch. Was I sensing just a reflection, or was I contacting Lilith?

Whatever I saw was just my height, and just my coloring, a pale face with a halo of cloudy dark hair.

I brought the spread fingers of both hands up to my face, trying to push the image away. The silver familiar streaked across my shoulders and down my arms to my wrists, like a mitten string inside your heavy coat. Only kids who'd grown up in a climate with cold winters, as I had in Kansas, knew that feeling. Instead of mittens, though, the familiar encased my wrists and first knuckles in chain-mail workout gloves. Cool but . . . impractical.

I spread my hands apart to study the effect, and the stainless steel wall in front of me split. The two halves of my reflection slid to the edges of my vision, and a 3-D version in living black-and-white, a knockout brunet Cinema Simulacrum, stood barring my way out.

I was eager enough to escape to push right into her, which might feel bizarre. Humans up top avoided contact with the CinSims, very aware of the zombie body in possibly questionable condition beneath the attractive monotone surface.

Dreading first contact was not necessary. Two hands in glorious living color grasped her off-white upper arms and shuffled her aside.

"Get lost, *chica de cine*," someone said.

Chapter Ten

THE MAN WHO stepped from behind the clawing glamour-puss looked confused, but unruffled as any man could who'd just fought off a sexy CinSim.

"Ric! Thank God. Somehow the familiar cracked the lid on my steel coffin."

"Delilah? How'd you get here? What do you mean . . . coffin? I just pushed the elevator Up button and . . . here you are waiting to pop out of the car like a jack-in-the-box."

"More like a Jill, I hope." I frowned at the femme fatale still trying to glue herself to his side. Was that . . . it couldn't be! Screen vamp Maria Montez.

"What are you doing here?" I asked him.

"Ah. Research."

"Does 'research' always make you look so sheepish, *amor*? And exactly where is 'here'?"

Looking around, I glimpsed black-and-white film vistas of native girls in tropical lagoons cheek by, uh, lower cheek with slinky dames on nightclub floors. Whether nature or nurture, the scenes were populated by gorgeous, more ungowned than gowned, Hollywood stars of the pre-Technicolor days.

Uh-oh, Irma warned. *Our main man has been window shopping on the naughty side of Vegas.*

This time Ric grabbed *my* upper arm. "I don't want to explain here, in front of the, um, populace. Let's just hop back into the elevator and get to the main floor."

"The main floor where?"

He looked startled. I usually knew where I was coming from, if not always where I was going.

"Delilah, are you . . . all right?"

"Pretty much, or so you whisper in my ear nights. Regularly."

Ric closed his eyes as if hoping all this, even I, would go away.

"So, Ricardo, you have some ' 'splaning' to do. Where are we?"

"At the Inferno."

Now it was my turn to be speechless. I turned to examine the bullet elevator. I'd never seen one like it at the Inferno, not even on the way to Snow's penthouse.

"Where did you think you were?" Ric asked.

"Maybe . . . in some fey-sprung time trap. Loretta Cicereau is loose and set me up for a big fall in mirrorland. You haven't seen her? She's out to destroy you and seemed in a big hurry."

"Maybe she can't find me."

"I sure wouldn't have been able to. What is this place and why was that CinSim siren pressing wrinkles into the left arm of your best suit?"

"Let's just get into the elevator and out of here, Del."

"I'm not anxious to hop back on the Claustrophobia Closet. Isn't there another exit?"

Ric looked around. I noticed some of the dark-haired CinSim honeys abandoning their exotic settings and gathering like the three brides of Dracula around us. Ordinarily I'd have loved to interview each and every one, unemployed reporter and rabid film fan that I am, but something was wrong here and it involved a "honey" of my own.

"I'm not leaving, Ric, until you tell me what this weird

place is. It can't be anywhere at the Inferno I've seen. . . ." The light was dawning and it was colored lurid red.

"It's the, ah, entertainment level of the Nine Circles," he said.

"The Nine Circles of Hell? I know Snow has a key club at the Limbo level, where all the noir movie sets are stocked with the appropriate CinSims. So what are these babes in the woods doing here on their own?"

"You do punch *L* on the elevator floor layout to get here," Ric said.

"Really? I'd thought it would be *B* for bimbo." I was beginning to get a dark suspicion.

Ric looked over his handsome tropical suit shoulder at the encroaching lovelies.

"It's the Lust level, Delilah, and these babes will eat a guy alive." He grabbed my arm and pulled us both back into the elevator car.

"What should I hit?" I asked, ready to split now that he'd confessed to Mama. I had a lot more questions.

"*M* for Main, I guess." Ric kept anxious watch as lily-pale hands with black fingernail polish reached out to stop the elevator doors from closing.

I pushed the button, and the doors shut out the longing, zombie faces of the Lust level attractions just in time. The elevator car didn't move, and my stomach indulged in the classic sinking feeling. Now we were both trapped.

"What button did you hit?" Ric eyed the lit board.

I pointed at one.

"Delilah! That's not an *M* for Main. That's a *V.*"

I leaned close to study it in the dim light. "I thought it'd been used so much only the middle of the letter was still visible. So what's on *V*?"

Ric put his palms to his temples to wash his face free

of the sudden worry lines. "*V* as in . . . Violence. I didn't get out of Jesuit high school without knowing my Dante's *Inferno*."

"Snow probably ghostwrote the whole thing. I don't remember a major class of damned sinners in Dante's map of Hell starting with *V*."

"You're right that; there's an invisible *M* involved. *M* as in *Murder*. Murderers."

The elevator decided it had tormented us enough by remaining shut but motionless. It whooshed down smoothly, then stopped with a jolt harsher than a condemned prisoner's body reaching the end of its noose.

By then I was the siren hanging on to Ric's right arm with my left. I was not letting him out of my custody until the Las Vegas Strip's version of Hell was behind us both.

The elevator doors parted. My other hand hovered over the floor buttons. I'd hit the real Main the instant the elevator registered it had reached this floor and was ready to rise again. I punched the right steel circle and . . . nothing happened. All I felt was a depressing lack of depression under my forefinger. Maybe the buttons were jammed.

"What the freaking hell!" a mad-bull sort of voice demanded from beyond the locked-open elevator doors. I looked around Ric to see a stocky guy wearing a teal velour sweat suit. His wet ringlets surrounded a bald spot and he was blocking the elevator exit, hairy hands akimbo on his hips.

"You! Girly. Look at me. I've seen your sweet kisser before and the circumstances were not good."

He glared at Ric next. "And you, punk, what are you doing on the spa level of my hotel dressed like a Cuban drug lord? I deal with your kind on less personal levels."

Now I saw that sweat was dripping off the man's nose,

onto the large gold wolf's head on a thick chain around his equally thick neck.

"You, punk," Ric said, pushing a palm against the guy's dry velour shoulder and intimidating him into a backward shuffle. "We took your kind down daily when I was in the FBI. Don't like my suit? Yours stinks. Literally."

"This is my hotel," the guy snarled, showing fangs. "I could have you torn to pieces in five seconds flat."

I'd moved forward with Ric to keep him from doing anything regrettable before we understood what was going down here, beside the elevator.

"And what hotel is this?" I asked, pretty sure all of us had been jerked into a non-Vegas venue, a fey purgatory, maybe.

The guy cast a quick, narrow glance around, then swiped one arm over his brow. He was starting to pant.

"Man, it is hot here. And I don't recognize the . . . hallway." He ignored Ric to fasten his confused brain on me. "You're that naked TV autopsy babe with the huge Internet fan club, minus the maggot beauty mark on your upper lip. Maggie. That's right. I had you in the palm of my hand. That Adam and Eve act with Madrigal would've gone mega-huge. The Gehenna Hotel would have been the number-one show spot in Vegas. But *you* wouldn't cooperate."

He tried to strut forward to grab me, to assert that unpleasant piece of my past when I'd been his prisoner. By now I'd recognized Loretta's father, Cesar Cicereau, fresh from a Gehenna spa workout room, hijacked to Hell as I had been.

Ric pushed back the head of the werewolf mob like he was a pizza deliveryman trying to pass off a cold pie.

"I've heard about your plans to use this woman in

your stage show against her will," he said in full law-enforcement mode. "Let's see, how many felonies does that make, Cicereau? How many life sentences—and you'll live a long time, from what I've heard—for kidnapping, human trafficking, false imprisonment, slavery—"

While Ric paused for inspiration, I leaped in. "Animal abuse . . ."

"Animal abuse?" Cicereau was indignant. "I have a hunting license from the state. And I *am* an animal, lady! Sometimes more than others. It's a family trait."

"I'm referring," I told him, "to the anaconda that served as my sole sarong during the run-through of that magic act you forced me into. No one got legal permission from the snake, much less me."

"Look." The salt-and-pepper pelt on Cesar Cicereau's chest was growing thicker and thornier. "This heat is . . . killing me."

His coarse features were elongating in the nose and jaw, and the middle-aged bald spot was lost in a widow's peak of furred thatch that dipped to the bridge of his muzzle . . . I mean snout.

Even Ric backed off from his macho nose-to-nose duel with the werewolf mob boss. The man was shifting before our eyes and the moon wasn't full yet.

The mob boss looked around, beady eyes glazed, panting painfully.

As a dog owner—companion—I forgot my major beefs with the guy, including his pack hunting me down like a wounded deer at Starlight Lodge—to feel, well, a teensy bit sorry for him.

"How'd. How'd I g-g-g-et heh-heh-here?" he panted, dropping into a crouch as long curved nails from his hands dug into his own thighs until they brought up blood.

I owed Cesar Cicereau one long revenge fantasy, but this was not it. More like him being hog-tied naked onstage by a boa constrictor that emphasized every fat roll and made his weenie look like an earthworm, but otherwise I'm not really the vengeful type. So far.

Ric pulled back to whisper something less than romantic in my ear. "I don't have any silver bullets in my semi-automatic, but I can probably strangle him if he goes lobo and attacks us. He looks more attacked himself than aggressive. What's going on here?"

I knew. And I knew we were next, Ric probably first. That would be Loretta's strategic mistake. Taking her revenge out first on her father.

"This elevator is disabled," I said, punching the Main button one last, useless time. "Maybe it only goes down. Loretta has got to be lurking somewhere."

"Then, let's force her into the open." Ric grabbed Cicereau's elbow and hustled him over gray slabs of slate toward an aurora of light dead ahead.

It was like running into a close-up of the sun, but that was a visual effect only.

After a few steps we had to stop. We stood on the brink of a river of blood, with corpses floating by just beneath the surface of the current. Cicereau seemed to recognize some. His clawed half paw reached toward the bodies rolling gently over as they passed.

"Victims?" Rick asked.

I eyed Cicereau, now cowering on his human haunches beside me. The atrocious teal of his sweatpants was turning black up to his knees as the blood river water lapped at his ankles like a liquid tongue.

"Murderers," I guessed. "He's offed a lot of other were-wolves and rivals and inconvenient humans in his time, most fiendishly his young daughter and her ancient vampire Romeo."

"And we messed with Loretta's plans for resurrection and revenge, so she's out for blood," Ric concluded. "Plenty of it here."

As we watched, a splash to our right let us glimpse a fresh body rolling into the river. The man lifted a horror-stricken face above the gentle waves, then an arm and shoulder.

Ric leaned forward, instinctively planning to drag the guy out. I grabbed hold of Ric's collar, fearing the worst. It came with the swiftness of a wedge of arrows that pierced the drowning man's arm, neck, and face. With a primal groan he swept past us, sinking.

More arrows shot into water, striking the submerged forms that rose up with horrible cries before sinking again.

"*Diablo!*" Ric swore. "Here they torture corpses. Is this truly Hell?"

I glanced at Cesar Cicereau, crouched trembling at our feet in a half-shifted state of overheated panting and shivering cold. The sharp sound of something hard striking stone echoed behind us. I turned farther to squint into the shadows behind us and jumped back to glimpse a seven-foot-tall naked male with long shaggy hair and a horned head.

"Centaurs patrol this place," Ric breathed, nodding to the boulder-strewn ground we all stood on. "Their role here is to torture the murderers."

Only then in the bloodred shifting light of the river did I notice the horse chest and body and hooves that made up the vision's lower half.

"*We're* not murderers," I told Ric.

"He is." He looked down at Cicereau, who seemed on

the verge of slipping into the bloody river to escape the hooved nemesis that shot the searing arrows.

Ric looked up at me. "And you are."

"Prince Krzysztof, you mean. But . . . he was slaughtering tourists and Cicereau's bodyguards. Krzysztof wasn't even truly alive. He was animated bone and pieces of ancient organs and skins from the mummifying process. I stopped . . . it . . . from destroying innocent life."

I heard the hooves of the single centaur drawing near behind me, and whirled back to face it. In the crimson light cast by the river, I saw the centaur had a rider, not a ghost rider but a physically solid girl.

Girls and horses had gone together like anklets and Mary Jane shoes since *My Friend Flicka* had been painted on a cave wall, but this girl wasn't standard issue anything.

Loretta Cicereau's long tangled hair still trailed the once-imprisoning webs of Sylphia as if she was wearing a macabre bridal veil. She rode the man-beast barefoot and astride, her floor-length blue taffeta forties gown bunched up bustlelike behind her bare flanks, an oddly Teen Amazon look.

She carried the arrow-strung bow while the centaur paused, snorting through his flared human nostrils, fists akimbo on his hips, which were also shining sorrel equine shoulders. He was naked skin and muscle above the human hips, nude except for the diagonal slash of a leather band across his chest that held a quill full of arrows an elbow bend away from him and right at Loretta's fingertips behind him.

"You and the centaur you rode in on don't have any power over us," I told her. "We're not truly dead, not fair game for your kind."

"But I can torture and kill you." Turning, she aimed the

bow past the centaur's broad shoulder, "and what would torment you most, murderess, is *his* death."

She drew back the bowstring, but I rushed the smooth-hided horse-belly she straddled, grabbing a bare foot to drag her off the bizarre mount and to the ground.

The arrow in her bow shrieked free, blurring as it passed the edges of my vision, aimed at Ric, who'd been standing right behind me.

I screamed and turned, still clawing for Loretta's bare ankle.

From my feet, a snarling lupine figure bounded up in attack, sinking claws and fangs into the centaur's left shoulder. The man whinnied as the horse's lower limbs stumbled sideways. I'd momentarily thought Quicksilver had attacked, but it was a half-werewolf Cesar Cicereau whose repeated, growling lunges drove the beast off its stride and to the ground.

Loretta was falling sideways toward me. I caught the ends of her long hair and wrapped it around my hand, jerking her head around and her body hard to the ground, my eyes fixed on Ric, still standing.

What had she done?

Ric held out his left arm, dazed by blood-river red coloring the inside of his pale jacket sleeve, the outside of the pale suit coat.

By then my boot was pinning Loretta's all-too-solid flesh, her bow-holding wrist, to the stony ground and the silver familiar was binding that same wrist to the empty half of the handcuffs I now wore. Despite being down and immobile, Loretta was screeching with mad triumph, a banshee announcing a fresh death.

I turned again to stare, horror-struck, at Ric.

He looked down cautiously, lifted his left arm farther out.

"I'm all right." He sounded more surprised than I was by those words. "The arrow . . . must have skimmed between my arm and torso." He pieced the action together as he continued speaking. "It burned like a meteor for a moment, but . . . it only nicked me."

The silver familiar stretched itself into something resembling Wonder Woman's lasso of truth to bind Loretta's arms tight to her chest.

Ric, no longer startled, spun to grab the rabid Cicereau by the hackles of fur above his sweat suit. He pushed the half-turned mob boss to the ground again. Then he seized the only weapons available, the arrows from the quill of the fallen centaur, now lying on its side in a tangle of hooved legs, weakened by long gashes in its equine shoulder.

"My aim was true," Loretta shouted, squirming to work her bare legs around to kick me. "And the next arrow would have skewered *you*," she told me.

Owie! Irma yelped.

"Not saving the first round for your hated father?" I asked.

She glared at the angry, bloodied half-were. "I want him to suffer longer. I can torment him anytime. You two I want out of my life. Now!"

"You came after us, babe," Ric reminded her. "How?" he turned to ask me.

"She caught me on the wrong side of the mirror. A lot of that territory is laced with ancient and abandoned fey paths."

"She's not fey," a hoarse voice declared.

Ric and I looked toward the centaur's pain-wracked face. It remained mute.

The voice came from the ground, all right, but the speaker was the wolfman visage of Cesar Cicereau crawling to get face-to-face with the daughter he'd had killed, who'd come back as a ghost to haunt him and his hotel.

Anyone expecting a feud to be settled or a tender reconciliation didn't know Vegas and didn't know mobster werewolf families. They gave dysfunction a good name.

Ric and I stepped back, relieved one Cicereau was hogtied with silver and the other was caught in transition.

"Why the centaur?" I asked Ric in a whisper.

"According to Dante, they're the bullying guards on the Murder level. They have chronic anger-control issues and shoot arrows into the passing flood of murderers to make sure they're in constant torment."

I could feel my features wincing. Sadistic horses just weren't in my worldview. Even now I fretted about the wounded horse part.

At our feet, Cesar and Loretta were almost snout to nose and both were showing their teeth. A crimson foam seethed between Cesar's fangs. Loretta still looked girl-gone-rabid-rabbit.

"How'd you get me to this hellhole, daughter?" he growled at her.

"It's for murderers," she snarled back. "You are one. I just had to wait for your errand girl to get near any fey paths and I could send any of you where you deserved to be. And I'm not your daughter. I'm a fey changeling now. They get my ghost serving eternally at the Dread Queen's court and I get revenge on everyone who ever hurt me and Krzysztof when we were young and in love."

"Krzysztof was a vampire. He was never young. He was hundreds of years old," Cicereau spat, spraying Loretta's furious face with blood drops. "He was an inappropriate suitor."

She didn't even blink. "You never cared what anyone

did, just that it suited your purpose. You wanted to humiliate the vampire faction and take over Vegas when it was just a sandpit in the dirt road."

"I did care! I wasn't going to have any mixed-super couples in my 'Family.' Crime lord lore is full of treacherous son-in-laws and take-over operations."

Meanwhile, the silver familiar had slowly retracted back to my wrist. Both Cicereaus had clawed fingers curled onto the rock ridges beneath their bodies and were holding their positions for undear life.

Ric and I were moving away like a ballet couple doing a particularly slow and soft-footed pas de deux. We knew each other's minds and moves without having to exchange a look or a word.

There had to be an elevator car in this ghastly place somewhere.

As the heat and roar of the river faded, so did the light.

"I guess 'hell is other people,'" I quoted Sartre as the warring Cicereaus remained snarling at each other belly to belly, like territorial crocodiles on the banks of the blood river.

"I see the light." Ric looked ahead of us and it was just like in *Metropolis*. The subterranean depths where the workers toiled harbored a sleek steel exit door with Circles of Hell labeled *M, L,* and one through nine after that.

"Mezzanine, sir?" I used an old-fashioned elevator-operator trill.

"You bet." Ric pushed the silver button with the lit halo of light and leaned on the rocky wall. "I'd go anywhere with you, as long as it got us out of Murderers Row."

"Loretta is right, as you said. I did trick her resurrected boyfriend to his death."

"You can't kill a zombie, you can only destroy it, and

we've both done that to survive. 'Murder' has a whole new definition these days, Del. . . . Great, looks like the elevator is behaving itself now. It's about to give us a lift out of here."

"Very funny," I began, when a speeding bullet . . . or something really fast, knocked me into the rock wall so hard it took my breath away.

Ric leaned to catch me before I fell, and that same something knocked him into me.

We regained our balance to see the elevator's steel jaws closing on a creature that looked like a mangled chupacabra. Its slavering jaws were grinning as it leaped to press a clawed paw against the floor button panel.

Last glimpse.

We looked over our shoulders. Loretta was crawling to tend to her fallen centaur and her father was nowhere in sight.

A bell *tinged* above us. Level number six was lit up, and stayed that way.

We heard a horrible scream echoing from behind the sealed elevator doors.

Apparently it was programmed to stop on every level and Cesar Cicereau was in for a rollicking time escaping six through one.

Chapter Eleven

W*E'RE MAROONED IN Hell,* Irma wailed.

I had no answer.

"We're lucky to escape," Ric said. "Loretta went from skeleton to ghost to physical again, laughing maniacally all the way."

"She is a pistol," I admitted to Ric, "loaded for vengeance. To think she was empowered by being exiled to wherever the fey have retreated! Once again, I tried to contain one of the Sunset Park couple from doing damage to humans and only made the situation worse."

"It's Loretta's vengeful spirit that's causing all the trouble, not you."

Ric punched his fist into the unresponsive elevator button and scowled upward. We could watch each of the previous six levels of Hell light up to spit out Cicereau. Presumably, he was able to claw his way back on in his quest to reach the main Inferno Hotel level.

How he'd make his way through the daylight crowds to his own Gehenna Hotel turf in his current condition was his problem.

"This dead-serious version of Dante's Hell can't be part of the Inferno Hotel," I said wearily, leaning against the rough rock wall that surrounded the sleek steel elevator doors. "Public taste these days can be dark, but a blood river stocked with thousands of undead tortured corpses of murderers would get monotonous. Are you sure you're not wounded, Ric, or bleeding? I saw blood."

"Delilah, I don't feel a thing."

"That might be some fatal poison from the centaur arrowhead working. We've got to get you back into Las Vegas central to make sure you'll all right."

Ric patted his left side. "Relax, Delilah. Loretta shot the suit, not me. For intent to do evil, Loretta lives up to her father's rep. In terms of effective, er, execution, she's a failure. But we do need to find an exit fast, something other than death by blood river."

I turned in a frantic circle. "Even if we had managed to snag an elevator ride, I think Loretta and the fey have some control there. But there's no other way out."

Ric looked left to the river of churning corpses, then right to the sleek metal elevator doors. Their closed state seemed like a slap in the face to our survival.

"They didn't have elevators in Dante's day," Ric pointed out.

"No. That's an extension the Inferno Hotel made into real, raw, raving Dante's Inferno territory. I curse the moment I suggested you drop in on Snow to watch a freaking movie. It's his fault."

"Delilah." Ric bent to kiss my cheek. Bent? Oh, right, I'd lost my sling-back heels on the journey to this hell-hole and was now barefoot. No wonder the rocky ground roughed up my soles.

His kiss descended to my neck, and clung.

"You came to Hell itself to rescue me," he murmured against my carotid artery. "The least I can do is spring us from this trap."

I jerked away. "You can do that?"

He shook his head at my doubt. "One sentence will

explain my plan. I agree this is not part of the Inferno's tourist attractions, although that elevator is. I don't even want to speculate on what our host, Christophe, did to set up his Millennium Revelation hotel empire, or what backers he used."

"Probably the Black Prince of Darkness," I suggested. "Opposites attract."

"Not relevant to our situation."

"Which is pretty dire. I mean, barefoot in Hell?"

Ric smiled "Listen, Del. I studied Dante's *Inferno* and *Paradiso* in high school, remember?"

"We got *Moby Dick* and *The Scarlet Letter.*"

"Sorry," Ric said. "I can assure you that Dante Alighieri did not have elevators in his hometown of fourteenth-century Florence or in his Inferno."

I looked around. "You're saying there are *service* stairs in Hell?"

"Not really formal stairs. According to the Jesuit brothers in high school, Dante's Inferno is shaped like the caldera of a volcano."

Do we do volcanoes? Irma asked.

"Too Science Channel for me," I told Ric. "Caldera is the inside of a volcano?"

"It funnels down inside the volcano."

Ooh, I get it. Think a really big zit after the gooky white stuff has burst and leaves this red pit in your cheek.

Irma's analogy was too gross to dwell on, and I was too weary to think with my left brain, and my blank face probably showed that.

"Think an ancient amphitheater," Ric said.

My mind was blank except for *Oedipus Rex.*

"A football stadium."

"Oh. Rings and tiers of seats, wider at the top, narrower

at the bottom. Why didn't you say you were talking martini glass? Hell is shaped like a shaken-not-stirred James Bond martini."

Ric grinned. "That's the stuff. It's a rocky road carved out of raw earth and stone, one really big and rough-hewn circular staircase. What spirals down, can spiral back up. Come on!"

He headed back to the bloody river, me on his trail trying to catch glimpses of the left side of his suit coat. It would be incredibly lucky if that point-blank arrowhead hadn't pierced more than tropical-weight linen-and-silk blend.

I stopped when we were close enough to see the upended centaur's lower four limbs still struggling to right themselves. Loretta had deserted her faithful steed to hound her father through other levels of Hell, no doubt.

Ric picked up the arrows he'd grabbed and the bow Loretta had dropped. He went over to study the creature's shoulder gashes. "Too bad Quicksilver isn't here to fix those."

"I only soothe scars, not fresh wounds," I said, although even that was enough to get me into trouble. "That's why I want you up top ASAP for inspection and treatment."

"I told you, Del. It was just a graze. Meanwhile . . ." Ric squatted by the downed creature, patting the glossy horse shoulder. "This big guy needs to get on his hooves again. The wounds are superficial," he told me.

To the centaur, he said, "I'm going to help lever your foreparts up, okay?"

Churning hooves quieted as Ric moved around to face the human torso and head lying sideways on the rocky ground.

"You don't want to be a sitting target on the banks of

the blood river for too long," he told the man's fierce, pain-frozen, and helpless human face. "I'll get you up on your feet again and return the arrows and bow that will rearm you . . . if you'll carry me and my companion to the top level. You can be down here again and be back on the job in, say, half an hour."

The man bared square teeth as blunt as any horse's, but nodded his stiff neck and flowing mane. The human part of the beast hated helping us. The horse part had been trained to do just that.

I watched the magnificent headless horse push itself upright into statuesque equine glory as Ric grabbed the man's mane and helped the combo-creature to rise as one entity.

As the centaur staggered upright, Ric easily leaped atop the bare back astride . . .

Wow. A two-man, one-horse open sleigh, Irma marveled.

Ric filled the quiver on its human back with the confiscated arrows, but prodded his shoulder blade with the pointed end of the bow as a reminder who was boss. He leaned down to extend me a hand. "I always said I was a hooves kinda guy."

Me, ride pillion? I usually like to drive myself, but there were no reins here.

So. Ride pillion on a centaur? Priceless.

I vaulted up behind Ric, glad I was wearing bell-bottom pants, since the astride position mimicked the thigh-stretching footprint placement for victims of a TSA full-body scanning machine.

Wait! Irma was insistent. *We did horses very well at summer camp.*

I clutched Ric like a life raft when the centaur swung

into a jolting trot, then got a mini-roller-coaster buzz when it began a canter as smooth as butter. As it galloped on alongside the river, the gait's rise and swell felt as sweet as a wave to a surfer.

I laughed with relief and an odd joy, my hair flowing behind me like a flag, my arms clasping Ric's ahead of me, our thighs and torsos conjoined. We had become a bi-beast, a hybrid rider on a hybrid steed.

We sped past levels of Hell at its most horrible, carousel passengers aloof from the angst and the agony. It was if we had been forged into a glass menagerie mythological beast of legend and time.

The heaving belly and pounding hooves beneath us finally slowed.

Ric slid off the centaur's smooth side and waited to catch me on my own dismount.

The centaur held out a hand and Ric delivered the promised bow to it.

"Wait," I said, eyeing the creature from switching horse tail to shoulder and then the human head and torso. "The claw wounds are healed."

The human head spoke for the first time, eyeing each of us in turn. "A good deed in Hell is unheard of. Sympathy heals, but there is none of it below, even for the sympa-thizer. Best not return, riders."

With that he cantered away to his eternal round of har-rying corpses.

I looked around to see an empty, steel-doored eleva-tor, doors starting to close. We leaped to get on the single car, where I confronted a floor selection panel with a lot of Roman numerals, not Arabic numbers.

"We're at the *V*, Vestibule level," Ric assured me. "That's above both Limbo and Lust. Hit *M* as in Main,

Delilah, and we'll be back in the real hell-raising Las Vegas, instead of the surreal Hell of Dante."

A *V* is inside an *M. V* for Victory. I hit the button on the floor panel. Ric and I ascended for several suspenseful seconds. When the car stopped, the doors opened on a mob of waiting tourists. We were back on Vegas street-life level again, where sin was still busy being born instead of being punished.

Sweet.

Chapter Twelve

"**D**OES MY BLOODY armpit show?" Ric asked as we speed-walked from the elevator area into the slip-stream of casino crowds.

I stopped to let him gain a couple steps on me, eyeing the left side of his suit coat, then caught up.

"Not at all with your arm down. The real question is, does it hurt?"

"Not at all with my arm down." His smile broadened to showcase the usual Montoya confidence, that smile like a scimitar slash of white lightning against his bronzed south-of-the-border complexion.

How could you not buy a used Lamborghini from this guy? Irma murmured.

"Honest. It doesn't hurt at all anymore," Ric was protesting. "Don't be such a mother hen, Del. You must have seen some illusion, a fluke, maybe some spray from the blood river."

I slowed my pace as his down-shifted to blend in with the tourists. By then we were among the crowds milling on the dance floor that surrounds the Inferno Bar and gives it that eternal one-o'clock-in-the-morning nightclub ambiance.

"Say, Daisy Mae," a familiar voice hailed me. I turned to see Nora Charles in a striped long chiffon evening gown heading for us in a whirlwind of gray and white. "Good to see you two kids together again, as they said of Nicky and me for movie after movie."

"Daisy Mae?" Ric questioned Nora's nickname for me.

Nora eyed my bare feet. "Daisy Mae, from that new newspaper comic strip, Li'l Abner. My dear mother, Delta Mae—honestly and truly that was her name—told me it's not good to be barefoot in a briar-patch world, dear, and especially on a dance floor. Here, take mine."

Nora stepped back beside Ric, leaving a pair of silver satin thirties pumps standing empty on the blond wood floor.

While I stared, aghast, at the shoes, Nora murmured to Ric, "I see your visit to the L level was productive, dear boy." I looked up to see her fingernails playfully running down his chest, just a centimeter away from actual contact, and Ric . . . blushing? Certainly his bronze skin showed a touch of burgundy. Nora was such a sophisticated flirt. Maybe that was why she was considered the perfect wife by men of her era. Hopefully that now didn't include Ric!

"I can't take your shoes," I told Nora.

"Of course you can! I have dozens from the finest Hollywood designers."

"But . . ." Balancing a hand on Ric's shoulder—the poor guy was trapped between us now—I poked the shoe vamp opening with a testing big toe.

Holy high heels! The thing was physical. I pushed my toes all the way in, feeling like Cinderella trying on the glass slipper. Not a bad fit. First I cop a pair of ruby red slippers from the Emerald City Makeover Experience in Wichita, and now I'm being loaned CinSim shoes actually worn in the wildly popular Thin Man movie series.

Once my other foot was shod I didn't feel shrimpy, and backwoodsy, next to Ric and Nora. Hey! That combo sounded way too good together. I slipped my left arm around Ric's right one.

"Thanks, Nora. I'll drop the shoes back to the Inferno Bar tomorrow."

"Please don't. I'm looking forward to an update in outfits and having no shoes will force the boss to order one."

She smiled and wiggled her barely gray toes so the frothy hem of her gown did the cha-cha. The skirt was a floor-brusher anyway, so Nora wouldn't look shoeless unless she chose to reveal it. With a swift turn and swirl of voluminous chiffon, she returned to the bar.

"Wow," Ric said. "Having Nora Charles for a fairy godmother must be a kick for a film nut like you. Sexy shoes."

I liked the glitzy shoes peeping out from my bellbottoms, but the nightclub dance scene always on around the Inferno Bar was way more formal night and day than my casual outfit.

CinSim fans, known as "CinSymbiants" or "CinSymbs," dressed up as their favorite movie stars to come here and boogie. That meant they painted their faces and any visible skin white and wore only clothing in white, black, silver, and shades of gray.

I tried to smooth my hair. "You're always Mr. Cool," I told Ric, "but I must look like a disheveled escapee from Hell the centaur dragged in."

As I spoke, the silver familiar shivered up my spine and draped my collar bones with some dressy bling.

"It's a tough job, being a mirror-jumping, life-saving do-gooder." Ric grinned as he tweaked the ends of my hair.

The teasing gesture had pulled my face up. I was about to shake my hair loose when I saw his expression, and then I didn't want to.

He stepped close, closer as the crowds parted expertly to flow around us.

"Actually, I'm more than in the mood for dallying with

an escapee from Hell. Before the floor dropped out from
under us on the elevator and put us on that murderous lower
level, I was forced to interview a bunch of hot screen mamas
from the forties serving as call girls in the Inferno's lower
depths. Those black-haired film fatales—Jane Russell, Ava
Gardner, or Yvonne de Carlo—couldn't hold a candle to you
You'd know all their names better than I would."

"Yeah? They were all probably Howard Hughes rejects."

"Not you," Ric said. "Even Hughes's old, broken-down
vampire self has a soft spot for you. Speaking of soft
spots . . ." Ric's hands on my hips pulled my pelvis against
his while our mutual gaze never broke.

I'd come a long way since I'd been a skittish virgin
and we'd first done the salsa among the werewolves at Los
Lobos nightclub just months ago. Our brush with danger—
and Ric's puzzling sojourn among the Lust level's available
females—had revved both our libidos.

I smiled like the Mona Lisa, put my hands on his shoulders, and let my CinSim-slipper-shod feet do the walking,
or shuffling, to the music we suddenly heard, "Bolero."
Those slow Latin steps in Nora's borrowed heels produced
a wiggle in the palms of his hands on my bare hips, which I
could feel going from cozy-warm to fever-hot fast.

"Get a room," a low ironic voice commented in passing.

I whipped my head around, indignant, only to see the
back of Snow's white-suited form threading through the
dancers like an unseen ghost. Some stopped in their tracks
anyway, as if sensing an invisible wind. Just as Ric and I
had stopped, melded together.

The nerve," I muttered. "He's on another of his ghost
walks through his domain, felt but not seen."

Ric nodded as he drew me closer. "The nerve. He wants
me to move in here to babysit the Silver Zombie."

"Live at the Inferno? As if I'd want you back where you were in a coma, inhabiting what amounted to an ICU in the hotel bridal suite."

"We could make it a bridal suite, period," he said, feet moving in the mock-intercourse rhythm that kept our hips swaying three inches apart and then glued together again in an altogether indecent way. Our conversation continued in that same tantalizing way, murmured, private, always sexy under the surface, each coming together in almost a kiss, but not quite. It was like the famous Cary Grant–Ingrid Bergman serial kiss dialogue scene when the decency code forbade long kisses.

"This isn't a proposal, *hombre*?" I asked, brushing my lips along his jaw.

"Only for dirty dancing. Seriously. Christophe offered me an entire floor, and you a private elevator entrance."

"After experiencing one of his private elevators today, I think not."

"Not a bad deal, Delilah." His mouth pushed under my hair so his words vibrated against my ear. "Your Enchanted Cottage is teeming with unseen little helpers, not to mention Hector's intrusive security-voyeurism. No real privacy. My house may be technologically smart, but it's not secure on a level to keep out Loretta Cicereau's fey new physical form, not to mention El Demonio's zombie legions."

"So you're actually thinking about changing residences?" I tilted my head to let his tongue take full liberties.

"Right now, *paloma*, all I'm thinking is that we *do* need a room . . . somewhere. And soon."

"Not here," I said.

Not with Christophe so close, Irma seconded for my

ears only. *The last time you made healing love to Ric here, our favorite hotelier paid the price in pain.*

Snow loved rubbing that in as much as Irma, now that we both knew the touch of my lips could undo the second-hand scars I'd unintentionally inflicted any time I chose.

Since any lip-lock mojo I had resulted from Snow's Brimstone Kiss in the first place, you could say I owed it to him. Even if I could ever zone out and regard such healing intimacy as not quite sex for me, I'd learned from healing Ric it would be certain orgasmic pleasure for him and that was a deal breaker.

I liked to think of myself as true to my friends and a one-man woman with a conscience. Snow seemed bound to prove that everyone had her price.

Past secret history apart, I could understand why Snow would want Ric on board. *Mi amor* had dowsed the Silver Zombie from the film screen, a fully 3-D entity. That was a first even in this newly paranormal world, and Ric was the only one in it who had a prayer of controlling her. Plus, I knew he felt obliged to help her, to help any zombie he'd raised.

Talk about voyeurs. Hector Nightwine was a piker. I bet Snow would love Ric and me getting romantic under his own admittedly big-as-a-small-country roof, knowing how creepy I'd feel about it now. Get a room! Somewhere else for sure.

"Delilah." Ric's desire-deepened voice thrummed on my throat and sent all thoughts flying. "We're safe now. The music is hot and so am I, if you haven't noticed."

"Oh, I'd noticed. You're carrying concealed . . . a dows-ing rod."

"That's right." His lips moved to my neck as his breath and tongue warmed my skin and inner chambers. Then he whispered, "I want you. I want you fast and flat on your back, under me. I'll take the Inferno bar for a bed right here and now if you don't think of a private place pronto."

This "under me" talk got me simmering now that I could finally make love on my back without panicking from my childhood phobia. Once a fear is conquered, the new freedom can become addictive. Doing it on the Inferno bar with the liquor bottles from my cocktail recipes winking above us sounded even hotter.

"You'd do that, would you?" I murmured. "Right here, right now?

"In a heartbeat."

I wished I was wearing flame-red chiffon and scarlet spike heels. "All right. I give up. We'll get a room."

"I don't guarantee we'll make it to the bed."

"Let's just make it to the registration desk and improvise from there."

Chapter Thirteen

A LONG, LONG hot walk later we were ensconced in a classy room at the Crystal Phoenix Hotel across from the Inferno. Neither of us had wanted to sleep where Snow had told us to, for mutual but different reasons.

We had made it to the king-size bed, if not fully undressed, and I had made it on my back like Everywoman.

Now we lay beside each other in dreamy satisfaction, gazing up at the gilt ceiling, a softly reflective surface of gold leaf.

"Gilt" was the right word. The Phoenix would never be so obvious as to install a mirror over its beds, but seeing our hazy figures reflected above us, I guiltily recalled Snow's first words to me, that our twined black and white long tresses would look sexy in the mirror above his bed. An even more evil thought, maybe Lilith could spy down on us. There wasn't mirror enough here to do more than glow, thank . . . uh, badness.

Back then, I'd had no clue about my paranormal partiality to silver-backed mirrors and other reflective surfaces. Right now, my silver familiar was a ring clamped onto my belly button, wearing a zircon teardrop. Or maybe the semiprecious stone was meant to emulate sweat.

Of course a rock star would have ambitions of bedding anything female new in town that moved. And of course said female would feel rotten for harboring any pulse of response to such a blatant booty caller.

Ric shook my hand, which was wrapped around his. "Now can we talk?"

"Guys never want to talk after sex. I read it in *Cosmo Unplugged*."

"Usually murderous ex-ghosts don't show up as foreplay."

"So we talk. Forget Snow's visions of making us in-house dependents. On to *Metropolis*. What did you think of the movie?"

"I didn't stick around to see it."

"What? I swallowed my pride and sent you up there specifically to see the complete, uncut edition. It's vital you see it now that Her Serene Silverness has imprinted on you like a duckling on its mama."

"That's exactly why *I* didn't swallow *my* pride and get herded into his penthouse theater for a long, awkward sit-down with him observing my every reaction. Plus, he had the robot there and she, uh, came on to me."

"What?"

"She sort of . . . wakes up when I'm around. I didn't want Snow witnessing that again, calculating how he can use that fact and me and . . . it. His penthouse has this vast semicircular screen and theater house with only six seats in the place. Kinda sad. I think he was expecting you to be there too."

"Well, here's to doing the unexpected. So you left?'

"Right. I wanted to thoroughly check out the 'CinSim experience' at Inferno areas other than the very public bar before I make any decisions about anything involving the Silver Zombie."

"For the big picture, you need to see the uncut film, *mi amigo,* and you just blew the one opportunity on the planet to do that."

"You saw it. I can rely on your reporter savvy."

"Secondhand won't cut it here. The Silver Zombie responds only to you. You need to know her inside and out."

Ric winced. "Not that intimately, I hope." He glanced at his suit coat, crumpled on the floor. "There's no blood at all there. Or on me. Satisfied?"

"Yes, but I did see it at the time."

"Must have been a reflection from the boiling river of blood."

"Is that the Styx?"

"No. The Phlegethon."

"Ick. That sounds like something green you'd cough up."

"The name is based on the word 'phlegm,' and Hell was *supposed* to be icky in those days. Dante wrote in his own Italian Tuscan language, not the usual Latin, and he used Greek mythology and words. I know one thing. Where we escaped from was not part of the Inferno Hotel's Dante theme attractions."

"We were deposited in the real Hell?"

"Maybe we'll figure it out if we discuss larger issues, like why and how you tried to contain Loretta Cicereau and how and why she got loose to track me through the Seventh Circle of Hell. You've never explained much about your solo adventures at the Gehenna Hotel. I respect your right to conduct your own investigations, as I do mine, but we weren't as together then. Now that my hide is on the line, Del, I need full details."

So I explained that the Gehenna house magician, Madrigal, had rescued two nestling fey he'd found on their own. His human touch banned them from Feyland, so they'd become eternally attached to him.

"Oh, yeah." Ric nodded. "I've seen the billboards. He's the muscleman illusionist and those two Tinker-Bell types are his tiny assistants."

"They may look 'Tinker-Bell,' but they're venomous . . . and jealously possessive of Madrigal. Cicereau had caught me snooping around his hotel and . . . this is where my mirror-twin, Lilith, comes in . . . she'd had an anonymous nonspeaking role on one episode of *CSI V, Vegas*. Our glass-coffin-ready looks and her lack of clothing made her a very desirable collectible image worldwide. Cicereau wanted to build a magic act around Madrigal with me as the hot new naked corpse from the *CSI* franchise."

"I've seen some of that, but the quality was so bad I never realized it was supposed to represent you. What nonsense!"

"What? You don't think I'd make a hot naked corpse?"

"Yes, but . . . no." He laughed and ran his palm down my arm. "I'm screwed no matter how I answer that question. Why would you want to?"

"I didn't. So what was 'nonsense'?"

"That show's crime scene procedure isn't authentic. Technicians don't act as detectives. So tell me how you avoided becoming an undead pinup girl?"

"Madrigal's fey assistants helped me escape from the Gehenna because they wanted me away from their man."

"So what has that to do with the mobster's daughter coming after *me*?"

"I used the fey girls to bind Loretta Cicereau in Madrigal's main mirror after I'd lured her resurrected lover, who'd been brought back as a killing machine of mismated bone and patchwork flesh, into a reflection of Loretta on the empty air outside Cesar Cicereau's penthouse floor."

Ric made the connection. "I get it. Loretta's reanimated dead love was the mystery meat at the coroner's facility when I met you there that time. How'd the gangster's dead daughter get out of the fey stir you put her in, and why's she so pissed at me?"

"For one, she wants *me* to know what it's like to have a lover offed. Also, she blames your dead-dowsing talents for raising her and her vampire prince, Krzysztof, from their undiscovered grave in Sunset Park. They had a horrible death—"

"Don't we all risk that?" Ric murmured. His distance-focused eyes were probably rerunning his tortuous time under the Karnak Hotel's ancient Egyptian–themed superstructure.

Every key figure in the rescue party—Sansouci, Snow, and Grizelle, the Inferno security chief—was certain Ric had passed the point of death when we finally found him. I still refused to believe my secondhand Brimstone Kiss had revived him when I hadn't been able to pound a heartbeat back into his chest and had given him a passionate farewell kiss. The usefulness of the so-called Kiss of Life had been debunked years ago, and that wasn't what I was trying. I wasn't a miracle worker who thought I could save Peter Pan if I clapped my hands or puckered my lips, although I did believe in fairies if they were the terrifying fey.

But somehow I did bring Ric back to consciousness.

"Loretta's fury springs not so much from the dying," I said after a silence, "as what was done to the victims beforehand. I have to say Cesar Cicereau deserves whatever she can dish out."

Ric eyed me again, quizzical. "You never mentioned 'beforehand' details."

"You weren't there and I wasn't eager to dwell on them. When I was 'exorcising' the Gehenna Hotel of Loretta's ghost, she accused her father of worse atrocities than fili-cide. He picked a vicious gangster way to punish the cross-supernatural pair, and probably to show his own lack of mercy. Cicereau's men castrated and killed Loretta's lover—" Ric's intent listening expression tightened. "I was about to say 'young lover,' but he was a youthful vampire several hundred years old. Then they raped Loretta right there beside his body and killed her too.

"She must have lived long enough to turn and clutch his body in her arms," I theorized. "That's why we found the skeletons embracing. That sight touched every Vegas crime professional involved in reclaiming the bones, except that sadistic cop, Haskell. So the young couple had been discovered making love, all right, but that moment was profaned. Maybe not such a great subject for postcoital chitchat, huh?"

Ric's frown of disbelief and horror had deepened with the details of my story. "Weird. That kind of gratuitous sexual brutality has ancient historic roots, and it's showing up again?"

"Hold that grisly thought." I rolled off the bed, grabbed my bell-bottoms, and headed for the bathroom. "Time to shower out the kinks and tune our heads into war, not love."

Most Las Vegas bathrooms these days could serve Roman emperors. I entered a wonderland of wall-to-wall marble and mirrors, soaking tubs and whirlpools, foot baths and anatomically adaptable massaging showerheads and driers, not to mention obscenely multifunction bidets.

Somewhere in all this in-your-face and funky excess were hidden extremely discreet actual toilets.

Ric followed me in, whistling at the shining high-tech water and action toys. "Do you think the master bath on my proposed private floor at the Inferno could have all this?"

"And more, much more decadent. Trust Snow. Also probably a stainless steel service bay for the robot."

"Now here's a good question. Do CinSims sleep?"

"Maybe standing up, like horses."

Ric began shrugging off his unbuttoned shirt, his only remaining article of clothing. I was relieved to confirm there was no blood on it, nor on his skin. Somehow Loretta had managed to wing only his suit coat. "I know humans can do other things standing up than sleep."

"Again?" I asked, pleased to find him unharmed but not unarmed, so to speak.

"The first time was fast and dirty. This will be slow and clean."

FRESHLY SCRUBBED AND fully dressed, and thus feeling extremely virtuous for fornicators, Ric and I lounged together in the bedroom sofa area before giving up the posh room that was ours until morning. This had actually felt like a mini-vacation, moreso than our recent road trip to Wichita.

"I hate to ruin the mood," Ric said, "but what the werewolf mob did to the teen lovers sounds like transferring life-force rituals for dead Viking chieftains."

"I have a feeling my stomach is not going to like this."

"It's . . . horrible and sexist, yes. A slave girl is sacrificed. It begins with her being raped by men in the chieftain's guard."

By then, I was pulsing with fury. "Yeah, testosterone-driven cultures always come up with reasons to torture and defile women."

"Then it gets ugly. She's sent into the tents of warriors and traders, who explain they're raping her out of love for their dead leader. Finally she is taken into a tent on the Viking ship bearing the chief's body, where six men rape her before strangling and stabbing her."

"Any chance you can raise some Viking chieftains to feed to Loretta and the fey girls?"

"That isn't so different from parts of Africa today, where men believe that raping virgins will cure them of AIDS."

"Some days I could sneak back into Dr. Frankenstein's lab under the Karnak Hotel and whip up a nuclear bomb that targets only testosterone-bearers, you excepted. Is there a reason you further ruined my view of the inhumane human race? Yes, Loretta was raped and shot. What are you saying? Cicereau is a resurrected Viking as well as a werewolf?"

"I wouldn't be surprised to find a long line of werewolves among the Vikings and other Northern marauders, but no. I'm saying the drug cartels' horrible violence to innocent men, women, and children in Mexico often repeats those ghastly primitive rituals. I've long suspected the drug lords are either employing academic experts in perverse human behavior or some sort of demonic sadism consultant. Perhaps they have since the early twentieth century. Look at the tribal wars in Africa. And Cicereau was a chieftain of his tribe, disciplining a disobedient child. Haven't you wondered why he's lived so long? Werewolves aren't ordinarily immortal, like vampires."

"I did wonder," I said. "Sansouci was with Cicereau back in the forties, but he was a hostage from the defeated vampires indentured to Cesar. So why has Cicereau lasted as long as he has? Maybe the Immortality Mob is involved."

"Or maybe the mob is the defeated vampires of seventy years ago in corporate clothing. Sansouci, along with Big Bad Howard Hughes, makes two closeted vamps operating aboveground in Vegas. I know you've found the Gehenna muscleman a handy information source, but a vampire could turn on you, or turn you, any time."

"No. Sansouci's got a constant blood supply. He's Sir Sipalittle-a-lot."

"Huh?"

"Vamp tramp pipeline. He's a gigolo with a string of willing clients, all donating just enough blood to make it exciting for them and sustaining for him."

"Good for him, as long as he stays true to the harem. I don't want anyone sucking on your neck besides me."

His lowering head nudged my chin back as kissing lips and tasting tongue forged a trail from the hollow of my throat to under my left ear.

While my heartbeat did a startled sprint, in the dark shadow of my hair he imprinted a love bruise on my ultra-white skin. It burned almost but not quite too much. Put me on an edge I couldn't resist.

Despite my lifelong fear of vampire bites—or maybe because of it—my body throbbed with liquid heat in all the right places. Ric almost never broke the skin, but these moments alarmed as much as they excited me. He pulled away, kissing my lips almost as long and hard, and ran a hand down my torso that had surged against his with a will of its own.

"You've really got to let us get back to cases, *chica*."

As if I'd started it again.

Really, now that I was out of my overaged virgin box, I was still freaked by how easily men spotted that and how much I was getting to like it. I was facing a whole new world most other people had long visited by my age of twenty-four, commonly called "carnal knowledge."

Loretta's ghost had once claimed credit for Ric's and my instant sexual connection when we met and dowsed together in Sunset Park. She told me her and Krzysztof's passion had leaped to us, and in this new paranormally quirky world, she might have had a point.

Thoughts of undying undead love were too morbid, or personal, for me. I pulled away from Ric, reluctantly becoming investigative reporter again.

"Sansouci called the double killing 'the Blood Price.'"

"That's a very Mafia concept, and now like the drug cartels too," Ric said. "Cicereau probably wanted a male heir, so the female, especially a disobedient female hooking up with a male not of his selection, was expendable."

"He certainly will force anyone to work in his Vegas empire—magician, vampire, or little me in the guise of my double, the *CSI* autopsy queen, Lilith."

"Why'd you keep that surprise under wraps for so long?" Ric asked, his dark eyes narrowed to indicate he was teasing. "Afraid of some really direct competition?"

"She's why I came to Vegas. Lilith supposedly was one of the TV series' actual corpses, who kill themselves for the immortality of being taped during their autopsy on the number one show in the world. But Hector seems to want me to replace her, or . . . find her. I don't know what he really wants, or what Lilith really is, spirit, doppelganger, sister, or evil spirit."

"Nightwine is a wild card among Vegas powers that be," Ric mused. "As with Christophe at the Inferno, exactly *what* paranormal he is, if any, remains a mystery. I knew Nightwine had some hidden motive for keeping you under his thumb and oversight at the Enchanted Cottage. Still, it's a cool place for you to live, cheap and secure. But playing landlord is not charity on his part."

"I could sue him for using my 'image' without authorization, and told him so when I first came to town."

"What about your mirror-chase of Lilith? Is she ever going to show up on our side?"

"I did confront her outside a mirror once, in a back alleyway. Inside or out of a mirror, she's rebellious, bitter, savvy, and in that alley she left me to the oncoming hyena pack from the vampire empire."

"Lilith. The rebellious teenager you never had a chance to be. Instead, you grew up as the innocent, loyal, inquisitive, defensive, smart girl."

"Sometimes you're eerily perceptive, Montoya."

"Try having a renowned child psychologist for a foster mother."

Mention of Helena Troy Burnside made me think of my CinSim foster dad, super defense lawyer Perry Mason. I wondered if he could force Snow to release a copy of *Metropolis* to us because we fought to help the Inferno head man keep it. No, even Perry Mason wouldn't intimidate Snow.

That idea led to another that perked me up like the Silver Zombie with Ric in the sights of her blank oval eyes.

"Ric! I bet I know where else we can see an uncut copy of *Metropolis*!"

"Back at the restored vintage movie theater near Wichita? No more road trips to weather witch country."

"Oh, this will be a very short trip."

Chapter Fourteen

LEAVING THE CRYSTAL Phoenix lobby, we soon found the world beyond the artificial novas of its glass and white neon-lit entrance canopy was—surprise—dark as night.

I looked up to check if the moon had risen high enough to be visible in the usually cloudless Vegas sky. Not yet. I wondered when, or if, Cesar Cicereau would get back to his hotel in time to go into hiding until he could finish his "shift."

I smiled. For now, the werewolf mob boss was facing job time conflicts like any other working stiff.

I checked my watch face. "It stopped."

"You can't rely on those vintage timepieces, Del." Ric pulled his cell phone from his jacket pocket. Then he frowned.

"I'm not getting a signal. Must be all the wattage. The Strip is famous for messing up cells. This movie thing isn't working out. We should forget it. It's later than we thought anyway."

I nodded. That comment cut a lot of ways.

"Besides, that thing is awfully long, isn't it?" Ric added.

I couldn't resist. "*I* don't think so. They never can be too long for me."

"I just think the timing is bad."

"Aw, c'mon, Ric." I draped myself over his shoulder, cajoling like a gun moll. "We've gotta do it sometime."

Revolting bimbo act, Irma confided.

"You folks need a ride someplace?" A cabbie who

had just unloaded his passengers at the Crystal Phoenix entrance idled his small yellow SUV beside us.

"Perfect!" I opened a back door and hopped in. I leaned forward to tell the gentleman originally from Oman, it turned out, our destination before Ric heard it. As an ex-reporter, I was used to chatting up people in the service industries, getting their life stories along with their cooperation, so Ahmed began a monologue. Driving a cab can be a lonely occupation.

Ric hadn't seen this side of me before. He settled back to eavesdrop as I elicited which hotels had the better occupancy rates, that Chez Shez was the hot new can't-miss offbeat spot on the Strip, and Madrigal's sparkly little assistants were really "puppets."

"Puppets, no kidding," I marveled, accepting the usual stream of both information and misinformation.

Ric, meanwhile, was eyeing the streets as we turned off the glare of the Strip.

"Nothing resembling a cineplex this way," he noted.

"I should just ask you to close your eyes until we get there." I shut up both Ahmed and Ric by pushing *mi amor* back in the seat for a make-out session. Sure enough, his eyes closed on cue.

"You're being impetuous and mysterious," he was able to murmur before I took total control. "I like it."

Ahmed switched on the solo driver's consolation and wake-up pill, Poxx talk radio.

MY SURPRISE WAS sprung when I had to use the tiny remote I worked out of my pants pocket.

Ric looked up to see the rearing forefeet of the Four Horsemen of the Apocalypse bronze sculpture looming over our vehicle.

The cab stopped inside the now-open iron gate.

"First the time got away from us, and now the place isn't right." Ric's frown barely dented his dusky Latino forehead, but it made him look intense and *muy* macho.

"This is one of the highest-security pads in Vegas," I pointed out. "Ours free for the duration."

"I don't want to owe anything to our ambiguously supernatural host."

"He can't be worse than the morning movie date you ultimately stood up."

Ric was teasing now too. "I suppose we have to do it sometime."

"*Umm*, yes, we do."

Ahmed's eyes were popping in the rearview mirror.

"For two hours and fifty-one minutes, you say?" Ric asked.

"And fifty-*two* minutes."

Ric groaned.

So did Ahmed.

"Twenty bucks will do it," Ahmed said. "I gotta leave." As Ric leaned forward to pay him, the cabbie rasped, "That woman is insatiable, buddy. Run for your life."

The moment our feet touched pavement, the cab's wheels squealed away like an abused Indy 500 stock car. The cab's taillights disappeared down Sunset Road. Ahmed's meter was now a tracking meteor.

"That's the nicest thing anybody's said about me since I left Kansas," I told Ric. "Now," I went on, "I need to quick-change into something more comfortable . . . and less wafting an odor of boiling blood. You can hang out in the courtyard for a sec. Look. Isn't that cute? Quicksilver's waiting for you on the stoop to play catch."

"Cute" was my way of kidding. Quicksilver was all

dog, and then some. The half-wolf part dominated his looks, and the half-wolfhound part accounted for his huge size and striking blue eyes to match mine, that being a rare wolfhound gene.

"You don't need to doll up for me!" Ric yelled as I raced inside the Enchanted Cottage, leaving him to confront a very bored guard dog in search of a little home entertainment, just like us.

In four minutes flat, I was back outside. Quicksilver was waiting by the Enchanted Cottage's hobbit-hole-shaped front door when I came through in one of my Hector-cajoling outfits.

The platform heels almost looked "today"—purple satin peep-toes with marabou feather trim over the instep. The knee-length forties frock of pale lilac print voile was short at the flutter sleeves and swing hemline. I had puffed my hair up at the sides into a heart-shape, thanks to two tortoiseshell combs, but it was down in back, falling like a curtain over the nape of my neck.

"Holy Hedy Lamarr!"

Ric had recently seen the real thing, so I was highly flattered. He was still under the influence of the Lust level; I could tell by how he eyed me.

My new yet discreet hairstyle, designed to hide any trace of his love bruises, was a private signal and a turn-on for him that would be wasted on our unsuspecting host. Hector Nightwine struck me as a leg man anyway, or perhaps, more accurately, a drumstick man.

"How do you manage these vintage transformations?" Ric asked. "I hate to say it, but you'd be the queen of the Inferno's Lust level in that getup, especially the silly shoes."

Apparently Ric's stroll through the Inferno's shady lady

section had upped his appreciation of vintage rags, if not footwear.

"Frilly, not silly, shoes," I corrected him. "My secret weapon is a long history of attending Wichita estate sales, added to an Enchanted Cottage wardrobe witch I never spot."

"I love how you look, but I hate that you gussy yourself up for that *CSI* lech, Del."

"He's genuinely fond of CinSims and their vintage appeal, Ric. I doubt he ever leaves his estate, and rarely his office suite. He likes being cajoled, but he'd never touch me and risk destroying the illusion. There are worse power mongers in Vegas nowadays. And I'm betting you'll get a chance tonight to research my favorite CinSim, Godfrey. Just don't mention to Nightwine that Snow owns a totally complete new version of *Metropolis*. Hector would chew on more than the usual *Survivor* reality show vermin atop his desk if he knew that.

"Come on, Quick." I turned to my patient dog, who'd been following our conversation like a spectator at a tennis match. "Time for us to get our due at the Big House."

Quizzical, Ric jammed his hands in his pockets and held his tongue too, trailing Quicksilver and me while we trotted across the driveway into the servants' entrance of Hector Nightwine's Sunset Road mansion.

Cameras on stalks rotated silently across the courtyard to follow us, reminding me of mechanistic alien eyes in a fifties science-fiction movie.

"Now you'll see what *I* have to put up with," I told him as I opened the kitchen door, "to live in high-end security."

"MASTER QUICKSILVER! MISS Street," Godfrey exclaimed, meeting us inside the door, as he always did.

If I didn't know that *his* master required him to dance twenty-four attendance on his apparently insomniac self, I'd think Godfrey lived by Nightwine's back and front doors, the eternal butler.

"And Mister Montoya," Godfrey acknowledged Ric with a nod of his head. "The master is most curious about the purpose of your visit. May I say, Miss Street, you look most like Miss Carole Lombard in that ensemble?"

"Thank you, Godfrey. That's an enormous compliment. Carole Lombard," I told Ric, "was Godfrey's love interest in the film named after his butler character, *My Man Godfrey*."

"Does Nightwine lease that Lombard CinSim?" Ric asked us.

"Alas, no," Godfrey said in his emotionless butler voice. "It might distract from my duties, and, frankly, the girl was a bit of what you nowadays call ditzy, and a pushy dame on top of it."

"She *made* Godfrey marry her at the end," I explained.

"Oh," Ric said.

"Mr. Nightwine is eager to see you, Miss Street," Godfrey told me, "but not Master Quicksilver. He fears competition for his favorite snacks."

"Quick prefers the prime cuts you feed him from the kitchen anyway," I answered. "Ric, why don't you and Quicksilver get acquainted with one of Godfrey's filling snacks while I pave the way with Nightwine upstairs?"

Ric nodded far more agreeably than I'd expected, so I left the trio and took the narrow back stairs to the level of Nightwine's office. There I knocked lightly on the huge coffered door.

"Enter," a robust voice commanded.

I did.

"Such a pleasure to see you back after your recent get-away, Miss Street. Sit."

I did, crossing my legs, which allowed display of the half-off frou-frou shoe dangling from my instep.

Nightwine sighed with visual, vintage satisfaction. He loved feeling like a detective in a noir movie receiving a femme fatale client. Nero Wolfe, perhaps, given he too was a housebound man of size.

"What can I do for you, Miss Street? Everything running smoothly at the Enchanted Cottage? No rogue gnomes or pixies showing up?"

"Peaceful as ever." I'd never told Nightwine that the hall looking glass had always acted more like a door than a mirror for me, but he probably knew. Someone had bought the Wicked Queen's prop from Disney's *Snow White* film. Who, if not Hector?

I had a bone to pick with Nightwine, but now was not the time to bring up touchy matters.

"I see the Cadaver Kid has escorted you here," he noted.

"Ric was called that in his very early days with the FBI. It's a dated term now, Hector."

"But so colorful, Delilah." He also loved it when our conversations evolved into first names, though they always defaulted back to more formal forms. "He would do very well as an actor in one of my *CSI* international franchises, perhaps *CSI Chihuahua*."

I didn't mention it sounded like *The Dog Whisperer* meets *Criminal Minds*. "I'm sure he's not interested."

Hector sighed. "I can always use my Ricardo Montalban and Cesar Romero CinSims, but fresh blood *feeds* successful TV series."

"And your frequent autopsy scenes provide plenty of that."

We were getting too close to the bone. My grievance: his already pimping existing images of Lilith and me for a new series. Time enough to broach that another day.

"We are so bored, Hector," I said, getting down to business by twirling my instep and putting the marabou on my purple peep-toe shoe in tremulous motion.

Hector's left eyebrow raised and his red Cupid lips pursed.

"I told Ric if anyone had the latest, most complete version of *Metropolis*, it would be you."

Hector beamed. "You never underestimate me, my dear Miss Street. Of course I do, but why is the Cadaver Kid . . . apologies, Mr. Ricardo—"

"Mr. Montoya."

"Yes, how careless of me. Why would your beau, who has always been rather indifferent to vintage films, wish to watch such an old, silent, and long example of the art form?"

"*He* doesn't, but I love the imaginative clothes."

"Yes, they are drool worthy, aren't they? I believe you know figures of influence in Vegas who'd be willing to re-create any of the garb, particularly from the Yoshiwara nightclub scenes, for yourself, if you but expressed an interest and a suitable gratitude."

Jeweled pasties and sheer concubine skirts, right. "I prefer my own collection and whatever the Cottage's clever resident wardrobe witch can produce."

"I do have an ample state-of-the-art home theater. I don't suppose you'd care to have me join you?"

"Ric is such a novice at silent films that you'd find the experience wearing."

"How can you consort with someone so lacking in that appreciation?" Nightwine shuddered as if he'd accidentally tasted a Cheeto. I fully expected him to display an orange tongue next.

"This is an educational outing for Ric's sake, Hector. You can help bring another soul into the flock of film fanatics."

"Play on my better instincts, will you? Very well. Have the lad up, but the dog must remain on the ground floor. I find him ungovernable."

"So do I," I said with a smile, rising. "I'm sure Godfrey will install us comfortably in your viewing palace."

Hector's smile grew sly as his chins dimpled against his brocade cravat. "You will adore it."

I smiled back. On this, we spoke the same language. Sometimes I forgot he was a really lonely man, or whatever, and that was why I cut him slack.

Chapter Fifteen

Ric watched Godfrey don an apron with aplomb and remove a platter of roast beef from the massive stainless steel refrigerator-freezer unit. A CinSim maid also clad in black with white cap, cuffs, and apron began making cold cuts for Quicksilver and a welcome sandwich for him.

Delilah needed a food break too. With all the morning's excitement extending into afternoon, they'd been too busy to eat. Or too in love. Ric's stroll on the Inferno's wild side had stoked his desire for Delilah and now that the hang-up against lying on her back had been exorcised, they had a lot more exploring to do.

Ric returned his mind to Nightwine's kitchen and found himself grinning like a Halloween pumpkin.

"Please sit down," Godfrey invited, pulling out a stool at the central island. "The master has ordered a viewing supper later for you and Miss Street. I'm told the film is almost as long as three hours of network prime time."

"Don't you find this role demeaning, Godfrey?" Ric asked as he sat.

"Why should I, dear boy? I'm a successful businessman with a social conscience for the devastated unemployed of my Depression times and now, yours. I played along with being mistaken for a homeless man and took a butler job because the family involved needed serious emotional and financial help."

"And you 'help' here too?"

"Indeed. The master is housebound."

"Some house." Ric eyed the huge, high-ceilinged kitchen gleaming with the stainless steel of innumerable gadgets.

"I do enjoy the surroundings."

"So you feel some sense of loyalty to your 'owner'?"

"Certainly. Loyalty has always been my greatest virtue. The self who underlies this incarnation got my ex-wife the lead female role in my namesake film because I recommended her for the job. And together we made screwball film history. An amusing sort of immortality, isn't it?"

"Carole Lombard was once your wife?"

"I see our Miss Street has been explaining my role to you. She was also my wife again, in the film, although Miss Street is quite right that the character bulldozed me into marriage at the end. Don't get yourself corralled in such a sneaky fashion, my lad."

Ric waved off that notion. "Do you miss . . . Miss Lombard? Would you want her on these premises?"

"Not necessary, although Miss Street was instrumental in getting my . . . er, cousin at the Inferno his screen wife and even the dog."

"Delilah got Snow to buy Nora Charles and Asta for Nick's sake?"

"Indeed. Miss Street could get Christophe of the Inferno to do a great many more things for her, should she stoop to flattering his ego. He is not a hopelessly bad individual," Godfrey mused while swiping a dishcloth over Quicksilver's already bare and washed plate. "More misguided than anything. Next to Miss Street and the master, no one in Las Vegas is as considerate of CinSims as he. We do not forget our friends."

"Are you familiar with the film Delilah and I will be seeing?"

"*Metropolis?* Of course. It came out only a few years before my best work."

"Godfrey, you seem much more self-aware than most CinSims."

"I am supposed to be the perfect gentleman's gentleman."

"Yes, but you know where your other . . . incarnations . . . are located in Las Vegas, and even recognize the actor beneath the character."

"We are not stupid, Mr. Montoya, just limited somewhat in our memories, and certainly in our movements, through no fault of our own. My master's love of film requires I discuss them with him and I've learned what many less advantageously placed CinSims may never access. Why all the personal questions, Mr. Montoya?"

"I was forced as a child to raise so many zombie 'canvases' that may have been used for CinSims."

"Well, you have a special talent, then."

"But now I've raised a CinSim directly from the screen and it . . . she . . . seems horribly dependent on me."

"Ah. Which version of the stunning actress Brigitte Helm are you referring to?"

"I don't know. The form is the silver metal robot zombie."

"Actually a plastic, wood, silver-and-bronze robot zombie, I believe."

"That doesn't matter! The point is her image registers as all silver on the old nitrate films used then. The point is I brought her to 'life,' personally. I've never done that with a film creation. And now she has a bizarre second life, thanks to me."

"It certainly will be interesting to see what she does with it."

"Is that up to her? Snow owns her."

Godfrey's head shook from side to side in a maybe-maybe not manner. "In a way. In another way, it depends upon what we CinSims are exposed to, as I'd mentioned."

"You're like children, then? You can learn and develop a sense of self?"

"It depends on the sophistication of our underlayment, as it were. On what we're exposed to in our environments."

"And if that environment is an elaborate brothel?"

"Oh, dear. Not my style. However, all Hollywood was an elaborate brothel when it came to female actors."

"And Delilah isn't catering to Hector Nightwine when she dresses up to see him?"

"The master is a viewer, not a doer. What harm does it do to invoke his favorite things?"

He glanced up at a callboard. "I see the office light is on. That means I should install you in the home theater. Any particular beverage you crave? Nick Charles would recommend oodles of Boodles for a three-hour film like *Metropolis*."

Ric shook his head in defeat. "Whatever you deem appropriate, Godfrey. You're the perfect gentleman's gentleman."

DELILAH WAS WAITING for him against a background of looming doors of gilt and carved wood, the pale purple of her forties frock intensifying the dramatic effect of her blue eyes and black hair.

"I'm supposed to pay attention to a movie?" Ric asked as he came up to her.

"I know what you guys go for in darkened movie theaters. Really, Ric, you *have* to pay attention to the film. This is an investigative outing."

"If you say so." He pulled the huge door handle open and they walked into what resembled a gigantic vintage jukebox, uplit columns and arches of intricately carved glass in luminous colors of poison green, hot orange, vivid red, and neon purple.

The theater house was a sea of red-velvet wave after wave of seat backs, enough to accommodate a couple hundred.

"All this for us?" Ric asked.

"All this is for Hector's aesthetic sense. I guessed from your morning activities you'd rather be obligated to Hector Nightwine than Snow."

"I'd rather be obligated to no one."

She led him halfway down the center aisle. "This okay?"

"I can snooze here as well as anywhere."

"Trust me. You won't want to nap through this film. Hector's print lacks six minutes Snow's has, but narrative title cards will bridge any gaps."

"Title cards? It's a 'movie' but not a 'talkie,' and now it's a 'readie'?"

Delilah leveled those police-car blue-light-special eyes at him.

"You've got to face the Silver Zombie in all of her many manifestations, Ric," she said. "What you raised in Wichita will incredibly complicate the human and unhuman world in Vegas, and she is definitely a package deal."

Chapter Sixteen

SOMETIMES OUR BELOVED Ricardo Montoya, Irma noted, *can be as stubborn as a chupacabra.*

So could I. We settled into the cushy seats, easing around the burl wood trays attached to one arm. I took advantage of the initial gawking period at the spectacular surroundings to study Ric's profile. What had he and Godfrey discussed? I wondered.

Godfrey and his own silver tray arrived fast on our heels.

"Master Quicksilver is watching *The Wolf Man* in both forties and 2010 reboot on the servants' quarters wide-screen TV," he whispered to me. "The next feature is *Ratatouille*."

He set out crystal martini glasses and platters of appetizers.

"No popcorn?" Ric asked.

"Mr. Nightwine finds crispy foods disruptive at film showings."

"So what are these pale, damp-looking worms?" Ric asked.

"Cheese curls, sir. There's Montrachet, English cheddar, verde capra, rustico limone, and drunken goat, for those well acquainted with El Chupacabra. No crunching to interfere with the exquisite symphonic score. Pop-up drink refills are on your left. Enjoy."

I smothered a giggle as Godfrey retreated. "He sounded so contemporary waiter."

"What the hell are all these cheese varieties? Drunken goat?"

"Delicious, I bet. I don't see any evident insect legs, so I think it's safe to snarf and sip."

I leaned back in the reclining seat and aimed my eyes at the huge black screen set between swaths of red velvet curtains.

"I'm glad we're not seeing this in Snow's penthouse," Ric said.

"I doubt it would be as pretentious."

"Did you ever notice the blood-bruise in the hollow of his lily-white throat?" Ric leaned close to whisper. "It seems new since Wichita."

"Ah, didn't notice it, really."

"That's a relief. No decent *chica* should. It was half-concealed by his rock-god black-leather collar. Some long-stemmed skank tried to suck the soul out of him. I bet she was a looker."

I cleared my throat.

Throat? Irma admonished me. *What a Freudian slip. You ever going to 'fess up to laying that mark on the dude?*

"Groupies are throwing themselves at Snow all of the time," I said, loud enough to drown out Irma in my own mind, desperately wishing for a program for the upcoming film that I could flip through to hide my lying-by-omission eyes.

And so are we, thanks to you. Irma was being merciless.

If I couldn't get me and Irma to understand why I'd ever thought taunting Snow with an irresistible turn-on was payback for my being in his total sexual thrall for the duration of what had seemed an endless Brimstone Kiss, I'd never convince Ric.

The BK had probably lasted a minute and forty-five seconds, one one-hundredth of the time the new, restored version of *Metropolis* would unreel. It had only seemed like a lifetime, as watching this early silent film would no doubt seem to Ric.

"This will be primitive," I warned. "The makeup was garish and the acting is broad, yet oddly intense despite it. Especially between the men. There's a father-son struggle and a romantic triangle involving a dead woman named Hel. One *L*."

"The usual melodrama. Any action?"

"Lord, yes. A towering city of the future, an underground city of enslaved zombielike workers, a heartless CEO, an angelic young girl savior who's turned into an emotionless robot, and a false double of herself to destroy the workers. Then there are riots, a flood, statues of the Seven Deadly Sins coming to life, and luxurious depravity at a nightclub."

"Sounds way too much like Vegas today."

"Look, Ric." I punched up an Albino Vampire martini that lifted from the wide arm-tray like a ballerina on a music box, sans cheap melody. "I sat through *Night of the Living Dead* for you outdoors in Dolly's front seat, in a hokey restored drive-in off a deserted state highway in Kansas. You need to see *Metropolis* to understand the creature you raised from the film Snow located and obtained back in Wichita. She's got a silver-metal crush on you and the demon drug lord who held you prisoner as a child wanted her really bad. But we've got her."

"Snow owns her, and the film."

"Snow needs us to control her, as only you can, and to decipher her role in this wacky mob-run supernatural hierarchy . . ."

"As only *you* can," he finished. "Okay. I'll watch this ancient and endless art-house flick. But I need necking and petting privileges."

I looked around. I had to admit the cushy seats and the dark empty theater was making me, um, pliable, way more pliable than any metal woman.

Ric took advantage of my silent okay to push away the hair on my nape and engage in his favorite turn-on, and now mine, a clinging, stinging kiss turned passion bruise. I was nervous about how close our ritual was to welcoming a vampire intimacy. Still, I'd become hooked on this shadowy secrecy, on hiding the visible proof of our passion, on the danger of edging near where vampires and vamp tramps went for sex and blood. Maybe I'd been a naive fool all my earlier life to fight the darker side of love.

His lips released. I felt a faint bloody rawness on the hot surface, glossing his lips as they moved along my skin. It wasn't a bite, merely sexy suction. He softly nuzzled his way onto the public side of my neck, lips lingering at the hollow of my white-skinned throat.

"You'd look hot with my mark here."

Matching hickeys with Snow? I felt a shudder of guilt and anxiety. I think not.

My fingertips shushed his lips. "Really. We *need* to watch this film. Self-defense."

"It's full dark and we're alone in a major luxe environment. And you just taste so good." He grinned. "All right. I'll satisfy myself with these gourmet cheese curls. Jeez! Hector Nightwine is one of a kind, taking the popcorn out of the pop culture."

I didn't tell him I hoped they were just cheese. Hector's appetite ran to suspect foods, like white-chocolate-covered maggots.

I sipped the Albino Vampire, leaving a lip-gloss imprint on the rim. Ric sipped his, leaving a similar but fainter version of my imprint, part my lip gloss, and not part blood, I hoped. Made me wonder about the whole history and point of lip painting. . . .

The movie screen opened on black emblazoned with white letters.

"Right off I can see this is going to be an action opus," Ric commented.

I gave him a friendly punch on the arm. "The first *Star Wars* movie used that pompous rolling text gimmick, remember?"

"Hokey," Ric grumbled, but he tilted back in his body-hugging leather seat. I did the same, feeling like tiny Dwan supported by the huge, padded leathery palm of King Kong.

Once the starring city of Metropolis in all its corrupt futuristic glamour of the world of 2000 as imagined in 1927 took center stage, it was impossible to take your eyes off the screen. The production was German, and the prophetic scenes of skull-capped male workers marching like convicts into the "forced" labor of the mechanical age was chilling.

Meanwhile, the white-clad, golden-blond sons of the corporate masters gamboled in Olympic-style games in an Eternal Garden—of Eden?—and were visited by gorgeous girls in evening gowns of sheer chiffon and feathers.

Ric leaned over to rest his head on my shoulder. "How come you don't wear any outfits from that era?"

"The style was 'boyishly' chic," I pointed out.

"Huh?"

"This was the first time women showed bare arms and legs. They were the major erotic zones of the era."

"If you say so." Ric shook his head. "Now that you mention it, that glitter hides the fact that all those girls' chests are flat as two-by-fours. Not my druthers."

"Duh."

"Who's the guy in the eyeliner and riding britches who's always swooning?"

"That's the hero, the evil manufacturer's son. Both genders wore liner in these early black-and-white films to make the eyes stand out."

The scene showed the young activist, Maria, crashing the Sons' party, a raft of Dickensian orphans clustered around her. She was all sweetness and pleading light, the dialogue box reading, "These are your brothers." Poor hero-guy was instantly smitten and set out to find her like Prince Charming with a hard-on for a glass slipper.

Some of it was corny, some of it was prophetic, and all of the sets were stunning.

We stared unblinking at Maria in her high-tech glass coffin as she transformed into the gleaming cyborg the mad scientist Rotwang had made . . . at Rotwang's neon and test tube laboratory transforming the sleeping Maria. Once Maria's essence is poured into the metal robot, it in turn becomes a human-looking false Maria who Rotwang sends out to incite the workers to self-destructive rebellion against the city's masters.

For the usual flimsy reasons, false Maria does a nearly nude stint as the whore of Babylon dancing for the leering moneyed class. All very symbolic but also the obligatory strip club setting we see on TV all the time today. Even Ric was mesmerized by Bad Maria's frenzied erotic dance. Some things never get old.

At last the workers finally realized they'd been had. Their rampage ended with burning the false and defiant

Maria at the stake, where she turned back into the silver metal cyborg before the false personality finally "died." The good Maria was freed to unite with her suitor and rebuild the leveled *Metropolis* as a really nice place to live and work. *Finis*.

When the film ended, Ric was leaning forward on the edge of his posh chair, arms braced on his thighs, hands laced together.

"That's all Brigitte Helm," I said, "from saint to seductress to saint again. Her false self sure whipped up that crowd of wimpy workers like Hitler on a tear."

"That's just it," Ric said. "This film eerily predicts what would happen in Germany ten years later when Hitler was in power. Speaking of power, I can see why Snow wants to reinvent that amazing towering Metropolis cityscape as a Vegas attraction. The dancing girls and even the Seven Deadly Sins are built in. Did he name his rock band after those creepy critters?"

"Don't know. Too bad the Sins' scene is mostly lost. We see them as gray, stone figures in a churchlike setting that come to life and walk toward the viewer, with Death as their sheepherder coming last, carrying a scythe."

"Snow's onstage backup group is a lot more sinful than those walk-off parts, especially Lust and Envy." Ric ginned as he named the two female members of the rock group.

"So you'd noticed those hip-swiveling hussies? I thought you weren't a fan."

"I don't follow Vegas stage shows, but when you admitted after I recovered from the Karnak ordeal that you'd had to submit to a Brimstone Kiss to get Snow to help rescue me, I caught a show to see what was involved. He bent down to do the Elvis scarf trick with the mosh pit groupies, but no kisses."

I allowed myself a mental sigh of relief. And since when had Ric started calling Christophe "Snow"? He'd been reluctant to sound friendly with the mogul-rock star in any way whatsoever.

"You must have been his last customer," Ric added with that deceptively casual side glance of a veteran interrogator. "Must have cured him of the habit."

"Maybe."

"I had to buy a used video of the show to get Brimstone Kiss footage. Just the standard long wet lip smack, but those women sure swooned like the hero of *Metropolis* kept doing. You figure out why, Delilah?"

Did I ever! And it wasn't fit for family consumption, much less one's boyfriend.

So I dismissed the strength of the effect. "The fans get overwrought when they have actual contact with an onstage idol. Every moment is magnified. It's a kind of psychic orgasm."

That was perfectly true, although in the case of the Snow groupies, the orgasms were real and serial.

"Not with you, though," Ric wanted to confirm.

"You know Snow's a power freak. A man, or whatever, who can call a dragon into being from a palmful of ashes would have to be. Me submitting to the Brimstone Kiss was his price for mounting your rescue expedition. He knew it was the most hateful and humiliating thing he could require."

"Does the kiss pack a kick?"

"Like with a groupie? No. Not with me. And I don't want to talk about it, any more than you'd want to reminisce about your enslavement to El Demonio Torbellino."

Ric nodded. "I've just noticed some tension between you two."

"True. Terminal lack of trust. Who'd put the stupid fairy-tale price of a kiss on rescuing a human from the vampire mob? Enough about that egomaniac. What did you learn from the film?"

Ric leaned back. I was thankful he'd moved past the dicey topic of Snow. "That Brigitte Helm was a hell of a performer. She was really just nineteen then?"

I nodded. "Ambitious kids today start on YouTube much earlier. She almost got the part in *The Blue Angel* that made Marlene Dietrich. She had first crack at the title role in *Bride of Frankenstein*."

"From Blue Angel to Mrs. Frankenstein. She had quite a range."

"Brigitte did what the old soap operas promised. As Maria, and as old film trailers boasted, she ran the gamut of human emotion. *Metropolis* let her turn it all loose. She's a saint, a protectress of the downtrodden, a Joan of Arc in a suit of sexy cyber-armor, a seductress from the Apocalypse upheld by the Seven Deadly Sins, a helpless prisoner, a manipulated tool of worldly powers, a deranged orator with qualities of the antichrist, not to mention a virgin and martyr. And she played that emotionless metal cyborg too," I added.

"I don't get why they needed to create a robot to re-create it as an evil but human Maria under their control."

"The robot was created to host the mad scientist's lost love, Hel, who'd married the heartless CEO, then died bringing his son into the world. Rotwang abandoned his idea of re-creating his soul mate and used the robot to embody a programmable Maria he could use to bring down the bigwig, at the cost of destroying the workers too. The robot plot was probably a warning that factory work was making robots of us all. The theme is announced on the first screen. 'The heart is the arbiter between the head and the hand.' "

"Not much heart in any world I've seen." Ric sat silent as he reran the script of his life and I reran mine.

"The dreamer and the maker, the brain and the hands, need to meet inside us," I said. "The dreaming-it-up and the making-it-happen parts. The head Wicked Witch of Wichita, Lily West, mocked her sister Lilah for believing that."

"I don't think she's mocking much anymore, now that we've defeated the weather witches." Ric took my hand. "You saved me when everyone else thought I was lost. I'll never forget that."

I couldn't help thinking, saved him for what? An even worse threat?

"So," he went on, gazing at the dark screen. "My altered silver vision"—he tapped his left eye socket where a brown contact lens obscured the new, mirror-bright iris— "brought the potent deposit of silver nitrate on the scenes featuring the Maria cyborg to independent existence here and now. How did El Demonio hope to use her?" Ric mused on. "How can we do that, and aren't we as bad as him, or Snow, for being willing to?"

"We don't have a choice. You called her off the screen. Now you need to bring out her better nature."

Chapter Seventeen

IT HAD BEEN a long day for both of us. Only security lights and stars were shining down on the darkened Nightwine estate, so Ric and I parted with a chaste kiss on the stoop outside the Enchanted Cottage.

"How're you going to get home?" I asked, suddenly aware of the logistics. "Your car must be in the Inferno Hotel parking lot."

A screech of wheels burning rubber into my driveway turned my head. Ric's bronze vintage Corvette was tooling up to my door.

"How?" I asked.

"Godfrey got his 'cousin' at the Inferno to contact your favorite parking valet." Ric smiled and went to open the driver's-side door.

"Manny!" I cried as the orange-scaled demon leaped out of the driver's seat. "Ric must owe you a huge tip."

Ric was already in the car and waved a single bill at Manny through the open window. I'd have chewed out the valet if he'd treated Dolly that way, but Ric didn't seemed bothered by the roar of his car's entrance. He liked to push the 'Vette around the same way. *Vroom.* Guys.

Logistics remained on my mind. How was Manny getting back to his post at the Inferno?

I glanced at the slim vintage watch on my left wrist. Wristwatches were a trademark of mine, despite cell phones replacing them among the Android generation. I had a large collection from all eras and they were also a perfect undercover form for the silver familiar. As now.

If I pushed Dolly a little, and she pushed lesser vehicles out of her majestic way, I could make the time limit.

"I'll drive you back to the Inferno," I told Manny.

His eyelashes fluttered over his golden cat's eyes. He had extraordinary long and lush eyelashes for a male demon. "A ride in the Queen. I could swoon."

"Please don't. I don't want you shedding any scales on Dolly's interior."

Manny, more formally Manniphilpestiles, grinned. "No, ma'am."

Parking valet demons in Vegas coveted Old Detroit steel. Manny always babied Dolly up the Inferno parking ramp because he knew I'd make Wiener schnitzel of his tail—the figurative *and* literal one—if he didn't.

Dolly was parked under the porte cochere so I zipped inside for my keys. I returned to find Quicksilver in the back and Manny riding shotgun. Wow. Quick must like the friendly demon to cede his place to him. Quick could make faster work of Manny's tail than I could.

Here's a secret to making sure that what happens in Vegas stays in Vegas: cultivate the hotel and casino staffs. Big shots and whales you have always with you and they come and they go, but the seemingly little fish are canny friends to have in a pinch.

"You drive like my aunt Zegaconphistia," Manny complained as I floated Dolly onto Sunset Road. He still wriggled down into the red leather upholstery like a cat in a faux fur shop.

Soon the lights of the Strip were getting us tourist stares, but Dolly cruised up to the Inferno's frenetic entrance unmolested. The moment I disembarked, Manny slid into the driver's seat.

"I know. No more than fifteen miles an hour in the ramp. Still the best ride in Vegas." He patted Dolly's dashboard and moved away at barely above idle.

Quicksilver had leaped out to escort me inside, so we joined the throngs shuffling in. It was nine-ten p.m., the start of Snow's break between the two nightly Seven Deadly Sins shows and I intended to have more than a word with him.

Quick got a lot of awed glances, but he was taken for a service dog. He had that all-business look about him, and his leather collar encouraged people to assume his thick gray body fur obscured a harness.

Of course, not everybody employed by the Inferno could be described as people.

One of them loomed into my path, a tall, sleek black woman wearing a short zebra-striped dress and fuchsia lipstick vivid enough to snarl traffic.

Ooh, our favorite fashion-forward shape-shifter is here, Irma warned.

"Fresh from a garden party?" Grizelle asked in a put-down tone.

True, nineteen-forties daytime frocks had a frothy, innocent air.

"No dogs." Grizelle's face and voice were harder than granite as her luridly green eyes moved from my floral print to Quicksilver's flashing fangs.

Snow's security chief cherished a major hate for me, one part deserved and three parts not. But that one part had been a lulu.

"I intend to see Snow," I said, scrupulously avoiding the verbs "want" and "need."

"Besides," I added, "Asta the wire-haired terrier is act-ing out just fifty feet away at the bar."

"He's a CinSim. Your dog is not."

Quick growled so deeply it sounded like he had laryn-gitis. He'd taken a hunk out of Grizelle's hide once when her inner white tiger had attacked me.

"No dogs," she repeated.

"I'll leave him with Asta, then. I'm sure you'll report my visit to Snow before I can reach the elevator."

Quick and I walked on, his growl still rumbling in his throat.

He peeled off at the bar, though, sitting beside Nick's stool where all the gathered lady tourists and CinSims started cooing at Quicksilver for being so big and strong and having such great hair. You'd think he was a Fabio CinSim, perish the thought. Thank God that had been a color film era.

The private elevator was waiting for me, doors ajar. I whisked up sixty-some stories fast enough to make my ears pop.

The elevator door opened on the penthouse foyer and rooms decorated like the interior of a giant ice sculpture snowflake, all white and silver and cold. Against this daz-zling background stood Snow, up close and way too per-sonal in his onstage outfit of skin-tight white leather open to the navel above a jeweled fly, the only color in the entire scene. I was amazed there wasn't a follow spotlight on it. Then I realized there probably was when he was onstage.

"Was it necessary to ruffle Grizelle's fur?" he asked.

"No, but it was fun."

"I have a feeling this visit will not be fun. At least not as much as our last encounter."

I was glad his back was turned as he headed for the glittering bar, though I couldn't help wondering if the whip-lashes I'd transferred from Ric to him were still present. I was startled to notice the *Metropolis* cyborg standing statue-still and apparently dormant beside the bar setup.

I wandered to the window wall that framed a black velvet painting of high-rise Vegas lights and glitter. Some buildings were dotted by functional yellow work lights and red aviation warning lights. They were still under construction, giant erector-set skeletons of vertical concrete columns intersected by horizontal steel I beams. I imagined the pharaohs gazing on such a sight and wondering how the heck our twenty-first-century civilization had built ladders straight up to the sky.

One such ugly behemoth crowded the fiery exterior sheath of the Inferno itself. Somebody somewhere owned every bit of near-strip land.

Snow appeared ghostlike behind me in the reflecting window glass. An opaque Silver Zombie glass seemed to levitate from his to my hand. His other hand held a milky Albino Vampire martini.

"I have thirty-five minutes," he said. "Will that suffice?"

"Easily." I turned from the bewitching nightscape and set the drink down on an end table by the cushy white leather sofas that undulated through the spacious room like a giant anaconda. "Just what are you trying to do, adopt Ric?"

"Excuse me if I sit." He did as promised on a sofa arm. "I spend a lot of time pounding hardwood floors nights." He demonstrated by lifting a foot shod in a white snake-skin boot. PETA would have his ass even though I wouldn't on a bet.

"You certainly don't tire of meddling in my life," I said.

"Works both ways, Delilah." Snow idly slouched down

onto the couch. "Inviting Montoya to move in here is purely a business offer. I need to protect the *Metropolis* CinSim and your . . ."

"Partner."

". . . your partner has had the bad or good luck to have a unique relationship with the most desired object in the supernatural firmament, which I own. The arrangement has nothing to do with you."

"I am not going to let you use Ric's powers to protect your greed."

"My offer would protect Montoya as well. You know better than he does what supernatural scum will be on his tail now. They mean to have the hidden power of the *Metropolis* robot, and they'll want the man who evoked and controls her."

"Ric doesn't get off on putting other . . . entities through the ringer, like you do."

"A better man, no argument, but neither of us can make use of a dead man."

That's a trick answer, Irma warned. *Snow may not be a 'man,' so he isn't really conceding moral superiority to Ric.*

While I searched for a withering retort, Snow's sunglasses took aim at my feet.

"What on earth are those?"

I looked down to confront the forgotten peep-toe heels with marabou insteps. I felt my face flush with embarrassed fury.

"I had to leave home in a hurry."

"Not a criticism. I can see some entranced lover painting your toenails scarlet in those shoes and then sucking them. The toes, I mean. One by one."

My damn bare toes shriveled back like the dying

Wicked Witch of the West's stripe-stockinged feet in the ruby red slippers.

"That kind of inflammatory chitchat is just why I don't want Ric under your roof. He wouldn't understand you're a . . ."

He waited, sipping the Albino Vampire. I eyed the raspberry liqueur shining like a lost jewel at the bottom of the martini glass. It reminded me of a tiny pool of dropped nail enamel . . . or blood.

"I'm a what?" The sunglasses tilted up, Snow's version of an innocent look.

The trouble was nobody knew just what variety of supernatural he was.

"A . . . debauched sensualist addicted to the adoration of groupies."

"Thanks, but I can be discreet around Montoya. Can you?"

"That makes it sounds like we have something to hide. He knows about the Brimstone Kiss."

"Does anybody really *know* about it, Delilah? Besides you and me?"

Long, guitar-string supple fingers lifted to the blood bruise on his throat, his head tilting back a bit, as if to touch a talisman. That damn sexual hot spot had nothing to do with his extorted Brimstone Kiss. It was a souvenir of a more recent encounter that was my fault entirely. The mark would drive the groupies crazy if he stroked it onstage and I wouldn't put it past him to put the gesture into his repertoire.

Why isn't your damn hickey fading? Irma was echoing my own question. *Although it does look hot. Leaving physical evidence of one of your more impetuous and misguided moments, how stupid is that?*

Now Irma was ragging on me. It was bad enough that Ric had noticed the mark, maybe even envied it a little. Lord, I hated this super-bite-human world, even when it was human-bite-super.

"That," I told Snow—and Irma—"is the unfortunate result of an experiment. I needed to know if any disastrous remnants of your damn Brimstone Kiss remained in my . . . system. Don't get your ego up. It was an experiment I couldn't try on anybody else. Responsibly."

"I could say that so was your Brimstone Kiss from me. An experiment."

"Good. Then any . . . side effects on either of our parts . . . were purely accidental."

"I wouldn't go so far as to call it 'purely.'" He sipped from the cocktail I'd named to annoy him. Now he had a means to annoy me.

"Why hasn't the mark faded yet?"

Snow shrugged. "An albino's skin is seriously sensitive. I thought you knew that, Delilah."

"You're about as sensitive as a Brillo pad. Ric told me you treat the Silver Zombie like an artifact instead of an unhuman being."

"He's right. I'm not sure exactly *what* I have in my possession."

"Well, it won't be Ric. Over my dead body."

"And none of us want that, do we?'

"I fought off half a dozen vampy boys in my Wichita days. No bloodsucker is going to turn me now. Maybe you *are* an albino vampire." I nodded at the glass in his hand, almost empty except for the glob of raspberry liqueur at the bottom.

Snow tilted back his glass and his neck to flaunt my blood bruise as he sucked down the last of the drink. Did I have damnably good aim. The mark was perfectly placed to make a pendant for the black leather collar he wore onstage. He set the empty martini glass on the same end table that held my untouched Silver Zombie.

"Whatever I call it, or her, I'll protect the Silver Zombie at all costs. And Ricardo Montoya too."

He stood, so I had to stand also to avoid communing with his crotch.

"I'm the only one in Vegas who has a . . . prayer . . . of doing that with El Demonio and the Immortality Mob and my rival moguls coming for it, and him," Snow said. "I'll even protect you, whether you like it or not."

His smile was tight. "Now do trot those impudent toes of yours out of my sight. I have a show to do and, according to you, groupies to grope."

I heaved a huge sigh as I checked my watch. The familiar had remained static in this form all day and night, but Grizelle would be waiting to pounce on me in about two minutes if I didn't leave soon. It was clear I'd have to convince Ric to stay out Snow's "protection" without confessing the rock star had a habit of compromising women, even me.

It's hard to be perfectly honest these post–Millennium Revelation days, Irma consoled me as I left the penthouse.

"It's hard to be that way anytime and anywhere," I muttered.

In the foyer, the elevator doors opened on a thankfully empty car and a Grizelle-free zone.

Time to collect Quicksilver and finally call it a night, with me safe at home in my Enchanted Cottage.

Chapter Eighteen

SO MUCH FOR anticipated sweet dreams.

I'd come home and thrown myself across the bed on my stomach to think, without changing clothes, but first I'd kicked the damn frou-frou shoes halfway to the baseboard.

I must have dozed off for a short time.

A nightmare woke me up not long after midnight. I'd witnessed the ranting false Maria about to be burned at the stake . . . and then she turned into me instead of back into the robot.

No reassurance was handy. Quicksilver was out. Whether he tracked down lady canines or rogue supers on these midnight expeditions, he had his own doggie private life to live too.

So, groggy and disoriented, almost sleepwalking, I found the toppled pair of heels on the cold wooden floor and jammed them on my feet before wandering into the hall to make sure I was still me and still here in the Enchanted Cottage.

Sure enough, there I stood in the funky-framed hall mirror, still wearing my Loretta-era lilac frock, only with nightmare-tousled hair.

I was just wondering where Loretta was now when my reflection made a face.

"Lame outfit."

It wasn't Irma talking so I wasn't surprised to face my

doppelganger mimicking me down to my feathery insteps in the mirror.

"You always hide in plain sight," I told Lilith, as I gazed at her . . . me.

"You're always too chicken to venture too far into my world, ducks," she complained in return.

"Loretta Cicereau is haunting it pretty hard these days."

"Are you afraid of that vintage prom queen? Or me?"

"Why should I mix it up with you in mirror-world? The only time you actually deigned to show up in person in my reality, a pack of fiendish hyenas on your heels drove me into the clutches of the Karnak Hotel vampire underground."

" 'Clutches,' " she mocked. "Kinda melodramatic for a former reporter. Face it, vampires and the Strip are more happenin' than *your* usual back-alley investigations. Come on, Dee. Come visit me and I'll take you on a real interesting trip."

"I don't do drugs."

"Yeah, another black mark on your record. The trip I have in mind doesn't require artificial enhancement, unfortunately. How'd you like to meet Mama?"

For a moment, words wouldn't come. "You've met her?"

"I know where she hangs these days."

"You . . . admit you're my sister?"

"*Ooh*, you should see your face, Dee-li-*lah*. As if you'd tasted a moldy pickle. Or something naughtier . . ." Lilith's puckered lips produced that calculated wicked expression I knew well.

"Don't go there, Lil," I jibed back. "I know you're mad, bad, and probably deeply sad."

"Oh, psych me out! I'm just sayin' we take a stroll on the Darkside of the mirror. You're the one who's got a knack for using those nasty biting-back fey paths."

"You can't go there?"

"I'm your mirror-image, Dee. I can't go anywhere without you. Don't you know that by now?"

"But . . . you claim to have led a separate life from mine, even back in Wichita."

"Yeah, I'm the tawdry side of uptight, all right, but I'm always on your invisible leash."

Lilith my own personal CinSim? Interesting possibility. I resisted her distracting taunts, working it out.

"I've only seen you in the mirror, only been able to mirror-walk since I came to Las Vegas."

"To find me, right? You had to want to do that to see me, and now you do."

I went silent. Lilith's existence depended on my will, my feelings? Poor thing!

"Come on, Dee, don't wait until I need to pee and vanish into a powder room. A reunion with Ma would do us both good."

"Why do *you* know about her and I don't?"

"Because *you* didn't want to until now."

"And you think I care now?"

"Care? No. I don't either. Why should we care? She dumped us."

"Maybe not entirely." I was thinking of my "scholarship" checks at Our Lady of the Lake girls' high school.

"Well, I'm ditching your *Alice in Wonderland* outfit. I'm not going to be seen like that outside your mirror."

Lilith extended ragged, grimy fingernails to me and the mirror's surface, my vintage outfit melting off my reflection as she moved. She looked lean and mean in her hipbone-hugging jeans and the same cheap, glitzy skull tank top I'd seen earlier.

"Something's missing in your look," I said slowly.

"Oh, how suspicious you sound. You look a little naked too. Where's your Snow-powered silver familiar?"

"Snow has no effect on the familiar. I have that from his own lily-white lips."

"You've had other things from his lily-white lips."

"Once. In an emergency. And you?"

Lilith laughed, then flourished a scrawny gym-graduate arm over her head.

Black inked patterns were climbing it like a fey thorn forest, images overlaying images . . . the tattooist's traditional barbed-wire hearts and banners, quickly followed by Egyptian hieroglyphics, Morse code, Dolly's license number, Celtic knots, signs of the Zodiac and the planets, Ric's phone number . . . and my locker combination from Our Lady of the Lake!

The twisting string circled around and around her arm. It could have been a Times Square messaging billboard . . .

"Think Mom will greet me with open arms?" she asked.

"So, you're a living road map of my life? You only record the minutiae, though."

By now Lilith's moving tattoos had congealed into an alarmingly 3-D eel on her arm. To judge from the pugnacious head and mouth on her flexing bicep, it was a viper moray with two sets of long, needle-sharp fangs. She flexed her muscle to make the fully armed tattoo jaws snap.

My silver familiar wasn't getting into any crude pissing contest, but it emigrated from a discreet garter under my dress that I could feel, but not flaunt, to a heavy charm bracelet I'd seen before, dangling a slew of mysterious items including a doghouse, ball chain and leg iron with lock, binoculars, wishing well with bucket, mummy case, globe, scissors, chariot, high-heeled platform sandal, and

wolf's head. Someday I'd solve the clues in that assort-
ment. Meanwhile . . .

"Okay, Mirror Me," I told Lilith, eager to meet her
on neutral ground that wasn't part of my everyday life.
"I'm convinced you're improperly attired enough to greet
monsters in the mirror-walk. Me, on the other hand . . ." I
held out my arms, indicating my Hector-cajoling outfit of
ladylike vintage frock, high heels, and charming bracelet.
Window dressing was always a great disguise.

"You'll confuse the hell out of them," Lilith said.
"Death by boredom, Little Miss Go-to-Meeting. Mom will
love your quaint apparel, girl. She always liked you best."

"How do you figure that?"

"You at least got a last name."

"Street? That was for where I was *found*. I was a *found-
ling,* Lilith. An abandoned infant. Where did you come
from?"

Her eyebrows waggled above over-made-up smoky
eyes that looked startlingly blue in contrast to the smudges
above . . . and below.

"Your worst nightmares, Delilah. You gonna be a big
girl and show me the way? I want to know why I'm stuck
with you as much as vice versa. Grab your cell phone and
join the party. You do have pockets in that loser antique
frock, don't you? "

I did indeed, but I had no reason to trust Lilith or even
to wish her well. She was not a sister in any interpretation
of the word and why would I care about the woman who
deserted me? Maybe because I did always want to know
who, what, when, where, and why, the reporter's bywords.

I ran back to the bedroom and slipped my PhD-level
phone into my dial-phone-era dress pocket.

"Stand back," I told Lilith on my return to the hall. "I'm

coming through, and if you make any aggressive moves, pussycat doll, I will stomp *your* riveted ass pockets with my World War Two pinup platform heels."

I PUSHED INTO the mirror as if going through a revolving door. At once, my arms plunged into tepid Jell-O and even the quality of the air thickened as I joined my mirror-image in the dim reaches beyond the glass.

This was scary. Crossing over had always been an airy process. This implied that Lilith might have real physical presence, not merely a psychic presence, like the ghost of Loretta before she'd struck her fey-changeling bargain.

A deep breath had me inhaling Eau de Motorcycle chick—gasoline, leather, and some heady cologne that blended musk and magnolias. Lilith's earthy scent took my breath away. She'd always been unreal before, an image just a thirty-second of an inch away in dreamland.

Only the silver familiar awakening to materialize around my forearm in a 3-D tattoo pattern of gleaming barbed wire shook me from freezing under the spell of a solid Lilith. I'd no idea it had a competitive streak. Maybe I did too.

"You have the coolest jewelry, though," Lilith said. Her debauched wink was just like the Bad Maria's in the *Metropolis* movie. "Does that tricked-out cell phone of yours get a signal in mirror-world?"

I had no idea, but the familiar reverted to a bangle bracelet as I pulled it out of my skirt's hip pocket and turned it on. My usual wallpaper of Rick and Ilsa's parting scene in *Casablanca* came up while the lyrics of "I Love Paris" played like a whisper in the vast, inhuman space.

"Mush," Lilith groaned, cringing away like a senior citizen at a rave.

No problem. While I watched, my settings vanished to be replaced by an eerie undersea cosmos of shifting greens and blues and red-orange hot Inferno Hotel firescapes. I was fixated when a golden version of the Silver Zombie materialized and stripped off pieces of the metal carapace until she was down to her skivvies—real gold leggings and a metal bra that made Theda Bara's hot-for-1917 *Cleopatra* version look wimpy. It was Beyoncé belting out "Get Me Bodied."

"Hey there, Delilah, that's way cool for you." Lilith was circling me while I watched my supposedly smart phone reinvent itself as a hard rock venue.

The rock audio-visuals finally faded.

I put my attention on Lilith, still circling like a street-gang shark, looking shorter than me in her scuffed low-heeled motorcycle boots. But she wasn't.

"Mom will like you best," she decided. "And I prefer it that way."

"We have to find her before she can play favorites." I studied my now-alien cell phone screen. I do believe it was currently on . . . Feynet. "I suggest we keep moving."

"Pump in 'Delilah Street.' You do know how to spell your own name?"

"I've done that. There are dozens of them. Some with nearby 'Lilith' streets."

"Spooky."

"I favor Corona, California. That seemed to ping a ringtone when I mentioned it to you."

"That was in the bathroom mirror in Snow's suite at the Emerald City Hotel in Wichita, Sis." Lilith licked her chapped lips. She obviously wasn't slathering them with Midnight Cherry Shimmer gloss like I had been. "I can never think straight when Snow's around. Can you?"

"Obviously, or I wouldn't remember our mirror conversation. I doubt knocking my heels together will get us anywhere in mirror-world."

"Pity-party time. The ruby red slippers were the coolest part of the whole movie."

"You. A shoe slut? Or was it the 'home' idea?"

"No place like it, I hear," Lilith said with a crooked grin. "So you're the mirror explorer. I just come when called."

"The phone is wonky. I use Groggle, but there's a Giggle search engine on this thing now. I'll try to zero in on the map location."

"Aren't you clever? Let's bounce outa here."

Lilith tried to lean over my shoulder to watch, but I shrugged her off. I hadn't forgotten she'd been lurking around the exterior of the Inferno Hotel when someone had downed one of Snow's mosh-pit fans with a blow to the head from behind. And that got "me" on the crime scene security camera.

I was getting dizzy from turning around to keep the info between me and my cell phone, so it didn't faze me when some loud, pulsing, lyric-less music (unless you counted "Uh-uh-uh") came screaming banshee-loud out of my overheating palm.

I looked up. The bland blackness of mirror-world was being stabbed with bolts of color vibrating to the frantic beat of rock music on speed. We stood in the middle of a jam-packed crowd of would-be cool clubgoers all wearing sunglasses.

"Where are we?" Lilith shouted in my ear.

I'd say a soundstage lined with scaffolding, with every kind of illumination—neon, spotlight, fairy lights, strobe lights, even cop car headache bar flashing lights—draping every surface. And they all reflected crazily in a huge mirrored ball rotating in the dark sky of the second-story ceiling.

Even the concrete floor beneath our feet vibrated.

"Hard-core," Lilith cooed in my ear.

I blinked my eyes against the kaleidoscope of violent light.

"You're too emo for this scene," I shouted back. "Let's bounce again."

I used my cell-phone camera to scan the room until the black hole of a possible door out of this madness was center screen. I took a photo. *Kazzam!*

We were standing in the cool night air, outside the box under the giant neon RAVE MACHINE sign. All that mania and high wattage was reduced to only the bass beat pounding to escape the windowless black metal door at our backs.

"Why'd we leave the rave?" Lil asked. "And how are you whipping us around this whip-ass place?"

I didn't answer. I needed to prove my suspicions: that my cell phone was infected with pixies. I walked through the jammed parking lot until I came to a curb where I could stop and figure this out.

Giggle operated like a fey clone of Groggle, so I swiped around and got up its map program . . . Terra Infirma. I made a face at the name, no doubt a jab at unmagic-bearing mortals. Those fey, on the mischievous side when they weren't being wicked deadly. I texted in the location.

"This neighborhood is just what it looks like," I murmured as much to myself as Lilith. "It's a light industrial area. Small manufacturing companies."

Even as I spoke, I recalled what Hector had called the Immortality Mob when I first arrived in Vegas. Could this be a secret outpost . . . or headquarters . . . for that mysterious operation? A Vegas version of George Lucas's Industrial Light & Magic company that offered special effects on a supernatural scale?

After remembering her presence I reported to Lilith. "The other buildings are deserted at night. The rock palace probably doesn't have any neighbors to complain. Doesn't seem a likely place to find long-lost moms."

"Then, let's head back to Rave Machine for some sure-fire fun. You can dance if you ditch the statement spike heels."

I wasn't ready to give up on the ghost in the machine.

I used the phone's camera to pan the area. It showed a few other boxy buildings, most one-story, dark, and surrounded by vacant parking lots. I walked along the curb until a sodium iodide light's peachy glow lit up the signpost.

"Delilah Street," Lilith breathed behind me. "So this is Corona, California. Home of raves and . . . us?"

"No home here." I studied the cell screen's list of businesses along this section of the street. Small manufacturing companies, mostly.

"What a snoozer street." Lilith was jigging from foot to foot, hands down her jean pockets, stuck in rebellious teen mode. "I'm heading back to the rave for some fun. If Mom's around here and worth finding, she'll show up there."

"Lilith." I sighed. "That's an unrented building, I'd bet. The current occupants are there illegally."

"Illegal is part of the thrill, but what would you know about that? The first man you ever got it on with is the Law."

"*Ex*-law enforcement. Ric's a private consultant now."

"Still has the soul of a *federale*, if he still has a soul."

"You have any other setting but 'taunt'?"

"Now's when you tell me I'm a very unhappy girl acting out." She pouted and turned her profile to flash the tiny blue topaz nose stud I used to also call mine before I discovered her.

What an odd feeling to want to slap yourself in the face.

"Why bother?" I told Lilith. "You dragged me here and now all you want is music, music, music. I'm going to check out the scene farther down the street. I'll pick you up at the rave on the way back, *if* my route happens to go that way."

In this deserted area, my every high-heeled step sounded as loud as a single clap of hands. After a couple yards, I could hear her emo-girl boot-drags fading in the opposite direction.

Without Lilith to worry about, my elation at this trip in time and space came bubbling out. Loretta Cicereau wasn't the only one who'd walked fey paths. I'd put myself and Lilith in California, three hundred miles from Vegas, in the blink of a smartphone screen.

A faint tinny sound was all that remained of the rave. I passed lit signs that hawked manufacturers of rubber products and energy food and drink lines. Did my . . . our mother toil at one of these places in daylight hours? Was she an assembly worker? A receptionist? Or a sales rep, maybe?

No. Not a sales rep. I wanted to find her in humble circumstances, a former unwed teen whose life had been a string of impulsive mistakes, like me and Lilith. I wanted her to be someone I could pity and feel superior to, glad I'd never known her. I was getting over what the social services in Wichita had done to me, but Mama was the First Cause. The Root of All Evil. I stopped. Looked at the phone I was clutching as if to crush it.

Unsettled anger issues, maybe? came Irma's chirpy tone. *My advice: lose the rage and stow the smarty phone in your pocket.*

"You're back."

You got rid of the doppelganger. Three's a crowd.

"Lilith was getting tiresome," I agreed, "but you are too."

Me? I'm your best scout. See that two-story building with the corrugated steel sides?

I looked, and nodded. "There are cars parked around it."

Cars? That meant . . . occupants. Now. At night.

I pushed my almost seventy-year-old shoes into a trot. I sounded like a hansom cab horse in a Sherlock Holmes movie, but in less than a minute I'd passed the sixty or so parked small sports convertibles, feeling a deep pang for the absence of Dolly's immense and protective Cadillac bulk.

The familiar chimed faintly on my wrist, like an old clock. I was so lost in my vintage dreams that what I actually saw when I made it around the building's corner hit me like a tidal wave.

The entire front facade was a dazzling plaid of colored neon you couldn't see from the back parking lot. I heard music on Delilah Street again, but this beat made my hips and skirt sway to the rhythms of salsa, cha-cha, merengue, sexy samba.

If only Ric was here. We could party.

That brought me back to "Terra Infirma." Hard.

"No," I said aloud to Irma. "The last thing I want is him messing around in mirror-world."

Or with your Mamma Mia.

Irma's words made me squint to see the front entrance, mirrored glass doors with a cursive neon sign above them: LA VIDA LOCA.

I straightened and swung my self-advertising shoes ahead of me one pavement-banging step at a time. This was the place that had paid for my costly sanctuary from the group homes, the nun-run private girls' high school where I'd been a charity student until I graduated, hit state college, and made it to a BA in journalism on my own.

Mama was . . . Latina? Then, where had my Black Irish coloring come from? Oh, my. I hoped to God I didn't have a supernatural father . . . uh, besides Him.

Meeting myself in the mirror before I swung the door open, I saw my flushed cheeks emphasized my black hair and blue eyes and made my glossed lips pale by comparison. My vintage forties ensemble was really . . . ugh, perky. What I do to keep Hector Nightwine from stomping all over my druthers.

I yanked the door open and entered.

Chapter Nineteen

A BORED GIRL at the reception desk yawned and slammed a clipboard toward the high counter and me.

She was wearing an orange tank top, enough butterfly tattoos to sponsor a Costa Rican tour, and her hair was striped magenta and blue.

I'd had too many doctor's office clipboards slammed at me during my recent traumatic sentimental journey back to Wichita, so I slapped it back down on her desk.

"Just visiting," I said. "I don't read any permission pleas. I don't sign any papers or pay any admission fees."

Her Slinky-supple spine straightened right up. "Uh, sure. Here's a visitor's pass, but it's only good until morning. You're late."

"Is that a personal message?"

"Uh, no. Only, the open house is almost over. You've got less than an hour to try us out."

"And what has La Vida Loca got I might want to try out?"

"Look behind you. Wall-to-wall classes. An awesome lap pool, and a totally *kew-ool* juice and wine bar." She narrowed her tar-pit eyeliner at me. "I see you shop last century. La Vida Loca will have you out of those nineteen-forties fat farm dresses and into sixties anorexic Alice-in-Wonderland white tights and French nape-bows in no time."

"Is this a chain?"

"Shut your mouth with duct tape!"

Somehow the imagery had turned very creepy.

"This is a one-and-only totally spa-experience health club," the receptionist said. "We specialize in after-hours workouts for the working girl."

"Who's the boss?"

"Our owner and CEO is leading the Zumba Zapata class and should be down in a few minutes. Step up to the bar and have an energy drink on the house."

Anybody is a fool for a freebie, me not excluded. I plopped myself on a bar-height stool at what looked like an old-fashioned soda fountain with chrome taps and stainless steel mixing machines.

Lilith was missing out on a fun detour down Delilah Street.

"What can I getcha?" The tanned, collegiate-looking blond guy wearing the cop mustache behind the counter looked so California.

I studied the handwritten menu above the work area. Between graphics of smiling and fan-dancing fruits and veggies I perused a funky list of smoothie names, like Bloody Mary Contrary and Vegetarian Voodoo.

"I'll have a Red Zombie." Since I'd created a Silver Zombie cocktail I was curious about the nonalcoholic fresh and fruity version.

"Freshly squeezed," he said with a wink.

"Pomegranate," I suggested.

The mixer machine was whirring like a speedboat engine, so I didn't hear his answer.

He turned to put a tall beer glass of scarlet liquid down at my place.

"Cranberry?" I tried next.

He shrugged and returned to polishing the chrome and

stainless steel for the next day. I'd just have to use my connoisseur's nose and tasting tongue.

I had the glass rim at my lips when a hand from behind me snatched it away.

"A glass of sparkling water for the lady," a low, contralto voice ordered. "She's the designated driver type."

I turned indignantly, already pointing at the chorus line of fruits and veggies on the sign above.

"Merely mixers, my dear, not the hard stuff actually on tap. Let's have a look at you."

I couldn't have put it better myself.

I slipped off the stool and turned to stand nose-to-nose with her. My designated fairy godmother was a tall brunette poured into a peacock-blue leotard. White skin, dark hair and eyes, with that coal-black mane pinned off her neck in a forties updo. Not a drop of sweat showed on her or the leotard she rode in with. Not a bit of a hitch in her breathing.

I managed to remain as cool as one of the line-dancing cucumbers above us. "The Vida in La Vida Loca, I assume."

Very red lipstick made her teeth look supernaturally white as she smiled, particularly the pointed canines. Or it could be Crest strips. And a genetic tendency to sharp incisors.

"Ihateyourguts," I got out and closed my eyes. "Just something I wanted to get off my chest once before I die."

She leaned past me. I peeked to see her claiming my abandoned Red Zombie.

"Welcome to Delilah Street, Delilah. Let's talk in my office. Take your sparking water." She eyed the bartender. "I'll lock up the health bar, Bane."

While I followed her past the steel-and-birch suspended

staircase, a flock of fit young women thronged up it in thong leotards and tights. All were pale, thin, muscular, wearing the same Revlon red lipstick as my hostess, the thick creamy old-fashioned kind that caked and would peel off with a bit of your lips as it got old. Kinda a metaphor for vampires.

They slowed, their eyes fixed on me as they ran into one another and formed a clot on the stairs, predatory pupils dilating, lips parted, and not from exercise.

"Come along," Vida ordered, emphatic.

I skedaddled after her through a pale birch door. Better one-on-one. The office furniture beyond was more silver-and-blond Nordic modern with accents of scarlet leather and silk. My hostess finished wrapping a sarong around her hips, Dorothy Lamour or Hedy Lamarr come to life from some native girl film of this woman's prime, the nine-teen freaking forties.

I stood with my back to the closed door. "You're Cesar Cicereau's Vida."

She froze like a statue of an Egyptian goddess. Her spine became stone, every disc visible and incised like a hieroglyph, and her voice came out raw and god-awesome. "Don't *ever* use a possessive of *that* name and *mine* in my presence again, Delilah."

She turned, smiling and gorgeous. "Now sit. I won't bite."

Her dark-chocolate eyes threw me a half-humorous, half-challenging look as sharp as a perfectly aimed dart.

I couldn't help admiring her style, maybe because we'd both adapted it from glamorous but hard-boiled forties film dames. The only difference was Vida had done it naturally in her time. I'd done it unnaturally decades later, hiding in dark empty group-home rec rooms, watching old midnight movies with a nail-file weapon clutched in my hand.

"You were expecting me?" I slunk to the red leather sling chair in front of the desk.

It might mean I was a nonchalant shady lady. It might mean I was scared out of my vintage-loving mind. Take your pick. Mom was my literal role model? And she could eat me. Gee, a whole bunch of fairy tales rolled into one.

I leaned forward to set my water glass on the white sharkskin desktop. "I'm well over twenty-one now, you know. What's the foamy red stuff about? Blood beer?"

"Never you mind." She leaned behind her and selected a crystal decanter from a line of liquor bottles. "Feel free to spike your water, since you're such a big girl now. Albino Scotch should suit you."

I shook my head, blinking. Red Zombie, white scotch?

"This *is* California." Vida sipped my former drink, my former supposed veggie refresher.

"Why did you leave Las Vegas?" I asked her. "When did you leave?"

"Don't you mean, 'Why did I leave *you*'? And Lilith. Where is she, by the way?"

I jerked my head to the vague air behind me. "Preferred the rave up the . . . street to exploring. I guess I'm glad she's safe, at least."

"Lilith is never 'safe.' It's against her nature." She smiled again, which was more disturbing than if she'd hissed and bared her fangs. "On the other hand, I always knew you'd find me, Delilah. You're the explorer."

"Vampires can't reproduce."

"No time for niceties, I see. What vampires can and cannot do is a tangle of mixed mythologies, my dear."

"And our father?"

Vida shrugged and sipped. "It's not for me to say. There are . . . candidates. Some," she added as her fangs showed, "forced upon me."

Oh, Lordy. First I'd worried for years I'd been raped as a child and I just get over that false assumption and now I get to worry I'm a product of rape. Can't women ever get free of such ugly personal histories?

"I saw a photo of you in the old days on Cicereau's computer," I told her so she'd know I was an effective investigator. "It was something of a family shot, if you include that to mean 'Family' in the mob fashion."

"How did *you* get access to Cesar's computer?"

"Broke in."

"To his office at the Gehenna? Nicely done." She leaned back to pull out a drawer. In a moment, she'd inserted an unfiltered cigarette in a long black holder twined by a rhinestone snake. It could have been flaunted by Audrey Hepburn or Cruella de Vil.

I went into knee-jerk covet mode. "That's from an old movie, isn't it?"

"One of the advantages of living near Hollywood. Lots of prop shops."

I frowned. "You shouldn't—" Then I shut up.

"Smoke? One of the advantages of being undead. I can continue bad habits." Her slightly opened lips emitted a serpentine stream.

"You *can't* smoke. You don't breathe."

"Think about vampires. We walk, we talk, we suck and swallow blood. Smoke is just a pale substitute."

I thought about it. Only air vibrating the vocal cords produced speech. Yet, party tricksters I'd seen blowing smoke rings didn't inhale. They just held the smoke in their mouths, puckered their lips and let it drift out in circles. A vampire's oral pleasures must be as fleeting.

"So . . . Lilith and I were twins of a nicotine-addicted pre-vampire mother."

"You preceded the smoking, but otherwise it was quite a rare situation, which is why I kept it utterly secret."

"Even from us."

"Especially from you."

"Vampirism isn't inheritable."

Vida shrugged. "Who's to say, if not you and Lilith?"

"That's it? You gave birth to us and called it quits? You don't care? Then, why did this place"—I nodded at the slick surroundings—"send money to help me attend Our Lady of the Lake, a Catholic institution that would be anathema to vampires, and vice versa?"

Vida leaned forward to tap an inch of ash off her cigarette. The ashtray on her desk was an open crystal palm, the head, heart, and lifelines etched deep and long. I watched with dismay. Mama looked like an under-thirty hottie. Lilith would groove on that, but I'd hoped for something cuddlier, or at least with a conscience.

"The Catholic church and vampires both have long, tortured traditions," Vida said mysteriously, "and more in common these days than you might think."

"I must have been born here in Corona on Delilah Street."

"No. I left you to be *found* here in Corona, on Delilah Street. The area wasn't much of anything then."

"And how does that leave me ending up in Wichita?"

"You know social services." Vida shrugged. "They take a lot upon themselves in dealing with helpless wards of the state."

"Don't divert my focus to little me. What about

prime-time you? In that photo from the nineteen forties, you were obviously Cicereau's shockingly younger arm candy."

"No possessives when you speak of him! There *was* life after Cesar."

"I was born in eighty-eight, twelve years before the Millennium Revelation in 2000 to 2001. You would have been . . ."

"Yes, Delilah. An older unwed mother." Vida simpered mockingly, more at herself than at my struggles to solve the logistics of my birth.

"Fifty-eight years old, if you were eighteen in Cicereau's photograph. It doesn't add up."

"That's right." Vida's long red-enameled fingernails probed her desk drawer again. She extracted something small and white and tossed it to the desk in front of me.

I stared at my own baby business card, three months old, designed when I hit Vegas and wanted to declare myself.

Vida sucked more smoke into her mouth. This time the stream puffed out with her words. "You bill yourself as a paranormal investigator these days, and I guess you did find me. More nice work."

I stared at my own name, sitting in a building with a matching street address, interrogating my own mother. So be it.

"Vida," I noted in my most objective reporter voice. "That's the Spanish word for 'life.' Ironic, isn't it?"

"No kidding. When I was your age I expected to have a long and happy one, I just didn't anticipate how very long it would be."

"What happened? In Cicereau's 'family' photo everybody looked content with their roles. He was the satisfied middle-aged mogul getting short on hairline and large on waistline. Loretta was maybe sixteen and glowing in probably her first long gown. You were chorus-girl gorgeous in your slinky long slit skirt with a lush silk flower in your hair. Even Sanscouci looked a tad younger, the silver streak in his forelock muted, and him looking all casual hand-in-dinner-jacket-pocket fully armed. The stalwart bodyguard."

Can a vampire's face go paler? Vida's was giving Snow's albino complexion a run for the money. She stood behind her desk, spreading her bloodred-tipped claws on the surface, glaring at me.

"I see you still believe in fairy tales, Delilah. Keep that snapshot in your mind's eye and forget looking for the man . . . or woman . . . behind the curtain."

"Nope. Pulling back curtains is my business. Besides, everyone in that photo is a mess. I know now Sansouci had been freshly indentured to the werewolf mob by his own kind. Cicereau slaughtered Loretta and her ancient vampire young lover not long after that."

Vida sat down slowly, leaning on her hands as if she was, say, eighty years old.

"Cesar killed Loretta?"

"How can you know about me and not about them?"

She sighed out some more smoke. "I wanted to forget about all of them. I couldn't forget about you. Cesar was power hungry and brutal, but I can't believe he'd kill his own daughter."

"Believe. I was instrumental a few months ago in finding Loretta and her lover's buried bodies in Sunset Park. Then Loretta's ghost went so crazy she conspired with the Karnak Hotel vampires to resurrect her boyfriend, now she's going after mine in the process."

"Karnak? Vampires? Not on my radar. Though, from

what you say, it's no wonder Cesar 'retired' me for a while soon after that photograph. I thought he just wanted an even younger woman, but he wanted witnesses gone."

Vida interrogated me in turn. "Who is he, your 'boy-friend'?"

"You wouldn't have known him. Ric is mortal. He's a crime consultant formerly with the FBI."

"Good family, then?"

That made me want to laugh. Here was Vida sounding proprietary about my associates after all this time, and me wondering whether to cite Ric's poverty-stricken peasant Mexican roots or his foster family's impeccable Washington WASP credentials.

He wouldn't deny either one, so I just said, "Good man."

Vida's tone turned cynical. "I suppose you don't exactly have family to brag about."

"Maybe I could, if I knew who my father was."

"Doesn't this cast of characters so far convince you that you don't want to know?"

"You mentioned Cesar took you back."

"He was a grieving father. He claimed Loretta had 'gone missing.'"

"Thanks to him. But thanks to Ric and me, she's back, and not the better for it. So I'm still doing the math. You remained with Cicereau for years, knowing what he was?"

"Knowing and seeing are two different things, Delilah. So he went off with the 'boys' to Starlight Lodge in the mountains for three days a month. My periods actually got in sync with the full-moon schedule. Convenient for Cesar."

"Creepy. And more than I wanted to know."

Vida smiled. "Odd how a woman's blood cycle unnerves

even other women. Now I know how to stop your incessant questions."

"What about Sansouci? He's the obvious suspect for turning you vampire."

Vida's dark eyes blinked twice in her impassive face. The involuntary tic broadcast a strong emotional reaction, from what I'd glimpsed of her. Her long fingers picked up the extreme cigarette holder to cover her discomposure.

"Sansouci. He tried to recruit me for his harem, but I was too savvy to fall for that."

"You stayed true to froglike Cicereau with a suave number like Sansouci around oozing forbidden sex for the price of a little blood? Why?"

"Simple, Delilah. I knew too much. Not about Loretta, or I'd have risked leaving, but too much about Cesar's shady criminal activities, not to mention the supernatural ones. I'd been 'dropped off' as an infant myself. All I knew of my family was a couple crazy old aunts in the Midwest and I ditched both of them when I was sixteen. I was on my own and doing my best."

I kept silent. That was as close to an apology as she'd come yet. I didn't believe her story about Sansouci. It went against human nature that a trapped and neglected trophy mistress like Vida wouldn't at least have revenge sex with her sugar daddy's handsome bodyguard, if not give blood.

Good question. Did daylight vampires ever have sex for the sake of it, or only when it netted blood?

Vida was watching me while trying to hide it. "How is Sansouci?" she asked too casually to feel that way.

"Same old, same old, I suppose. Hates Cicereau, loves women."

"You said his forelock has more silver."

"Only to a very keen observer, like me, after seeing the sixty-five-year-old photo."

"His daylight lifestyle will shorten his immortality."

"By a century or two, maybe. He doesn't seem worried."

"He never did. Does he like you, Delilah? You look quite a bit like me. Especially in those vintage rags you're wearing."

"Why should you care?" These were the first roster of questions she'd asked about me, besides wanting to know Ric's history.

Then I got it. Sansouci could be my father! He was Black Irish. He'd been around Vida for years. He was the one who'd want revenge sex . . . with Vida. He had good reason to cuckold Cicereau even if a blood donation wasn't in the picture.

The idea of Sansouci as Daddy made my skin crawl and wrung my stomach. Vida was right. He did act attracted to me. Still, Cicereau was more likely to be my father when you looked at the Gehenna Hotel habitués. Another revolting, stomach-churning idea. I recalled his lust for the *CSI*-autopsy image of Lilith, aka me.

This cast of likely suspects for my father was getting more twisted than the family freakiness in *Oedipus Rex* and *Hamlet* put together.

"You have no reason to be honest," I told Vida, forcing myself to be so hard-headed I sounded cold. "You've let Lilith and me fend for ourselves since infanthood and grow up in a separate nest of lies. Maybe you fooled yourself into thinking you were doing the best for us, but you got out of Vegas, got out of motherhood, and now you're running some chichi California fitness club, and you're out only a few thousand dollars for my high school scholarship. I appreciate being your charity-of-the-month for four years, but all I want from you is our father's identity, Lilith's and mine. Then I'll vanish like a bag of trash left for the garbage collector. I won't even tell Lilith, so she won't bother you, not that she'd be inclined."

Vida leaned her gorgeous, made-up forties face on the elbow she braced on her desk.

"I'd like to help you out, Delilah, but you really ought to leave now."

"I'm not leaving until I have the answers I need."

"Too bad, because my workout girls are all done with their routines and hepped up and about to harvest the rave attendees up the street. Just up Delilah Street." She pointed beyond me with a sharp scarlet fingernail. "I own both enterprises, you see. It works out very well. That's one thing I learned from Vegas and Cesar Cicereau, owning competing venues just ups the ante for the savvy CEO."

I was on my high-heeled feet. "Your vamps are hitting the rave club? You let Lilith stay there?"

"No, my dear. You did."

I ran to the door, pausing when I heard high-pitched tittering outside. Excited feminine twittering.

I turned my back to the door and faced my mother as the silver familiar abandoned its old-timey charm bracelet and reshaped itself into a dagger in my right hand, a dagger with a cross-shaped haft, of course, as hokey as that old superstition was.

"You must have been the one," I told Vida even as I realized it, "who was made vampire so Howard Hughes could get turned by a beautiful woman."

I didn't need a confirmation. A look of paralyzed fury froze her face into a horrific mask. Mama as a snaky-tressed Medusa would never leave my memory.

"That's the beauty of being undead now. I don't need men anymore, Delilah, I prey on them. Exclusively. My girls are not so persnickety."

I turned and yanked open the door. Zombies on speed were one nightmare I'd already navigated. Aerobic vampire chicks were about to become another can of worms entirely.

Chapter Twenty

THE SCENE IN the health club lobby was like being trapped backstage at a major beauty pageant. Thin, fit, tall, busty young women were milling everywhere, wearing full makeup that concealed their undead pallor.

They lounged at the health bar, warming up with bottled blood in trendy concoctions that abused fruits and vegetables. They used the metal railing along the stairs to the second floor as a ballet barre, stretching toned torsos, endless legs, and supple arms into supernaturally unnatural positions that would have snapped human bones.

They gathered at the front glass doors, prancing and preening like racehorses at the starting gate.

And I had to get through them.

Bursting out of the boss's office door gave me an edge of surprise. For about fifteen feet.

I shook my hair to fall into my face and kept my head down, squared my shoulders, and slammed one foot down in front of the other so my heels echoed rifle-shot-style on the terrazzo floor. Concealing my silver dagger-bearing right hand in my ample skirt folds, I lifted my left hand high and slowly lowered it, pointing imperiously to the front door.

Vida herself had said I looked like her. Maybe enough to pull off a short stroll.

Around me, I sensed these self-absorbed beauties pausing in their occupations, turning their attention on me. The ones crowding the door parted for my passage. My left hand pushed the left glass door open so hard it banged against the glass window-wall.

A cracking sound cascaded into a shower of broken glass that tinkled like the very highest keys on a piano. I was still striding away toward the street, Delilah Street, not daring to look back.

When the second of the double glass doors resounded as it slammed open, I broke into a full-out run. Thanks to GPS, I had an aerial memory of the area's layout, and I angled across to the next dark building. I dodged around the Dumpsters at its rear, my footsteps obscured by the sharp high yips of once-human hounds.

Speed was not on my side, and I knew they could scent my blood, but my shortcut had zipped me into the back parking lot of the Rave Machine. Darting through the highest SUVs and pickups, I noticed a lot of non-California license plates. These patrons were unwary tourists who didn't know Corona supported a hornet's nest of vampires. All their black-clad mock-Goth and high-sepia steampunk fantasies were about to come to life in living color, red bleeding into the monotone crowds.

I burst into the back hall, bouncing off lines holding up both sides of the walls . . . the restroom queues.

"Go to the end of the line," a few wasted girls in black lipstick snarled at me.

"Just what I intend," I snarled back. "I'd stay in the restroom if you don't want to be vampire bait."

Meanwhile, the bleary-eyed guys, some in black eyeliner, whistled and noticed me.

"Schoolteacher," one drawled, and others took up the refrain. "We'll muss you up, teach."

One guy with a leer and abs of corrugated cardboard tried to block my way. When I elbowed him hard, he folded and slid down against the wall. You just can't drink and drug and then molest women properly.

"Vintage is a waste on punks like you," I told them.

Irritating, immature blowhards they *might* be, but pathetic victims-to-be they were *sure* to be.

The relentless screeching of the music in the hollow two-story box ahead was already filing my nerves to the quick. Was the high-pitched end of the clamor the first wave of vampire victims or just bad-rock white noise? And where was Lilith?

A ring of deserted tables hugged the walls. Everybody was dancing. I guess it was either move with the hyperactivity or sit on the sidelines and go blind and deaf to stay sane. Okay, I'm a party pooper.

I glided by some tables, snagging a faux leather jacket to cover my out-of-sync dress.

A central open staircase mimicked the La Vida Loca layout, so I fought my way to its foot, being drawn into crazy mob moves on the way there.

A pale hand grabbed my shoulder.

I turned.

"Sorry. I thought you were a guy," one of the workout-gear-clad vamp chicks said.

I knew what she was right away. Her eyes widened with lust as her mouth gaped open until the fangs appeared, heading for my neck. In the hectic lighting, I could see drops of drool on the fang-tips. Seriously unsanitary.

My silver dagger stabbed through the flimsy shiny fabric of my borrowed jacket. I was scared enough to stick it in under her rib cage and twist, hoping the silver familiar knew what it was doing. The feel of blade tip rebounding off bone and then sinking deep into gushy heart of darkness was so repellent, I stopped the attack.

A horrid burnt acid smell and a stream like Vida's cigarette smoke rose between us while our eyes held. Her pupils vanished up into her eye sockets as blood suffused the whites, whose blood, I had no idea. Not mine seemed enough to hope for at the moment.

She fell onto the first steps as I skirted her form and galloped up the stairs two at a time, soundless in the cacophony, desperate for an overhead view. How would I ever spot Lilith in this crowd? She blended in like pot in a look-alike spider plant field.

From the second-story balcony, I saw that the vamp girls were not only already inside, they had mingled, warming up their victim's blood by boogying them into a dance fever. Their colorful workout wear made them stand out among the undertaker-black clad clientele like carnivorous Easter bunnies in a bat cave.

Great. Up here, I had a bead on every one of those fanggirl, grrrl-power bloodsuckers and no anti-aircraft guns to mow them down with. Even if I'd had a flamethrower handy, I'd do as good a job killing their victims as they would.

Helpless witness is not a role I care to take.

A pair of icy hands grasped my shoulders from behind.

I spun around and away from the two-story drop over the railing, punching my forearms outward to break the contact. My college martial arts moves were rusty, but a sideways kick caught the shadowy form in the abs.

"You are *mean* on the other side of the mirror," a voice huffed out. Lilith's.

I kept my dodging, defensive crouch. "You oughta know mean. What're you doing up here?"

"Quick smoke. They don't allow it down below."

"That's the only thing they don't allow."

Lilith edged into the light reflected from below, crossing her bare forearms over her lean middle. Figures like spiked worms were churning over her flesh.

"I managed to hurt you?" I tried to sound disbelieving. Our mama was a vampire. I knew I wasn't one. Didn't mean Lilith was taint-free.

"Not that bad." Lilith showed her teeth as her breath hissed in. They were reasonably square and blunt. "If I don't hold my defensive ink back, you'd be baled in barbed wire. Guess I startled you."

"We've never . . . touched before."

"And won't do it again," Lilith swore. "I won't bite, promise."

"Unless you're a vampire."

"Not yet. I wanted to ask you—discreetly for me—where the Phi Delta Dingbats cheerleader types on the dance floor all came from. They look more your style than mine or Rave Machine's."

She joined me at the railing, curling her hands around the top round bar.

The phantom tattoo poured over her hands like living lace and vanished into the dark surface. Her body ink must be metallic-based, discharging into the nearest inert metal. It made me wonder if my recently discovered trick of converting an involuntary copper intrauterine device into sterling silver endometriosis was a unique feature in Vida's offspring. Maybe I wasn't the only bionic baby.

"Have your dark tattoos always been mobile?" I asked.

"They come and go like a rash, without my asking. Why?"

"Inquiring reporter."

"Right. Hold it over me that you're a professional at something besides being a hard case, why don't you?"

"Good sister, bad sister," I said with a grin, feeling oddly mischievous, considering the situation. Lilith smothered a smirk.

"You're okay, I'm okay," I told her, "but those 'dingbats' below are a bunch of vampire girls about to go wild."

"No shit! That's why you retreated up here. Great view of the carnage."

"No retreat. I'm a proactive chick. I'm trying to figure out how to stop them all. Right now they're busy enjoying toying with their food."

"You get down there and manage to stake one, the others are going to eat fast and run."

"No staking. Like the metal railing in your hands, everything in this building is constructed of glass or metal. That's what I'm seeing from up here. Not one sliver of wood. It might as well have been built as a vampire people-trap."

"By who?"

"Whom."

Lilith stuck her tongue out at me. Black Old English script read "Screwest thou." Kinda demony, Sis.

"That should be reading 'Mothersucker,'" I said.

"Huh? You sorta swear? Ms. Goody Two-hundred-shoes?"

"Mother is a vampire and she runs a health club just a few doors down Delilah Street for awesomely toned girl vamps. I'm surprised you opted out from meeting her."

"I don't care what she is and what she does where. This is your quest, Dee."

"Her name is Vida and I have a picture of her on my

computer. It's several decades old, but she looks the same."

"Hope those genes run in the family," Lilith quipped, but she was keeping her billboard tongue bridled. She leaned over the railing. "Those dippy college types are really going to make this party into a bloodbath?"

"As soon as this set ends."

Lilith looked around what would be the flies area in a theater, the dark top story above the stage where backdrops and other theatrical effects would be stored out of sight, out of mind.

We were on a level with all the light fixtures.

"What about that gigantic cheesy mirrored ball in the center of the dance floor," Lilith asked. "Can't you do some mojo with that?'

"I could try exiting through it, if I wanted to come out on the other end fractured into tiny pieces."

"You're stuck here, then. Good. I hate to watch massacres alone. Look. There's a mirror behind the bar."

"Not glass I can use. Highly polished chrome. It distorts, see? I'd come through the S-shaped woman."

"Oh, yeah. Kinda cool. Everybody looks like pig faces in it already. Some of these lights might hurt the vamps."

"Neon hasn't kept them off the Vegas Strip. Strobe lights only mask how superfast they can move when preying, or fighting. It also makes their pale faces look sexy to humans, so they can paralyze prey before the kill."

"Sunlight can kill them, though?"

"Supposedly. Don't you know the common remedies? "

"I've been locked up in mirror-world."

Now was not the time to explore what my remote "twin" had been up to during my twenty-four years of existence. Still, Lilith's simplistic questions reminded me of

Sansouci, the "daylight" vampire. Sunglasses allowed him high-noon strolling time.

"Maybe you could use your superpowers to smash a huge hole in the roof—" Lilith was saying.

"And let the starlight in? Three hundred million light-years isn't going to make any planet-Earth vamp go nova."

I couldn't get lost in centuries of legends and hearsay about what killed vampires. Vida was right. Yet Sansouci was a new-model vamp and he'd kept sunlight from his eyes. Sunlight had to be bad for vampire eyes, at least.

With all these lights here . . . and still the vamps were hopping around like Paris Hilton in a Manhattan nightclub spotting an *Excess Hollywood* camera. When the strobe light hit them, I noticed that their fangs had come out to play. Zero hour was approaching fast.

Their dance partners, male and female, were too busy being cool in black leather and shades—cat's-eye-shaped shades, Snow-type expensive European shades, mirror shades, eye-slit shades, wraparound shades, round scholarly John Lennon shades, Sansouci aviator shades, glitter-framed shades, *Matrix* shades, cool hot shades—to notice anything outside their rum-and-Coke and cocaine hazes.

I had to escape looming doom mode and think like Vegas thought. Corporate. I had to get into the head of Forties arm-candy Vida knuckling under to Cesar Cicereau and watching hard as he took over what would become Vegas when it was as low-end and unglitzy as Delilah Street—pardon my low-esteem self description—was today. Or a few years ago. Vida the entrepreneur, building a new immortal life in California.

That's when I realized that Rave Machine had to be the

first club she'd owned. The gym down the street was the new, improved version, with a vamp-only membership. This had been a real health club she'd bought and had now turned into a literal tourist trap.

I turned to Lilith. "Where were you getting your quick smoke? There are smoke alarms all over this ceiling."

She eyed the dark spaces between the huge light fixtures. "Yeah, I saw them. I thought they were security cameras at first, but then I tumbled. So I ducked behind one of those doors."

"What doors?"

"Step back from the railing and this pit of whacked-out lights and you'll be able to focus on them."

Sure enough, we were standing on a balcony. A row of blank metal doors were set back about ten feet.

I eyed Lilith's skin-tight everything. "Where do you carry smokes?"

She worked something out of her front jeans pocket with a mighty wriggle. To some—men—it might be provocative. To me it was a time waster.

She finally withdrew a slim rectangular metal case. "Vintage, baby. The lighter is built into one end. Isn't it cool?"

I raised an eyebrow she couldn't see in the shadows. Maybe there was hope for her yet.

"So the doors are unlocked. What's in there?" I asked.

"I don't know. Crap. It's dark."

"Not if you light one candle in the darkness."

"Religious crap."

I grabbed her elbow—I almost got a shock—and pulled her to a door. "This one?"

"I guess."

"We haven't time to play 'you-don't-care.'"

I grabbed the nineteen-thirties cigarette case from Lilith's hand, my palm loving the incised Art Deco lines it felt, the sleek compactness . . . thinking Vida would know and love this artifact of her era . . . rats, sentimentality sucked! My thumb found the strike wheel and pushed hard. A sturdy little flame flared into life . . .

. . . and its tiny glare reflected off long glass tubes lining the top of a bullet-shaped coffin on the floor in the small chamber built to house only it.

"The vampires sleep in this space cocoon thingie and there are roomfuls of them up here?" Lilith asked, sounding in awe for the first time I'd ever heard her do so.

I didn't have time to explain. "Help me drag this out of the room."

"It looks heavy."

It ain't heavy, it's my maybe baby sister, and she is sometimes very dense.

Thanks, Irma.

"You like to flaunt those hard-candy girlie biceps?" I challenged Lilith. "Use 'em."

Together, but mostly me, we manhandled the awkward "coffin" out of the room and through the open door. We heaved it upright on the outside wall, where it looked mighty like a space-age mummy case.

I raced back into the room, striking Lilith's ninety-year-old lighter time and again before it ran out of fluid, hunting two things: a loose old-fashioned male plug lying around and a female receptacle, known in the building trades as an "outlet," in the wall.

Sometimes they are pain in the neck to connect and sometimes they make beautiful music together.

I returned to the balcony flushed with effort. Lilith was leaning her crossed arms on the railing, looking down. "The vamp girls are really slingin' hash now. And those dumb guys are keeping their sunglassed eyes glued on the girls' gyrating hips, baby, not their lips. That's guys for you."

"Stand back by the doors," I said.

She turned. The upright tubes lining both the bottom and the top of the plugged-in case were tinging and buzzing and blushing pink and yellow. "You don't tell me what to do, Dee."

"Lilith! What happens next could blind you. Nose to the wall. Cup your hands around your face when you get there."

"And you?

"I'm gonna aim this little Venusian Palace death ray and then do the same as I told you."

Lilith was boot-scuffling her way to the wall like a reluctantly obedient three-year-old. That girl had issues. "The Venusian Palace is a Vegas Strip residence tower behind the Gehenna Hotel."

"Right. Remind me to tell later you how it made the news. We are about to invent Vampire Fire."

She reluctantly helped me (so much for her muscle tank top) manhandle the "coffin" (so aptly named by Lilith), to face the *Dancing with the Stars* super-ultra-huge mirror ball trophy hanging above the crazy-lit floor below.

"Now," I ordered her. "Nose to the wall, eyes shut, and hands cupping your face."

She cozied herself up to the painted concrete like it was a six-foot-two hunk. "I'm going to think beautiful thoughts. Of *your* boyfriend."

"Whatever makes you docile."

Every muscle in my body was shaking from overextension as I turned myself into the wall and cupped my own hands to put my eyes totally in the dark.

Below, the music was reaching its climax with the shrill of police sirens amping up the mix. I could picture the gyrating couples, vampire and human, reaching the end of the set with a mutual—but so misguided on both sides—mass predatory pounce . . . except the mirror ball was (I hoped but dared not look) broadcasting a strange new light into the frenetic mix below.

The sirens and guitars shrieked and my spine burned with the bites of a thousand fire ants as a totally atonal mass scream of dying vampires joined the last chords.

I heard an electrical apocalypse.

All the breakers in the place burned out at once, even through the light-reddened flesh of my hands I glimpsed when the house went dark as the vampires went down.

First, there was silence.

Then, the buzz of people muttering discontent. Questions floated up.

"Where're the freaking lights?"

"We're blind as bats."

"This is a gyp joint."

"We want our money back."

"The band's *really* unplugged!"

"*Eeew*, goo."

"Yeah. What's the gunk on the floor?"

I kicked the electrical cord out of the "coffin" with its blackened glass tubes and ran to the balcony railing, gazing down.

Some of the lights were slowly warming up and coming on again.

I'd hoped for nice tidy Buffyverse piles of dust. Instead, I saw puddles of bloodred.

Dazed, formerly cool ravers had ripped off their sunglasses and were wandering the half-lit dance floor, keeping their dancing shoes out of the vamp girl Jell-O.

"What is this stuff, Silly Putty?"

"That hot babe I was dancing with ran out on me when the lights all went out."

"Ouch. Mine gave me an Indian burn on the arm when she vamoosed."

Up in rafters, I commented to Lilith, "More like a sunburn."

"Awesome." She leaned so far over the railing I had to grab the back of her low-rise jeans. "What did we do?"

Now it's 'we,' Irma pointed out, *when it was really thee and me.*

And mostly me. I was almost too exhausted to explain.

"When this was a real health club," I said, "it was so totally California it offered suntanning machines that are banned nowadays. They use ultraviolet light, the artificial equivalent of sunlight, deadly to vamps. The mirror ball fractured that lethal light into a thousand laser stakes spinning down onto the dance floor in a few seconds."

"So what's the Venusian Palace effect?"

"It's one of those new hotel-condo towers, part of a nine billion dollar development."

"I hear that right? Nine *billion*?"

"It was built before the Great Recession. Anyway, the hotel-condo walls were all made of concave curved glass. When the Nevada sun hits the surface it creates a beam of concentrated solar energy that can melt plastic and singe hair. It was burning the patrons in the pool area. You get the same effect when you focus a magnifying glass on a piece of paper on a hot sidewalk."

"*You* focus your stupid magnifying glass on the

National Enquirer pages on the Las Vegas Strip. How that burning hair thing happens is way too nerdy and painful for me," Lilith said. "You ready to blow this joint? If I only had one in my hand."

"Now that the vamp girls are history we could go down the street and confront our mama together, safely."

"Not interested. I'll let you keep on doing the heavy lifting, Dee. Click those simpy heels together and get us home to Vegas."

"I'm not sure I can."

"What? I'm stuck in this nowhere town on a street with your name?"

"Maybe if we walked back to the exact place we showed up along this street."

"I am not an 'exact' chick." Lilith frowned. "Besides, that's quite a hike and we'd have to go through all those geeky guys looking for Ms. Goodbar down there. I'm just along for the ride," she said.

Dare I say 'whined'?

I shook my head at Irma's comment and pulled my cell phone from my pocket. The address on Delilah Street in Corona, California, was still on the backlit screen. The folks living here would have no idea what lurked around the corner. What would Vida do now?

Or us? We weren't on fey paths anymore. How would we get home? These heels of mine were just anonymous vintage wear. They didn't have a "click" option.

My smartphone did, though.

I wandered toward my own improvised Venusian death ray—the open, upright tanning bed. All right! The vertical bulbs' blackened centers acted as a mirror backing. I could see my image vaguely reflected in the vertical glass array, with Lilith shadowing me.

In for a penny, out for a pounding. Could I make another giant leap for humankind, or would I zap us both into scattered atoms of fairy dust?

I sighed and pulled up Vegas on the phone's map app, targeting Sunset Park.

No way did I want to aim exactly for my front door and have Hector Nightwine's ever-present spy cams reveal his Enchanted Cottage was far more than a reconstructed movie set.

I closed my eyes and hit the button and wished on a star—or a planet, my inspiration, Venus—for good luck. I may even have clicked my peep-toe heels together *ever so softly.* . . .

Nothing. I felt nothing, not even a breath of wind.

Then I heard something pounding toward me and opened my eyes.

Wow. I saw an oncoming bolt of cold lightning, greyhound big and fast and, duh, gray. It almost knocked off my heels. Also, it battered my ears with barking and a bunch of really too hot, slimy, and thorough ear licks for a public park.

"Quicksilver, *down!* Good dog. *Down.* Happy to see you too. You're my ever-lovin' American Express card. Shouldn't have left home without you."

He finally obeyed and gamboled around me in circles of joyful greeting without jolting the phone out of my hand or me off my feet.

Me.

Solo.

Lilith was nowhere to be seen.

Don't worry. We're not going to lose that psycho hitch-hiker this easy.

I did worry. I'd gotten Lilith and me to the current

address of our foggy vampire roots. Vida. I kinda felt for her. I kinda feared her. Now what were we going to do about it?

Me. I. By myself. Not quite.

I still had a long high-heeled walk home ahead of me. Me and my succulent toes.

Which Quicksilver, confined to the ground by my command, had done a play bow to lick.

I doubted that was what Snow had in mind, but it sure did tickle.

Chapter Twenty-one

"**B**IG DAY YESTERDAY," Ric's voice told me.

"*Mmph,*" I told my cell phone.

It read 12:52. Why was Ric calling me so late at night after what had truly been a long day?

Wait! Sunshine fell on the bedroom floorboards. Quicksilver lay curled around his giant stainless steel water dish by the dormer windows. It was not last night, it was morning.

Or what passed for it with me, which appeared to be the afternoon.

"Delilah? Are you awake?"

"Barely."

"I know we need to do a postmortem on Loretta in Hell and me on the Nine Circles' Lust level and seeing *Metropolis*, but some honchos from D.C. just hit town wanting to meet on an emergency consultation about smuggling zombies in from Mexico."

"I saw you speak on that subject," I murmured. "You were very good. *Muy* commanding."

"You did? I've never given a formal speech in my life."

Oh. That had been a dream. Right.

"Well, you'd be very commanding if you did."

"They're flying people in from the West Coast and Midwest, so this could run late into the evening. I hate to leave our own matters hanging."

"Such as . . . ?" I began, still wondering how I could

explain my freaky mirror-trek to California and a maybe-vampire mother.

"Dealing with Snow's astounding offer of sponsorship, what's best for the Silver Zombie, and how much danger raising her put me in from Vegas bigwigs will just have to wait," Ric said impatiently.

I yawned. He didn't know I'd been to the West Coast and back already that very early morning. "I agree. We don't want to jump on Snow's bandwagon without plenty of research. It's okay, Ric. We'll check in tomorrow."

Besides, Snow wasn't the only one worried about Ric.

We cooed our good-byes and I rolled over to sink into that most luxurious of feelings, a long nap in a sunny room.

I should have been wondering what was up with Ric and his government contacts, but my mind was on a maternal vampire—mine!—and recalling how I'd stumbled to find mother substitutes in my early years.

Discovering an apparent vampire mother also ramped up my growing anxieties about Ric, worries about his soul I'd buried under a white-knuckled dedication to his physical survival.

When an unadoptable orphan—whose closest thing to a mother most of her life was shared with Mr. Spock (and look how he turned out)—is all grown up and has an intimacy "issue," who's she gonna call on?

As usual, I was more comfy with film people than the real "family" folks in my life . . . like some hard-hearted group home supervisor.

Spock's human mother, as played by Jane Wyatt on *Star Trek*, was formerly the mother on *Father Knows Best*, so she had to put up with a lot of male domination in her day. She remained my model of mature sweet reason. God knew I could use such a woman in my life.

The vamp in California was not my role model.

Our life was way simpler when you were still a virgin early last spring and had nil intimacy, much less other issues, Irma popped up to remind me. *So who's our go-to gal now? Helena Troy Burnside has my vote. She's only a long-distance phone call away, or we could video conference.*

"No Skype," I told Irma. Helena had spotted only Lilith lurking in my psyche. "If she finds out about you, I'll be certifiable in her book and no fit, uh, partner for her foster son. You are not going share any screen time with me. Who do you think you are, Irma . . . Lilith?"

Come on, Helena's an open-minded lady.

"She's my lover's foster mother, Irma. It would be embarrassing to look so green in front of her, and I don't want her to worry about Ric."

If you didn't lock me out when you're gettin' down with Mr. Yummy Montoya, I'd be all you'd need to advise you, girlfriend.

"I seldom have luck locking you out totally, but keep your comments to yourself right now."

I drifted off into dreamland and a sleep level they call "fitful."

A couple hours later I woke up, knowing exactly the right person to call for a spontaneous meeting and an emergency consult. I just needed to wait until it got dark so no one would know about it.

And Irma was back then too.

You're gettin' out your black leather motorcycle jacket, mama? I do wanna go where you're going. What kinda shrink digs in-your-face?

"It's not a shrink in the traditional sense," I told Irma.

"And you're gonna love the leggings, if you could see them," I said, firmly slamming the door of my mind shut on her.

I tossed the jacket down on the bed after a try-on. Vegas nights did cool down at times, not in summer so much, but I was after effect, not comfort. I wasn't content to leave my appearance to the wardrobe witch tonight and waved away the Goth T-shirt she'd produced on the hanger rack next to my closet door.

My black leggings had tiny skull studs down the sides that coordinated with the buckles on the ankle-high genuine motorcycle boots. That was Goth enough. I shrugged into a white ruffled shirt that would suit a pirate or Mrs. Peel. Then I buckled one last buckle, or swashbuckle, a black leather collar around my neck.

A savvy reporter knows how to dress up or down for the assignment.

My role on this occasion? I was a would-be bad girl going to a bad part of town to meet up with a big bad player. I was glad even Quicksilver wasn't around to give tails up or down on my look.

No sooner had I buckled the bad-girl collar than the familiar curled around it as a gleaming circlet alternating studs with spikes. At least it felt at home. Too bad Quicksilver wasn't purse pooch material; now our collars matched. I was glad that thought reminded me to take a wrist wallet for essentials. The top of my right hand already bore my homemade tattoo.

I firmly refused to even think of Jane Wyatt, Helena Troy Burnside, or Irma and her reaction, grabbing the jacket and heading out to my date with Mr. Wrong.

HE'D PICKED THE place since this meeting needed to be secret even more on his account than mine.

Now that I stood in front of the off-downtown location too close for comfort to the nomadic Sinkhole, I regretted my agreement. The giant bunker that passed itself off as a nightclub squatted on a parking lot that stank of spilled four-dollar-a gallon contraband gas, beer and stomach contents. The place boasted a big charcoal-gray metal door guarded by three hulking CinSims, all duplicates of six-foot-seven James Arness as the Thing.

They weren't terribly articulate beyond *Argggh*, but one held up an infrared device to scan the membership ink on my hand.

I'd downloaded the spider-on-a-skull logo from the club Facebook page—so much for social networking trumping security measures. Then I duplicated it in the invisible ink formula I'd heard about from my pal at the city morgue, coroner Grisly Bahr himself. Murder victims turned up regularly with the club's reentry imprint on their decomposing skin, visible only under black light. Classy place.

I breezed by the Three Arghmigos. Inside, screaming guitars and pounding drums easily drowned out any editorial comments from Irma. The scene was Rave Machine meets Vegas motorcycle club. My vision adjusted to the combo of stuttering off-and-on strobe lights and that stripper-bar staple, black light that made white skin and shirts, like mine, gleam the same electric blue as my eyes. I spotted other women present with lots of glitter on eyebrow-raising places, but they were all way less dressed than I was, if you didn't count ankle-to-eyebrow body ink.

I'd wanted to be instantly visible to my interviewee in this crowd, but my signature look was immediately mobbed by dudes in biker chains. These growling urban werewolves were hoping for an impending full-moon night out to howl while they could still have human intercourse, in both senses of the word. Before I had to impress a few more dents in their gypsy leathers, they peeled away right and left as if Moses was coming along putting a long straight part in the Red Sea. My source was here and announcing himself.

"Bitchin outfit," Sansouci said when he alone stood before me, the other guys skedaddling history.

I recognized vampire fight mode. He seemed taller, wider, stronger, wilder. His eye whites caught the black light too, gleaming blue as he elbowed away the competition.

"Do you know what you're doing?" Sansouci asked, shifting down into the usual merely intimidating Vegas muscle mode again. He steered me through the crowds in his custody and bent down so he could admonish and question me through the high-decibel rock band wailing from every wall.

"When you set this meetup, I wondered," he said. "You doing crazy-ass things is my greatest entertainment form in the world entertainment capital. Montoya know you're off your monogamy leash?"

By then, we'd reached one of the luminous giant skulls suspended on chains at various heights around the vast dark space. I'd checked out the setup on the Spider Skull Bar website, so wasn't surprised when Sansouci steered me to a swaying skull booth a couple feet off the floor.

Entering it was like stepping up into Cinderella's pumpkin coach from Hell. Sansouci's hand under my elbow boosted me inside. We were scooped onto a semicircular red velvet "booth" as our weight swung the skull's jaws snapped shut. The macabre capsule whisked up over the dancers' heads to rock gently in the dark.

Whee, Irma managed to blurt.

Whee, indeed. My stomach did that involuntary adrenaline swoop you get from Ferris wheels or sexual attraction. At least I recognized both sides of "thrill" now.

Inside, we sat at a small circular table with a black glass top as round and perfect as a gun barrel. As soon as the swinging-on-a-skull effect slowed, Sansouci used the remote control on the table to shut off the piped-in racket.

He leaned back on the tufting to inspect me from head to boot. So I surveyed him with Vida's eyes. He was still a handsome green-eyed guy with a slash of silver in his brunet forelock. His black turtleneck shirtsleeves were pushed up to the elbows to reveal a landscape new to me, forearms with matching iridescent green tattoos of snaky Celtic design.

He'd recently made no secret of being attracted to me, so I'd resolved not to fidget under his own assessment, half impersonal surveillance and half lust. Wondering if he could be a remote candidate for Daddy dearest really upped the ante on my nerves.

What I wanted—needed—to know from him was extremely personal and even more confidential. Girlish hesitation wouldn't get me anything from a man or supernatural like him. I had to extract my information in a way that seemed to feed his desires, but also addressed my increasing fears.

Lucky for me his was a new breed of vampire—developed to go public these post–Millennium Revelation days. A gigolo vamp who liked and lived off women, a few drops at a time, was easier to relate to than the usual desperate lunger.

A screen inset on one of the skull's eye sockets burned into being, showing the impassively perfect face of the joint's virtual cocktail waitress. "Your order, please?"

Sansouci cocked a dark eyebrow my way. "You're the star Inferno Bar mixologist."

My answer lofted that eyebrow to new heights. "I'll have a Virtual Virgin." I ticked off the ingredients. "Six ounces of no cal, no sodium, no caffeine cherry cola, an ounce of lime juice, and a slice of lime."

"Is there any octane at all in that drink?" Sansouci asked.

"Add two ounces of UV cherry vodka," I suggested.

"That'll do for mine," he said, nodding at the screen. "Skip the lime garnish."

Our virtual waitress vanished.

"Virtual Virgin." He savored the name. "You sending a message?"

"I wanted to invent a drink for the sober that could go country or pop."

The eye socket blinked open with a red flash. Two cocktails in tall, footed glasses sat on a black glass tray. Only one had a skewered lime slice on a swizzle stick.

Sansouci handed me that glass and took his own as the skull's socket went opaque black again, tray gone. He clicked off the skull's other . . . porthole, as I'd prefer to think of it.

We were swaying in a sensory deprived environment again except for a black-light blue glow that amped up my white blouse and skin and our teeth, of course. We each sipped our light, and loaded, versions of the Virtual Virgin. I was beginning to regret my nervy attempt to sucker the werewolf mob house vampire into any kind of confession for anything.

"A toast," he said, "to whatever you think you want from me this time."

I clicked glass rims and talked fast.

"Why did you c-come . . . show up . . . if you weren't willing to give me information? You know that's my job."

I wished Irma were there to sing, *Wrong start*.

He smiled at my clumsy attempt to dodge any inciting double entendres. Sexy guys made me nervous. Blame it on my convent school education.

"Fair enough," he said. "I patronize this private club. These suspended skulls are as secure as the grave used to be. I was curious to see what you'd wear to semi-seduce me, but not really mean it. You never disappoint me there, Delilah. No skin but a whole lot of attitude. I can't resist a virtual virgin." He shrugged and lifted his glass as an example. "And I'm bored. Should I say, bored out of my skull?"

I quirked a pale smile at his jest. To get info you've got to give info. I ignored the inciting things he'd said— everything but the last phrase. I leaned my elbows on the table and bent in confidentially even though he claimed the skull booth was eavesdrop proof.

"You and your skull are not going to be bored in Vegas very long. Christophe's come back from Wichita with something that will blow the local supernatural mobs off the map."

"What, some new venue or power? Out of Podunk Wichita?"

"Wichita is my home town." I was surprised to hear myself defending a place I once couldn't wait to leave. "We were just there, Ric and I. And Quicksilver. And . . . as it turned out, Snow."

"Hmm." Sansouci gazed down my waterfall of front shirt ruffles as if it wasn't there.

I sat up tall and adjusted them, like it would do any good.

"Sorry, Street. Christophe may have sold you a fairy tale, but I don't believe any of them, except for the big bad wolf. Mine's named Cicereau. I notice you're not wearing red tonight, except in your lip gloss. Or am I supposed to go beneath the surface and think creatively. A scarlet satin thong?"

"You should think with something besides your . . . your gigolo jeans." I decided to commit truth. "Yes, I know you like me. I'd like to think it was me and not my, okay, girlie attributes. You hate being held hostage to the Gehenna's Cesar Cicereau and his wolf pack. I'm here to say you could do something about that now.

"Snow has a secret weapon Ric, ah, unearthed, something snatched from the clutches of the drug lord El Demonio that would have every overlord in Las Vegas panting to capture and use it, from the Immortality Mob to Cesar Cicereau.

"Snow is offering Ric sanctuary from all those forces, and he might offer you that too if you went over to his side."

"What could be that powerful," Sansouci scoffed.

"Not what, who." He still looked unconvinced, so I sold harder. If I told Sansouci a secret, he might help me with mine. "This is big. You know what reach and power El Demonio's cartel commands in the whole Western hemisphere. That demon covets what Ric raised to the dark bottomless depths of what would be a soul in anyone else, even in any other doomed supernatural in Vegas."

I stopped for breath. And then caught it.

Sansouci's head was down, hovering over the glass he held in both hands. His thick black hair with its silver streak reminded me of a wolf's pelt, of Quicksilver's paler version of it. Oh, no. I'd offended him. Wasn't a vampire just another doomed soul too?

The silence lasted long enough for me to realize I was breathing heavily.

And so was he.

Just as Mama said, vampires may not live and breathe, but they had to suck air to speak.

When Sansouci looked up, his eyes were rimmed in bloodred.

"Do you believe that I ever wanted this, that I was always this?" he demanded, his voice so low I had to lean closer to hear, much as it scared the hell out of me.

"Do you believe a vampire *ever* forgets being human, any more than a plague victim forgets a whole skin and being able to breathe, to the very end . . . for six or seven or eight hundred years of the very end, with no cessation in sight but some fanatic striking out centuries of half life with a stake or a beheading sword? To finally wanting, needing immortality, if only as a way to hold off total damnation? By God, you're lucky I've had a hundred years to live off what you call my gigolo jeans."

God? Damnation? What kind of vampire was this? What shocked me most was his taking the Lord's name in vain. A vampire? Calling on God in any way? Even I was edgy about doing that anymore. And I was only recently a postgraduate virgin.

Sansouci's low mutter continued, as rhythmic as a familiar prayer. "Do you dare to think I'm some kind of chained bear whose entire being doesn't scream out every day for vengeance on its tormenters? Do you presume to think I've come to your rescue a time or two just because I like your ass in a city showcasing whole chorus lines of them? Do you think I tolerate your feeble attempts to use me because it's fun to see an amateur try to fire a forty-five magnum? To judge me, use me, *snow* me?"

Again the silence spoke only of my shock and terror.

And it was utter silence. I ached to hear the shrill pulse of the half dozen rock bands writhing to the beat outside the skull, for the screen to brighten with the waitress's supernaturally perfect face offering a refill.

I was sure my heartbeat was audible too, especially to him, and shut my eyes.

"Who the hell do you think you are, Delilah Street?" the harsh whisper came again.

"Desperate?" I tried. "And overconfident."

I heard the movement of fabric on velvet. My throat tightened against my damn flippant Goth collar, anticipating the fanged assault.

A bit of light flickered over my closed eyelids. I eased them open a slit.

Sansouci had finished draining his glass and called up the virtual waitress.

"Two doubles," he snarled at the screen as it illuminated his face, emphasizing broad cheekbones, a bone-snapping strong jaw, and the widow's peak of his black hair against pale skin.

No wonder I'd taken him for a werewolf, as everyone else did.

His face turned my way. The redness rimming his eyes had shrunken and darkened, like dried blood, but his eye whites still glared blue from the black light that penetrated even the skull booths. "Meanwhile, why am I here, now, at your service?"

"I tend to give people the benefit of the doubt."

"Or maybe you will make up my mind. Decades are weeks to the immortal."

His laugh held overtones of a melancholy lilt. I guessed that some inborn ruefulness of his particular vampire history and nature kept me alive and untouched right now.

"Well, hold onto your virtual virginhood," Sansouci advised, "because you're going to get more 'story' than even you wanted now."

I glanced up. He looked just as intense and grim as before, but a tiny emerald gleam sparked deep in his eyes. "Guess your method works, Delilah Street."

I cautiously changed position to ease my frozen muscles, but he wasn't looking at me. He was staring into the skull's black portholes to nothing.

"I'm not Dear Abby, Delilah. I'm not your big brother, but you seem to think I can tell you what you're so eager to know. Time for the hard stuff, so drink up. And then I'll tell you a night's tale you won't soon forget."

Chapter Twenty-two

My FINGERTIPS INCHED the cocktail glass Sansouci had put dead center on the little table toward my side of it. The flavored and colored vodka, added to the innocuous cherry cola, had produced a bright bloodred brew suitable for virginal wedding nights and vampire orgies.

I didn't dare look at Sansouci, and that wasn't totally about him being a vampire and also a vampire angry with me.

It was about *me* being angry with me.

"I'm sorry. I do that," I said, not looking anywhere but into the cherry-amber depths of my drink. "That's what I was trained to do as a reporter. Approach story subjects in a mode they feel comfortable with and then get their stories."

"And why do you need stories?"

"It . . . they explain things. About the way the world truly works, about what this person has gone through and knows that other people may need to know and . . . benefit from."

"You're an idealistic tattletale?"

"Not anymore." I dared one sip of the strong drink, lowering my head to the glass, going for being as low-profile as dirt. "Now I do it to save my sanity and maybe a few people's, um, lives."

"You mean their mortality, their humanity? Everything I *don't* have."

Ouch. "That's my mistake. I don't think of you that big-oted way."

"What way do you think of me?"

"If the Las Vegas Strip was a line, with all the people and paranormals I know on either side of it, I'd want you on my side."

I could feel him shift position, lift the glass, and drink deeply.

"I've taken a lot of lives, and you've saved lives." He observed this as an interesting phenomenon, not as murder and not-murder. "You saved a bunch of tourist lives at the Gehenna when you exorcised Loretta's ghost in that spectacular fashion."

"Really? She's managed to come back in physical form and wants to destroy Ric and me."

"Didn't you listen to her story? I could have told you lovely little Loretta was and is as willful and power-hungry as the gangster father she hates. Being Cicereau's victim only deepened the blood fury already in her."

"I've seen a photo from the nineteen forties of Loretta with her father, you, and a good-looking woman."

"Girl," Sansouci corrected.

"Girl?"

"Cicereau's arm candy. She was only a few years older than Loretta, whom he had killed at age sixteen. So?"

"You were there as a bodyguard. I can almost see the outline of the gun in the dinner jacket pocket your right hand was in."

"No, you couldn't. I wouldn't do that. I carry it in an underarm holster or the small of my back. Keep that in mind if you ever get the occasion, or urge, to pat me down." He had resumed flirting, a mode I could handle. "Loose guns go off, slip out of your hand. Your imagination was running away with you. But I'm intrigued that you looked me over so thoroughly."

"And that chorus girl . . . ?"

"Vida. An aspiring actress. Don't laugh; she had some chops and Cesar had promised her auditions outside his master bedroom."

"What happened to her?

"She . . . moved on. He was not a monogamous mobster. None of them are. No need."

"When did she move on?"

Sansouci consulted his very long memory bank. "After Cicereau went berserk over the Loretta business."

"That was after you were indentured to him?"

"Same time. It was one big ugly meltdown."

"You admitted that you witnessed Cicereau kill his own daughter so viciously."

"I was there under duress. He was teaching me a lesson too when he killed Prince Krzysztof."

"What lesson? That he could cut off your blood supply, your harem?'

"No. I can always revert to draining the traditional single source, and they're everywhere, my dear Delilah. Why all the questions?"

"Maybe Cicereau killed Vida too."

"Maybe."

"You don't seem concerned. Didn't she . . . like you?"

"Maybe." Sansouci shook his head. "Cicereau had fourteen master vampires buried and held in concrete coffins somewhere in the Mojave. I was the sole one aboveground. One werewolf was released . . . and sacrificed to the vampires in exchange for the masters' voluntary 'hibernation.' A part-time blooder like myself was of value to neither side, except for Cicereau's amusement."

"Why were you saved?"

"If you can call it that. The vampires thought I would find and release the masters."

I caught my breath. "And have you?"

"Not yet."

"Will you?"

"Time will tell what I will or will not do, Delilah Street, not you. Cicereau, being werewolf, did unto his competitor vampires as he'd do unto another pack. He scattered and buried each one. Vampires, though, are lone wolves who usually prey individually. Then came the Millennium Revelation of the many supernaturals who had hidden from the humans. The old-style vampire wouldn't fare so well today. Besides, they tend to bicker when gathered in political groups. They're on separate power trips. What I do takes discipline."

That's something the huge "pack" of organized vampires right under the Strip had, but I was here to learn the lay of the land, not utterly remake it.

"Is it possible," I wondered, "that suspending those vampires' lives and power gave werewolf mobster Cicereau some extended mortality?"

"Maybe. I was expendable because I wasn't like them. I remembered I wasn't always vampire." He stated the obvious with a mocking sideways glance. "Several hundred years ago, give a century or two, I was the second son of a landowner in Ireland."

"I *knew* you had Black Irish roots like me," I couldn't help exclaiming, like we were distant cousins. I could hear Irma saying, *Back off, girl.*

Sansouci wasn't buying either. "You gonna put that on the nightly news, Delilah? This is *my* story, not yours, for a change."

I winced, but was relieved to hear him use my first name again, so relieved that I sipped my fresh drink again. The added alcohol warmed my insides, but my fingers were still ice white and ice cold on the glass.

Sansouci addressed his tale to the skull's interior facade of molded plastic bone, the reverse of the Silver Zombie's robot suit. A faint Irish accent embroidered his tale, something I was always a sucker for.

"The eldest son got the fiefdom, with the might of England soon to come at him. For me, it was either the Church or the itinerant sword—"

"So you became a mercenary, and still are to this day."

"Street, shut up. You must have been a lousy reporter. Why didn't you just make it up yourself?" He eyed me, hard. "So I became a monk."

"You?" I flash-carded my visions of his Las Vegas blood harem, all lounging belly dancers wearing no more than veils and glittering coin belts, like the *Metropolis* Whore of Babylon. "Monks are . . . poor and lorded over by the abbot and the order rules and—"

"Celibate." He grinned with rakish pleasure as my illusions came tumbling down.

"How can . . . how could—?"

"Story? Mine?"

I relaxed a bit. Everybody ached to tell his or her story. Sansouci was enjoying shocking the saltwater out of me. That was what a good reporter wanted, an interview subject invested in amazing and surprising his audience.

I nodded and supported my face on my fists, a rapt audience of one myself now. I finally had *my* Interview with the Vampire. Anne Rice, eat your new, angel-hooked heart out!

"The Church was a refuge then," he said. "My vows

were solemn. Poverty, obedience, celibacy. Obedience was the hardest."

If Irma were here, I'd be rolling my eyes at her.

"I was sixteen. We worked from sunrise to sunset then. I was hoeing the chard patch, meditating on Our Lord's crown of thorns like a good boy. I'd forgotten that vespers might toll for evening prayers in the monastery, a severe failing for a monk."

I nodded, spellbound.

He reached out, his hand huge, I noticed for the first time. His fingers brushed back and replaced the hair falling onto my shoulders. His cold undead thumb found my carotid artery with its first gesture. My skin felt clammy, but I'd worked myself up into quite an anxious fever, I told myself. I could use a . . . cold compress.

Yikes, Irma broke through. *He's got us by the pulse point.*

"You've never felt a vampire bite," Sansouci said as caressingly as his thumb rested on my neck. "I don't know how it is for anyone else, but in my time and place, there was no sensation at first, just a barely sensed pressure." His thumb pressure intensified. I felt the tension all through my body. "Then the slightest . . . tingle and then the imping-ing edge of something . . . small but hard, though not like steel."

His thumbnail impressed my skin.

"And then a flood of what doctors now would describe as anesthetic with an aphrodisiac overtone, but in my time and with my youth I only knew it felt like . . . surrender. The surrender of sleep, even a spiritual surrender, as an acolyte gave to the will of God and the abbey. My vows lulled me."

I knew certain martial arts grips could stop the flow

of blood to the brain. I felt dizzy and breathless, but Sansouci's touch hadn't tightened. I was doing this to myself, and I almost sensed craving the sort of surrender he was describing. Utter.

So I let the vampire gaze at and touch the side of my naked neck, nostalgically. He was trusting me with his story, the most important thing in his long immortal life. I let him speak uninterrupted. A reporter has to take big risks for the big story.

The pressure of his thumb relented. His hand stayed anchored on my flesh, his red-rimmed eyes still stared intently into mine.

"I woke in the neighboring woods, hearing the monks calling as they sought me with torches. My hoe lay in the chard patch where I'd dropped it. I heard the rustles of the night as I never had before, thirsted for what I thought was the body and blood of Christ as I never had before.

"One monk had found my abandoned hoe and began circling the spot after the others had vanished around the abbey's great hulk, their calls growing faint, as was any sense I had of belonging to that scene, to those people, to those mortals. Do you feel faint, Delilah?"

I did. He spoke on.

"A shadow crept up on the lone laboring monk. I could see as never before in the dark. I could see what had happened and what I was now. Only the shadow of myself. I crept up on the alien shadow."

My instincts urged me to bite my lip from the suspense, but I resisted.

"The shadow felled the monk, and I felled the shadow. I broke the wooden hoe handle over my robed thigh and impaled the monster's chest with its thick, jagged end. It had carried a sword. I dragged its body into the woods and cut off its head, then stripped it of clothes and donned them, leaving my empty robe beside it. I returned to kneel over my former fellow monk.

"Then I drank him dry between mutters of *miserere cordias.*"

God have mercy on me. I knew that's what the Latin phrase meant. On me too.

I sat, breathing and wishing I could disguise that function. And this had happened centuries ago. Centuries. I was speaking to the last living witness, a vampire.

"They never knew you . . . remained?" I asked.

"Staked, headless vampire. Drained monk and robe. An uncommon couple, yet the only two-plus-two their superstitious but holy medieval minds needed. They burned the bodies and my robe, and put up a gravestone for me on an empty plot."

"What name did it read?"

"None of your business, Delilah Street. I have lost everything of my past. Concealing my original identity is the only thing I am pleased about."

"After all these centuries? At least you have an identity to guard. Even my name isn't really my own," I admitted.

His thumb stroked my neck, the callus on it oddly human, then withdrew. "Stage name?"

"I said I was a reporter, not an actress."

"Could have fooled me, drama queen."

He was trying to distract me, but I wasn't buying it.

"I was an abandoned infant supposedly found on Delilah Street, only there's no such address where I grew up, in Wichita, Kansas. You want to forget who you were and I want to find out who I am."

"'Aren't we a pair'?" Sansouci quoted the melancholy classic song, leaning back in the velvet banquette.

He was showing some of the lazy surrender he'd been recounting during his tale of his simultaneous first time of being bitten and biting, of his virtual virginhood lost. He was the usual cynical Sansouci again. Maybe.

Either my cocktail recipe or telling his tale had returned Sansouci into the deceptively laid-back persona he automatically used to lull human or werewolf fears. He'd had centuries to perfect that. I could see how modern women got hooked on the tension between his sensually knowing exterior and deeply dangerous needs. It was tantalizing.

He licked his lower lip without being conscious of the fact, considering me. "No more questions?"

"Dozens. How did you . . . live?"

"Animal blood repelled me. I soon realized I needed a large supply of victims who wouldn't be missed. I'd chosen God as a master because I knew my temperament wouldn't bow long to any temporal lord, but I'd shown a knack for swordplay. Can you guess? We're talking the fourteenth century here."

"*You're* talking the fourteenth century. I can't believe the changes you've seen. From . . . warlords to twenty-first-century gangsters."

"That breed has changed the least of all, Delilah. What did I do with myself for the next seven or eight hundred years?"

"I have no idea."

"You're an inquiring reporter. You pride yourself on putting two and two together. You tell me. Psych me out."

He leaned back, narrowed eyes challenging me to "undress" his mind-set, even his soul, to dissect his vampire nature overlaid on a young, naive, obedient, chaste monk of an unthinkably alien time to modern me.

Kinda like me a few months ago. I'd let Sansouci unnerve me. It was time to reverse the situation.

"The Irish then were disenfranchised in their own land," I said. "First by the Normans, then by the English. They became wanderers, like the Jews. Bards and . . . mercenaries roaming all lands even into the nineteenth and twentieth and twenty-first centuries. Even today, a lot of the freelance journalists braving the Mideast wars and meltdowns to report for the American news networks are Irish. Still, you didn't crave pay or treasures to live, but blood. Do you play an instrument?" I asked, hunting clues.

He considered, then said, "Only women now."

His voice, the tone, the implications were meant to distract me. They did.

How did a monk learn to be so sexy? *To eat, dummy!*

Paging back to my Our Lady of the Lake convent school classes allowed me to access a lot of religious history.

I closed my eyes and recited. "It was the end of four of five hundred years of rabid Viking butchery and terrorism in the British Isles and Europe, but the developing nations were seething with war, even to sending knights on crusade to the Holy Land, the Middle East."

My fingers tapped on the table.

"What instrument are *you* playing?" Sansouci taunted me.

I studied their dark reflection as my fingers pantomimed a riff on the black glass.

"Castanets," I said, realizing what my unconscious was telling me. "Spain was under siege by Moors in that period. Wait." I sat up straight. "Yours isn't a *night's* tale, like around the campfire. It's a *knight's* tale. You joined the monk warriors who fought to hold Muslims back from Europe and reclaim the Holy Land."

"Because . . . ?"

"Battle was butchery then. Blood was everywhere. Your liquid diet would go unnoticed."

"More than that, we battled for the cause of heaven. Our foes deserved to die."

"Maybe their leaders did, not the foot soldiers."

"It was warrior to warrior then, knight to Saracen. Drinking their blood only further eradicated them from the face of the earth."

"You didn't turn any?"

"Never. Why? A vampire turns a human only from desperation."

"What makes a vampire desperate except lack of blood?"

"Utter hatred or revenge . . . or establishing a link with a mortal he or she can't bear to lose. It's always beauty that destroys the beast, Delilah."

"Then you never had any human connection in all those centuries?"

"Only brothers at arms, and they came and went, as the wars came and went."

"Why were you turned in the first place? You were already dead and out of the way."

"The most common of the seven deadly sins. Greed."

"Greed? You were a penniless monk.'

"I recognized my assailant after I staked him, a trusted retainer of my elder brother's. Apparently Gowan feared I'd tire of the abbey and take what mere happenstance had earned him. I was his superior in everything but order of birth."

"I don't doubt it. He's long moldering in the grave and you've lasted." I sipped again. "How did you . . . convert from battlefield to bedroom?"

"The times did it for me. I ran out of 'holy' wars sometime in the eighteenth century. Then I looked for 'just' wars on the side of the foot soldiers, not the rulers, and finally I realized by the mid-nineteenth century that war was just war, no 'justice for all' in them at all. I hadn't chosen to be a vampire but I could choose to dine from humanity's enemies until the modern age made it clear they weren't to be found on a battlefield."

"So you turned to literally living off women."

"No. I still honored my vows of poverty and chastity."

"You?"

"You're not the only aging virgin to hit Las Vegas, Delilah."

"Oh, come on! Your harem?"

"By the earlier twentieth century it was harder to find anyone deserving to die in war, certainly not enough to keep me going. Women, however, were starting to discover what they wanted, including passion that included a controlled bit of danger. I discovered I could survive on multiple small doses of blood."

"That doesn't make you a virgin."

"I've never had sex without blood, without involuntary need. For that reason, I consider myself true to my vows of celibacy to this day. I've never really made love to a woman, just for the sake of it. I have never loved. I think you might know what I mean now."

"And, in your eyes, that makes you a virgin?"

"A virtual virgin, anyway," he said, with a wry twist to his smile and a raise of his glass. "Just as you still are, really."

"So in your mind virginity has to do with innocence despite experience. Or experience despite innocence."

He nodded. "All you are now, Delilah, is an experienced virgin, in my expert opinion of the same state."

That reminded me of the Silver Zombie, who combined the extremes of innocence and experience through the actress and split personalities of the saintly and salacious Maria character. I wondered if that's why she disturbed me so deeply, along with her obvious dependence on Ric.

Sansouci's head lolled back against the red velvet upholstery. He did look like a knight, a Technicolor effigy of a stone knight in some aged graveyard forever England or Ireland.

"Now," he asked. "What did you really want from me other than a very long life story?"

"The doctors wouldn't let me donate blood to Ric when he was drained at the Karnak. I want to know what's wrong with it."

"Your blood? You want an in-the-field analysis? You want me to make it?"

"I know you can . . . control yourself."

"Maybe not. You're obviously worried that something is up with your blood. I might go berserk. I do scare you, don't I?"

"Sometimes."

"Good."

"If you were to take a sample . . . a tiny sample, where would it be?"

"On my tongue."

"I meant on me."

"Oh." Sansouci obviously relished the chance to inspect me again. "Any erotic zone will do." His eyes made a leisurely Grand Tour. "Lips. Neck." They followed my snowy ruffles halfway down. "Breasts."

I was shocked enough to show it. Blood as mother's milk.

"De*l*ilah." His gently corrective voice was even more

seductive. "Are you going to force me to say nipples in mixed company?"

"Oh, shit."

He shrugged, continuing. "Tits."

Oh, *shit*!

"Fingertips. Navel. And, my favorite, thighs." His expression turned smugly angelic. "Inner thighs."

"I meant places that are showing. *My* favorite is a fingertip."

"So school nurse, Delilah. Sterile. Impersonal."

"Exactly. And where would *you* learn about school nurses, Brother Monk?"

"From one of my circle of current donors. Oddly, she prefers the fingertips too. Must like role reversal. Not on your luscious glossed lips, Delilah? That's the only place you need or use cosmetics and you do them up right."

"Thank you, Mr. Urban Decay. I love your Pocket Rocket lip gloss too. I recall you being afraid my Resurrection Kiss might have the reverse effect on you. It could put you back where you belong. Really dead."

"I said I wasn't *sure* of what your kiss would do now. I'm not afraid."

"It might be lethal."

"You need to know this. Your kiss has already revived Montoya. He's immune. You'll never know if your kiss can thrill or kill another man if you don't test it out. Try me. I like danger."

"Such a brave little lab rat. Fingertip," I said severely, extending my forefinger, print up.

He took my hand in his, his thumb caressing the inside of my wrist, which felt way too good. I liked danger too, I was discovering. His dark head bent to my fingers. I felt like a medieval lady having her hand kissed. All the paintings of that period teemed with languid ladies being led around by the hand. Sanscouci would have had a field day if he hadn't been hunting the battlefields then.

"You'll feel a tiny prick, like from a school nurse, Delilah," he murmured. "Your fingertip will hardly sense it."

And he was right, it didn't, because he pulled my hand and arm over his shoulder to draw me into his arms. His lips were on mine before I could say "Close sesame."

I could have elbowed or kneed him, but I'd never let another man kiss me besides Ric—Snow's Brimstone smooch certainly didn't count. I couldn't be sure Snow had ever been human, and Sansouci had. I needed to know what about my blood was so exotic or toxic it couldn't be transfused to Ric. I now feared it could have a vampire taint. Would my half-vamp fading Brimstone Kiss have special effects on someone other than Ric?

Amazing what situations the ace reporter's "need to know" could get an inquisitive woman into. I no longer wondered why the combination of scared and excited was so many women's downfall.

I wasn't falling at the moment, just a very close observer testing as much as Sansouci was. His tongue-tip slicked back and forth along my closed lips until that relentless tickle made them part. His tongue plunged inside for one hot, deep moment, mimicking a much more intimate incursion, before withdrawing. What a tease he was.

Sansouci sat back, visibly tasting me on his own lips. Tease.

"I avoided taking advantage," he said, "by prolonging the contact past the anesthetic phase to the aphrodisiac effect. Anything you're feeling now is purely natural." His quickly lowered eyelids failed to conceal desire-swollen black pupils. "Perhaps not *purely.*"

"Besides a quick kick, what did you get out of it?" I asked.

He nodded like the connoisseur he was acting as at the moment. "Very rare. New to me. I've dallied in an intercontinental pool of blood over the centuries. You're type AB. Maybe AB positive. Very rare," he repeated.

I frowned, making a mental note to look that type up.

Sansouci rinsed his mouth with a swallow of the Virtual Virgin loaded. "For the record, your period is coming in six days. The flow will be heavy and the expected painful. I'm not getting the usual coppery tang. Somewhat metallic, still. Silver? Some vampires may be weakened by silver but I'm feeling . . . none of your business. Each person's blood reminds me of a distinctive color. This is silver blue, like that zombie cocktail of yours, but not anemic, quite a hearty and even robust overtone. Rich but not cloying."

"Who's the freaking school nurse now?" I asked, feeling my cheeks warm at the mention of my period. I didn't want to even think why a vampire would be able to sense that.

His laugh was low as he leaned near again. "Piqued, Delilah? I'm being too analytical? I admit I enjoyed a unique effervescent quality some might become addicted to. I might too, but I don't want your blood. How was the taste test for you?"

"Quick and dirty, as I expected. Grow up, Sanscouci." I knew my request was ridiculous to a seven- or eight-hundred-year-old vampire, but guys will be guys.

"You're not retching with revulsion."

I rolled my eyes. "You're an expert at this, right? Like a dentist."

I was pleased, though. As the lyrics in the classic

Casablanca movie song went, "a kiss is just a kiss" and that's what I'd wanted to know. Sansouci had enjoyed that moment on the level of a stolen sexual buzz, but didn't find it an orgasmic occasion. I was no longer passing on any remainder of the Brimstone Kiss effect to the man in the street. Or vampire.

At least not on the lips.

"So this is what you do. Kiss and run. Tell me about the harem."

"They're ordinary women with no men in their lives, for some reason. Young. Old. In between. Maybe they were abused when children and need the edge of mock violence to feel alive. Maybe they've lost someone who can never, ever come back. Maybe they're just too busy to meet and date and mate. Maybe, Delilah, they just like me and what I do for them."

"What do they get out of it?"

I was asking an existential question. He wanted to take me down to brass tacks. What does that mean, anyway? I was about to learn what it meant to Sansouci when he was ready to play me.

"I'll show you." He reached into the side pockets of his light cotton jacket and started laying items on the black glass where their reflection made twins of everything. "This is my tool kit now, not lances and swords and daggers."

I recognized the first item, a flash drive lozenge.

"Dirty movies for the cell phone?" I asked.

"No. A vibrator, and not just any vibrator." As he picked it up the surface shimmered through an electric rainbow of colors changing form in his hand. "This is the Swiss army knife of vibrators, small and portable but with eighty-six different shapes and functions."

I tried not to stare at it bug-eyed. Huh? Call me an amateur. I'd just achieved supine. He pushed forward some
small round rubber bands. I was thinking condoms, but
was glad I hadn't tried to be the A-student and sung out
my guess.

"Silken bonds, expandable to any length or situation.
Second-most popular. Of course you've never . . ."

I was taking the fifth.

"A pair of chorus-girl earrings?" I gawked when the
sparkling pair of three-inch red-carpet shoulder-dusters hit
the tabletop next.

"We're back to that naughty word again, Delilah. Nipple
clamps. Vibrating. Unisex too. They also work as actual
earrings. They'd look hotter than hell with your current outfit. I don't suppose you'd . . . ?" He held them up so they
caught the light like Whore of Babylon pasties.

By now my cool white skin had overheated with a
blush. Heartland-naive sucked.

"Yes," he said, a wicked spring-green sparkle in his
eyes, "that's the effect I'm going for, but it's called a flush.
Just how far down do your flushes go?"

"You're teasing me in payback for prying your history
out of you," I accused.

And, I realized, it was also because little boys like to
torment little girls they like with scary objects like frogs
and snakes, that Sansouci's display was an adult version of
the same scenario.

The next item was a nest of tangled chains of various
lengths. "Some of my clients have numerous piercings and
rings. These offer myriad decorative and functional com-
binations with onboard equipment. Your silver familiar
ever assume any titillating forms?"

"Never," I said, vehement, only then remembering a

time or two . . . I felt my blush go scarlet. "I hate that," I ground out. "I hate that my skin type does that."

"I don't. I find it charming, and very telltale." Sansouci laughed as he swept his display off the table and back into his pockets. "These are only the easily portable . . . accessories of my trade. Care to know more?"

"No," I swore. "I think I'd better leave."

"Not before you tell me *your* real story,' " Sansouci said softly. "Your real reason for why we're here, your interrogating me."

He suddenly pulled me close again with one arm while his other hand lifted the hair off my nape. My face was smothered in his jacket shoulder. In an instant I was held immobile, although the skull rocked after his sudden move.

"I thought so," he murmured in my ear. "You didn't ask about this, and here I am an expert at your disposal, fearless reporter. Señor Montoya's been sampling your tasty neck. Regularly."

"It's just a hickey. Hickeys," I mumbled against his jacket. "I hate that word."

"Not just a hickey. Hickeys." His thumb stroked the freshest one and I couldn't stop a wince. I jerked away, but he held me tight.

He whispered the next words into my hair, but I heard every damning syllable. It was a taunt and an intimacy and a diagnosis. "Can't deny it. Broke the skin, Luscious."

I pushed off, fighting his custody, more flushed and angry and anxious than before. "As if you wouldn't," I hissed back at him. "He gets . . . overenthusiastic. A bat bite in the Mexican desert spurred his first wet dream, okay? It's a tiny, harmless kink."

God, why was I telling him this?

"Like you'd know, virtual virgin."

"He doesn't have . . . fangs."

"Teeth enough to be interesting. You let him?"

"I love him."

Sansouci let me go. The silver familiar lay coldly around my neck. I put my hand up to feel a bristly crown of thorns. It had allowed him to touch me when I'd wanted to intrigue him into testing my blood, but this was too much for us both.

"Manhandle me like that again," I told Sansouci, "and you'll lose a body part."

"No desire to, now that I know what I suspected is right. This is serious, Delilah, and you know it. That's why you cozied up to me to pry out some facts of vampire life, so to speak. You're like any vamp-tramp-in-training—"

I belted him in the mouth before I could even think.

The shock shut him up, and me too.

Not very ladylike. I didn't approve when women did that to men who said things they didn't like in forties movies. It made them "dames," I guess.

Sansouci felt his jaw. "Bit my tongue. You drew blood, Delilah. How does that feel?"

"Annoying, like your behavior. You're the only vampire I—"

"Trust?"

"Don't fool yourself. The only one I know I can ask."

There was always Howard Hughes, but asking lecherous Uncle Howie about plain sex, not to mention vampire sex, was way too icky. Warped, even. Especially if he was my father. At least I was convinced that Sansouci's attitude toward Vida was far too neutral for him to be a candidate.

"You weren't going to tell me the one piece of information that really mattered." He sat back, shaking his head. "I overstepped, but it was for your own good."

"The bastards always say that. Ric is not a vampire."

"Let's say not. But you're worried sick. Vampires did drain him dead."

"Maybe. . . . I'm not buying that. Whatever happened, they didn't . . . turn him."

"You just don't want to accept responsibility for raising the dead. Why not? Your lover does? He dowses for them."

"If it was me who brought him back, maybe I shouldn't have."

"I saw it. Snow saw it. The Gehenna werewolves saw it. Everybody in the rescue party did. One of the great love scenes never on the silver screen." He picked up his drink to toast me. "Here's looking at you, kid. You willed Ric Montoya back from the dead. Now you have to live with it. Everybody throws that term around. 'Turn,' like it's a damn dance move."

I shook out my hair to make sure my nape was covered and sipped my Virtual Virgin. Was I starting to be sorry about what I'd named the drink. . . .

"I don't know about those things," I said. "I only know the vamp boys in the group homes were always after me and I would die before I'd be bitten." I sounded weary, a mistake in strategy.

"You're right. That's not a real bite on your neck, just a love nip, huh?"

"They say . . . I've heard . . . People can be turned if a vampire drains all your blood, or you've been bitten and you then bite the vampire. Or from toilet seats. I don't know!"

"And you hate that condition more than anything," Sansouci said with a quirk of his lips. "Not knowing."

I was relieved to spot no blood on them. "So what's it like being a vampire forever?"

"Like my brother figured when he wanted me more than dead and out of the way. He wanted me to suffer. He knew that the religious vocation I'd chosen would make my undead eternity as a bloodsucker into unliving hell."

"Ric would be like that." I shut my eyes.

"I don't think he's a vampire." Sansouci's hand covered my fist on the table, his thumb stroking mine. It was truly a consoling gesture.

"Not?" I looked up, my eyes full of question and hope.

"But it's not good. I said your blood had an intoxicating effervescence."

"I've got pink champagne in my veins?"

"That, and circumstances. Part of the vampire/prey dysfunctional relationship is that being bitten can hook you on biting. You mentioned a boyhood vampire bat bite. Then the Karnak vampires made it a group party. It's possible Montoya's becoming addicted to your blood, which would make him your personal human 'lifestyle' vampire. All addicts want more and more. All addicts have a built-in denial factor for why they do what they can't resist. For a girl who hated the idea of being vamp-bit, you're on the royal road to serious risk. It's not his fault, but it's a fact."

My fist lifted to shake his chilly vampire hand off mine.

I hit it down again so hard the black glass cracked from rim to rim like an instant spiderweb.

Sansouci's head leaned back against the red velvet upholstery. He did look like a knight.

"Love the new cracked glass tabletop, Delilah. Now. Here's the way it is, the way I see it, and you're going to have to deal with it."

I listened with all my heart, and my head.

"Montoya loves you."

I knew that.

"I want you."

I knew and used that.

"And Snow . . . Snow needs you for some reason even I can't guess."

Need? Snow? That one had me stumped.

"Unless you're willing to juggle lovers, and I doubt you are . . . yet, you're going to have to decide who you're safest with, and who's safest with you."

My only answer was silence. It was time to head home and mull what Sanscouci had told me and what he'd told me without knowing it.

He drained his glass. "Even your Virtual Virgin packs a kick, but a tentative one."

"It's the cherry vodka you laced it with, not my innocent nonalcoholic recipe."

"Cherry vodka." He repeated . . . caressed . . . my words with a searching look.

My inner alarms went on red alert. I was Sansouci's chief prey these twenty-first century days. For all his apparent sophistication and benign blood-drinking, he'd been a savage warrior many more centuries than he'd been a dedicated monk or a cultish "life coach" for lonely ladies.

"I need to move on," I said.

"In your life, or at this moment?"

"Both. How do I . . . we . . . exit this Goth carnival ride? And I like my life," I announced, sitting forward on the banquette, in case he had any doubts.

I needed to pass him to get out.

Put me on hold and put yourself in a cul-de-sac with a vampire, right. Irma was back, gloating.

"Excuse me," I suggested.

Sansouci tilted his head, as if analyzing a lot more about me than my words.

He has us at his mercy. Umm.

"Sure thing, Luscious." Sansouci's smile was as smooth as corn silk. He cracked the skull's tufted velvet doors and the jaws yawned open, admitting screams of laughter and tortured electric guitars.

His exit left the suspended unit swaying hard. I poised on the booth's bottom lip trying to gauge the jump to terra firma. I made the leap unassisted, taking the impact with my bent knees.

"Impressive," he said.

"I'm used to exiting hovering helicopters. A state-fair ride is a snap."

"Helicopters?"

I'd truly surprised him, since most such exits happen during troop deployments during wars. I was a veteran of the journalism wars.

"The WTCH-TV 'copter. Weather coverage was a big deal in Wichita when I was a reporter there."

"Weather. TV-station 'copter. Right. Let me get you to the door. Spider Skull gets . . . raucous after dark."

I sensed the female-unfriendly eyes all around. Or too friendly, I should say. Even today, women on business errands at night were considered fair game.

"No one will mess with me," he assured me.

Count me out on that.

Irma! Some support here?

"Did you say something?" Sansouci leaned nearer to hear my words.

"Nope."

I was still frothing at getting Irma's usual sass in a situation that was making me uneasier by the second. I'd thought I could handle Sansouci. Maybe if I somehow finessed him into a fatherly role . . . which escorting me to the door surely was.

We were there, at the usual blank steel-door nightclubs this town favored.

I heard murmurs behind us complaining about my leaving.

Sansouci blocked all that noise and ugliness with his body, his big warrior's body pinning me to the steel door, protective as a wall, intimate as a . . . well, my mind didn't want to go there.

His eyes searched my face, marking my panic with a look . . . a look somehow both satisfied and . . . tender.

I felt all the superhuman strength I'd told him I'd want on my side when worst came to worst and it was holding me suspended in a bell-jar moment I'd never anticipated..

I had the most awful suspicion . . . instinct . . . that Sanscouci wanted to . . . kiss me . . . good night. Like a freaking prom date.

He didn't want to taste my blood, which should have been a relief. He wanted to taste my emotions, which were even more intimately mine, far beyond some fluid pounding through my veins.

"I'd consider breaking that vow of mine for the first time with you. No blood, just what you're sensing now." His husky undertone seemed to vibrate in my bones.

"Gee, thanks. What part of 'taken already' don't you get?"

"Undead life is long."

I averted my face. And his followed like steel to a magnet.

"Delilah," he said, willing me to look at him.

And nothing more.

I'm outta here, Irma announced, fleeing.

I wasn't breathing, I was panting, a wild animal, cornered.

His expression melted with mine, his face following my evasive features as I turned my head left and then right and found only a steel door against my fevered cheeks, his eyes locked on mine, a dark emerald forest I was plunging into like a hunted animal. A unicorn. Virtual virgins.

If I kissed him . . . if I let him kiss me . . . now, here . . . *No!*

Nothing was keeping me pinned here but me. I forced my eyes to focus far to the side and addressed the empty air so I didn't have to see him, to see what was coming.

"I've been here before," I said, my voice hard and cold. "Before I ever bled for the first time. In the group homes with the sick, crazy vamp boys pinning me against walls, wanting my blood both ways. Hungry. Horrible. They smelled of death and murder, old blood and new lusts. Their skins were moonscapes of scars and pus-oozing pits. They were revolting and I only had a diamond-dust embedded nail file to fight them off. But I did. So. Let me go."

I felt his presence retreating before it was physical fact. It was if I'd knocked a moon out of orbit around a planet it had been bound to by gravity.

One furtive glance at his face caught a fading gleam of something green and tentative as a root in his harsh gaze.

He hadn't lasted all those postvampire centuries because he had kept any nugget of humanity that could be read as . . . hurt? No. I was thinking in my limited human way and that was no way to survive among unhumans.

"Get out." His voice was harder and colder than mine had been.

"I was planning to."

"Get. Out."

I saw the blood tide, maybe the cherry vodka from my Virtual Virgins, rising in his eye whites and yanked the door handle open behind my back, slipping through, heart pounding so loud I knew he'd hear it for yards, as he'd scent my blood for a mile, maybe.

Dolly waited to enfold me in the parking lot, her neon chartreuse halo of pixie dust security announcing she was no Eldorado to mess with. She had never looked more like a fortress.

Chapter Twenty-three

AFTER HE'D LEFT the Spider Skull, Sansouci had made an immediate blood and booty phone call to Carmella, the three-time divorcée, a handsome but stringy cougar of a woman in her late forties.

Carmella was the only one of his blood "wives" he didn't like.

She was also the only one who craved being drained to the very edge of mortality. Sometimes he needed to remind himself of the centuries of raging, senseless survival. Especially after seeing, flirting with, wanting Delilah. She got under his skin the way he was supposed to want to get under hers. Like an addiction.

He did all the things with Carmella he supposed Delilah was imagining he did. Twice.

He left his client when she was sated in every way possible and he was sick of himself. His ancient, wholly human shadow-self seemed to be tailing him through the glitz of the Las Vegas Strip.

Sansouci decided to finish his unhappy evening out by stopping for a nightcap at Chez Shez. He could atone there for what he'd refrained from doing—and what he'd just done to make up for his restraint—by patronizing the artificial blood on tap. Penance, they'd labeled it when he'd been a monk. Nowadays even that word was out of date.

Gentle Fawn, the day-shift employee Shez called Fawnschwartz, had been replaced for the evening hours by a tall black woman with green eyes who suspiciously resembled Grizelle, the Inferno Hotel's security head. Had the ancient Egyptian godling developed a crush on a twenty-first-century shape-shifter?

Good luck with that, Sansouci thought.

He hunkered over the stone cup inset with semiprecious stones and filled with the chilled bloodwine "Hastur" had given him before disappearing into the shop's rear. The smooth jade felt cold in his undead hands, though the artificial bloodwine inside tasted like lukewarm cinnamon mouthwash.

Could he live on this swill forever? Or for as long as Delilah lived her mayfly's seconds of existence until . . . 2168, say? Delilah would be old and frail and he'd be . . . sorry he hadn't turned her and facing more centuries of mere survival alone.

His hands lifted back from the goblet in fists of frustration. What he treasured about Delilah was her smarts so oddly combined with innocence and integrity. Giving her his endless blood-craving life would destroy that.

"The bloodwine does not appeal?"

Sansouci looked up to see Shezmou, once Lord of the Slaughter and now Vegas Strip huckster of fine wine and oils, standing behind him. Looming, rather. He was the living flesh of a god from a long-dead civilization and the city's latest buzz-worthy supernatural.

"It sates without satisfying," Sansouci admitted. "Like my recent date."

"Dates. Ah. I know this word. There are many palm trees in this great city of eternal lightning and sprouting water and artificial thunder, but none offer the sustenance of dates."

Sansouci smiled. How could you not like this ancient big lug Delilah had hauled back from the Karnak Hotel's sinister vampire empire? The "thunder" Shez referred to was the roar of the Mirage's Strip-facing volcano erupting on schedule.

"Have you seen the Mighty Delilah of late?" Shez asked.

Sansouci smiled again. He knew his private obsession had earned the undying public gratitude of the chained god she'd freed from millennia of captivity.

"Yes," he admitted.

"She was in good health and state of mind?"

"When I left her."

Shez's brow wrinkled under the shoulder-brushing white linen headdress that reminded Sanscouci of the kepi caps the French Foreign Legion wore in the desert.

"You should not have left her if there was any question about that," he told Sansouci.

"She was safer after I left her."

Shezmou hauled him off the zebra-hide stool by the nape of his modern turtleneck knit.

"*You* would endanger the Mighty Delilah?"

Sansouci twisted out of the god's choking grip, relishing exercising force against him. "Why do you call her 'the Mighty Delilah'?"

"She freed me from four millennia of immobility."

"Delilah's merely mortal. How'd she do that?"

Shezmou pulled another stool up to the bar and braced a hip on it. "You must understand that what you see before you is a mere sliver of my former self."

"An impressive sliver," Sansouci conceded, eyeing six-and-half feet of terra-cotta-colored muscle wearing only what would be called a skimpy kilt these days and eyeliner, plus collar and headgear, including a heavy braided wig that mimicked a lion's mane.

"We gods are supposed to impress mere mortal men," Shez said.

"I'm not mortal anymore."

"Once you were. I accept the company of a foul blood-imbiber only because the Mighty Delilah says you represent a powerful mogul in this city, one called Caesar. Even while imprisoned in my pillar image, I'd heard that name mentioned. It was used with fear by the debased Egyptian sect of blood drinkers who'd infected an entire once-proud race of my subjects."

"My 'Cesar' is not your 'Caesar.' Julius Caesar lived two millennia ago. Cesar Cicereau has been a force in Las Vegas only since its founding seventy-five years ago."

"A paltry span," Shez noted, "even for a human."

"Too long for my taste," Sansouci said. "Cicereau's an entirely inferior modern breed of dictator. I work for him only to pay a debt owed by my . . . tribe."

"All bloodsuckers."

"We all started as mortals. And were converted forcibly."

"Not I, though I must admit it pains me to think that the Mighty Delilah may soon falter and pass away. I owe her my freedom and the restitution of justice to the ancient beliefs of Memphis and Thebes."

"How'd she actually free you?"

Shezmou rose to go behind the bar and uncork a lavishly bottled and labeled wine. He filled another jeweled cup and returned to sit on the stool, staring reflectively into his image in the polished sheet of bronze behind the various containers of wine and oil and manufactured blood.

He lifted large, cupped hands. "My likeness resided on a pillar twenty feet high. I was depicted standing in the boat of the sun, fully human, with twin stars above my headdress with the sacred cobra rising at its forefront. Unlike all the other pillar gods in that vast temple underground, my wrists and ankles wore manacles connected by chains of gold. Well, a layer of gold, the flesh of the gods, over silver."

"Gold overlay on silver. That's called vermeil nowadays," Sansouci said. "Silver's more Delilah's style, and I'd think that underlying metal was the key to your release."

"There is some reason the Silver Pharaoh exists, but I'm not yet sure why." Shezmou sipped reminiscently from his cup. "That last sentence was good. I used a contraction. That would please the Mighty Delilah." He smiled. "She is small, but curious and agile, like a . . . a monkey."

Sansouci interred a smile behind the cup of his palm. Shez didn't have a notable sense of humor. Monkey was hardly the animal he'd associate with Delilah, although it was a good standby for any smart human in the mind of an ancient god.

Shez continued to reminisce between sips of wine, like any modern dude in a bar.

"She alone," he went on, "of any human worshipper in thousands of years, climbed the stone-etched trunk of my leg and swung from my insufficiently golden bonds, breaking them. I heard a crack as of ancient thunder between my stone ears. My fleshly representation fell to earth with the broken chains, and I was there with my strong arms to catch and break the fall of my fragile mortal rescuer."

Sansouci sipped too, unaware of the taste in his mouth,

coursing through his veins. Delilah's sense of adventure and enterprise had freed a god from bondage. Could she free a vampire as well?

"She freed me," Shez's deep Darth Vader voice mused. "I saved her. Now she is my"—Shezmou frowned—"personal representative who seeks peace and unity between my local sponsor and all your powerful Las Vegas lords who desire to sell the profitable fruits of my mighty winepress."

Sansouci nodded solemnly, drawing more artificial blood into his system.

"Then, of course," Shezmou added with a windy sigh, "if the current debased pharaoh corulers return to their foul blood-drinking ways, I will rise up to my full form as Lord of the Slaughter and pull off their heads and those of their evil minions and throw them all into my relentless winepress for crushing."

Ouch. Sansouci's steamy dreams of being rescued and rescuing crashed to the Strip like the body of Loretta's reanimated dead lover. Delilah had yet another dedicated protector, besides Ric and Quicksilver, and this one hated and destroyed vampires.

"So," he told Shez, "you're like the giant up the beanstalk, crushing our bones and drinking our blood."

"I do not . . . don't . . . know your myths and gods and your hierarchies. Only the Mighty Delilah."

"You called her fragile yourself."

"Might is more than physical durability, friend. It is what you will to make of yourself."

Sansouci gazed into those utterly dark, ancient eyes. "What if I choose to . . . convert from blood to . . . this." He gestured at the bland contents of his jeweled cup.

"Then Shezmou would declare that you have done

more than his entire debased race of worshippers have done." His huge hand clapped Sansouci's shoulder, nearly dislocating it. "This is just what the ancient one atop the Karnak has accomplished with his blood-hued brew. You know who I mean, the living mummy, ho-war dhu-ooz. I will create a tablet for you, Sandsoozi."

Sansouci blinked, interpreting as fast as he could. "Thank you, Shez. I think you mean you'll set up a tab, so I can patronize your gilded cobra heads daily for bloodwine. And your mummified patron is called 'Howard Hughes' in this incarnation." He doubted Delilah knew how much he knew about all her contacts.

"Why do you wish to make this transformation of yourself, Sandsoozi?"

"I was once a Lord of the Slaughter myself."

"Indeed. In what time or place or cause? You were not a god, as I am."

"No, but I served one. I took the life and blood of his enemies in war, and called it just. Like you, I'd once wielded sacred oil and water during peacetime, but it was war that made my method of existence possible."

Shez thought, then nodded. "I too would rather mash grapes and seeds than the heads of the damned unjust. Their blood as it spatters my lips tastes foul. I must brew much wine to banish the inadvertent sins that have tainted even so little of my flesh."

"You can . . . taste who is damned from their blood?"

"A mere . . . what you say, side effect, like the inebriation that results from too much healthy wine. Forget the tablet. I like you. I wish to aid you in your quest to be worthy of the Mighty Delilah."

"I didn't say anything about my reasons."

"You did not have to. Who does not aspire to She Who

Frees a God? You are my guest whenever you choose to drink at Chez Shez."

"Thanks." Sansouci raised his glass of Blood Lite.

"It is good when gods and men can sit together and talk." Shez nodded his head until the beaded ends of his heavy braided wig danced on his doughty shoulders.

Sansouci was getting mighty tired of feeling outclassed.

Chapter Twenty-four

Now that my dreams had ditched the alien abduction and examination mode, there was no place my subconscious could not go.

I woke up the next morning with a grab bag of horrible memories fading from my mind.

Dr. Frankenstein had me on his ancient Egyptian blood-letting stone slab again, only he was showing an unnatural interest in my toes . . . Loretta Cicereau and I were twin sisters in the mobster's family photo from the 1940s, with a young, lanky Howard Hughes replacing Sansouci and Vida morphed into a busty Jane Russell. Only Cesar Cicereau was unaltered except for wolfish fangs. . . .

So when my old-fashioned white phone rang in the Enchanted Cottage bedroom I picked it up with relief, hoping Godfrey had dialed me from the main house with news I was to breakfast in the servants' quarters, my favorite way to start the day.

It was indeed exactly that invitation. I sighed as I hung up the receiver and lay back. Godfrey and the maid, Molly, fed Nightwine's occasional guests and Molly made popovers to die for.

I idly tested inside my lower lip for sore spots, but Sansouci's "sampling" procedure had been alarmingly symptom free. A vampire bite that went down as smoothly as aged scotch was a thing to respect and fear.

My cell phone yodeled from the pocket of the leather

jacket I'd used the night before. I hated to leave my comfy bed to hear anything that might interfere with a sunny, chatty breakfast with my favorite CinSims. I sighed again and rolled over to snag the bag without getting out of bed. In a moment the hopefully normal again little rectangle was clamped to my ear.

"Good you're awake so early and rested up," Ric's voice boomed in my ear. "You'll never guess who paid me a surprise visit last night."

Uh-oh, Irma warned. *We know a truckload of folks who could tell tales on you to Ric.*

"Uh . . ." I said.

"You and Quicksilver would kill me if I didn't share the pleasure of my unexpected company. Breakfast?"

"Um . . ." I was being really brilliant.

"I'll swing by and we can decide on the place then."

"Ah, Ric—"

But he'd hung up without giving me any clue to whom I'd be meeting besides him and where we'd be going and what I should wear.

I'd dropped last night's outfit on the bed's end. Since the wardrobe witch hadn't had an invisible hand in selecting the clothes, they were still piled there. I checked the empty chrome dress-shop rack on the wall outside my bottomless closet.

Empty no more. From it hung a plain white shirt, a black "boyfriend" blazer, and gray boot-cut jeans.

Was I supposed to go as a CinSim?

I might sleep in a high four-poster bed under the cottage eaves, but the attached bathroom was high tech. I was sure it had more showerheads than Vida's all-girl health club, and an infrared drying system that reminded me of the abandoned tanning beds at the now-defunct Rave Machine.

The familiar disliked getting wet so it morphed into a banana clip to hold up my hair. I liked the effect so much I told it to "stay" as I would Quicksilver, not expecting obedience, as I didn't with Quicksilver.

Surprise. It remained in place, allowing me to keep the tumbled curls down the back of my head effect. I grabbed some fresh underwear, dressed, and jammed my feet into boot-style mules, ready to greet whosoever or whatever showed up with Ric in my driveway.

As a last thought, I used the bureau mirror to tease the curls forward on my neck, realizing how accustomed I'd become to hiding what I refused to call hickeys. Loathsome word. And maybe deed. Sansouci's admitted self-interest didn't mean he'd lied about what dark and dirty things Ric's little quirk might lead to.

I glowered at the idea, glad to see my image mimic my emotions. No Lilith here. I didn't so much as glance in the hall mirror when I left. I'd had quite enough of my so-called kin for a while.

Clattering down the stairs, I met Quicksilver grinning and panting at the bottom. He knew he was invited, wherever we were going. With whomever. I could always stop at the mansion's kitchen door and take a rain check on the (sob) homemade popovers.

Ric's Corvette was already idling in the driveway, as throaty as a movie queen. Quick perked his ears and I raised my eyebrows when we saw that Ric wasn't the only figure unkinking a tall frame to exit the low car and greet us.

"Tallgrass!" I IDed his companion with welcome disbelief. "What lured you out of Kansas?"

Ric's former FBI mentor hitched up the belt under his belly to match his standing position as he adjusted his

straw cowboy hat into its groove in his thick black hair.
Otherwise he was lean and well-done, his Native American skin seamed with sun and wind and wisdom.

Quicksilver rushed to greet him with a nudge of noses,
paws momentarily braced on his shoulders like a bear's.
Both were pretty prominent in the nose department.

"So where are we all going for this breakfast outing?" I
asked Ric when Quick put all fours back on the driveway.
"In that car?"

"You and the dog can take Dolly."

"I propose we take a stroll across the courtyard instead.
Godfrey and Molly can lay out a spread for us all. Quicksilver's welcome there, unlike in most restaurants."

Ric looked from me to Quick to Leonard Tallgrass.
"You'd have a chance to see some well-established Cin-
Sims at work," he told his friend. "The ones you saw in
Wichita were fresh out of the film canister."

"Sure." Tallgrass winked at me and Quicksilver. "If
these two didn't have blue eyes, they could almost pass as
those black-and-white movie escapees. I sure didn't know
CinSims can cook."

"They can do anything humans can do," Ric said. "And
when it comes to human and unhuman trafficking and the
sex trade, that can be a big problem."

So we moseyed over to the back door, an appropriate
verb since Tallgrass and I both sported boots of a sort.

Ric hung back momentarily so we were following the
other two.

"You sure this group feed is okay with the resident
CinSims?" he asked. "And what about Hector Nightwine?
Doesn't he have a spying fetish and the high-tech toys to
indulge it?"

For the first time I considered that this might not simply

be a visit from a vacationing buddy Ric had reconnected with during our recent Wichita road trip.

"Tallgrass is here on business?" I asked.

"Yeah."

"Molly's blueberry jam is primo."

"All right." Ric pulled me close. "After breakfast, though, I want to take Tallgrass for a spin on the Strip."

"Dolly always likes to show off. Why is Tallgrass here?"

"Not you and Dolly. I need a jaunt with just him and me," Ric said. "I want him to see the real deal when it comes to world-class entertainment venues and the works of superhuman moguls."

"He's not a hick," I pointed out.

"CinSims are a new breed of being. When I was a kid, I used to think I just needed to stop the zombie trade to end all the evil on earth. I thought on that happy day that all the CinSims should be unchipped, unplugged, retired to a refrigerated warehouse, buried, or whatever. Now I'm seeing it's not that simple. We'd both miss Godfrey. It's great that Tallgrass can meet a CinSim who's not a public curiosity, but who holds an actual position, right here and now."

"So," Ric stood back to let me follow Tallgrass and Quicksilver into the Nightwine kitchen. "Bring on breakfast."

Fine. I was thinking I might want to be off on my own for the day anyway.

Chapter Twenty-five

BLUEBERRIES AND POPOVERS and Vienna sausages, oh my!

We breakfasted family style in the kitchen while scents of fresh coffee and fried bacon incited our appetites. Godfrey, with his apron donned over his shirtsleeves, was still formal yet breezy. Molly prepared and helped serve everything as they waltzed around each other with the cheery efficiency of long-time employees.

While I'd think nothing of Nick Charles holding a scarlet cocktail in his pale silver-screen hand at the Inferno Bar, to see Molly's monotone flesh tones deliver platters bearing fluffy yellow clouds of scrambled eggs and ruffled ribbons of red-brown bacon strips to our table felt a bit odd.

Everything was scrumptious, especially the airy popovers with butter and blueberry jam filling every crevice.

Quicksilver had long gotten used to CinSim food servers. He provided entertainment while chasing and gobbling dozens of short Vienna sausages around a huge pewter tray on the floor.

Afterward, the four of us gathered a moment in the courtyard before Ric and Tallgrass took off in the 'Vette.

"I like these CinSims," Tallgrass said. "Why didn't this Nightwine bigwig join us?"

"He's a hermit," I said. "Godfrey and Molly tend his few needs and he treats them very well."

"Other than chipping them in place," Ric noted.

Tallgrass shook his head. "Those Emerald City Cin-Sims fresh from the farm didn't seem happy, or even quite all there."

Ric answered before I could. "Godfrey's alter ego at the Inferno Hotel, Nick Charles, explained that it takes a while for CinSims to take hold on a placement."

"Nick Charles?" Tallgrass sounded impressed. "The elbow-bending gent detective from the old movies? That guy was a hoot."

"We'll stop in and see him. We can order one of Delilah's Brimstone Kiss cocktails there."

"'Brimstone Kiss.' That sounds like real firewater, Miss Delilah."

"Rick Blaine from *Casablanca* loved it," I bragged.

"It's a lot early for booze, Ric," Tallgrass said, "but anything Humphrey Bogart goes for is good with me."

So off they went. Quicksilver barked once and ran around the cottage to the back. I suspect he had pestered Woodrow, the yard troll, into playing fetch with him.

I returned to the cottage to start a find-and-interrogate list.

With Ric doing the town with his mentor, now was a perfect time to delve into the pesky question of who might have fathered me. I didn't want to introduce Ric just yet to the idea that my mama was a vampire. Encountering Vida in the absurdly long-lived flesh had tweaked more than my overdeveloped curiosity bone; it had quadrupled my fear factor.

I came up with a long roster of hair-raising prospects for Daddy Undearest, starting with Cesar Cicereau, Vida's werewolf sugar daddy.

I'd already tackled number two on the list, Sansouci,

the werewolf boss's involuntary enforcer and indentured vampire stud.

Also on the Gehenna Hotel roster, I could list the indentured house magician with the twin fey accomplices, Madrigal. An unlikely suspect, but he'd been there when Vida and Loretta had owned expiring life spans. I smiled to think that Cesar Cicereau just couldn't kick the women out of his life without their coming back . . . and back.

Moving on, there was the pre-vampire Howard Hughes, buying up Vegas properties in the sixties and growing more isolated and phobic every day, aiming to hang on to his empire by being turned vampire.

And I couldn't eliminate Vegas mover and shaker Hector Nightwine, another film and media empire force, so eager to provide me with room, board, and constant surveillance. Although imagining Hector fathering anyone except by test tube was a disturbing vision.

Finally, there was Snow, mystery supernatural, age and aim unknown, but way more invested in me and the future than any Vegas figure of the past was, including Vida.

All of them could have been around long enough to sire me. All had offered me opposition, attempts to make me play prey to their predator, and had claimed to have my best interests at heart, or to sell me on the idea that their best interests were also mine.

All of them radiated the various degrees of lust from knee-jerk pseudosexism to something much more personal that came naturally to being a power on a guy's playing field like Las Vegas. Two didn't stand a snowball's chance in hell. One was likely an ice king in Hell. One I actually liked.

I'd found my way to Vida, so it was time to connect her to all the usual suspects and find what had made the

two and two that became me and Lilith. I didn't expect to
unbuild Rome in a day, but I expected to find some unexpected possibilities.

So I donned my general-purpose spandex black-leather
leggings, a trapeze-shaped turtleneck thigh-long top that
hid my pared-down version of a cop's duty belt under it,
and ballet flats covered with suede gaiters to the knee. I
had to wear something vintage as a lucky charm.

The familiar obligingly tarnished to black with faint
rainbow highlights and formed a chain-swagged steampunk epaulet on my left shoulder.

I was a either a vain cat burglar or a woman not worth
the trouble of tangling with.

QUICKSILVER SURVEYED MY new look, and then sat in front
of Dolly's massive chrome grille, refusing to move.

"No," I said. "Nix. This is a solo mission. It's investigative, not dangerous. I don't need an escort."

I had to circle way around him to get to the driver's
seat, and then he leaped into the passenger side through
the open window. We had a stare-down, but I finally pulled
onto Sunset Road with him still installed, feeling good and
guilty.

Not much later I reluctantly left him guarding Dolly in
a low-rent parking garage so I was able to join the women
slipping into the shade of the Chez Shez royal awning to
buy lotions and bath oils. They lined up two deep along
the counters, sipping gratis wine while buying the rare oils
and costly perfumes. The combined scents were sublime.
Like a Goth shadow I slipped around the end of one counter and into the shop's rear.

Shezmou was far back in the manufacturing area,
laboring by oil-lamp light, working his ancient grape

press. The sack that held the grapes or oil seeds he crushed was dyed dark bloodred from centuries of usage. Ancient Egyptians favored red wine and extreme afterlife intervention.

I could easily imagine torn-off human heads inside that sack, being crushed by the steady power of Shezmou's broad, muscled shoulders as he worked the two wooden poles like opposing oars to twist the sap out of the sack.

The liquid that dripped down today was clear and golden. Olive oil.

I could inhale through my nose again.

Shez gave the sack a final, emptying wrench and stepped back to squint at me. I must be silhouetted by the lamplight at my back.

"Who dares to intrude on Shezmou at his press?"

"Sorry, big guy. I need a quick favor."

He wiped his palms on a piece of white linen. "The favor of the gods always pours down on the Mighty Delilah like the finest embalming and funerary oils."

Oh, goodie, Irma said.

"Really, Almighty Shez, you can stop calling me Mighty. I am a mere pipsqueak compared to your power and nobility. And your customers will find the usage . . . unfitting."

"What is a pipsqueak?"

"Something insignificant that your sandaled foot could crush like a grape."

"Or like the heads of the damned." He grinned with the zest of a proud craftsman.

That had been the dark side of his godly role . . . acting as Osiris's headsman and using damned heads as twist-off caps to throw into the bottomless pit of the Egyptian underworld.

Right now, I needed to persuade Almighty Shez to be my doorman.

"What then should I call you?" he was asking, polite in the way of demon gods who can grease their skids with your own blood.

"Delilah would do."

He inclined his head. "So, pipsqueak," he said instead with relish, "what favor can I perform for you?"

"First, how did you find your new shopgirl?"

"Hastur came to view my product . . . line?"

I nodded. Shez needed to update his ancient formal manner of talking, and get with his new career as entrepreneur.

He spoke on. "She seemed an excellent canvas for the new powdered Jewels of the Nile Eye you encouraged me to create. I wish to impress the emissaries of the other foreign powers when they come to sue me for custom."

I nodded. The semiprecious stones in the broad Egyptian collar he wore formed a natural palette for a killer eye-shadow collection . . . malachite green, amethyst, lapis-lazuli blue, deep red carnelian. Shezmou was an unemployed god I was responsible for jerking into the twenty-first century. The least I could do was to find him a commercial niche.

"They don't want to sue you for custom," I told him. "That could involve legal action. They want to sew up your franchise."

"I am not sure I wish strangers to sew up anything of mine, including this 'franchise.' "

"That merely means they . . . pay you tribute, massive tribute, for the honor of selling your unique wares at shops all over the world."

"Even in Phoenicia?"

"They call that . . . ah, Phoenix now."

"Nubia?"

"New . . . Newport Beach."

"Persia."

"Palm Beach now."

"The Nile must have risen alarmingly high during my endless imprisonment."

"The world is completely different, Shez. You're adapting to it very well. It was smart to hire Hastur. She has the look of a supermodel."

His tilted his head to question me.

"Ah . . . a queen, as does Grizelle of the Inferno Hotel."

"Grizelle." He intoned her name with more than relish. Reverence. "She is the equal of Nefertiti, a word that means 'the beautiful woman has come' in my language. And you have also," he added with a majestic head nod.

Beauty is as beauty does. Grizelle had always kept me in her guard-tiger sites, but I could see that a guy who'd been chained to a pillar for four millennia might respond to the statuesque black shape-shifter in her tall, lithe human form. Not to mention her own goddess attitude.

"I have met with the Gehenna city's Sandsoozi," Shez went on. "Apparently Gehenna is a later version of the Egyptian underworld. It is gratifying to encounter one whose ancestors go back a few centuries. I am puzzled that I find the same condition that destroyed the Egyptian royal house for millennia is . . . passable in this Sandsoozi and my esteemed sponsor."

"It's *San*souci. He's a customer of yours?"

"He samples the latter-day bloodwine my esteemed sponsor is creating and bestowing on his many subjects."

Shez was living in a dreamworld long gone. His "sponsor," the now eternal vampiric Howard Hughes, was still a controlling power in Las Vegas, even though few knew of his continued existence. And Sansouci? Throwing back Howard Hughes's synthetic bloodwine with Shezmou? Nothing good could come of that.

"I'm so happy for you all," I said to move on. "That's where I need your assistance, Shez. I must consult your sponsor. Getting to his secret digs atop the Karnak Hotel means going through the hotel's main attraction floors. I'm not exactly welcome to the current administration."

When Shez remained politely silent I named names. "I mean the twin reigning pharaohs, Kephron and Kepherati."

"Those unnaturally eternal betrayers! They remain in the living world as careless consumers of the blood of innocents. Yes, I remember that your companion in freeing me and the blood slaves had recently escaped their lowest unnatural appetites."

"My companion was Ric, Ric Montoya."

"A name that rolls off the tongue. And where is your small Anubis?"

That stumped me for a few seconds. Anubis was the god of the dead. Sometimes shown with a jackal or dog head.

"Quicksilver is guarding my, um, chariot."

"Most wise. Then I will commend you to the protection of my little brother. His position as court entertainer allows him to come and go and be seen in strange company."

Shez's traditional Egyptian kohl eyeliner gave him a Captain Jack Sparrow–come-hither-or-run look. He squinted at me as he would a plump grape for the squeezing.

"You look sufficiently unlike yourself when you last

visited the Karnak in the skin with silver stars all over it. No guard god will recognize you."

He referred to the steel-studded impenetrable black bodysuit I'd been given at the Inferno. Star-studded skin sounded much more impressive. I thanked him and left, heading on foot for the Karnak, counting on a raunchy fertility god to get me in, and out again.

Chapter Twenty-six

"WHY THE POSTADOLESCENT noisy sports car?" Tallgrass asked Ric after breakfast was just a fond memory.

"I was not much more than a postadolescent when I bought it?" Ric suggested as he cruised the Corvette through the concrete canyon made by massive pyramids, domes, towers, and 3-D billboards known as the Las Vegas Strip.

"So. Why aren't Miss Delilah and what that butler-sorta fellah, Godfrey, calls Master Quicksilver with us on our sightseeing expedition?"

"I have a big decision to make, Tallgrass."

"So? I'm an ex-coworker. I don't share your soul and I sure as hell don't sleep with you."

"It involves what I brought to life in Wichita. You were there."

Tallgrass's espresso-dark eyes bored into Ric's eyes, looking for his soul. "So was she. I think the phrase today is 'significant other,' *amigo*. Is that 'she' Miss Delilah, or is it that damn ghost of a machine?"

"It's that I might be poison to associate with *because* of the ghostly machine."

Tallgrass lifted his deeply seamed palms. "Stop the sports car. Let me out. I am good enough to swallow poison, and Miss Delilah is not? I would like to hear her opinion on the subject. Did you even ask her?"

Ric put the 'Vette through the purposes it was made for,

a slash across four lanes of less gutsy traffic and into the long drive up to the Inferno Hotel.

"I need your opinion on something," he said. Admitted.

"Some thing?"

"Some one. Maybe a something."

"Miss Delilah is full of opinions."

"That's the problem. She may be prejudiced."

"If she wasn't, she wouldn't be worth much." Tallgrass grinned. "These days are not for those who weigh left hand against right until they are paralyzed. It is a time to act."

"Exactly." Ric nodded as Delilah's favorite parking valet appeared in a puff of STP-scented cologne at the 'Vette's driver-side door. He handed the orange-scaled demon a twenty-dollar bill.

"You mind if I rev her up the ramp?" Manny asked, a devilish arch to his green eyebrows.

"Be my guest," Ric said.

"Bonsai tree!" the demon shrieked from the driver's seat as the 'Vette vanished in a cloud of genuine gas exhaust.

"Self-indulgent and not very green despite the valet's eyebrows," Tallgrass decreed.

"Wait'll you go inside," Ric promised.

As Delilah had pointed out, Tallgrass was not a hick. He observed and nodded sagely as they entered the Inferno's interior glitz.

"IT'S TOO EARLY for the Boss to be up and receiving guests," Grizelle said, eyeing Tallgrass after Ric had her paged.

"You're a shaman," Tallgrass told her. "What is a creature of earth and sky doing caged in all this artificial light?"

"I'm security chief here. Chief."

He nodded. "Of course. You are like that Corvette sports car Ric drives. There is a tiger in your tank."

Grizelle slashed Ric a look, part awe, part anger. "Don't make me show my claws," she told Tallgrass.

"Nor me, mine," he said.

"Neither of you needs to resort to postadolescent noise," Ric said. "Christophe made it clear that I was welcome at any time," he told Grizelle. He *might* call the Inferno boss Snow to his face, as invited, but he preferred thinking of him as the mogul Christophe.

Grizelle inclined her elaborately decorated braids. "May I offer you earplugs for the elevator journey?" she asked Tallgrass.

He snorted.

Ric had thought Delilah tweaked Grizelle's tail. Tallgrass jerked her braids.

"Most impressive," Tallgrass muttered in the short elevator spurt to the top.

Ric wasn't sure whether he referred to the Inferno Hotel, or Grizelle.

Christophe was waiting as the elevator doors opened like a stainless-steel stage curtain on his dramatically bizarre figure of white skin and hair. He wore a white linen Cuban guayabera shirt with its subtle four pockets and pleats, but the long sleeves were rolled up in a display of casual cool.

Ric was annoyed to see the Inferno bigwig sporting a classic item of Hispanic menswear with such aplomb. His own tropical suit the color of a cappuccino latte seemed formal and stuffy by comparison despite the open neck of his silk shirt.

And Tallgrass. He looked fresh off the ranch. Not that it bothered Tallgrass one whit.

The Native American had not doffed his pale straw Western hat in Christophe's quarters, as Christophe recently had kept on his riverboat-gambler white hat at the Emerald City hotel-casino he'd bought in Wichita.

So it would be a battle of white hats.

"I understand," the ex-FBI man opened the parlay, "no one knows what brand of supernatural you are."

"That disturb you, Mr. Tallgrass?"

Christophe led them into the expansive living area and gestured to an arrangement of leather sofas so supernaturally white they must have come from ghost cattle.

Ric wandered to the window wall to survey the Strip from this spectacular viewpoint.

In daylight the framework of the neon icons looked as drab and shabby as the half-constructed hulks of glamorous towers-to-be, including one so close Ric could count the rivets on the I beams. He wondered how the rock-star mogul liked having his hotel crowded by another new Vegas venue going up.

Probably as little as Ric wanted to be crowded by him.

"Not much disturbs me, except labels," Tallgrass had responded, stretching out his untidy middle-aged frame dead center on a curve of the endless sectional sofa. "No one can figure out what tribe I'm from. Most of my kind has vanished from my home state."

"Which is Kansas," Christophe stated, sprawling on another long sofa dead center, but opposite Tallgrass.

"Maybe." Tallgrass's smile was short and not very sweet at all. "Our people were moved all over the map by the US government, usually with some excuse that it was for our own good."

"I see Mr. Montoya has brought a private contractor to eye his possible future property." Christophe turned to quirk a white eyebrow at Ric over the rim of his black sunglasses. "I'm glad you brought your agent into our discussion."

"FBI agent," Ric said. He had to smile to himself at how each man had spread his arms and legs to occupy the most territory on his chosen seat.

"*Formerly,*" Christophe noted, "the way I like all my agents. Those who've fled overcontrolling entities best suit my purposes."

"And you're not overcontrolling?" Ric asked, pacing behind Christophe's sofa.

The rock-star mogul kept his face focused on Tallgrass. "That's why it'd benefit your friend's interests to deal with me. The devil you know, and all that."

"Are you a devil?" Ric had stopped behind Christophe, bracketing his hands on the sofa back on either side of him. Now Ric leaned close enough to knife him between the shoulder blades, claiming his own negotiating territory.

"Depends who you ask." Snow's sunglasses lifted and aimed to the side of the room. "It seems you have a groupie of your own."

Ric jerked his gaze in that direction to spot the Silver Zombie moving smoothly across the white plush carpeting toward their conversational gathering. Toward Ric.

"Still silent," Tallgrass observed.

Ric stood, partly because he would when any lady entered a room, partly in the nervous awe she always stirred in him.

The other men also stood, as if he'd cued them. Tallgrass turned to Ric, nodding and brushing his palms lightly together. "She moves with a whisper like soft sandpaper, a slight snare drum brush."

Trust a veteran tracker to notice. Ric realized he heard that too.

Tallgrass had seen the *Metropolis* robot in the guest penthouse atop the Emerald City hotel-casino in his home city of Wichita. In this more sophisticated yet austere environment, all laboratory white, she shone like a polished suit of armor walking through a snowstorm.

She stopped in front of Ric. "Master."

"No one's your master now," he said.

Her streamlined metal features turned to regard Christophe and Tallgrass before returning to face him. "I must answer to my maker, my caretaker. If not you, who else?"

It was her first sentence.

Ric found Christophe's head and sunglasses bowed, looking down, staying neutral. Tallgrass's dark eyes, often so noncommittal, had gone blank with shock.

There it was. The quandary.

If Ric didn't use his natural power over this complex homemade CinSim, this brave new creature who was as diverse as mogul Christophe/rock star Cocaine/acquaintance Snow, who or what would fill that vacuum? She could be Good Maria/Bad Maria/robot/actress.

"Thank you . . . Brigitte," he said, using the actress's name to establish himself as . . . director. "You may go."

She turned and strode away to the ajar double doors Ric knew led to the home theater. Could she even sit down in that wooden bodysuit? Did CinSims need to?

Tallgrass released a windy sigh. "Certainly not one of the spirit-walkers of my forefathers."

Snow looked up at Ric, smiling. "In this case, looking out for my own interests dovetails with your needs, Montoya. Who can argue that this entity *doesn't* harbor a demon, as the drug lord Torbellino maintained. He'll want her and his cartel has limitless reach. You need powerful allies too."

He directed his gaze at Tallgrass. "You might have need of a dragon again," Christophe added, referring to a recent battle with El Demonio's forces in Wichita.

"And you, Mr. Christophe, of a Wendigo." Tallgrass smiled.

"HE'S A SUPERNATURAL something," Tallgrass told Ric once they'd reached the Inferno's main floor again. "That's my opinion. We know Christophe's powers are impressive. You'll never know their extent unless you watch him as closely as he seems to want to watch you."

"'Watch over me,'" Ric said. "That's his claim."

Tallgrass grinned. "You already have Miss Delilah doing a much more personal job of that. It's hard to tell these days, Ricardo, who or what has anyone's best interests at heart. If you can strike a mutually advantageous deal with this smooth operator, you're doing well. I worry about you too. Meanwhile you and me have to keep the government working for us as we work for it. That's our priority now."

"Before we leave, want to meet Godfrey's 'cousin' at the Inferno Bar?" Ric asked.

"Home of Miss Delilah's Albino Vampire martini?" Tallgrass's laugh boomed out, attracting amused stares. "She nailed Mr. Christophe but good by inventing that at his own bar. Sure, if they serve plain spring water. We'll need our sharpest wits soon."

"That's all right. We can let Nick Charles do all our drinking for us."

Chapter Twenty-seven

THERE WERE A lot of reasons a venture to the Karnak
Hotel made me edgy, and a few hundred of them had
fangs. Just because the Karnak was a relatively new kid on
the block in Vegas didn't mean it wasn't chock-full of the
evil dead.

In "middle-kingdom" Las Vegas, when the hotel-
casinos first aspired to be modern architectural marvels
instead of hyped-up motels with attached casinos and
nightclub acts, the main hotel-casino buildings were set far
back from the Las Vegas Strip.

More people drove than flew to Vegas then. Land was
plentiful and cheap. Like aristocratic proprietors of country estates, the owners of major properties wanted long
driveways leading to the magnificence of their main buildings, something impressive on the scale of the Roman
Empire, say, of which Caesars Palace was the first and best
example.

And even Caesars had installed a moving sidewalk
from one corner of the Strip to the front facade early on.

So tourists had hoofed blocks along the Las Vegas Bou-
levard sidewalks and more blocks along driveways to reach
the first hint of air-conditioning, the fabled *zing, zing, zing*
of slot machine coins, and leggy cocktail waitresses bearing free drinks.

Call it sweat equity. Tourists consider the sweltering
heat part of the experience.

Then some accountants realized the time the customers spent hoofing could be more profitably used having them cool and relaxed indoors, betting and spending money. Newer properties had entrances that cozied right up to the Strip, more like the long established Riviera and Flamingo hotels.

That explains why the Egyptian-themed hotels like the Luxor, Oasis, and Karnak planted their main entrances right out front, where a pyramid, an obelisk, or a temple would be only a short stroll away. No grandiose avenue of the sphinxes like in the ancient days.

At the Karnak Hotel you were immediately deposited by cab or walking in from the Strip among the massively thick and high crowded pillars duplicating a mammoth hall in the ancient temples of Karnak. And, incidentally, you were instantly immersed in cool, blessed shade, even outside.

Since I'd dressed for my undercover outing in heat-absorbing black I took to the shade like a mallard to marsh. I wove from one clot of tourists to another through the lobby and registration area, not pausing to gawk at animal-headed gods twenty feet high.

I was looking for a much lowlier deity.

And having zilch luck.

The crowds came and went, too thick and furious for a pipsqueak figure like Bez to stand out. I needed to avoid catching the eye of any hotel staff in linen kilt and braided wig who weren't just local color, but whose kohl-outlined eyes would be scanning for suspicious characters like me.

I was more familiar than anyone besides Ric with the Karnak's hidden vampire court and underworld, from which Shez was an escapee, thanks to me.

A cold wet nudge in the palm of my hand made me

pause my weary tourist shuffle and step out of the traffic flow to snuggle up to the base of a towering statue of Anubis.

"Quick! No dogs allowed," I said, grabbing his collar and kneeling so I wasn't a target. At least his wet nose told me he wasn't dehydrated after following me from the parking garage.

I felt a tug on the silver bangle on my left wrist. It melted down through my fingers to make a shoulder-circling semiprecious stone-studded collar on Quicksilver. Darned if he didn't resemble the ancient god Osiris wearing his ceremonial doghead on his handsome broad human shoulders, of course.

Before I could lecture the both of them, Fido and familiar, the crowd around us milled with murmurs of annoyance. They parted, unhappily, to provide a path.

In moments, a short stocky figure about the height of Quick's head was facing me.

The deity know as Bes to the ancient Egyptians and—less reverently to me as the second headliner in the act of Shez and Bez—tucked the cell phone in his hand into the decorative horizontal band of his wrapped linen kilt. I'd glimpsed a screenful of Egyptians hieroglyphics before he'd hidden the screen.

"Hail, Mighty Delilah and Quicksilver the Clever. My heart-brother, Shezmou, alerted me to your advent," he noted in the formal way of ancient Egyptian gods.

If I resembled Snow White, Bez was one of my seven dwarves, short, stout, and cocky. Too cocky. Since Bez was an ancient fertility god, one attribute was outsize and often a bit too obvious. He was not the lean-hipped he-man tomb paintings used to portray Shez and most male Egyptians. Bez was muscular, but stubby and hairy, even his face surrounded by a curly mane and beard. He was more reminiscent of your neighbor's cute pot-bellied pig that had grown larger and noisier than advertised.

"I came to escort you to the peak of the Karnak," Bez said, ogling my outfit. "I see that I will not be able to look up your skirt as easily as you could look up mine, if desired, as I am sure that is. You are a strange woman from this strange land and wear twin snakeskins on your legs. Which I, however, find most interesting."

"You kilt is safe from any sneak peeks," I told him. "I need to reach Shez's top-level workshop from inside the Karnak."

I had no idea if Bez knew who or what Howard Hughes was, but I did know the undead mogul was backing Shez-mou's less lethal efforts both in his private quarters and on the Strip. He was quite the inventor and medical research sponsor, our Howard, in his twentieth-century heyday, and even moreso now that he'd become eternal.

Bez beckoned me to bend down deeply to receive a private word. While doing so, I caught him trying to peer down my top. Where is it written that fertility gods have to be four-thousand-year-old dirty old men? Probably in all the ancient books.

"Our high and mighty rooftop deity has installed a secret path to his throne rooms," Bez whispered in my ear. "Follow me."

Quick and I did, getting sour stares from women tourists as Bez tweaked any passing hems, be they on skirts, skorts, or short-shorts. I hoped they took the little lion god for an unmanageable kid, because they sure glared at me like I was the world's worst mother.

"The souvenir shop?" I questioned when I realized that was where we were heading. "The only souvenirs I want to take out of here on this visit are Quicksilver and *me*."

"Tut," Bez said, mischievously grinning up. "This place holds the cleverest innovation to the Karnak yet."

Like the Luxor's main floor attractions, the Karnak souvenir shop was designed to put the visitor inside a pyramid, with faux stone and scene-painted walls and shelves crammed with reproductions of Nefertiti heads and King Tut's golden death mask.

Bez seized my hand, Quicksilver acting as a guide dog on my other side, and led me through the crowds and small mazelike shops. The culture-vulture tourists in the shop area were too busy ogling glitzy reproductions of the glory that was ancient Egypt to donate a glance to any passing dog-and-pony show like my party.

We came to the deserted restroom area and passed it.

Quicksilver whimpered in confusion and I was starting to wonder if the randy little clown was just trying to get me alone with him.

Bez abruptly got on his knees and then mane-butted the lowest fake-stone block. Just as Quick and I exchanged mutually mute and puzzled looks, the stone swung inward into the dark, into which Bez was disappearing except for his unhappily exposed rear end.

I looked back for witnesses, but realized this spot was beyond any viewing angle from the shop area.

What a disgusting sight. All fours, Irma noted. *Not dignifying.*

At least Bez isn't *behind* us, I told her. Close your eyes and think of England.

My "snakeskin" leggings proved useful as I knelt to wriggle through the opening, Quick panting on my heels. The other side was as black as, well, a tomb.

I stood cautiously. No head or body bumps. There was room.

A moment later glowing amber light revealed everything. I saw Bez standing, arms akimbo, dead ahead. I looked back to see the entry stone had shut behind us. More of the gigantic sandstone block walls and a paved path angled upward to our left.

The most amazing object was an exquisite wooden bench with arms and legs carved into the likeness of lion cubs. It seemed suspended against the far wall, like an abandoned amusement park ride seat.

"Hop on," Bez urged, jumping up to install himself next to the wall.

I looked up the grade and spotted parallel dark lines painted along the bottom of the wall opposite where we'd entered. Then I looked harder. The lines weren't painted. They were *fastened* to the wall.

"This is an inclined elevator, like in the Eiffel Tower in Paris," I exclaimed, mystified and charmed at the same time.

Not another step, Irma warned, *this looks like the way to a fertility god's bachelor pad. That imp Bez is always on the make.*

I ignored her and sat next to "that imp."

"I know only," Bez said with a wicked leer, "to touch the magic button."

His stubby thumb depressed a gold circle atop the seat's inner arm. A buzz of bees, almost as soft as silence, accompanied us as the seat glided upward.

Howard Hughes invents again, Irma noted with a sigh, and shut up.

Quick huffed out his doggie disgust at the mechanical route and trotted up the incline well ahead of our conveyance.

Riding up the inside of a reconstructed ancient Egyptian pyramid passage was an experience I didn't want to hurry. Bez grinned like the grown-up child he was beside me. I recalled that Karnak Hotel's exterior concealed the top of an interior pyramid. Howard Hughes must have secretly constructed this inclined elevator so employees could sneak in and out of his top floor quarters without the resident vampire court far below the hotel's bustling main floor suspecting anything.

When the elevator mechanism hushed and stopped, Quicksilver lifted his forepaws and leaned on the fake stone wall. Again, it swung inward, revealing the elevator door and foyer outside Howard Hughes's most upscale lair.

Hesitating, I saw Bez gazing back down the illuminated slanted pathway. "If only they'd known about this when constructing the Great Pyramid at Giza." A sigh ended his wish.

Once I moved into the foyer, I immediately faced the familiar double doors to Howard's suite.

I knocked.

Theda Bara, the silent screen vamp CinSim, flourished open the doors still wearing her notorious *Cleopatra* costume, or lack thereof. It was actually more concealing than the similar outfit Bad Maria wore in her Whore of Babylon production number with the Seven Deadly Sins doing backup at the *Metropolis* nightclub.

Theda shrugged her disappointment at seeing me again, her A-cup metal bra shimmying at the gesture. How sad to think that female competition never died. Also metal bikini bras.

Howard awaited me in his cushy living room, his gaunt form attired in a burgundy brocade dressing gown. Its color tastefully echoed the clear plastic bag of blood suspended from the IV stand always at his side.

After forty years of afterlife as a vampire, he had the burned-out rock star look down pat. His rutted face seemed to have been caught in a fire in the wax museum on the way to the plastic surgeon's office. Bald-doll wisps of dull hair framed those ruinous features. A shrunken head would not be an out-of-line comparison. His surviving body was scrawny to the point of lacking any muscle tone at all.

If this was my secret father I was going take an even-more-assumed name and hide out in Iceland for the duration of the twenty-first century.

"Delilah!" Howard exclaimed on seeing me. He waved the usual set of busty *Playboy* vampire nurses to his side. "See what my guests would like to drink. Water for the dog, I'm guessing. A good four-thousand-year-old red wine for our friend Bez, the god of luck and love. Perhaps a Shezmou three-zero-forty-one B.C.? And for the very modern Miss Street?"

His shaggy eyebrows elevated on a forehead terraced with frown lines and hovered there, awaiting my answer.

"I could probably use a good belt of plain scotch," I admitted, taking a deep breath.

"Johnnie Walker black, neat, four fingers." He waggled four of his. "With any luck, it'll knock her on her ear so I can whisper sweet nothings in it, which is all I'm good for these days."

He sighed. "I know drinking from the tap"—a long horny fingernail indicated his neck—"would be much more fun in my current incarnation, but the germs nowadays! Bedbugs, would you believe? In the twenty-first century? Not in *my* hotels, nor beds. And dust mites. Have you seen those monster faces close up? Uglier than anything in the grossest slasher film. Which, of course, you and I never watch, Delilah. What can I do for you?"

"You also assume I want something when I visit."

"Well, everybody does."

"Is that why you became so distrustful of your starlet dates back in the day?"

"My dates? My stars, Delilah, you're interested in my dating life? Are you jealous? I certainly made the rounds of Hollywood."

"I know all that. You gave casting couches a bad name. Why have you allowed the Inferno Hotel's Christophe to corral all your old girlfriends as sexy CinSims in his Lust level at the Nine Circles of Hell?"

"He's done that?"

"So I'm told."

"What a power freak, as they say now. Merely mogul envy, my dear. Must be deficient. Trust me. They didn't call my founding business Hughes Tool Company for nothing."

I'd heard the emotionally stunted Hughes had been physically far from stunted, but before this topic gagged me, I had to settle another interesting oddity.

"They're all brunet," I added.

"I did have that weakness," he said, gesturing a raven-haired nurse and her tray to me. His attempted wink turned into a blink. He was, after all, more than a hundred years old even by normal standards. As a vampire, though, he was an infant.

"However," he added, "I never turned away a willing blonde. Jean Harlow. . . ." His voice and memory faded at the same time.

What an interview subject he'd make . . . except for the frequent fade-outs and the fact I was no longer a TV reporter.

"Think of me as an aviator who has crash-landed atop a volcanic mountain in the uncharted Pacific islands," he rambled. "Would any reasonable man say no to the native girls who thought he was a god?"

"You don't have to justify your past lifestyle to me, but it all seems compulsive and controlling and sad. Three wives, dozens of actresses as mistresses. You wanted to keep everything, but you didn't want to commit to anything."

His head leaned back as a nurse bent close, loosening the clamp on his IV tube so sterilized blood leaked into his delicate veins.

"Not my issue with money," he mused. "There I anticipated many opportunities. Why should you care about my Hollywood hit list, Delilah? We are all so over."

"You never had an heir."

"No! And especially not the losers who showed up after my supposed death to claim they were my inheritors. Luckily, law firms are as eternal as vampires. My secret enduring estate is still well guarded while the public estate has dwindled into bankruptcy."

I couldn't help thinking that his life and afterlife was the reverse of that. "How did you manage to transfer your wealth along with converting to an undead lifestyle?"

"Thinking of going vamp, Delilah?"

"You never know."

"My nurses are very well paid."

"You and Hugh Hefner." Something in his expression tipped me off. "No! You've helped set Hefner up to follow in your fang marks?"

"Perhaps not under the same persona . . ." Hughes pursed his lips and looked smug.

"My biggest question is, why wait?" I said. "Why not make the change before you look like something from a horror film vault?"

"Looks are so common. Nowadays any obsessive cheer-leader is getting nose jobs and Botox at sixteen. Besides, in my day, or the decade I purportedly died in, the seventies, the undead were only thought to exist in those horror films you mention. Even in my youth, I had always been original in my thinking and grandiose in my plans. I became the richest man in the world. Then I became eccentric."

"You became mentally ill, an obsessive, phobia-ridden hermit," I corrected him gently. "You were powerful enough to order legions of underlings to fulfill your every whim and weak-minded enough to be taken extreme advantage of."

Howard leaned close, his faded pupils afloat in liquid. Tears, or just weak in the lamplight? "So they thought. In 1953 I created a nonprofit entity no one much noticed but it's the only thing that bears my name today."

"The Howard Hughes Medical Institute. I know. It's a world-famous biomedical research facility that sponsors research from scientists across the globe. But you can't have anything to do with it now."

"Bah! Humbug, I would say, but that's true. The basic research I wanted done there was to probe the genesis of life itself. However, to prolong my own life I had to explore the darker side of the street where scientific research meets what some would call quackery, or superstition. I secretly started another small company. I had a . . . last, lovely contact I could trust who had a head for business and even science. She was able to assemble a team of . . . shall we say . . . less reputable European doctors and researchers—"

"She? *You* hired a woman to head up your real dream team?"

"In the thirties I pretty much lived with Katharine Hepburn for four years, Miss Street." Howard's vampire strength made his knotted hands compress the sofa cushions as he threatened to push himself to his feet in anger. "Even Spencer Tracy couldn't manage that at all."

I held up my palms to lower the volume before something in his fragile, undead frame broke. "Hepburn was no cakewalk, I know that."

He fell back into the cushions while his glaring nurses surrounded him, showing me the fangs he'd never let pierce that leathery hide of his because his aversion for germs had outlived his death too.

He rallied to snarl, "Privacy" at the carnivorous nurses. To me he said, "I hired whom I could trust. And . . . someday . . . that might be you."

I wasn't going to ask for trouble by saying this, but that job offer was no prize.

However, the identity of his long-ago secret henchwoman was a tasty appetizer for my reporter instincts. Say she was young at the time, something of a given with a chronic womanizer like Young Howard. Thirty, say. She could be alive at ninety today, by the usual methods, and certainly would be by unconventional ones.

So who could run a fledgling early fifties company formed for cutting edge biomedical research with a staff of eager researchers?

Nineteen fifty-three? *Nazis!*

I was so appalled I repeated the word aloud. And then said, "You hired ex-Nazis."

Howard looked thunderous again. "And what was the federal government doing at the very same time? I ought to know. I had enough defense contracts with them."

Bizarre movie titles that would describe the start-up scrolled through my mind. *Mother Was a Nazi Organizer. I Led Three Reichs. Startime for Hitler.*

Could this woman have been Vida? She was a proven

entrepreneur in Corona. She would have been young and his type. Was the California setup a reward for her role in his escape clause from his disintegrating human life? First, she'd headed his new company; then she'd become vampire to bring him over to eternal life.

Howard was acting too coy about the woman's identity. He'd been the kind to brag. If I could figure out which of his many women had worked for him, she might lead me to answers about my parentage.

"You're not listening, Delilah." He lifted a scrawny forearm to speed the drip of blood into his veins. "I know you need to find out the *true* story." He cackled. "Finding a double of myself to play Dead Howard was easy on any skid row. Transferring me was the simplest matter. Can you guess?"

As fascinating as the process of becoming the late Howard Hughes, eternal entrepreneur was, only one detail in his saga could help answer my questions about paternity.

"You admit you've set up the perfect retirement plan, keeping your money *and* your life. Would it hurt to help a poor orphan resolve her issues?"

"All I can say is you surely have family somewhere, Delilah. Besides, I'm better now. Fresh blood, you know." His shaking arm rattled his IV tube and stand. As it has been said, "all is vanity," and Howard was vainer than most vampires. His need to talk about himself, though, may have given me a couple of hot clues to what I really wanted.

I slugged down some scotch. "So. Vida."

Howard summoned the energy to elevate just one thin eyebrow. "The word means 'life' in Spanish."

"The word meant 'mistress' in the forties when it came to Cesar Cicereau."

"That Johnny-come-lately werewolf trash from France! They'd been hanging around Nevada for decades, trading with the native population. There were no wolves in England, an island kingdom, but the Continent crawled with them, therefore, werewolves as well. I would never allow myself to be bitten into a werewolf. All that hair, although I admit could use some." His taloned fingernails ruffled the three visible coiled white hairs at his scrubs neckline.

"But werewolves are so impotent," he went on. "Three days at ultimate power and then you sink back into common humanity. Might as well settle for one, er, major rising a month."

His gaze shifted. Hughes avoiding plain talk with me? Did he indeed have protective feelings toward me? Paternal feelings?

More scotch, fast.

"My dear, you mustn't gulp Johnnie Walker. Savoring is the secret of life. And undeath. Now, why are you so interested in this woman, Vida?"

"She's apparently my mother."

"Impossible! That would likely make that low-life werewolf Cicereau your father, a fate to be escaped at any cost. Oh."

He snapped his fingers but lacked the strength to make sound as well as gesture. A nurse hastened to his side to produce an auditory snap.

"Mainline level, please," Hughes croaked. "I'm suffering a terribly distressful thought."

I waited while Howard gathered strength and spittle. "You can't seriously suspect that unprepossessing *frog* might be your father?" he demanded finally.

"That's a very biased way to refer to Frenchmen, Mr. Hughes. But you're right. I don't want to think that."

Howard's features squeezed into an expression of pleased calculation. "You came here hoping *I* had that honor. That you would inherit?"

"Please. You 'died' childless without a will more than thirty years ago. Your 'heirs' unto the third generation and their lawyers number about a thousand and your last asset is a plot of Vegas land that lost most of its value in the Great Recession and is owned by a bankrupt corporation."

"You cared enough to look that up," he said, smiling sideways at me like a shy suitor.

Ugh.

"I'm an investigator. I investigate." I eyed his white-uniformed attendants. Real nurses wore colorful scrubs nowadays. "We need to speak privately," I told them. "Could you run off and sterilize blood or something?"

Howard cooperated by nodding vigorously. "I haven't been alone with a living single woman in years," he told me. "You are so obviously after my money, Delilah."

"Me expect to inherit from a vampire, especially one so careful about the purity of the blood he takes in? Never happen. Besides, I don't want your blood money."

"Then, what do you want?"

"Your guess on my parentage. Vida is more than vague about when her fertile and vampire years intersected. But I do know that someone had to turn you. I heard you had a beautiful woman made into a vampire to make the process more inviting. That was despicable, Howard, even in a life that used women like the tissues you relied on during your last live years to keep your fingers germ-free. There is still innocent blood on your hands."

"Don't say that!" Howard began wringing his cadaverous hands like the sleepwalking Lady Macbeth washing them in Shakespeare's play. "I have even more money now.

It could all be yours. All you have to do is think well of me, flatter me. You do resemble my fondest loves, but, of course, I can't consider any carnal activities nowadays. Germs. You could be my virgin mistress."

"Some things you can't buy, even after death."

Like really old people his moods shifted fast. "I can destroy you," he threatened.

I wouldn't have come here if I'd taken his moods seriously, although he was probably right.

A deep growl to my right drew my gaze, and Howard's.

Quicksilver was stationed by the IV stand, black lips drawn back from white fangs, his major canines poised to cut the tubing.

His eye whites showed as he turned a questioning look my way. To bite or not to bite.

"Get that monster dog away from my blood line!"

"Now *I* can destroy you," I noted. "Your so-called bloodline is what I'm asking about. Am I in it?"

Howard's teeth were chattering, his eyes pinned on Quicksilver's teeth. For a huge dog Quick had a grip as delicate as a Chihuahua's.

"All those women, Howard, those flattered, suckered devoted starlets and actresses. Never a pregnancy, never a hidden birth, an abortion? Birth control was more primitive then. You favored actresses who looked like me."

A smile trembled around his chattering teeth. "It had not escaped me, but parentage is not possible, Delilah. There were two or three attempts to claim my paternity before you were even born. I was, ironically, sterile long before I became . . . senile."

I nodded Quicksilver to back off now that Howard was sharing his most intimate secrets. Maybe. When I maintained silence he went on.

"Syphilis."

For a wild moment I thought of Madrigal's fey assistant, Sylphia.

Howard confused my continuing silence for ignorance. "Syphilis was the AIDS of the centuries preceding the nineteen eighties."

I knew what it was. I had just gone stone cold at any possibility that my "inheritance" from Hughes might be that devastating venereal disease. It would certainly explain most of his mental and physical degeneration over the decades.

"Yes," he went on, "any genuine heir of mine would bear that inescapable curse. My nurses can take a sample of your blood right now. A DNA test comparing yours with mine would settle the issue. It's unlikely, but I'm willing if you are."

I eyed the nurses lingering in the archway to the next room. Two were edging nearer, heavy lipstick clinging to their bared fangs and scary-large syringes drawn from their side uniform pockets like ever-ready revolvers from a cowboy star's hip-slung holsters. I imagine they were on a diet of Shez's bloodwine and welcomed any crack at the real thing, even through the intervention of a needle.

Quicksilver produced his bigger fangs and they stopped, eyeing Howard.

"Not necessary," I told him. I definitely did not intend to submit my blood sample to one more vampire in this town. "I'll take your word that you paid for the sins of your youth early, with interest."

His skeletal hand waved off the attendants again.

"So you *had* to turn vampire," I noted when we were alone. "It stopped your deterioration. Your life was really screwed up from the beginning, wasn't it?"

"Not my fault, say the shrinks. It's a kick to talk to a thorough researcher like you who sees the whole picture."

"You're like Elvis, Howard. So many exaggerations have been written about your life . . . and death . . . that the truth is still out there."

"Elvis did not have the foresight to fake his death and live on as a vampire."

"Elvis was surrounded by vampires at the end, as were you."

"Ah, human vampires. A minor variety compared to the actual thing. I did do some good in my life."

"What about the nest of unreformed vamps you're sitting atop?"

"They'd be up here to stake me and my attendants in a second and take over the overworld as well as the underworld, except for you and your handsome lover, Ricardo Montoya. And your big dog too."

Rumors abounded that Hughes had been bisexual, but his tone when he mentioned Ric had been more envious than lustful. Once *he*'d been the handsome young adventurer and he'd owned the skies, the most money, and the most beautiful women in Hollywood.

"Why thanks to me?" I asked.

He leaned toward me, looking alarmingly like a reviving mummy whose case had just been cracked.

"Shezmou!" he cackled. "You freed the demon god who can cast them all into hell. Shezmou is the only thing left on this earth they fear. It's why I installed a workshop for him adjoining my suite in addition to that silly little enterprise you talked him into opening on the Strip. His presence is my guard dog. Nice puppy," he crooned at Quick, earning an operatically sustained growl that made him grin, showing not great teeth.

I was struck to realize that Vegas moguls were busy inviting live-in neighbors, like Shez here and, at the Inferno, Ric, to protect their empires and . . . perhaps themselves.

Hughes was sitting atop a powder keg. The imperious ancient vampire empire under the Karnak had to scrounge for prey in the surrounding desert now that Ric and I had freed their food supply, an entire class of nonvampire Egyptians bred and kept like stock for that sole purpose.

Only the fear of Shezmou reaping their immortal heads and sending their souls on to Orsiris and a judgment that would cast them into eternal darkness kept them going along with Howard and his artificial bloodwine campaign.

So . . . why did the great and powerful Christophe need Ric? Sure, *mi amor* had soaked up some of my silver medium powers, but I still had my modest original silver mojo, plus the familiar transformed from a lock of Snow's hair.

"I'm tired now," Hughes muttered. "You may leave."

Apparently girls weren't considered ace supernatural guardians.

I should be so hurt that Cesar Cicereau hadn't invited me to be his in-house guard when I'd saved his hairy ass twice.

Speaking of hairy asses, as I'd recently had the unhappy occasion to glimpse, Bez was waiting outside the suite door to see me and Quicksilver out when we took our leave.

Chapter Twenty-eight

*G*EE, IRMA ANNOUNCED, *when we weren't looking, someone turned the lights out.*

I took a deep breath.

After a fun ride down on the Hughes-built automated chair, Bez left Quick and me to navigate through the Karnak crowds and the oppressive exterior pillars outside. As the casino chill faded in the warm dry air, we gazed on the overlit dark of the Strip, now the world's biggest and most expensive velvet painting.

I actually liked the effect of night scenes etched with luminous chalk on a black velvet background. It wasn't the Hope Diamond on red-carpet jewelers' velvet, but it was . . . Vegas.

Meanwhile, Irma waxed guilty for a change.

I sort of feel like I should have stayed to keep the old guy company.

"He's power-mad Howard Hughes, world's most unattractive vampire," I pointed out.

All he needs is a good listener.

"Fine. Do whatever you do to take over an innocent mind. Howard just reminded me what I do best."

Attract lonely old moguls?

"Research, baby! My next project is to figure out the identity of the woman who helped Hughes die and live again. If it wasn't Vida, and I doubt that, thank God . . .

who was it? That might explain a lot about pre– and post–Millennium Revelation Vegas, maybe even the Immortality Mob."

But . . . it was late and tomorrow was another day.

AND THEN QUICKSILVER and I returned to the Enchanted Cottage to find Ric leaning, arms folded against his chest, against his 'Vette in the driveway.

Talk about a velvet painting. Add it up. Bronze car gleaming under the soft security lights. Bronze-skinned guy with the day's tie in his jacket pocket and his cream-colored shirt opened three buttons down. The glints in his hair and his eyes both simmered like hot black coffee.

Quicksilver took one look, bolted over the wall, and headed for Sunset Park. He knew my weaknesses.

Going off leash was illegal and I should chase him down and get him home.

"Got all night?" Ric asked.

On the other hand, if Quicksilver couldn't take care of himself, who or what could?

IT ONLY TOOK a quarter of the night for Ric to soften me into an utterly agreeable state and whisper the bad news in my ear.

"I'm going to hate to leave town tomorrow, *chica*."

I paused in doing passionate things to his navel.

"Tomorrow? Leave?"

"An out-of-town consultation gig. It's secret government work. I can't tell you anything."

"Anything? Now that's a challenge." I moved my mouth lower. "Where?"

"I'm not supposed to say . . . Delilah! It's just Texas."

"Texas? What's in Texas?"

Lower.

"El Paso. Zombies. Smuggling."

I had him down to one-word answers, then paused to give him time to catch his breath so I could learn more. El Paso sounded innocent enough. Until I realized what was opposite El Paso.

"Juarez!"

"Delilah! *Ouch*."

I put us on serious Pause button. "You're going back to the worst killing field on the planet and you weren't going to tell me!"

"Just for a couple of days."

"And nights. If you want any more of them with me, you'd better take me along."

"I can't. It's not just me involved."

"So that's why Tallgrass showed up. You guys put on the foot-shuffling male-bonding act so I'd only be able to kick up a ruckus about being left behind when it was too late.

"I don't even have a passport," I said bitterly.

"Delilah, you're an ace investigator and have more *cojones* than most werewolves, but the officials we work for wouldn't understand what you could do for them. This is an all-human, unofficial covert paramilitary, *not* paranormal, force and operation. "

"All *male*," I grumbled.

"There will be some female troops, but you are not an enlisted woman."

The finality in his voice was something I'd never heard before. This was FBI Ric speaking, laying down the law in an area where men were mostly men, discipline was strict, and rules were not broken.

I sighed. There was no stopping him, I could tell.

Might as well make the most of these last hours before he left.

I wriggled farther down his body, tossing my hair from side to side as it trailed down too.

"That's a good girl," Ric murmured after a deep intake of breath. "That's a very, very good girl."

He had no idea just how good I could be when I was bad.

Chapter Twenty-nine

WHEN THE LOVE of your life insists he's going off with his one-time FBI mentor to find his demonic worst enemy in "the murder capital of the world," a city that boasted almost five thousand murders last year alone, and you will damn well stay home safe in Las Vegas, what's a modern woman to do?

Argue herself pink, purple, and puce to no avail, and then say, "Yes, dear."

So he soaks up the supersteamy farewell sex while you soak up his mushy vows of love and a swift, safe return.

Then you check his cell phone and email in the middle of the night when he's sleeping sounder than an exhausted sultan after you gave him his third orgasm.

And then . . . you wait a few hours after he heads for the airport, take your hundred-and-fifty-pound wolf-mix dog and ex-reporter savvy, and follow the cocky son-of-a-gun right on down to Mexico and Door Number Three, the murder capital of the world, Ciudad Juarez.

Just for the record, and I know where to find hard facts, Las Vegas averages fewer homicides in one year than the City of Juarez averages in one month.

I MADE THE twelve-hour drive on Highway 93 and I-10 to El Paso in ten hours flat.

No way was Quicksilver shipping in the belly of an airplane. Besides, he was great company on a road trip and loved riding shotgun.

And no way was I leaving my Cadillac Eldorado convertible parked at the border, so I found Dolly a good long-term garage in El Paso for the duration and stored Quick's car-riding sunglasses in the glove compartment.

Before moving on, I tipped the garage attendant royally. I trusted Vegas's valet parking demons more than the usual humans, but Quicksilver had shown this guy the size of his shark-worthy fangs.

His friendly parting grin had turned the Anglo attendant a whiter shade of pale. He definitely got the message about what would happen if we came back to find Dolly violated in any way, including a joyride.

Twilight was stretching long shadows even longer as we walked the mile to the border. I hated splitting with Quick a couple blocks from the international bridge. I'd have to walk over the Rio Grande River alone.

"Sorry, boy," I knelt to tell him. "It's swim or confiscation."

For the first time ever, I unbuckled the black leather collar he'd been wearing when I'd adopted him at a shelter event in Vegas's Sunset Park so soon after arriving in town that I didn't even have an apartment yet. The volunteers had me when they said such a large dog was so tough to place he was slated for so-called euthanasia right after the event.

Quick was a major reason I'd accepted Nightwine's offer to live in the Enchanted Cottage on his estate. I couldn't rent anywhere else with a big dog in the package.

As I slipped off Quicksilver's collar, he growled, the first time ever at me. My fingertips polished the silver moons that circled the wide black leather.

"I don't want that death-ridden river tainting your lucky

charms, *amigo*. Bad enough you have to swim it." Given the strife of the border wars, I wouldn't be surprised to find the Rio Grande a bloody boiling expanse sweeping thousands of visible corpses along.

Quicksilver arfed eager doggie agreement to my scheme, narrowing his eyes at the stream of cars and pedestrians crossing the bridge. Being mostly gray with touches of beige, I knew he'd blend into the water in the fading light. I hoped my copped ID would also pass better muster at twilight.

"Ric was right. We're both taking a big risk being here," I whispered into Quick's wolfish perked ear. "You don't have to go with me. Ric and you came into my life on the same day, and I couldn't forgive myself if harm came to either of you through me."

Yeah, dogs don't talk, but they do sense more than we can know.

Quicksilver was not a smoochy dog, but he answered by head-butting my shoulder and taking off at a trot, losing himself in the throng of people, heading right for the banks of Rio Grande . . . Rio Bravo to the natives on the other side.

Too late for me to get cold tootsies. Besides, that was hard to do in the cut-down ankle cowboy boots I'd bought to look touristy-fashionable and harmless. They'd still protect my legs from the brush I expected to encounter. I'd stuffed denim jeggings into them, tough enough for a tromp in the desert but not as hot as heavy-duty jeans in this heat-and-dust soaked climate.

In ten minutes I was filing forward in a line of tourists wearing shorts and sandals, visiting Juarez no matter the death toll and time of day, drawn by cheap prices on Mexican tooled leather, sterling silver, and dentistry.

My silver familiar had tarted itself up as a cuff bracelet

inset with lurid blue glass 'stones' instead of turquoise . . . nothing anyone would want to steal, but useful proof of presumed previous jaunts to Juarez.

I slung my backpack over one shoulder like a hobo bag and clutched the laminated key to the city in my right hand. My tan-shy white skin wore an air-brushed patina of bronze. Gray contact lenses hid my vivid blue eyes.

With my thick black hair, I looked Latina on first glance, which was important not only for general under-cover purposes, but because I held the passport of a Poxx TV News researcher named Ashley Martinez.

An American crew fresh from Juarez had been purging their minds of the horrors they'd seen there in a dim El Paso hotel bar. An ex-reporter like me could blend in and ask questions.

"Plan on paying *mordida*—bribes," said a woman who was a smidge heavier, older, and less blonde than most female oncamera TV reporters. "Tell me you're not a stringer or freelancer?"

"My crew's already in Juarez, but this is my first trip down. Delilah Street, WTCH-TV, Wichita." We shook hands.

"I'm Louise Dietz," she said. "So *Kansas* is sending crews to Juarez?"

"The drug lords' smuggling routes cut through the heartland, and so do the addiction and gun-running prob-lems these days."

"That's for sure." She sipped a spiked lemonade. "That's another thing: buy bottled water or canned pop and drink only that."

I pulled an Aqua Fina bottle out of the backpack at my feet, which was loaded with high-protein energy bars and foil-packaged dog food.

"You look prepared," she admitted. "I've been doing news for more years than you've known how to write your pretty first name, Delilah. I anchored in Santa Fe in my glory days, but I like hard news reporting better. I live to expose the bad guys. You're not driving in?"

"No. Walking the bridge."

"So you're meeting the crew muscle right on the other side?"

"That's the plan." News crews on dangerous turf hire locals as guides-cum-bodyguards. Quicksilver didn't speak Spanish but he sure spoke intimidation, and he was waiting outside the bar.

"You're lucky your dark hair passes around here. Still, I wouldn't send a woman crew member on foot alone across the street in Juarez," Louise said. "If the pollution from the burning tires and junker cars don't get you, the crazy traffic or the kidnappers will. You've got nerve."

"I've got a mission. Like you say, there's a lot of pollution in Juarez that needs to be exposed. And stopped."

She was silent for a moment, measuring me. "Most of it's human. Or are you one of these New Agers that think a bit of the unhuman is messing in our world since the Millennium?"

"I think bad is bad, whatever its origin."

"Look for it at every step, in every face, and you'll do all right down there, kid."

Meanwhile, I'd been watching a young Latina woman about my size who'd been flirting with the beach-boy handsome videographer.

"Thanks for the tips," I told Louise in good-bye, in pursuit of my oblivious prey. *She* should have been watching every step, every face. Especially mine.

I followed her into the ladies' room.

Señorita Martinez had closed her eyes to reapply Urban Decay Zero eyeliner to her lids, a faux decadent beauty product line so appropriate to this time and place. I was heading into the Zero Zone all right. Zero safety. Zero protection. Zero humanity. First I had to get in, so I slipped the tourist card out of the passport in her unzipped purse while her eyes were closed, getting pretty. Back out in the still-sizzling late afternoon sun, I collected my furry escort.

Tourists *from* the United States weren't subjected to as much scrutiny as those wanting in. Still, me and Ashley's tourist card, which allowed a stay of more than seventy-two hours, merited a hard look. My small backpack got a total feeling up. Martinez was a surname that could cut both ways.

"Researcher?" the border guard asked.

"I hope to become a reporter, meanwhile I tote and type up things on my laptop for the glamour guys and gals on camera."

My notebook computer was getting a thorough check too.

"A woman crossing over alone with night coming on . . . that's beyond dangerous."

"I'm meeting the crew right on the other side."

"Anybody who goes into Juarez these days is crazy."

"I get you. Hopefully they'll give me a ton of stories to file and I'll be back over tomorrow."

"Trust no one."

"Thank you, sir." I accepted custody of my phony tourist card and backpack. "I don't."

Crossing the bridge, I was charmed to see Mexican children of all ages wading in the Rio Grande shallows as the shadows lengthened. I paused to enjoy the evidence of kids playing in these brutal times in this godforsaken city.

I noticed a small boy holding a squirming puppy maybe six weeks old. How cute, how sweet . . . I'd never seen

Quicksilver at that age. A lump thickened in my throat to see innocence in a war zone.

The boy hefted the pup and threw it far out into the river.

No!

I breathed again to see the tiny head surface. The pup swam hard back toward the shore and the boy . . . when it got there, it was again picked up and thrown into the current. Again blind instinct homed it right back to its tormenter.

I curled my fingers in the cyclone fence towering over the walkway. "No!" I cried.

The child looked up, grinned, bent to pluck the tiny pup from the water, and threw it in farther. Even at such a young age, the puppy regarded a human as its pack leader and would return, no matter what.

Already the cultural divide was staring me in the face. Small boys could be cruel, but moreso in a land where families were gunned down and men dumped in acid and beheaded and young women tortured and raped and buried in the surrounding desert. This was where Ric had been sold into slavery by his own kin at the age of four, long before the cartels had become so unbelievably brutal and bold.

"No," I screamed again, pulling American bills out of my backpack and rolling them up to stuff them between the twisted wires, hoping they'd drift down to the kid, bribe him to be good. He knew he was upsetting the privileged *americana*. The puppy would soon tire, sink, and be swept away.

In the middle of the broad river another puppy paddled along, it too heading for the tormenting boy. Was an entire litter being slowly drowned? With human life so cheap, I was witnessing the ghastly trickle-down effect.

The next dog-paddler finally reached shallower water. The forehead I'd spotted rose slowly out of the water. A huge canine body came lumbering onto the shore, the water-logged pup a dripping, scruff-of the-neck burden in the big jaw's delicate grip.

Quicksilver!

Quick dropped the exhausted puppy on the sandy shore, then stood to his full height and shook the water from his fur until his wolfish hackles stood high and almost dry. His jaws grabbed the boy by the scruff of his T-shirt, and, with one toss, hurled him into the river deep enough to sink and rise and tread water, then swim furiously for a distant shoreline.

A preteen girl who'd been watching the entire drama got the courage to wade ashore and cradle the rescued puppy.

Quick gave one wolfish howl that made every playing child pause in saucer-eyed awe. He spun and streaked away, the sunset haloing his fur with an eerie rose-silver light. I was sure the kids had a new legend to report to their families: seeing the guardian spirit of the river who tolerated no rough play with helpless animals.

Awesome work, dude.

Since Quick was my guardian spirit too, I wondered how or when we'd reconnect.

I finished crossing the bridge, newly wary. This was not Texas anymore. Soon I was swallowed into the crowded commercial streets of the city. Restaurants along the main drag were lighting up for the evening, with hookers appearing in shady doorways. I wondered that they dared, but need drove them to risk being inevitable targets. Or their pimps did.

Low-rider cars, rusted and burned-out American classics like Dolly, and taxis loaded with American tourists, cruised by the women, seeking sex, or even a murderous desert rendezvous, for the night.

I walked briskly, hunting the motel I'd found on the Internet.

Sounds of merciless male laughter and gunshots punctuated the growing dusk.

Cars idled alongside me, male passengers shouting out words I'd seen only in my street Spanish dictionary, mostly *puta* for prostitute. How did the young women who had to work in the border's American factories put up with such nightly harassment? Puppies and women didn't fare well here, and the cartels' Reign of Terror only upped the atrocities.

No wonder Ric hadn't wanted me here, but he didn't realize how far I'd gone to save his life. I wasn't going to let him lose it now. I'd probably already crossed any normal line between life and death to keep him here and with me.

A scabrous nineteen-seventies Chevy had blocked my path.

"Get in," a voice ordered in English.

Uh, no.

"Puta!" another male voice labeled me.

I looked around. People filled the street. Nobody glanced toward the calls or the car. Or me.

Okay.

I kicked the opening passenger-side door shut on the emerging man. He yowled at his smashed hand, cursing with impressive bilingual zest. Meanwhile, I dashed into the slow-moving traffic, doing the *paso doble* through a sluggish parade of big old heavy cruising Detroit metal, ending up on the opposite side of the thoroughfare and down a side street.

Cars thronged the main streets. Here people crowded these narrow side streets, too many to permit rapid changes of direction. I returned my attention to locating the *Motel de los Flamencos Rosas*. That echo of the Strip's venerable Flamingo Hotel had somehow seemed comforting.

Someone bumped my backpack. I whirled, ready to fight for my vital belongings.

Quicksilver, dry and bright-eyed, grinned back at me.

No one would dare call me *puta* now.

Ducking into the doorway of a closed dentist's office, I pulled his collar from the backpack.

"Here's *your* brand of silver mojo," I said, buckling it around his neck.

Under my fingers, the silver circles swiftly shrank to three-quarters full to mimic the moon's current phase. The collar's "coins" tracked the moon's phases, a phenomenon I didn't understand but accepted, like many eerie happenings these days.

"Come on," I told Quick, standing. "I've got a motel reservation. You'll have to wait outside while I claim it, but then you've got an inside bunk."

ACTUALLY, I'D LIED. I just wanted to claim a roof in Juarez with a key to a door. Sleep wouldn't come until much later.

"Quick, I need you to track down Ric and Leonard Tallgrass," I said after I sat, gingerly, on the one lumpy armchair in the motel room. "I couldn't bring any weapons across the border into Murder City, so it's just you and me."

I pulled my leather workout gloves from my pack while the silver familiar arranged itself into a major spiked forearm band on my left arm. The left one. I knew why:

so I could grab cartel killers with my right hand and put their brutal faces through the cheese-parer of metal on my opposite arm. Mean place, mean weapons.

Seeing Ric's childhood enslaver, El Demonio Torbellino, in Wichita recently, I knew I'd viewed the ugly face of ultimate evil. If I ever encountered it again, I would not leave it unmarked.

Quick was turning circles on the battered linoleum floor and eyeing the door, slavering.

He either needed a potty break bad, or to sink his teeth into some handy murdering gangsters, and this was the place to do it. Killers teemed only blocks outside our door, where the native Juarez cartel and the Sinaloa group dueled each other to commit the worst atrocity of the day.

Torbellino was probably planning to make them all look like hothouse flowers of evil. *Flora di mal.* The Spanish I'd learned when Ricardo Montoya came into my life and love life seemed natural.

We had to save ourselves for the main event.

"Just find Ric," I told Quicksilver. "We make it up from there on."

I undid the three door locks, fastening my secondhand cop duty belt and black leather motorcycle jacket around my hips for the certain cool of the night coming to hot Juarez.

Quicksilver trotted ahead of me through the thronged streets, tourists even now hunting food, bargains, and prostitutes. I figured we were headed for the outskirts. Juarez, aka *El Paso del Norte*, housed one-and-a-half-million people, most in poverty, fear, and corrugated steel barrio shacks. Juarez remains the most violent site in the world outside of declared war zones. UN intervention had been called for years ago.

The beige-uniformed police had been the only middle class in a town where rich *Norteamericanos* had set up factories and fancy homes since the forties and fifties. Now the cops were not only corrupt, but any honest ones were an endangered species.

Quicksilver and I dodged patrolling army troops as we passed through mingled commerce and squalor, barely sensed shadows ourselves. We were silent, fast, and broadcast a Don't Tread on Me message to both human and canine as we passed the slums.

Thousands of young women who worked in the hundreds of border factories traveled by bus at night. They had died here for two decades, some said as many as five thousand. Most were rape victims who'd showed signs of "torment and torture," news stories reported, making me shudder to wonder what the possible difference between two such dreadful words could be.

Most were presumed to be prey of human and unhuman traffickers like Torbellino, the ones who refused to go quietly into that degraded slavery. Ric hadn't been in Torbellino's brutal hands then, having been rescued as a "wild child" by the right upper-middle-class Washington professionals before the "femicides" began.

The other most likely suspects were the drug gangs with initiation rites of raping and killing a girl or woman, no matter how young or old. The Mexican police either joined the gangs in their brutality or were targeted by them for death if they didn't.

Miserable, starving dogs slunk around the thinning buildings and hovels, too cowed to attack living prey. No children haunted the darkening streets, all corralled in whatever homes they had. The homeless ones were in the brighter, all-night border streets, selling themselves. This place made my traumas at the hands of mid-America's children's services seem minor.

Quicksilver was leading me into the so-called city suburbs where the femicides had taken place near dirt roads. In the desert beyond, most of their bodies had been buried and later discovered. This place was so crammed with human evil and darkness it must have kept even the predatory supernaturals out.

Quick whimpered beside me.

"Yeah, it's a dark time in a dark place. You picking up any scents besides rotting things?"

His gait, always a fluid trot, kicked up into a hard-driving cantor. I began jogging, glad for the Dr. Scholl's insoles in my motorcycle boots.

Don't call me wimpy; call me prepared. I'd gone solo on some dicey crime scenes when reporting on paranormal activities back in Wichita. Some would call me crazy for going alone into this meat grinder of a landscape, but when your partner goes off to the crime capital of the continent, you're supposed to do something about it, according to noir detective Sam Spade. Unlike him, I wasn't waiting until my partner was dead. Or dead again.

My boot heels beat out a rhythm. Ric-is-just-around-the-bend. Come-on-creeps-and-meet-your-end.

Quicksilver had lived up to his name. Our feet were already pounding into the hard-packed sand of the countryside. Away from the glare of city commerce, my only guide was the moonlight winking off of his collar. A high-intensity flashlight was tucked in my backpack but I wasn't slowing down in rattlesnake and scorpion country to crouch and dig for technological help.

I heard lightning crackle in the distance and stared up at the starless night. We were still close enough to

Ciudad Juarez that the city lights made stars hard to see.

The lightning snapped again and again. I slowed my pace, Quick idling with me.

Was it lightning I heard, or the crack of El Demonio's thirty-foot bull whip? He must be encamped near the city. And Ric, of course, would be hunkered down right on top of his immortal enemy.

My boot soles scraped sand as I hustled up a sage-covered hill, realizing Quick's feathered lower legs would be picking up burrs and cactus thorns. No insoles or ankle boots for dogs. I wished for the booties the search-and-rescue dogs had used at Ground Zero in 9/11, but my idea came a little late.

Quicksilver would have scorned such niceties, anyway. Now on the scent, his churning legs were kicking up sand and rarin' to breast the brow of the hill. I charged up alongside him, only to teeter on the brink of a pit. I surveyed a stretch of shifting, sizzling, hissing sand quivering with nocturnal desert life, moonlight scintillating off scales and shiny shells.

Leaping lizards and tarantulas and scorpions and rattlesnakes! It was a desert vermin convention. What would have the local toxic nightlife scrambling to escape en masse?

Chapter Thirty

QUICKSILVER SAT, HIS head almost comically tilted, to view the mess. Claw and fang weren't going to do much against this seething mass.

Following the moonlit reflections to either side, I saw the living floor of crawling insects and reptiles wasn't confined to just a piddly gravel pit.

My gaze scanned a gash in the earth that ran as far as the eye could see in both directions. The creatures struggling to escape the deep depression seemed unable to get traction on each others' amassed bodies. Some jointed legs and clawed limbs tried to scale my boot-toes, but they slid back.

With all the teeming nightlife of the desert assembled before me, I dropped my backpack behind me on the ridge and crouched to dig out the binoculars I'd brought. These weren't the government-issue night-vision binos Ric and Tallgrass had used in Wichita, but they and the almost-full moonlight were good enough to show how far the living line of desert vermin extended. And, maybe, to reveal what had caused them to cluster like this.

I put the binoculars to my eyes, scanning the distance, then was jolted into dropping them.

A solid form knocked me off my precarious balance on my boot-toes and confined me in a bear hug. I sensed as much as saw Quicksilver leaping at a second form clambering up the ridge behind us. Over and over I rolled, trying to dig my boots into shifting sand as sagebrush crackled under the weight of two bodies locked in battle embrace.

I was planning on a knee to the stomach and then the ribs, followed by a boot-toe killer kick in the groin, when I heard the man still atop the crest laughing softly.

"Oh, *Ty-ohni*, I know you are glad to see me, but enough tongue on my night-vision goggles."

At the sound of that familiar but foreign word, I tried to twist my head around, but my captor had me rolled up like Cleopatra in a camouflage-patterned rug. Then I realized what this roll in the sand was all about. The bastard was trying to protect me!

I flailed free and turned to look up the slope. Only one man called my dog by a Native American word for wolf. Yup. Quick had led us to Leonard Tallgrass and . . .

"Ric." I whispered, but harshly, to my recent "rug."

"Why did you sneak up on me?" I demanded.

He was as pissed as I was. "And you didn't do the same? I can't believe you'd do this, Delilah. Be all okay with staying behind and then slip down to Juarez anyway. It's dangerous and juvenile and it jeopardizes the mission."

"Maybe you should have confided 'the mission' to me. It's dangerous and juvenile for you to come back here right where El Demonio wants you."

The chuckles behind us continued. "You hotheaded kids." Tallgrass used the same forced whisper we had. "The mission will be fine if you quit trying to out-protect the other. Come on. Time to crawl for your country. They need us on the ridge to see if there are any cartel movements around here."

"You all right?" Ric mumbled in my ear. He was not only wearing camos, but the moonlight illumined a face painted in dark patterns like cracked dry earth.

"Don't growl at me. I'd be a lot better if I hadn't have been given the bum's rush down a desert roller coaster."

Grabbing the leather jacket that had fallen loose, I struggled into it without lifting too high from the ground, now that I knew this was a scouting party. Tallgrass's black jeans, boots, and Western shirt faded into the sky. He crouched to dig in his backpack and threw something down at me.

"Camos. Too small for me, and I don't need 'em any more than Quicksilver does. Fasten your duty belt over them."

I didn't argue, but struggled into the equivalent of desert warfare pajamas. By then, Quicksilver had already belly-crawled back to the ridge top. He and Tallgrass kept low enough to blend with the terrain.

I made a face no one could see at the thought of overlooking those millions of roiling spiders and snakes and scorpions as I dug in my knees and elbows and worked back up the slope like a recruit in boot camp.

Ric was still mad, because he got there first and didn't look back. Fine with me. I planted myself on the other side of Tallgrass with Quicksilver.

Leonard Tallgrass had been friends with Rick when he was a whiz-kid FBI profiler with a knack for finding buried bodies. I wasn't sure of the guy's tribe, but he was as pure a Native American you saw these days off a reservation, and pure Kansas cowboy too. Quicksilver had cottoned to him immediately, which had miffed me some. Quick and I were an unofficial K-9 team. Still, Tallgrass was hard not to like, and harder not to trust, which did not come to me naturally.

At least he didn't treat me as too fragile to go into the field. He passed me a pair of really powerful binoculars without comment while he and Ric lowered their bone-sensing night goggles from their foreheads to perch onto their faces.

Now I saw the reason for the vermin traffic jam. The binoculars showed a plain below pockmarked with mesquite trees and sagebrush and behind any smidgeon of cover sat duffel bags of probable weapons. A secret army was assembling and preparing to dig in.

On the horizon, heat lightning stabbed the dark night sky.

"What's going on here?" I asked. Only the vermin had ears and they weren't the enemy.

"Smackdown." Ric's voice was still low. "Secret combined US-Mexican government operation. That's why I couldn't tell you. This is an official consulting job for Tallgrass and me. The joint military forces have run a sting that will lure all the firepower of the Juarez and Sinaloa cartels into facing off ten miles north of here."

"What's the bait?" I asked.

"A juicy set of visiting state department hostages-to-be, worth millions in ransom," Tallgrass said, "and it's working. The bastards from both cartels are setting up major operations to grab the visiting honchos and families."

"It'll take them another day to muster all their men and weapons to go after the same target," Ric said. "Then the combined government forces wait until they take each other out and scoop up the survivors."

"Smart." I heard the crack of thunder in the distance. "I was afraid Torbellino and his bull whip were involved."

"They may be," Ric said. "He's certainly not falling for wasting his forces against the two warring cartels while they slaughter one another, as Washington hopes. That action is way north of here."

"You told them," Tallgrass muttered, "that wouldn't work."

I had one question. "If all the action is moving north, who's going to take on Torbellino's gang of zombies on speed?"

Ric lifted his bone-seeking night vision goggles and pulled them down to his neck. I could see he wasn't wearing a concealing contact lens over his single silver iris.

He focused beyond the ridge, facing the dark and the distant lightning.

"Me."

Chapter Thirty-one

"**N**OW YOU SEE," Tallgrass said to me.

Did I ever.

Ric was sweeping his unprotected gaze over the legions of teeming beetles and spiders and lizards and snakes and scorpions like an invisible searchlight while I watched through the binos.

I gasped as their scales and carapaces and even fuzzy black tarantula legs changed in a dazzling wave to sheer silver. The wave reversed course, sinking down the slope on our side and cresting the opposite ridge of the gash, overflowing onto the flat desert plain beyond.

Ric followed them down like a shepherd, a dull mottled figure behind the sparkling living metal.

I watched Quicksilver slink around the edges of the mechanistic silver wave, forcing the components into tighter formation. If Quick could herd the robot vermin, Ric could perform more wonders to stop Torbellino.

Tallgrass stood slowly, but he'd kept his high-tech goggles on. "He's just letting his new powers out to play. The vermin was massing to escape the action that's agitating their territory. They sense it's more than the gangs or the cartel hitmen using their range to bury the latest bodies."

As I watched Ric herding the silver tide south, he explained. "The military honchos thought Ric and I'd serve best as guides, Ric because he knows this terrain from his childhood indenture to El Demonio, me because I have Native American tracking blood as well as FBI creds."

"Kinda stereotyped expectations."

"Kinda dumb. The border crime and military types never believed us when we said El Demonio was more than a power-mad cartel king who used superstition and gory rituals to control his men and the Mexican authorities and population."

"They're still in denial about the Millennium Revelation?"

"So are these cartel drug warriors. They're so busy being bad they think they can conquer anyone or anything. What we have here is uptight military might versus gangster ignorance. The human cartel bosses fell for the trap."

"The inhumanly cruel cartel bosses."

"Ric and I never figured on El Demonio Torbellino doing anything but hanging in the wings and offing anyone who was left and taking over everything. That leaves us to stop him."

"And this will happen when?"

"Tomorrow night. Now we have the lay of the land. Ric has been testing his new powers."

"Gained through me."

"Maybe so, Miss Delilah, but he needs to know he can use them solo. This is the one chance he has to put down Torbellino forever, on the turf where their dance of death began years ago."

I looked at the silver-armored army Ric was scattering into the brush, the shining effect fading as the myriad tiny components separated. I had no doubt he could call up all these slithering toxic beasties any time he needed them.

"Ric somehow . . . contracted . . . my affinity for silver," I told Tallgrass. "Maybe that's why I feel so responsible for him."

"You feel responsible for him because you love him, Miss Delilah." Tallgrass touched my elbow. "Let's get down to the Jeep so we're ready to get out of here when Ric's done seeding the desert with his allies."

His hand gave me the slightest of shoves, but it got my feet moving and then momentum took us both down the steep rise until the ground was flat and the sagebrush was about my height.

Tallgrass's scuffed boots crunched cactus until we reached a certain clump. He began pulling camouflaging masses of sagebrush aside. They lifted and rolled away, just tumbleweeds. A standard open Jeep painted camouflage colors awaited passengers. I scrambled into the back while Tallgrass took the Quicksilver seat. With city lights out of sight, moonlight poured down on us, as if the moon, pregnant and almost at the full, had broken its water.

I trusted Ric's ability to safeguard himself out here, believe it or not, and Quicksilver was just another guarantee of my judgment.

"Ric is seriously angry with me," I told Tallgrass, leaning forward as he twisted in the front seat to face me. "He's never . . . we've never—"

Tallgrass's palms came up, patting the air and me into silence. "This is between you and him. I am not Dear Abby."

I blinked. He'd echoed Sansouci's exact words to me. Was I looking that in need of counseling these days?

"No, but you're an objective witness," I said. "Since our battle with the elements in Wichita, my silver powers have blended with Ric's ability to dowse for the dead. You've seen the Silver Zombie he raised off the *Metropolis* screen."

"Yeah," Tallgrass grunted. "I find it hard to relate to

such a piece of . . . sorcery. To me, a mechanized creature born of a mechanized process hails from the alien realm of automated beings and figments of film. My culture roots its power in nature. We've never embraced the age of machines as a people. Torbellino harnesses demons to do his evil work, but they too are creatures of spirit, or the unclean undead, not robots."

I had to admit the *Metropolis* CinSim robot was inhuman, but she was also the silver loving cup that held the spirit of the film's virginal heroine, Maria, as well as the now-dead Brigitte Helm, the actress who'd worn the Art Deco Joan of Arc suit of armor. Much as I sympathized with and liked the Vegas CinSims, that silver metal woman freaked me out.

"The Silver Zombie is more unnatural than even the most bizarre CinSim," I agreed, "such as Frankenstein, though they both were 'brought to life' in laboratories. Partly it's because she thinks—if she thinks as we know it—that Ric, having raised her from the screen, is her master."

I hated that concept. And, if I was honest with myself, maybe the competition. The Silver Zombie existed in a 3-D reality beyond all the rules of making CinSims that the mysterious Immortality Mob had perfected. Who could she be, what could she become?

Tallgrass seemed to understand my concerns.

"A century ago," he said, "my people believed a photograph stole and imprisoned a soul. They refused to pose for pictures, like the aborigines in Australia. I've studied this belief, because nowadays 'souls' are 'stolen' every second, and the photographs posted all over the World Wide Web. The native people's fear of photographs is based on the mystical properties of mirror."

I audibly caught my breath but kept my mouth shut. Tallgrass had no need to know about my mirror-walking powers.

"You are not unfamiliar with such marvels, I think." He lifted a hand, waved it at a space beyond my shoulder. "I see you with a slight double vision. I can't quite focus on you, Delilah Street. Never could. Ric doesn't see that."

"He knows, though. So you studied up on mirror images because I'm involved with your former protégé?"

Tallgrass laughed. "Protégé. No such fancy word for it. I was teacher, he the student. Now perhaps that is reversed. Such is the way of life . . . and death. All things reverse. And nowadays, it's a two-way street. Death and dissolution can result in life and restitution."

Crap. That meant death and resurrection could also reverse itself.

"Who says?" I asked.

"The Mayans for one."

"The ones who said the world would end in 2012? It's 2013."

"Thirteen. An unlucky number."

"I don't believe in luck. I believe in effort."

Tallgrass ignored me. "The ancient Egyptians, Greeks, and Romans used reflective surfaces to predict the future. Scrying, they called it, in ancient times."

"Minor league. I can travel through reflective surfaces."

"Can you, Miss Skeptic? Ric never mentioned that."

"He's just . . . learned about it."

"Then, are you a god or a saint?"

"Heaven forbid! Neither. I'm just a child of the Millennium Revelation stuck with some weird talents. Didn't you get any?"

Tallgrass's lips smiled, but his eyes didn't. "Mayans

believed mirrors opened portals into the Otherworld, allowing ancestors and gods to pass through between the two planes. They believed when praying to a saint, the soul leaves the body. To help the soul find its way back into the body, mirrors are placed in front of saints' statues to reflect back the soul."

"Mayans didn't have saints."

"They did after they were conquered by the Spanish. Here in Mexico, there are still towns where photography is banned in churches. The old cameras, and even some SLR digital ones, still use mirrors. And then there's voodoo."

"What? That's an African and Caribbean belief, sticking pins in dolls and other primitive notions. Nobody's going to stick a pin in El Demonio or the Silver Zombie."

"Sympathetic magic assumes a powerful link between entities that look alike. That's why voodoo dolls are used."

Lilith was my very own voodoo doll? Or could be used as such? Not something I'd considered. I shivered . . . but the night had grown cool. Still, I wore two layers of clothing.

"I see why you might distrust CinSims," I finally said. "If they have souls it's wrong to create and employ them. If I ever discover who or what runs the Immortality Mob I'll give them—or it—a good strong lecture. All that aside, there's never been a CinSim with as many layers of cinematic life as the robot from *Metropolis*. She'd better keep her silver-screen metal gauntlets off my man. Meanwhile, I'm worried about Ric's private war, even though his silver powers have probably outstripped mine."

I didn't tell Tallgrass he may have had to come back from the dead to do it.

"Are they enough to vanquish Torbellino and his forces?" Tallgrass asked.

"I don't know. But . . . I wish Ric had included me in his plans."

"Now you've taken care of his omission yourself." Tallgrass slid a carefully neutral glance my way. "Think he's going to like that?"

"Not at first," I told him.

"And in the long run?

"I still have some powers of persuasion myself," I added.

And smiled.

Chapter Thirty-two

THE MOON HAD visibly moved across the sky before Quicksilver came bounding through the sagebush to greet me and Tallgrass with triumphant pants and wags. That big tail could really whip your legs with "happy." Ric joined us soon after.

"Let's roll," he said, leaving all the enthusiastic reunion greetings after their trek back from danger to Quicksilver.

Subsequently, Ric kept silent as he and Tallgrass stowed their gear in the army Jeep.

I was happy to have even this rough ride after hoofing it through Juarez to the desert killing ground both old and new, and for a rest for Quicksilver's pads.

My dog leaped into the backseat with me, wanting to sniff noses to gauge my state of "okay." Smart guy. He knew Ric and I were not speaking. He'd acted fast to join forces with me and delay any messy public scenes, such as harsh words spoken in front of Ric's mentor.

If Tallgrass sensed any forthcoming fireworks, he was too savvy to show it.

The jolting journey back to Juarez postponed chitchat anyway, except for my shouting out the motel address to the GPS on the cell phone Rick wordlessly held up over his shoulder.

"Gadgets," Tallgrass shouted back to me from the shotgun seat, shaking his head. "Another invention that just ain't natural."

But the GPS worked like a magical charm. Within half an hour the Jeep was growling in idle outside the gaudily painted adobe-and-neon facade of the Motel of the Pink Flamingos.

"Get yourself and the dog a room," Ric told Tallgrass. "I'll escort Delilah to hers."

Escort, Irma huffed. *What are we, the* Queen Mary?

Quick flicked me an inquiring doggie look that meant "should I take this ingrate off at the knees, or let you handle it?"

Ric turned to shoo Quicksilver out. He got a fang brush and throaty growl for his trouble. Quick jumped over the Jeep's side, high-flagging his tail, the perfect raised third-finger salute, canine-style.

Tallgrass smothered a smile but lifted shaggy eyebrows at me in silent question too. I had to admit I wasn't looking forward to this solo reunion with Ric after kissing him sweetly good-bye and then heading right down to Juarez anyway.

I shrugged at Tallgrass, so he left the Jeep to do what Ric had said. Ric and I'd never had a serious argument, but I wasn't about to apologize. I gestured to the right motel door, and, when he parked in front of it, hopped out with my backpack hitched over my shoulder and the room key in hand.

Not looking behind me, I unlocked the painted metal door and went inside first. *Whew.* It smelled both moldy and dry after the clean desert air we'd been breathing. The air conditioner rattled and dripped. I couldn't wait to whip off the borrowed camos but needed to avoid any appearance of something as provocative as stripping.

Once inside the room, Ric locked the three possibilities: chain lock, bolt lock, and bottom chain lock. You'd think this was a major metropolitan tenement instead of a border motel.

I waited in the center of the small room. Ric turned to me, his face a stone mask of anger carved into Aztec warrior ferocity.

"You! Out of those filthy borrowed camos."

My heart hiccupped and my own adrenaline surged in a nasty confusion of defiance, anxiety, and excitement tinged with an undeniable sexual edge.

"So," I answered in a voice as guttural, "you're pissed at me because I tagged along without official permission, or more important, *your* permission, Señor Montoya, sir! I thought you didn't go into the military like your foster dad wanted, but now you've turned into an ungrateful, backass-ward martinet as far as I'm concerned."

I snapped off a mock salute as a muscle in Ric's cheek pulsed, Clint Eastwood-style.

"Isn't that a tad hypocritical?" I demanded further. "After all, you and Tallgrass did the same thing to the whole undercover raid unit, and followed your own private mission. To say nothing about the dog, what *my* dog thinks about that too."

He stood there, wide stance braced, glowering.

"So," I said. "*You* first! Out of those filthy camos."

"With pleasure!"

His hands lifted to undo the top closure, then ripped right through the fastenings to bare his body from throat to hips in one tearing gesture. Speaking of ripped . . . A veil of sweat still glistened on firm pecs nicely accessorized with rock-hard nipples over subtly six-packed abs. The effect was so romance-cover drop-dead, I gulped.

His hands reached for the pants drawstring below his navel, but if I saw one more hard thing I was likely to lose my self-respect and throw myself at his naked, um, feet.

"Stop," I ordered. "I could say 'God, you're beautiful when you're angry' but I won't do fight club sex. It's an unhealthy distortion of the power exchange between a couple."

Ric approached me, laughing. "You never miss the nuances." His fingers toyed with my camo top opening. "Take off these filthy clothes, *por favor, paloma*. You need to get naked, and clean."

"So saying please is going to make me cooperate?"

He took my balled right fist and stroked it down from his collarbone to hip bone. My fingers uncurled at first touch to give my palm a languorous, warm, skin-tingling, undulating ride. "Slowing down will make you see reason."

"Fine. But I get the shower first."

I stomped away, bulling through the first shut door I saw. I hoped to God it wasn't a closet because I dearly needed a dignified exit.

The shower stall was tiny, but tiled, at least. After losing the clothes, I teased a feeble cold stream out of the corroded head. With pipes clanking, it finally worked up a warming gush. And this was a three-star motel in *Rough Guides*! I shut my eyes to let the dust and ugly gruesome sights of the day and night wash away.

Something big and bare and dry pushed me face against the shower wall. I wasn't exactly surprised. I'd already turned my cheek to one side, welcoming the expected full body press. Ric's thumb streaked the available cheek, his voice even more caressing than his gesture.

"With that tan spray on you remind me of the old Hollywood pinup I encountered on the Inferno's Lust level, Maria Montez. New look. Almost a new woman, *chica*. I hate that you came down to this hellhole, but I love having you here. We're going to need a discussion, after I get off my standard three. You set the bar high the night before I left for Mexico. No wonder Samson couldn't resist Delilah."

"Kinda tight in here," I pointed out.

"Why do you think I came?" His voice went even lower, intimate. "You still made an unauthorized trip across the border. I'm going to have to do a serious body search on you."

He turned me into his arms. "The mouth is often used to conceal forbidden objects." His search was thorough and probing. His hands paused on my breasts. "Definitely contraband, requiring careful inspection and attention."

A pulse between my legs was pounding in rhythm with my heart. We were safe, we were alive, and we were in total sexual sync.

He drew away, resuming his role. "I'm afraid I'll have to finish up with the standard procedure. Assume the position, face the wall." He spun me into place.

He pulled my hips far from the wall and pushed the half-damp hair off my neck. In a few seconds I was coming myself, loving his lips, tongue, and teeth doing shivery things to my nape, his pelvis locked and rocking with mine.

"New place, new position," I agreed, breathing hard.

"Besides, we won't want to sleep on the bed. There are sanitized sleeping bags in the Jeep. I'll bring one in. No reason we can't share."

"Information too," I said pointedly, but he was turning me around, pulling me into his arms and the skimpy shower stream. I had to close my eyes again as warm water rinsed my tan-in-a-bottle away and his kisses washed over them.

"Mi virgen, mi amor, mi mujer, mi vida," he murmured. "I missed you already. I didn't want to leave you behind. It's just that I'd go crazy if anything happened to you."

I think he tasted my tears of joy in the cascading water.

"You like our little game, yes? Why not reverse roles next time. We're an equal opportunity couple, right?"

"Right. And I promise to speak softly and carry a big nightstick."

Ooh la la, Irma sighed before I could shut her commentary down cold just as the shower did the same thing to us.

I couldn't help thinking Sansouci had been right. I'd let myself be lulled into sexy mock-vampire turn-ons. Who hadn't these days?

Not me, Irma boasted, *but I wanna be.*

I ignored her. I'd interviewed enough psychologists, and confided enough in Ric's foster-mother shrink, to know that love and trust were part of any erotic game. As kinky went, this interlude was minor league. As for me realizing that Ric would love and want me even when I'd pissed him off, it was major.

I DREAMED THAT night I was the Silver Zombie.

Maybe it was because I was sharing a sleeping bag with Ric, which is such close quarters. Maybe I'd been obsessing about it . . . her . . . too much.

Somehow I was inside its glamorous shell, even inside its unplumbed mind. . . .

I LIFT MY mechanical metal arm, strong and smooth. I notice my house of elaborately sculptured wood has received a brand-new coat of sterling silver, so it shines like the carapace of a bug.

I'm trapped inside, body and soul.

I've heard of a girl named Alice who outgrew a house once, but I have always lived inside, it seems. I'm not growing or shrinking, I'm getting no smaller, no larger, imprisoned upright in the dark like this. Buried alive like a gagged mummy in a case leaned against the wall.

I must stand and wait.

My memories are a jumble of fresh and incredibly stale.

One memory is of movement, awkward, stiff. I'm a knight in a ponderous suit of armor made of plaster and plastic wood. Another memory is of dancing, as light as air, wearing only scarves of silk chiffon. Blue chiffon. Like a Blue Angel.

I'm an idealistic girl stung by social injustice. Haunted children look to me for salvation as to a mother. Now I'm a powerful and seductive goddess or a cabaret chanteuse . . . maybe even, someday, a monstrous bride of a famous monster.

I can be anything anyone would care to make of me.

For a moment the dancing angel's free, soaring movements make my prison a smothering coffin again. I feel the plaster, wet and heavy, wrapped around my face and body like a mummy's bindings. No! I am not a mummy! I am young, *young*. I need to move, breathe.

Oh, but I am old, *old* too, shrinking like that girl, Alice, my body the walls that are collapsing around me.

The biblical Tower of Babel flashes through my mind, and a shining city where trains fly alongside aeroplanes, an entire towering futuristic city made from hubris and light, like Lucifer, the fallen angel. I see screaming thousands rioting and drowning. I see a woman in a green gown and a man all in white, like a ghost. I see world war and world peace.

Perhaps . . . I am eternal.

Who am I? What am I? Who will tell me? Who will shape me, free me, use me, destroy me?

I glimpse again the man with the searching eye of a camera . . . the one with a silver eye that sees past the plastic and wood of my coffin to my hidden human heart beating inside.

WHAT A NIGHTMARE! Buried alive.

I blinked awake, trying to figure out if I was dreaming or hallucinating. In the dim light, I searched for the vague bulk of Quicksilver sleeping in front of the door. No, he'd stayed with Tallgrass tonight.

As my eyes grew accustomed to the night lights of Juarez leaking around the skimpy curtains over the window, I made out Ric's sleeping form next to me. One way or another, I had my nightly guard.

I was surprised to see a supple silver chain linking us, my familiar reaching out to Ric in the night. Was that why I'd dreamed of the mechanical woman from *Metropolis*? That idle thought made my dream seem more like being in a comic book rather than a movie. Maybe I'd snagged a small part in Superman's Depression-era Art Deco "Metropolis" that was inspired by Fritz Lang's *Metropolis* film.

By now Ric's profile was as clear as if outlined by a thin wire of neon, every feature sharp. I could see his eyelids vibrating with the hyperactivity of REM sleep, the dreaming stage I'd just left. I wondered what dreams, or nightmares, he was having tonight. Me in his arms? Or has the Silver Zombie seized his subconscious, the way she'd mastered mine?

HE'S A BOY again, in his seventh year of captivity to the human and zombie trafficker named Torbellino and his gang of coyotes.

Our Lady of Guadalupe has come to his dreams for years, perhaps even to his waking moments, her face melting with compassion for his loneliness, her pressed-together palms praying for him.

Now he's mesmerized by the woman's tantalizing image behind the smoke of a dirty magazine's cigar ad. Now *she*'s come to life, dancing for him in her sheer skirt with her bare breasts gleaming at the tips. He's mesmerized, never having imagined anything like this.

But he likes it. He likes it even when he feels the needle fangs of a vampire bat he hesitates to tear away for fear the almost-naked woman gyrating in the cloud of smoke will vanish if he wakes from his dream trance and moves.

Pleasure seeps from him like smoke, and then he wakes up, pulling the soft bat body from his neck with a sharp spasm of pain. It flies away, but the woman has vanished, as he feared. Maybe he should feel shame. He's seen the women dragged into the cabin of Torbellino and his men and has clenched his fists and squeezed his eyes shut, but this woman is different.

She likes him. She likes what she does for him, likes to ease his pain and fear.

He doubts the Virgin of Guadalupe will ever appear to him again.

But this vision will.

Chapter Thirty-three

A KNOCK ON the door caught me slapping on some lip gloss late the next morning just as my stomach was growling up a storm.

So was the other side of the door.

I opened it pronto to find Quicksilver on perk-eared, lifted-lip alert next to Leonard Tallgrass. He and Tallgrass managed to look both worried *and* sheepish.

"So . . . how are you guys?" Tallgrass asked, not examining the room behind me with his usual law-enforcement sweep.

"Starving," I said. "Ric will be out of what passes for a shower in a minute. What brought you two here?"

"The need to kill time," Tallgrass said. "If your stomach is growling, we know how to feed it. The sun is shining. It'll be a fine day. We could do the town until the heat of early afternoon, then take a siesta until it's time to go back to the desert and kick butt."

"Sounds great," Ric said from behind me. "I worked up quite an appetite last night."

"Scouting on the desert," I added quickly.

"Peace at any cost," Tallgrass murmured. "You two ready to do the Ciudad Juarez tourist shuffle?"

BREAKFAST WAS A very late brunch in the open patio section of a giant restaurant complex off the Plaza del Sol called Mariachiville.

More English than Spanish echoed off the colorfully tiled fountains, while parrots chattered in the surrounding jacaranda trees. Those gorgeous lilac-blur trumpet flowers were blowing in the wind with mariachi band fervor. Scents of hot peppers and cilantro mingled with the perfume of tropical blooms. The waitstaff was young, vibrant, and bilingual. I was ready to book a return trip to Juarez for a romantic getaway with Ric at a five-star hotel.

Dream on, Irma advised.

Over glasses of Negra Modelo beer Ric and Tallgrass were muttering about "rendezvousing" with military "big shots" and "borrowing" some firepower bearing numbers and alphabet letters instead of names.

"Quick and I go along tonight, no matter what?" I inserted into their intense, whispering dialogue.

Tallgrass looked at Ric, who nodded impatiently. "Of course. You and the dog have your built-in defense systems. You've proven that time and again. I get to solo head-to-head with El Demonio, though." His expression relaxed into a grin. "Unless my ass is being whupped. Then, I expect all of you to play some really killer backup."

The technical talk ended when the waiter wafted platter-size dishes of heavy pottery holding the kind of ammunition I dig—nachos, fresh guacamole, fiery salsa, tomatillos and chipotle sauce, enchiladas, tacos, jalapeño and habanero peppers.

This menu could melt down zombies, not to mention start a hot border war with the digestive system. We finished with smooth, sweetly bland crème caramel all around.

"I can see why tourists won't give up on this border city." Ric's smile lit up the entire area and even the big blue sky above it. "I won't give it over to the gangs and cartels either," he added, his glance darkening.

"Softly," Tallgrass cautioned him. "Enjoy the day, *amigo*, with great simple cuisine, an old friend, a beautiful woman, and a loyal dog. What more could a man ask? The night will bring the closure you seek."

"*You?* Talking about closure?" Ric teased Tallgrass. "Sounds like you've been powwowing with my foster mother."

"Wouldn't mind if I did." Tallgrass winked at me as I lifted my bubble of a margarita glass in a toast to Ric. "Is her husband involved in the US side of tonight's action?"

Ric shook his head. "Burnside is really and truly retired. It's better that way. He never knew why I was enslaved by Torbellino. Discovering my dead-dowsing abilities—or even my civilian efforts to bring down the Torbellino cartel—would bring out the army mule in him."

"Do you regret he never really knew you?" I asked Ric.

Now that I was starting to wonder who had sired me, I was realizing I needed to find that out as badly as Ric needed to stop his lifelong lethal enemy. My father might be someone I knew and would never suspect, or ever respect. He might already know me and not be willing to admit it.

Ric shook his head. "Why regret it? My foster dad's a suck-it-up kind of guy. He wouldn't have wanted any whining."

I exchanged a glance with Tallgrass. This man was Ric's soul-father. I could only hope to find one as wise and supportive as he was. I again recalled my brushes with the Perry Mason CinSim, and smiled. Couldn't ever be for real, but I could always rely on Perry as paternal backup if my freewheeling investigation work got me into any tangles with the law.

I realized that Ric's resting hand was warm over mine,

the hot dappled sunshine sealing our mutual thoughts with the kiss of contact.

"I've had way more in the way of parents than you have, Del." His smile was as healing as my lips and Quicksilver's tongue could be at times. "Sometimes great, sometimes not so. Remember that."

What struck me then, with surprise, was that Quick and I shared that oral healing thing. I'd never quite focused on that before. Poison dog lips? And mine? I stared into my dog's blue eyes, blander and paler than my own.

He laid his snout on my knee and gave me his clearest mountain-lake gaze.

This tableside love fest was getting sweeter than tooth decay. I shook off my mood with Quick's snout and Ric's hand.

"What do we do next?" I asked.

"Shopping," Ric said.

I didn't think he and Tallgrass had silver and sombreros in mind. Besides drugs heading north and dead bodies, Juarez was most noted for being the busiest illegal weapons purveyor on the south banks of the Rio Grande.

"THIS PLACE IS called the *Valle de Guadalupe*?" I repeated to Tallgrass, stunned.

Night had returned to Juarez, eclipsing its sunny side.

I was back in Tallgrass's loaned camos and we were back on the ridge where Quicksilver and I had intercepted him and Ric the previous night, smelling creosote bushes and tented by small cold stars and a moon so big it seemed blurry.

"You asked me where our party was gonna make our stand," Tallgrass said. "All the military intelligence targeted this place southeast of Juarez as the most violent

drug-war zone. You have something against the name Guadalupe?"

"No. I just hope that means we have the Virgin of Guadalupe on our side."

"We all met up last night a bit farther north, but this is
that same long ridge where Ric is sure Torbellino's soldiers
will hunker down, ready to mow down escapees from the
Juarez and Sinaloa cartels clash up there."

"And the Mexican-US forces will stay north to capture
whoever survives the cartel war too, entirely unaware of
this side of the contest farther south?" I wanted to get the
combatants and the geography straight.

"Yup. Torbellino will form an unsuspected trap south
of the action, offing any rival cartel men who escape the
government trap. That'll make him chief dog in the border
smuggling trade."

"So two guys, a gal, and a dog are going to take out
Torbellino's army?" I asked.

"It was supposed to have been just two guys," Tallgrass
reminded me sternly. "And Ric only wanted me along as
backup."

"Talk about a Lone Ranger. Maybe he has some secret
weapon."

"Maybe you." Tallgrass chuckled. "I suppose you were
too busy using your feminine wiles last night to get all the
logistical details out of him."

"Wiles take time. I prefer truth. I never thought Ric
could or would keep something this big secret from me."

Tallgrass shook his head at Ric's solo act. "The gal and
dog weren't in our original plans, but we four did pretty
well against Torbellino's Wichita posse. All I know is Ric
wanted to wait and take El Demonio down on their common ground where he'd once been a helpless child."

"Ric's personal crusade is the source of his greatest personal danger," I told Tallgrass. "He'll never allow anyone else to be enslaved as he was, and he's absolutely fierce and fearless in going after the exploiters. That's why I *had* to follow him here. By the way, I love the new accessory you guys got me during your spending spree in town. It really looks cool with my camouflage jammies."

I saluted the night vision goggles casually stationed atop my head where California women wore sunglasses 24/7.

Then I lowered the goggles to focus first on the heat lightning doing a war dance on the night horizon, then far closer and below, on Ric and Quicksilver. Funny, Ric hadn't been upset about the *dog's* presence here, in the heart of battle, I couldn't help grumbling mentally.

Together the hunting pair had reassembled the panicking desert reptile and insect life of last night into a thin silver line down in the sand canyon's crease. Together, they were belly-crawling up the next ridge, which was the only cover between here and the Valley of Guadalupe.

There the sagebrush stations of hidden weaponry were now shaking with the emergence of a low-profile army of drug-and-zombie smuggling gangs and hitmen.

The silent night was abruptly interrupted by distant automatic gunfire chattering amid the spectacular fireworks of exploding grenades and shoulder-launched missiles. Out of sight to the north the warring cartels were fully engaged and clashing like an electric storm, harried into mowing each other down to escape a pincer operation of combined government forces.

The rumbling north of this valley obscured the vibrating *chirrs* and humming and scale-scrapings of the agitated and silver-armed insect and reptile foot soldiers Ric and Quick had gathered until they were poised like the top curl of a gigantic surfing wave about to wash over El Demonio's forces.

"Let's bring up the rear here and put Torbellino's ass in a silver sling," Tallgrass hissed in my ear.

A rear in a silver sling. Nicely put.

Tallgrass grinned up at the fading northern fireworks in the sky above one last time.

Then we turned sideways to crest the ridge behind the one Ric held now and maneuver down the steep sides of the earthen gash, our booted feet moving fast to catch up to the advance party of two. We knew that Ric's show-down with his childhood enslaver had to put him first and foremost in the confrontation and that Quicksilver was the best scout in the party.

Soon we were approaching the quivering and broad-ening silver band making a do-or-die border like the Rio Grande. The maraca racket of all those metal scales and wings, feelers and legs, quieted and stopped. Like an ice-frozen river, the living shimmer of creatures stopped.

Tallgrass and I hastened to reach Ric's back, Quicksil-ver sitting beside him.

The lightning on the horizon ahead of us grew bigger and snapped like a chupacabra twitching its tail. Yet we faced a vastly different scene from last night.

Across the wide valley massed the forces of hell.

Talk about a rag and a bone and a hank of hair. Row upon row of feral zombies, a standing army, twitched and writhed like giant maggots, all white bone and bared red muscle in the moonlight. Only then did I see the black iron shackles that made them into chain gangs.

Any remaining flesh gleamed in the moonlight, reflect-ing the actual maggots burrowing through what was left, ready to drop off on living prey.

"They're . . . dancing?" I wondered aloud. Then I got it.

We were confronting an entire army of the new-generation zombies El Demonio Torbellino had created, hop-heads jived on crystal meth, a perfect meshing of the drug and the zombie trades.

"I'm going down," Ric announced, turning so I could see the lightning flashes reflected in his exposed silver iris. "You two hold the high ground here until I get something going down there. Proceed at your own discretion. Be advised *I* don't intend to be heavily into discretion tonight."

He started down the incline to the Valley of Guadalupe, his every step pushing the silver wave of desert vermin at his feet ahead of him.

I lowered the high-tech binos that read bones, not heat, to my eyes for an ugly, close-up view.

"That's it?" I asked Tallgrass. "Those are our only marching orders?"

"It's mano-a-mano now. Our boys are both in the ring."

Now I could see El Demonio had arrived at the jitter-bugging zombies' forefront. He sat on his traveling throne, the trunk of a black sixties Lincoln Continental convertible, his feet planted on the backseat. He was riding the stalled car like the grand marshal in a grisly parade of death, greed, and utter evil. He also was committing vintage car abuse.

I'd never forget his face as I first saw it in Wichita. At this safe distance I could study it longer. The brim of his flat-crowned black leather hat cut across the satanically arched eyebrows overhanging his hooded gaze. Thin high-flared nostrils made his nose as flat as a snake's, his lipless mouth a raw slash like deli-sliced rare beef.

Why hadn't I recognized who Torbellino looked like before? He was the spitting image of the sinister corporate muscleman in *Metropolis* who was only known as The Thin Man. That reminded me of the film title that had introduced my CinSim friends, Nick and Nora Charles, to an adoring public. Weird that something so innocent and light echoed something so evil.

Two chupacabras flanked the car, their eyes gleaming red with smoke steaming from their scaly hides like a visible stink. This multibreed creature resembled a small dinosaur with leathery gray-green skin and sharp quills down its spine and tail.

Despite the lizardlike quality, its fanged face, smoldering red eyes, and black forked tongue gave it demonic cast. To underline that, I can speak from experience that a chupacabra's every exhalation broadcast the hellish and overcoming reek of sulfur.

I had reason to know chupacabras weren't the biggest and brightest monster at the matinee, but they sure were among the ugliest.

Tallgrass was shaking his head at the opposition. "I didn't believe in chupacabras until I saw that one in Wichita. Just how dangerous are those mythical beasts? It's not a native Midwest monster."

"A monster it is," I agreed, "and mythical for too long. The real ones had a great cover all these years. Cheesy tabloids kept producing what people found and called chupacabras, dead coyotes ravaged by mange. You'd think they'd realize that creatures reputed to suck the blood out of goats and other stock had to weigh more than thirty pathetic pounds."

"People want to believe folktales that look safe and are in somebody else's backyard," Tallgrass said. "The more lethal and unkillable the monster, the less we want to believe it's really out there."

"Some of the worst monsters aren't supernatural."

"That's for sure. Look at these cartel mobsters."

"And we call unhumans inhuman." I surveyed our immortal enemy on his throne.

El Demonio's thick bull whip draped the car's front seat, windshield, and long, shiny hood before it coiled down to the desert floor. The last three feet of thirty—which Ric had often felt the slash of—swayed upright, an animated leather cobra ready to strike. Torbellino was a demon with an exterior tail.

And with every sway of the hypnotically moving whip end, lightning sizzled and danced in the sky, obscuring the stars and stabbing at the moon.

Ric marched closer to the drug lord's battle line, Quicksilver nipping at the sides of the silver wave to shape it into an advancing U-shape.

"Great strategy," Tallgrass observed. "We need to move to the ridge Ric left, pronto."

He slung his bulky new rifle over one shoulder and sent sand chunks tumbling as he hurtled down with a sideways gait.

I followed his example, stumbling and having to abrade my fingertips on the sand a time or two. Getting up the last ridge was easier, and we lay just under the crest, breathing hard.

Apparently it was going to be a battle of words before action.

"How do you like my wheels?" El Demonio's basso voice jibed across the barrier of stalled silver desert life.

I followed Tallgrass in sticking my head above the ridge to hear the cartel boss's rant.

"JFK bought it in this car. Jackie crawled where I'm sitting. The conspiracy nuts thought it was the mob, but they had the wrong *mob* in mind."

"Wrong," Ric shouted back. "That car's a museum piece far away and you soon will be too."

"Hola, mi niño pequeño," he taunted in tones of false fondness. "How you have grown. Every inch of height you gained must have stretched the welts from my whip on your back."

The crude Kennedy car reference had made my blood boil and now it boiled over. I scrambled to my feet and used my strongest voice from when I was at the back of a noisy press conference.

"Those evil marks are gone, you monster," I shouted. "What monsters make can be unmade."

"Ah. The Wichita *bruja.* Maybe the marks on the flesh can fade, but never those on the soul."

I knew that *bruja* meant "witch"—and didn't I wish I had those powers!—but I could use the ones I did own.

I shook out my spread arms. I felt the familiar stretch across my shoulders under my two layers of clothing as it streaked down both arms to escape the big, ugly camo shirtsleeves. Butts of solid silver filled my leather-clad palms with sleek and icy metal power.

Tallgrass muttered in his native tongue to see me holding twin braided silver whips, twelve feet long.

I raised my arms high and gestured sharply down, like a conductor. Narrow whip ends touched earth and snaked up again toward the sky, conjuring an arch of snapping, sizzling blue lightning above us. An electric branch of storm lightning fanned out a hundred and fifty feet in the air from the ends of each one, surprising even me. My familiar was rising to the challenge.

"Now Ric has some flashy Vegas neon backup," I told Tallgrass.

El Demonio seemed to welcome my showy defiant gesture. His right arm lifted far back before snapping down. The long, heavy whip arced high, poising for an instant right over Ric before snaking into its natural curve to curl down toward his back.

Ric held his ground, but lifted his right arm.

I'd expected his gesture to repel the whip. Instead it summoned a heavy gust of wind that spun the desert surface into dancing legions of swirling silver insects and reptiles. The hissing, spitting, biting toxic dust devils numbered almost as many as the massed and leashed zombies.

The last ten feet of the demon drug lord's whip curled into a spiral, caught in the mini tornadoes' eddies. Through the dancing dervishes of dust, I glimpsed the zombie chains falling to their feet. They were loose and rushing forward into a semicircle to hem us all in.

Tallgrass squinted through the eerie, murky yellow light the dust devils cast, then ran down the last ridge, his heavy hip-held rifle spitting rapid rounds through the dust, blasting the limbs and heads off the frontline zombies.

I snapped my arms in unison again, my silver whips lashing lightning straight at El Demonio's car, striking a chupacabra on each side. They curled into smoking remnants the whirlwinds spun away.

My next target would be the demon himself. I shook my arms but my hands were empty. I shook my arms again in frustration.

The damn silver familiar was now a spiked left forearm guard, useful only for hand-to-hand combat. By the time it rent any Torbellino henchman at the rear, I'd be downed and gnawed to death by oncoming zombies.

I looked to see how many I might be confronting and how soon.

An agile gray form advanced and retreated from the

forward zombie force, Quicksilver gnawing legs off to create a fallen wall of zombies. It was like any other war since time began: the others just marched over their fallen comrades' disintegrating forms.

Tallgrass, still shooting zombies, backed up in the shifting sand. I called Quick to join us, but the wind whirled my voice away.

"Why aren't you shooting?" Tallgrass yelled at Ric and the similar weapon slung over his shoulder.

Ric shook his head. "No need. The dust devils are vacuuming up the front lines. They're thinning out the zombie noose even as El Demonio tightens it on us."

He gazed up at the sky. The moon had broken through clouds, painting them into a silver sea above the agitated dust storm below.

A full moon had always reminded me of Bing Crosby's face crooning *ba-bub-bub-boo*, like a fairy godfather about to bibbity-bobbity-boo a barrel cactus into an escape carriage and lizards into snorting steeds with a desert fox for a driver.

"Don't shoot through the dust," Ric ordered Tallgrass. "I think . . ."

And then the moon's size enlarged and lengthened like the melting diamond pendant in the thorn forest.

I tried to decipher the face I saw in it now, for it was different. . . .

The moon grew so bright we lifted our arms to fend off the pain to our eyes, at least Tallgrass and I did. Quicksilver came bounding around the line of dust devils, joining us to sit and lift his throat to the sky and bay at the swelling moon.

Distant coyotes joined in as the rasp of insect legs and wings from our barrier wave surged louder. If sheer noise would repel zombies, we had it made.

Most of them didn't have ears, though. The smaller parts are the first to rot.

Even now the gap was closing.

Meanwhile, Ric was moon-gazing into the blinding light.

I ran to shake him out of his trance, but he turned eerie eyes on me that had Quick leaping to my side. Ric lifted his fists, nails digging into the palms until I saw blood running. Then he spotted the jagged spikes of the silver familiar on my arm and wrapped his hands around it.

"No!" I screamed, looking wildly for Tallgrass, who had lowered his weapon in confusion.

Blood was pouring from Ric's hands as he released them from the familiar. I gazed down at my forearm guard to see bright scarlet tipping every point. Then the silver melted like the moon and slithered up my arm in a network of fine chains, leaving my forearm bathed in nothing . . . except Ric's blood.

I looked to heaven for help, for hope, and was horrified.

The swollen face of the moon was the visage of the false Maria from *Metropolis*. Her slanted eyebrows and pouting lips and halo of a headdress were the face of the Whore of Babylon performing for the male patrons of the elite and decadent nightclub, who'd been hypnotized by her bared breasts and undulating pelvis, frozen by lust.

I needed more than this sky-borne CinSim from *Metropolis* to counter real evil. El Demonio's cartel killers and zombie forces didn't freeze at beauty bare.

Unlike the men in the nightclub, I could tear my eyes from the sky-borne seductress. I noticed the clouds on the horizon piling into the shape of the pillars supporting her hooch-koochy dance stage. The crouching hills beneath them became . . . the film's Seven Deadly Sins.

The Sins below her crouched on their haunches, supporting the platform the movie-screen succubus danced upon. Five robed men and two women, they were all as massive and muscular as Atlas upholding the world and now they stood and advanced as one. Their ghostly gray robes resembled a huge thunderous fog bank rolling across the land.

Behind them strode the stormy blue-black hooded figure of Death, its silver-bladed scythe sweeping left to right.

The creepy film figures—actual, not SinCims—rose to the top of the sky, and rolled over the human cartel killers at Torbellino's back. Guttural screams choked under the heavy tread as storm troopers of Envy, Anger, Greed, Lust, Gluttony, Sloth, and Pride found and crushed the human bodies that harbored them.

That shattered Torbellino's ranks to the rear. What about the forefront of the army massed just behind El Demonio and his rolling thunder car and crackling lightning whip?

Oh, God!

Ric had turned to face the undead army, putting his arms straight out like a zombie from a corny old movie. Or like Frankenstein's monster.

He moved toward the meeting walls of dust devils and zombies. With El Demonio watching through binoculars from atop his black Lincoln, Ric's extended hands dripped fresh scarlet in his own tracks.

Quicksilver gave a blood-thickening howl and hurtled around the outside edge of the dust devils to lead their advance. Tallgrass had somehow come beside me, holding me prisoner in his iron-armed embrace as I lunged forward to help.

"Look!" he shouted in my ear, but I could barely hear. "Look at the ground behind Ric."

I couldn't tear my eyes from Ric's vanishing figure as a curtain of dust devils and the evil yellow light obscured him. Tallgrass's big hand grabbed my head and pointed it like a gun where he wanted me to look, in Ric's sandy desert wake.

Bloody hands were breaking through the sand that had spun into the dust devils. Human fingers stretched out like fans of playing cards, reaching up into the dust until they became arms and then facial features broke through the shifting sands behind them . . . foreheads, noses, open mouths frozen in silent screams.

Ric was zigzagging back and forth among the wind-eddied rows, a shadow I could barely see. I was reminded of a farmer sowing seeds or a harvester of the dead or Death itself on another stately but implacable rampage.

"Tallgrass!" I screamed into the wind. "Let me go! Ric and Quicksilver, I can't lose them."

He pressed my head against his chest and I smelled ironed cotton. *Crazy!* It was blood and bone and guts all around us. I should have smelled rotting mortality. He ironed his shirts? Such a weird detail to circle in my brain, but maybe I needed to cling to any shred of normality.

"Have faith."

I heard Tallgrass's voice gusting away from me even as his words sifted through to my dust-beveled mind. I struggled to break the ex-FBI man's grip, but it was as implacable as Ric's methodical progress, every stride taking him a precious two feet farther away from me.

"You look but don't see," Tallgrass shouted in my ear.

I looked again, through the sandstorm tears blurring reality into a fun-house mirror.

And I saw naked female forms undulating upward from the bloody sand, a bizarre bony, ragged forest raised by blood and sucked free of the earth by the dust devils. They were mere pieces of people, not visibly rotting like the zombies, but bruised, mutilated, burned, and broken. I wanted to turn my eyes away in pity and revulsion.

But I couldn't. The silver familiar had formed a thick high collar on my neck, forcing me to watch the end of all I loved as man and dog vanished into a meeting wall of sand and cloud, earth and sky, dead and undead.

And . . . it had become impossible not to watch the resurrection before me.

The rising female bodies spun as the light enveloped them, clothed by the dust and blood into glowing orange figures as fierce as fire.

The light brightened and purified until it seemed they danced in an eddy of moondust . . . they one by one became whole as burnished silver metal replaced the ruined and missing pieces . . . a breastplate here, a jawbone or forearm or thigh-piece there, all elements of the *Metropolis* robot.

They'd been reborn into a patchwork robot zombie army, gathering speed, hurtling like the silver wave of desert reptile and insect life toward El Demonio's command post.

A shrill scream shattered the desert night.

The army of femicides Ric had raised swept over the zombies that fell into blackened ashes at their passage and beyond to the murdering human men behind them.

Ric and Quicksilver were standing together behind them, dark shadows against the light that seemed a bloody silver sunrise on the western horizon. I stumbled forward.

Tallgrass was running with me, his—I finally remembered the damn name—M249 SAW assault rifle braced on his hip spitting ammo.

Torbellino's devil whip lashed once against the advancing fire and dust.

I cracked my left arm and the familiar finally took a single whip form to meet it, shaking Ric's blood off itself into a circle of seething acid that shriveled the Demon's horrible weapon into a dried length of brittle leather.

This close we had to advance over zombie bones.

"El Finado, El Finado," I heard the cartel men cry as they turned to run but fled into the ensilvered embrace and grinning skulls of the risen corpses. These slavers and rapists and murderers were hailing their own deaths.

They were finished. *Finado.*

Torbellino was standing in his parade car, his eyes scarlet, his empty whip arm pointing a clawed forefinger at Ric. Demonic gunfire blasted from his being in the form of a fiery hail of bullets stitching the air as it took whip form.

I watched Ric jerk and spin in that immaterial onslaught of power, my own body shuddering with sympathetic pain.

But as he turned in that circle of torment and death, his head swung left and then right and left again. A luminous silver-blue lash like a laser cut through El Demonio's neck, severing his head from his body, and then back again, cutting his torso in two.

Like the whip and the chupacabras, Torbellino shriveled and blew away into fading smoke. In the desert behind him his followers went down, their forlorn cries of *"El Finado"* dying with them.

Ric had sunk onto his knees in the sand, Quicksilver's sturdy shoulder beside him the only force holding him up.

I ran to him, sliding onto my knees beside him, grabbing his hands and once again surveying the price of his dead-dowsing powers. His own blood. I madly patted the bloody camouflage jacket to find the deadly on-target wounds from El Demonio's very being. He'd been strafed before my eyes by weapons both physical and supernatural.

Ric swayed, most of his weight on my shoulders. And then the burden lifted.

"Delilah," he whispered.

The demon's last attack had failed to bring down his prey.

I looked up to see the moonlight clear and pure, liquid silver on the desert.

The hellish wind had been snuffed out like a candle flame.

The metallic insect hallelujah chorus was silent and I could hear my own breath panting, and Ric's, and Quicksilver's. Only Tallgrass stood tall and stoic.

"Justice," he said, "is a mighty power to invoke." He bent to pick up a palmful of desert sand. "May they rest in peace." The grains fell to the ground, captured before rejoining the desert waste by small upsurge of wind.

I looked at the desert floor behind us. Spotlights of red shimmered in the silver moonlight and faded, softly. A chorus of sighs rode on the night's back.

"Those are their graves." Ric's voice was hoarse from not having spoken for so long, and from his exhausting role in the mass rising of the dead. "Tallgrass, you report that when we get out of here. Tell the mission forces where to come to find and honor the Juarez dead. They'll believe you're an expert tracker. Torbellino?" he asked last.

Tallgrass shook his head. "Gone with the wind. *El Finado*. Still, a demon knows how to vanish when it's outspelled. But he'll have a far harder time than you raising another army."

"I don't want armies." Ric struggled to his feet with my aid. My pat-down of his torso found no obvious wounds. A miracle. "I want one evil demon eradicated from the earth."

"Perhaps he is. If not, next time, *amigo,*" Tallgrass said, touching his shoulder.

Quicksilver was lapping at Ric's slack hands, looking more doglike than he usually deigned to appear. His healing tongue would erase Ric's physical wounds from raising the murdered women.

What would heal Ric from drawing on such unhuman power, I didn't know.

Chapter Thirty-four

THE JEEP BOUNCED our weary bones back to Juarez and the Flamingo motel for what was left of one more night.

I drove while Tallgrass updated me on what would happen next. Ric lay more drained than sleeping in the back with Quicksilver.

The government commanders and their troops would be fully occupied for a couple days, rounding up the quick and the dead from the cartel war they'd engineered and won, for the time being.

Fringe support people like Ric and Tallgrass were free to leave, the earth-shaking stand they'd taken against an underestimated drug lord named Torbellino merely freakish weather effects to the official armed forces from both sides of the border.

Quicksilver and I had never been spotted.

Apparently the military mind was the least vulnerable to—or most prejudiced against—Millennium Revelation influences, just like Ric's foster father, the retired military man.

"Good thing," Tallgrass said when I mentioned that. "Official forces have to obey orders at once, without hesitation. The brass doesn't want unhuman hocus-pocus distracting them from their mission."

"So the destroyed zombies they find are—?"

"Opposing cartel fighters their flamethrowers and

handheld missiles *really* bent out of shape," he answered with a chuckle.

At the motel, he hauled Ric into our room and installed him in the single sleeping bag on the floor without comment. When Tallgrass bid me good night, Quicksilver followed him to the door and then sat on the floor and moved no farther.

Someone had lost a roommate.

"Lock up good, Miss Delilah," Tallgrass told me, giving me a forefinger salute before shutting the door behind him.

IN THE MORNING I drove the Jeep across the international bridge.

Tallgrass insisted Ric and I cover our clothes with camos. That and some official military personnel papers Tallgrass produced got our party through the border stations with only a cursory inspection of the vehicle.

Quicksilver following every move of the border officers with eyes and slightly open jaws speeded up the routine considerably. As for the duffel bags harboring any suspect items, I assumed the guys' weapons were buried deep in the desert with the femicides.

Me, I was just glad that I didn't have to produce a passport. Even if I'd taken Ashley Martinez's passport, its theft had surely been reported by now.

When we got to the El Paso garage where I'd parked Dolly, Ric and I stripped off the camos to our street clothes. Quicksilver jumped out to inspect Dolly's chassis from chrome bumper bullets to rear Cadillac insignia on the trunk.

"This where I say adios," Tallgrass told me and Ric. "I got a short walk to a shortish flight to Wichita. You good for the long drive, amigo?"

"I did it solo and can again," I was quick to point out.

"I know, Del," Ric said with a flash of returning humor. "Make a guy feel redundant, why don't you?"

I stepped close to rub my thumb under his lower lip and feel the rasp of that sexy three-day smudge of beard growth. "No worries. I just like to feel this guy."

Tallgrass cleared his throat.

"Ric, there may still be some . . . lingering presence of El Demonio out there and after you," he warned us. "Losing any confrontation just makes his type of supernatural more vicious if he shifted into another form, so be careful."

Ric nodded, clasping forearms with his one-time mentor.

Tallgrass tipped his straw Western hat to me. "You let that dog take care of you, Miss Delilah, and you'll never go wrong."

"I take care of him."

"You think."

He turned and left us beside Dolly. We listened until the echo of his cowboy-booted amble faded entirely. Quicksilver whimpered.

"I drive first," I said, not looking at Ric.

"Yes, ma'am," he answered in mock military tones. "Just as long as I drive last."

FUNNY, IT DIDN'T work out that way. I guess raising a killing field of zombies can wear a guy out. Not to mention what I put him through before and after in that sleeping bag.

I never thought seeing the neon fireworks of the Vegas Strip quivering like the aurora borealis on the night horizon would make me feel the relief of coming home.

From a distance, the place didn't look infested by werewolves, vampires, and even completely human corporate-greed moguls.

"Okay if I drop you off at home?" I asked Ric, who was stretched out in the roomy Caddy passenger seat, dozing. Quicksilver did likewise on the rear seat.

I felt good about handling the last leg of the trip while my guys slept. The bad taste in my memory of being left behind like a girl had evaporated.

"Makes sense," Ric murmured. "Then we both have wheels in the morning."

Another bad taste in my memory had not faded. I knew I'd have to do something about it. That would be *my* show-down in the Valley of the Virgin, but it could wait.

Meanwhile, Ric was reviving nicely. He pushed him-self upright.

"You feeling okay?" I asked. "No remaining pain from your hands, the impact of Torbellino's magic bullets?"

"I'm coming back fast, *chica*. It was a good sign that the showdown with El Demonio took place in the Valley of Guadalupe. We had the blessing of the Virgin, who visited and comforted me during my childhood enslavement."

"But . . . but that's not what unreeled in the cloud cover over Juarez."

"Sure it was, Del. You saw it too. Haven't you ever seen a holy card of the Virgin of Guadalupe?"

That comment stunned me. "Remind me again how the Virgin manifests herself. She was the first and last Latina manifestation of the Virgin Mary, I know."

I also knew that, while driven by El Demonio's whip to raise zombies in the Mojave Desert, the child Ric was sure the Virgin of Guadalupe had visited him in the goat pens at night. So he ought to recognize her when he saw her.

Hmm, Irma mused. *You do also recall that his last*

*vision of the Virgin coincided with a vampire bat bite
and the photo of a female hottie from one of the zombie-
runners' dirty magazines? Hello, first wet dream. Bye, bye
Our Lady of Guadalupe. Until now?*

I glanced at the passenger seat. Ric's narrowed eyes
were fixed on the gleaming towers of Vegas growing closer.
His face broadcast pleasure as he consulted his memory.

"I saw this beseeching . . . compassionate female face
of transforming beauty. Our Lady of Guadalupe folds her
hands before her. Her form in its heavenly blue cloak of
sky is hallowed with golden rays. She comes with the scent
of roses in the desert, which she let tumble from her cloak
for the peasant Juan Diego."

"The guy who was secretly Zorro?"

"That was *Don* Diego." Ric looked over and saw I'd
been teasing. "Okay, *chica,* maybe only my subconscious
conjured her when I was a prisoner of Torbellino and his
gang, but it helped keep me sane. She'd told Juan Diego
she was 'Entirely and Ever Virgin and your compassionate Mother,' so Mexicans have prayed to her for protection
from all evil for more than five hundred years."

"And they need it now more than ever," I warned. "Your
psychologist foster mother would tell you that if ever there
was a kid's wish fulfillment fantasy, an exploited child's
patron saint, it would be that paradox of endless virginal
purity and boundless maternal love."

"Yet fate sent me an aging virgin," he said with a wink.

"Not *that* old, Montoya!"

"Modern rationalizations like yours don't work nowadays. I was a child when I first saw the Virgin of Guadalupe. What I saw in that cursed place in Juarez tonight,
above those hundreds of unmarked graves of violated girls,
was like the Virgin, but pale-skinned, Anglo not Mexi-

can, more a peasant Joan of Arc, who was also a warrior woman and a saint. This figure of the clouds and the moon didn't look modern, with her simple gown and hair. She seemed an ordinary young woman, yet her encompassing arms sheltered a horde of cowering children."

I recognized the Good Maria from *Metropolis*, of course, but I kept my mouth shut. Like a virgin.

"That vision," Ric said, "gave me the strength to drive my nails into my palms until the blood flowed and the dead returned, like roses springing up in the desert, alive again and lethal to evil."

I'd seen a lot of bizarre and terrifying and impossible things since the Millennium Revelation had sprung a whole new supernatural dimension of life on earth on us all. Just before he'd raised the femicides, I'd thought Ric had gone mad.

Afterward, Quicksilver's healing tongue had erased the stigmata on Ric's palms. Most people would say he'd been hallucinating, except I'd shared his sky-borne vision.

Only *I* hadn't seen *Metropolis*'s saintly working-class girl, Maria, obviously a Virgin Mary stand-in, begging the heedless rich to pity and help the poor children.

Silent now, I let my brain attempt to superimpose the Virgin Mary over the drive-in movie screen-in-the-sky image *I'd* seen . . . the virtually nude, jewel-draped, pastie-wearing pagan goddess-cum-Folies-Bergère chorus girl, the Whore of Babylon from Revelations in the bible, another face of the same actress from the same film. Brigitte Helm.

Just as the dancing girl Maria seduced from a stage upheld by the Seven Deadly Sins, her sky-cast image had transfixed Torbellino's hundreds of human cartel "soldiers" in suspended motion to be mowed down by Tallgrass's bullets and the resurrected femicides' power to avenge.

What had really happened there?

All other CinSims were the image of the actor and the role. The Silver Zombie had many roles and a silver metal face and form to hide her true intentions behind.

Ric's religious vision of the Virgin Mary made more sense and soothed the savage soul he'd had to resurrect to destroy El Demonio and his human and unhuman armies.

I'd never forget that swarm of avenging Amazons, hundreds of brutalized girls rising strong and whole, clothed not in the "sun and stars" of the Virgin Mary but in the piecemeal Joan of Arc armor of the shattered Silver Zombie as she drew on the might of machine to vanquish the demonic lord's robotic male zombies and also used the hypnotic succubus powers of the Eternal Feminine to destroy brutal human men and the demon who commanded them.

In my mind's eye, our insubstantial savior had been one hot mama with the sensual, paranormal power of a succubus gone CinemaScope. That's what I'd seen Ric animate with the gaze of his silver iris, magically, without resorting to dowsing rod or blood, as he always did.

So the three faces of Maria in the film still lurked in the sky above and haunted and worried me. When she was good, she was very good. When she was bad, she was catastrophic. And when she was the link between the Good and the Bad, the anatomically correct sexy silver robot destroyed at the film's end—and the tool of somebody else—she was badder than anything.

Those thoughts jerked me out of my speculations. I had my own secret moments of being badder than anything, especially if they involved Snow.

During the duel in the sky, Ric had unconsciously drawn on both sides of Maria, saint and succubus. The Seven Deadly Sins' featured appearance, however, could have only been sent by the resident power at the Inferno Hotel, Cocaine, who played the lead deadly sin of Pride in the rock group's lineup and was *my* Silver Zombie.

Snow.

El Demonio Torbellino, or whatever remnants of him that might still be circling out there like a mist of evil struggling to take physical form, was not sitting down for a debriefing with me, but I could certainly put Snow to the question.

He always enjoyed destroying my illusions about my world, and myself. In this town, that meant that he was also the best thing that passed for truth.

Chapter Thirty-five

"GODFREY," I SAID.

He stood at my Enchanted Cottage front door, as formal as usual in white tie and black morning coat, but held a most unusual silver salver in one hand. His pencil-thin mustache took a stern downward turn.

I wasn't dressed for company, wearing my Betty Boop sleep shirt and a bedhead.

"Miss Delilah, a personal invitation for you was delivered to the main house. I saw early this morning that your Miss Dolly was parked aslant in the driveway and her normally shiny black coat was dulled with dust. I took the liberty of assigning an individual named Woodrow, who was idling about the area, to have her seen to."

"Oh, you didn't, Godfrey."

"I just told you I did."

"Woodrow is a yard troll. If it's green and growing, or, eh, brown and dirty and in need of picking up, he will do that, the brown part very reluctantly. *Dust* in *any* form is not on his duty roster."

"Apparently he found some unemployed pixies to handle the chore. Miss Dolly is her usual self again. I'm afraid I can't say the same about you."

I'd slept about sixteen hours and stumbled down to the kitchen for a hearty breakfast of sliders and McDonald's fries from the kitchen witch. Apparently she was annoyed with me as well. Quick and I were about to

make short work of the fast food when the doorbell had
rung.

I gazed again at the salver. At least somebody wasn't
A large square envelope was centered exactly on its
center, held in place by a slender Mexican quartz letter
opener.

"You say that's for me?"

"If you are Miss Delilah Street and not some unkempt
pretender."

"Can it, Godfrey. I've had a rough road trip to Mexico
and back."

With that I snatched the letter opener and pushed it
through the heavy rag paper so hard I got a jagged edge
instead of a neat slit.

I pulled out an embossed card on pristine white stock
and read the wedding invitation script very slowly, because
it was so ornate it was almost unreadable.

Christophe invites you to be his special guest

at a private party at 8:00 p.m. tonight

for the unveiling of a dazzling new Las Vegas landmark.

The Penthouse, Inferno Hotel and Casino on the Strip

Black Tie

"Nerve incarnate," I complained. "Not even an RSVP
as if he was certain I'd come running. Who delivered this?"

"A most unique individual from a messenger service."

I believed I'd received something from just such a mes
senger once before, the silver familiar.

I looked at my wrist, which was . . . watchless. Godfrey

lifted his left arm, shook down his formal white cuff, and offered his round-dialed wristwatch for my perusal.

"Four fifteen? Must be p.m.," I mumbled.

A nearby whimper made me wake up even more to spot Quicksilver beside me, presenting Godfrey with a furry and furrowed brow.

"Master Quicksilver, good afternoon," Godfrey said. "Thank you for the heads-up. Miss Delilah, you're exhausted. Why didn't you say so? Do sit down. There's a clever little bench just inside the door."

I took his advice, surprised that my knees were a bit wobbly. No food in sixteen hours will do that to my metabolism. For some reason Godfrey was reluctant to cross my threshold. I didn't know if it was because a proper butler would never do that, or because, as a CinSim, he wasn't chipped to roam that far.

"May I see?" Godfrey extended a hand. It did not cross the threshold.

I handed the card over it.

"I see," he murmured after a couple moments. "Rather formal for a piece of public relations ballyhoo. Are you going?"

"Of course not." I pushed a hand through my hair. Hornet's nests would be more manageable. "It's unspeakably rude."

"Certainly on inexcusably short notice."

"As I said, rude."

"Inarguably."

"And I could never get ready that fast."

"The last straw."

"That's right, Godfrey. The cardinal sin against Miss Manners. How could I possibly attend a formal affair tonight? Last night I slept in a sleeping bag on the floor of a fleabag motel in the murder capital of the world. The night before that I was up to my knees in rattlesnakes and lizards and tarantulas, big ones, Godfrey, running behind an army of desert dust devils and—"

"Please." Godfrey's palms were raised. "No more sordid confessions of the great outdoors. I am an urban animal, Miss Delilah. However, if your emergency is of a social nature, I'm your man. I'll return to the main house to organize the troops and arrange for a car to pick you up at seven thirty."

"Dolly's all bathed and polished, you said—"

"A lady does not drive herself."

He was gone before I could set him straight on that. My head was whirling. Food. That's right. I sleepwalked through the front parlor, past the high-tech office/home theater to the kitchen.

Where Quicksilver was wolfing down the last of the sliders and fries.

"Quick!"

The microwave tinged. A heavenly scent of beef *bourguignon* filled the air. I got it. The fast food had gone cold. I took out a savory, steaming dish and headed, salivating, for the kitchen table.

A martini in a chilled glass sat beside my empty place with the sterling silver tableware.

Apparently the kitchen witch had undergone a change of menu.

My cell phone rang. I couldn't remember where I'd left it, but Quick dashed out of the room and returned with it in his mouth, smiling around the case.

"Uh, thanks." I eyed the screen. Ric? Ric!

"I just got this crazy-assed invitation," he began.

"Me too. Who brought yours?"

"I'm going to sound like I'm hallucinating. A little green man."

"Did he wear silver sandals and have hairy hammer-toes?"

"I don't check out feet and shoes first, Del. He was some kind of benign troll with rubbery green skin, in matching lederhosen."

"That's Mercury Express, Homegrown Delivery Service. A lot of the Strip joints use them around town." And one in particular from my previous experience.

"You mean enterprises *on* the Strip."

"That's what I said. I'm still tired as hell, but I'm also as curious as hell."

"You game? I haven't gotten my tux out in year."

"You own a tux?"

"Yeah. Business reasons."

"I love men in tuxes."

"Down, *chica*. I am not the Godfrey type. No little bow ties playing peekaboo under *my* five-o-clock shadow. It's more actors at the Oscars style. Regular tie, a little black satin here and there."

"Like your sheets. Yum. Oh, and don't shave off all that bandito beard-growth you cultivated in Mexico."

"So you're into black satin and beard burns, huh?"

"No comment. It's just . . . we deserve to put on the Ritz. Celebrate being alive. Find out what Snow's up to. This sounds like a mega-event."

"Like the Oscars. We haven't had a real night out for a while. You deserve to dazzle the Strip, *amor*.

"Anyway, *my* Godfrey is sending a car for us."

"So the night's on Nightwine and Christophe. Sweet. Bring on the spice."

I put down the phone and dug into dinner. It was delicious. I could hear the spa bubbling upstairs and took my martini glass with me. When I walked into the bedroom, my ruby red slippers from Emerald City Hotel and Casino in Wichita were sitting under the wall-mounted clothes rack, from which hung the scarlet silk velvet Nora Charles gown that was a prize of the city's estate sales, like Dolly.

I dropped off Betty Boop on my bedroom floor on my way to the bathroom.

IF YOU'VE EVER seen the Disney *Cinderella*—and what girl child hasn't, even me in a group home—that's how everything went. I bubbled, I showered and washed my hair, I blow-dried it, I put on party makeup . . . for me just eye shadow and lip gloss and . . . dazzle dust here and there, but I didn't do it.

Maybe invisible little birds did it with their tiny beaks and tiny wings, maybe bluebirds that fly over the rainbow, but the blow-dryer magically put every hair in its fluffiest, shiniest place. The lip gloss wand rolled into my hand in a prechosen color. Ravaging Red, I saw when I looked. The clear mascara skated onto my naturally black eyelashes and shaped my eyebrows as if they'd been plucked by Kevyn Aucoin to look just like Elizabeth Taylor in her prime. It was a reality TV fantasy.

The red sequined slippers fit perfectly, and I even got a matching Snow White headband with the stubby little bow at the top. Cutesy, but so classic. And on my dresser top, another estate-sale prize, the familiar going red carpet as a small rhinestone-covered nineteen-thirties bag just the right size for my cell phone, credit card, driver's license, lip gloss, and forty bucks to see me through any transportation emergency if my date acted up. As I hoped he would.

I checked my gown out in the mirror, red, yes, with full

sweeping sleeves and long, rhinestoned cuffs at the wrist. No watch. A high-collared neck and long, trumpet skirt. Discreet slits from shoulder to cuff and nape to waist, but otherwise as modest as a nun's habit.

What was this? Maybe Group Home Girl finally free of her past and slaloming Olympic-style headfirst into her future. Heigh-ho the evil demon is dead. Ric is free and I am home free.

I tripped down the stairs (you can do that only in Disney movies) and ran to the front door, where a man in a chauffeur's cap waited like Godfrey.

The Lincoln Town Car also awaited, the discreet celebrity choice. Godfrey would never endorse the ostentation of a limo.

Ric was waiting inside.

"Hombre," I said, "you rock me," as I sank into the backseat and his arms.

And we were off to see the wizard and his mysterious unveiling. Maybe he'd even reveal just what kind of supernatural he was.

Chapter Thirty-six

"I'M IMPRESSED," RIC said.

"By what?"

"You know just where the penthouse elevator is at the Inferno. I had to hunt it up."

"But you'd used the Nine Circles of Hell elevators when I caught up with you."

"Before that, I mean," he explained, "when I checked out Christophe's personal setup before I investigated his entertainment section."

"It's good you've at last had a chat with him, man to man. Or whatever he is."

"He does play the mystery card, doesn't he?"

"So you went from the penthouse to the Lust level? Anything he said?"

"I visited the Inferno Bar too, to check with Godfrey's alter ego, Nick Charles, and company. That Asta is cute, not to mention Nora, but Quicksilver, of course, is Serious Dog."

"You *are* the thorough investigator. We'd better plan for a second act tonight," I told him as the elevator arrived and swallowed us up. "This announcement and celebration is scheduled for the break Snow has between evening stage shows. It's just a stop before we move on elsewhere to party hard."

"Okay. Time to flaunt our fine feathers and for some bubbly and a toast to the latest Christophe triumph, and we're off to where . . . ? The Venetian?"

I nodded happily.

"I'm not moving in with Christophe," Ric whispered in my ear. "Trust me."

"One thing about that facedown in the desert. What does *El Finado* mean?"

"What?" Ric mocked. "You're not keeping up with your Spanish dictionary?"

"El Demonio's real men, the actual human vermin, were chanting that as they perished."

"Did they? I was in my own Zen place then. They must have gotten the gender wrong. You know Spanish has masculine and feminine words."

"Sí, señor." I copped a feel of the Spanish masculine.

"Del." He laughed and swung his hips back. "The elevator has a security camera. Concentrate on your Spanish grammar until later. *El Finado* is like *El Muerto*. My culture doesn't fear death and the dead as Anglo culture does. We personalize concepts like Death."

"Like *El Muerto* is Death, our guy with the scythe, only he's got the grinning skull down cold."

"Right."

"So if *El Muerto* is Death, who is *El Finado*?"

"A corpse. *The* corpse. That's what a corpse is called."

Oh. My heart stopped.

Maybe I was *La Finada*. That's what the dying men would have called out if they were addressing the femicide army. Or maybe not. Some words don't have a feminine version in Spanish.

The elevator spit us out into the White Zone.

Snow wasn't immediately visible, as he usually was, like Godfrey. I felt a ping of unease as Ric and I moved into the main room. Maybe everybody was *finado*, and it had all happened while we were riding up in the sixty-story elevator.

I'd expected a murmuring, champagne-swilling crowd and waiters skating by with appetizers and Appletinis. The place was as silent as a tomb, a gorgeously designed and posh tomb, but deadly quiet nevertheless.

The penthouse was . . . deserted. I was walking through a dream.

"There's one thing I envy Christophe," Ric admitted. "I love the view from here." He swept me to the window wall.

Far down the Strip I spotted the huge lit billboard for Madrigal and the fey girls. Once it had advertised the iconic big cat magicians Siegfried and Roy, a sad reminder of how even decades of Vegas headlining could vanish in one tragic moment. Nothing lasted.

"It's a shame," Ric said, "that huge construction next door is blocking our view."

"I'm amazed Snow would tolerate that kind of infringement. I guess somebody paid a bunch of billions to smuggle their new concept against the Inferno."

"Let me tell you, the Lust level right here is pretty spectacular. *What?* Delilah, I'm saying you should take a stroll down there, *chica*. Discover what, or who you find. It's pretty illuminating."

I knew I should give him heck for that when I heard the elevator arrive.

We turned.

Another couple entered the foyer.

Grizelle and . . . Snow in full white leather rock-concert regalia.

Ric took a deep breath next to me. He'd never seen Snow's raunchy rock uniform up close and Grizelle was wearing a strapless sheath of magenta sequins that showed lots of her black skin with its glistening pattern of charcoal gray tiger stripes.

They made a spectacular pair. Both tall, she black and runway-beautiful. He platinum blond-on-blond.

"This is it?" I demanded.

I looked around, then realized why the place felt so deserted. No Silver Zombie was plunked against the wall like a family suit of armor.

But the bar, I saw, now boasted a silver ice bucket on a tripod and a bottle of Cristal champagne. And four flutes full of bubbly all in a row.

"This is it?" I asked again.

I was right. Ric and I *were* the show break.

"Grizelle," Snow invited his security chief-cum-arm-candy.

She plucked up two of the flutes to give to me and Ric. Seeing the haughty shape-shifter fetch was worth about ten cents.

Snow ambled to the window, Tallgrass style, a champagne flute in his pale, ringed hands.

"You're here for the birth of a billboard," he said, nodding to the Strip scenery.

Even as he spoke, of course, there appeared a Times Square scrolling–light billboard, with a scarily larger-than-life-size image of Snow prerecorded with audio that was piped onto the Strip and into the penthouse.

Way to hold a press conference, dude! I downed some champagne.

"Ladies and gentlemen," the filmed Snow far below but way larger than life announced. "I give you the Inferno's newest expansion and Vegas's most dazzling must-see, must-go-to venue, the *Metropolis*."

Half the view outside the window shifted, crumbled, sank, as if the earth had set on the moon. A total reverse of reality.

The massive construction framework next to the Inferno melted as the concealing curtain it really was—painted with a faux facade—fell like a finished Christo building wrap.

Behind the curtain towered a golden glass and metal skyscraper surmounted by a five-tiered horned-roofed Babel, all from the silent film, *Metropolis*, except it was maybe sixty-five stories high.

What an astounding, instant Dubai architectural-excess sort of monument. This was definitely Ric's and my week for seeing giant icons in the sky, and I for one was sick of it.

"There it is," Snow said. "My new Metropolis Tower. Casinos, nightclubs, five-star dining venues below, lavish suites above. All yours, Montoya, except for the profits, of course, which you'd never take anyway. Below the pinnacle, a Vegas landmark that is protection in itself. Above, your own penthouse, a floor for the Silver Zombie. Utter security. A headquarters for your new crusades. Every technological and magical investigative tool you can imagine. You're King of the World."

Ric turned to pin down Snow with a hawkish gaze. "And you're not overlord of it? You're not even on the premises?"

"You rule. Call me a . . . neighbor . . . with a financial interest in the crass commercial machine that will fuel your work to destroy the zombie and drug trade."

"You're serious?" Ric responded to the one thing that tempted him, not beauty and excess and money, but power against evil. "I can continue my incursions against the cartels?"

"Expand them, Montoya. Think as big as the edifice I've built for you."

Ric hesitated, cast me a glance. "And Delilah?"

"Your partner. Your lover. She can live with you there, or be a frequent visitor and ally staying low-profile and down-Strip on Nightwine's secure estate. Nothing changes but your immense resources in the fight against international crime.

"Grizelle." Snow turned to order his security chief. "Second-show performance time nipping at my heels. Take Señor Montoya and Miss Street on a tour of this new facility, and his new possibilities."

Ric hesitated, stared out the window at the glimmering golden vista, and then turned his gaze to me. He wore his brown contact lens and looked perfectly normal, as well as perfect.

"Go ahead. I'll be right along." I lifted my Lalique flute. "After I finish the expensive champagne."

Grizelle glared at me, and then at her boss, but took Ric's arm in hers.

"Consider me your personal wiki on all things *Metropolis*," she told him in a royal white-tiger purr few mortal men could resist.

Ric could, but he was taking some time to measure the law enforcement benefits against the personal debits. Still, Grizelle had major femme fatale paws on him and used her hypnotic green gaze to put him into a limbo of confusion.

The private elevator opened its stainless steel maw to swallow them.

I turned on Snow to present my own stainless steel maw.

"You're quite the seducer." My crisp cool voice matched the champagne without the producing any heady bubbles.

"I just didn't realize you targeted men as well. An entire Las Vegas tower as a funding agency and headquarters and home base? What is that new Metropolis tower, really Christophe, The Daily Planet?"

Snow strode to the bar and returned with the champagne bottle to fill my glass to the brim.

"You're not tired of champagne, Delilah, but you're aching for battle for some reason. I've finessed your high card from you, admit it. You should also admit that protecting Ricardo Montoya comes second to safeguarding your ego. I can offer him so much more security than you can."

"Speaking of seconds, don't you have another show to do?"

He refilled his own glass and faced off against me. "You know I have a CinSim substitute available to play me onstage. I can stay here and argue with you all night if you want. And enjoy it. As you will."

I eyed his obvious, post-Elvis getup. "No wonder a Cin-Sim can step in for you any time. Your act is a flashy, cheap, neo-Strip cliché, and so are you. Ric is not an attraction to be bought away from a competitor."

"And you've always been my competitor."

"Hardly. You're a leech. I created two cocktails on your premises and you copped them for the profits."

"The Albino Vampire cocktail was your admittedly inspired way of flashing me the bird of paradise," he said. "The Brimstone Kiss was an accidental tribute . . . to *me* and my stage show, used to . . . seduce . . . a hard-boiled CinSim at my Inferno bar into giving up some information that would save your sacred Ric. Who is used and who using? Are you so pure, Delilah, and I so damned?"

He went to a white Louie XVI desk I'd never noticed

on the fringe of his main room, ripped something off a horizontal notebook, and returned to flourish it in front of my nose.

"That gown you're wearing is seriously schizophrenic, by the way, as modest as a red lamé bikini on a nun. I like it way too much for anyone's sanity."

The check drowned out all commentary. Forty thousand dollars. My ears buzzed.

"Your royalties so far on the Inferno house cocktails," Snow said. "More will ensue. I pay my debts."

"I don't want your money," I said automatically.

"Better to take that than what you really want of me."

"This is not about any of us or what we want. It's all about Ric."

Those words came from the most fearful voice of my heart crying out, much as I hated to parade that raw fear in front of Snow.

"Ric can't be killed," I said. "I've seen it twice in a few days. The first time was the Murderers Level Seven in your ersatz Hell. A poisoned centaur arrow couldn't down him. I wanted to believe it was a surface scratch, but I later saw there was no mark at all from a wound meant to torment even dead men and that would be devastating to mortals.

"I saw it again against El Demonio. Ric cannot be killed. El Demonio is dead, maybe, but . . . *El Finado* isn't."

"El Finado?"

"At first I thought the phrase referred to a defeated Torbellino. *Finished*. But no, it means 'corpse.' It's what the cartel scum called Ric in Juarez when he took El Demonio Torbellino down . . . just two nights ago. 'The dead body. Corpse.' "

I froze like the Silver Zombie at attention, feeling the enormity of my fear and the suspicion I'd repressed so fiercely and at my idiocy in downloading it here and now.

I let Snow lead me like a lamb to the bar and refill my champagne flute even though my head was reeling almost more than my emotions. I drank and started to feel my fingertips and toes again, but my heart remained ice cold.

"Ric doesn't need me, or you," I told him. "Or your Metropolis Tower, or the bloody Silver Zombie. He can*not* be killed. He's a vampire. I made him one by bringing him back from the dead. I can't allow myself to be . . . fed upon. I just can't."

I stood panting, emptied, exhausted by the truth I'd fought to keep from touching me.

Snow edged away, then circled my tensed and furious form.

"You won back Ric's life . . . forever. That should make you very happy," he said. Carefully. "It's everything you fought for with every fiber of your being, with every beat of your human heart, everything that you believe in."

I took a deep breath, but it shook, and shook me. "You've always known what he had to become to stay alive, Snow. I hate you for knowing that and letting me dream on, but that changes nothing. What matters is that Ric's not . . . normal anymore."

"And you are?"

"I never was, was I? But Ric had . . . overcome all that. He'd sailed through the Millennium Revelation. Turned tragedy into triumph. Predestination into freedom. An ancient folk ability into a modern phenomenon. He's taken on the supernatural drug lords and human traffickers and won. Yet now he's not mortal! They won. He's no longer human."

"And you are?'

"I don't know. I do know I can't be . . . drained, for love or money. I am more than my blood, or my bloodline. Sansouci claimed you needed me. You, who need nothing. You with your Hell below and your Metropolis above. Tell me what you need me to do, Angel of Death, to make Ric mortal again."

"Can't be done, Delilah. That was over under the Karnak Hotel even as you transferred my Brimstone Kiss to his lips. Impossible desire can't reverse anything."

"I kissed him alive. What can I do now to kiss him undead?"

"Even true love is sometimes lust, Delilah. The Seven Deadly Sins must always have their tribute. Fortunately, you have tendencies despite yourself."

"Tendencies?"

"You're far from perfect, and that's perfectly human."

Why did he have to rub in that I wasn't a supernatural, like him and Sansouci and everybody I knew, including . . . Ric now.

"And you don't really hate me." Snow moved toward me. "Hate is inspired by something you see of yourself in someone else that you're not ready to admit."

If it wasn't Snow I hated, it was the damn calculated stagy sexiness of a breed I despised, a woman-using rock star who actually had the charisma and—could it be?— the *soul* to seduce the upright, maybe uptight, liberated woman I liked to think was me.

Oh . . . *not* God.

Champagne is a fast drunk. And anger is an aphrodisiac.

I learned that lesson for once and all when I stood hypnotized, watching Snow's white snakeskin boot-toes slide across the plush carpet. I couldn't read his intentions . . . hostile or worse, personal.

I wanted to face off Snow, to lift my eyes to his cheatin' heart and sunglasses, but they insisted on keeping a groupie's mosh-pit-eye view and moved from those boots up to his white-leather-clasped thighs and . . . tight-stretched leather-swathed pelvis and . . . torso bared from the hip-slung belt above the jeweled fly to sculpted chest muscles endorsed by Jack Frost with jagged edges of scar tissue and . . . to a corded neck branded with the cheesy purple passion emblem of my most inflamed soul kiss at the hollow of his throat . . . to his pale white lips . . . that a woman might want to kiss until they reddened . . . or to bite until they bled.

The Snow groupies online had called him Ice Prick. I liked the sound of that, ice meeting fire, ice melting into me. They'd tossed around imagined dimensions, as if for rainfall. Didn't matter, just the sky raining down moisture, just the earth giving ground.

I could see why the groupies found him totally tasty. I'd already dipped an 'impudent toe' into that pool of sexy whitewater and found it unforgettable. I'd seen how my mouth and lips could blaze a hot, warming trail over his albino skin, his scars, his Sanscouci tits, over the entire bleached, muscled, beloved Carrara marble of Michelangelo's *David* come to life.

Did I want him groveling at my feet—toes would do—or conquering me utterly?

I was your typical conflicted modern woman. And he knew it.

His hand cupped the back of my skull, brought my lips to the hollow of his throat. "Yes, I know."

I told you he was obvious.

I tried and failed to shake off his erotic spell. My lips met the familiar cool skin—once surprising myself at the Emerald City, now surprising no one here, neither of us—and fastened hard with intent to suck another soul-shaking orgasm out of him. Just to prove . . . I didn't know what, that I could be a vampire too? That I might as well be one now?

At this moment I believed he'd let me chain him between two pillars, his dark-glasses-shielded eyes blinded by the light, and die from pleasure. I wanted to feel those pillars shake, rattle, and roll, because of me.

Except . . .

Shoot. Biblical femme fatales weren't my style. Not really.

I broke the contact and stepped away, admiring the still smoldering trace of my handiwork on his perfect body.

"So I'm human," I said. "You're not. How can I help Ric be even better than both of us?"

"Admit the truth about him, as long as you're at it." Snow stepped back, unshaken by my about-face, to drain his champagne glass.

Every little thing he did was magic, or so I thought, watching my blood bruise seem to throb on his throat as he drank. I was developing a serious addiction problem. I understood Sansouci now.

Ric loves you.

And me, him.

I want you.

And I like him, an honest vampire in a naughty world, bless him.

And Snow needs you.

That is probably true, but I don't know why. And not knowing why is my most unacceptable condition.

Snow began pacing the lush carpet. "You can't hide from me or yourself anymore, Delilah. You have to understand what's happening. In the desert, Montoya called on the Silver Zombie. You called on me."

"No. I didn't. I'd never ask you for help."

"Never? Why, Delilah? Why never?'

"I . . . don't do that."

"Maybe you should try it sometimes. Everybody needs help sometimes."

"Even you?"

"Especially me now that I'm . . . defaced."

Oh, kick me in the conscience, why don't you? "I didn't consciously call on you." I'd remembered calling to the heavens for help, to any force anywhere.

"You did. And I came."

Well, that was unfortunately too true, a few days before in Wichita.

"I just wanted to save Ric. He had the Silver Zombie to call on. You're saying you had to butt in with the Seven Deadly Sins because of me?"

"The Sins only come when called." Snow paced close again, tossed his long hair so the very ends sizzled across my skin. "And only you can call on me."

"I didn't ask for that favor. It was Ric drawing down the power of the Silver Zombie that saved that situation in the Valley of Guadalupe."

"He *survived* it, Delilah. We all need more than mere survival."

I recalled a favorite line: "Pay no attention to the man behind the curtain."

Snow had certainly been that man tonight as he rang down the false front to reveal the new Metropolis he'd already built with a lot of money and also magic, probably.

Now Snow stood watching me. Waiting for me. I eyed the pulse in his throat and leaned forward to place my fingers on the beating blue-purple bruise.

"Why won't this fade?" I asked.

"Maybe a succubus comes every night to renew it. Do you have any succubus tendencies, Delilah?"

"In your dreams."

"That's the place."

I managed a smile.

Sansouci's mantra replayed in my head.

Ric loves you.

I want you.

Snow needs you.

And I needed, maybe wanted, all of the above.

"You *are* the Silver Zombie, Delilah." Snow had recognized my confusion and indecision and zeroed in. "*You* are the bleeding-heart purity of Mother Maria and you are the hot-blooded temptress who drives men to extremes, maybe bad, but maybe good despite themselves. The Silver Zombie is celibacy and sexuality in one contradictory, addictive package. Don't think I don't know all about that. But *you*, on the other hand, know nothing of my curse."

"Curse?" That sobered me up fast. I stepped back. "You've been cursed. For how long?"

A white eyebrow lifted above the black sunglasses. A reporter soon learns nobody ever wants to tell you his or her age. Especially nowadays.

"How?" I asked next.

"Isn't it obvious why I keep the groupies in their mosh pit forever? I can only give pleasure, never receive it."

No! Yes. That would explain the Brimstone Kiss, the ultimate dead-end pleasure trip for women. It wouldn't explain . . .

"But . . . when I . . . we—"

Can a smile both calm and sting?

"Every curse has an antidote, Delilah," Snow said. "That's the quest that keeps me going for . . . however long I have been. You can always find an antidote. Some*time*. Some*where*. Some*body*."

I'd truly been shocked sober.

"You're going to have to decide who you're safest with, and who's safest with you." Sansouci's words again.

Or, I added mentally: who I most want and need to save and who most wants and needs to save me.

Not a cakewalk.

No, indeed.

I left without another word.

Finis for now.

AT HOME IN the Enchanted Cottage, I worked on dozing off with my e-reader on my stomach.

My red velvet gown had disappeared into the cottage's bottomless closet, probably snuggling up to the green silk one from Wichita and the ivory satin thirties wedding dress Ric had unbuttoned all seventy-two buttons of, up the sleeves and down the back. The Mrs. Peel section was Sansouci's. I've always been a versatile chick.

I've set the ruby red slippers on my dresser as a reminder.

No, they're not a reminder of the night's intense discoveries.

What I need to remember was that Dorothy had finally got her head and heart together and figured a way home from Oz.

Ric had called to say he was trying out an overnight at the Metropolis. He sounded as eager as a Boy Scout on a camping trip. I'd promised to come and see in the morning.

Sansouci was somewhere in the night ministering to needy cougar and choir girl alike, imagining I could someday be his sole companion for a short off-road idyll in his long, long life span.

Snow was still onstage, his unhealed back wounds massaged by tight leather, making him writhe even more incitingly for the groupies in the mosh pit. In post–Millennium Revelation Las Vegas, someone's pleasure is all too often someone else's pain.

Quicksilver is lying under my bedroom window, gnawing on a treat whose source I don't want to know.

"Me Delilah, you Quicksilver," I say.

He looks up with those winter-blue eyes, jaws calmly cracking unlabeled animal sinews.

"I rescued you in Sunset Park, you rescue me everywhere else."

Chomp, chomp. Smile, smile.

"I master. You . . . sidekick."

Pause. Paws crossed. Really adorable posture, not so adorable expression. Silence.

"We both should leave Vegas and relocate to a monastery in Tibet. What do you say?"

Pause. Growl. Leap up, nose open window. Vanish for the night to exercise his needs to chase prey and enticing bitches.

Males! Can't live with them, can't live without them.

Correction: given recent events, they can't live without me.

So I finally exit to Dreamland, where I'm climbing the seventeen-foot height of the Caesars Palace reproduction of Michelangelo's *David* like I'd once climbed the pillar likeness of Shezmou to free the chained demon god of the slaughter by bringing his avatar to earth and commercial success on the Las Vegas Strip.

Michelangelo loved men and the male form. I'm not indifferent. In my dream, I find I can turn David's sculpted muscles of white Carrara marble, cold stone, into living flesh tones with the kisses of my brimstone mouth, but it will take a really long, long time to cover all that territory.

I guess I can make the climb with a little help from my friends, lover and would-be lovers, and my frenemies.

Delilah's Darkside Inferno Bar
Cocktail Menu

Virtual Virgins
Invented in *Silver Zombie*

"Love it. A Virtual Virgin, wouldn't that be fun to dabble in again?"
—Psychic psychologist Helena Troy Burnside in *Silver Zombie*

Virtuous Virtual Virgin
3 ounces chilled Dr Pepper or cherry Coke
3 ounces chilled lemon-lime sparkling bottled water
1 ounce Rose's Lime juice
1 ounce Rose's Cranberry Twist mix

LAYER ALL INGREDIENTS in a Tom Collins glass, with ice to fill and a long-stemmed fresh Bing cherry garnish. This dark brew reminiscent of a hopped-up cherry Coke allows you to sip in sinless certainty.

Virtual Virgin Vixen

3 ounces of chilled Dr Pepper or cherry Coke
3 ounces of chilled lemon-lime sparkling bottled
  water
1 ounce black cherry vodka
1 ounce lime vodka
1 ounce Rose's Lime juice
1 ounce Rose's Cranberry Twist mix

LAYER INGREDIENTS AS above. This alcoholic version allows you to look soda-pop innocent but drink like the Devil.

Silver Zombie
Invented in *Silver Zombie*

*We have got one hot little Roomba robot vacuum cleaner
on our hands. Master? I wonder if she does dudes.*
  —Irma, Delilah's alter ego, in *Silver Zombie*

3 ounces chilled Fuze blueberry raspberry bottled
  water
3 ounces chilled lemon-lime sparkling bottled water
  or champagne
1 ounce Jose Cuervo Silver tequila
1½ ounces lime vodka
1 ounce Alizé Bleu with vodka, cognac, and tropical
  fruit

COMBINE ALL INGREDIENTS, then dribble a dash of blue curaçao down the inside of the glass to sink to the bottom. Be careful that *you* don't sink to the bottom in the snare of the real Silver Zombie.

Vampire Sunrise
Invented in *Vampire Sunrise*

"Umm. Subtle yet spicy . . . for modern women like us."
—Psychic psychologist Helena Troy Burnside in *Vampire Sunrise*

  6 ice cubes
  1½ ounces pepper vodka
  ½ ounce DeKuyper Hot Damn! Cinnamon Schnapps
    Liqueur
  4–7 ounces orange juice, well shaken
  1 ounce Alizé Gold Passion orange cognac
  ½ to 1 ounce grenadine

PUT ICE CUBES in 12-ounce highball glass. Pour in pepper vodka and cinnamon schnapps, add orange juice to fill to desired level. Add Alizé. Last, pour in grenadine, which will settle to the bottom. Keep adding ice to this classic brunch eye-opener and daytime drink as it melts . . . for a longer, more sensual experience to the very last drop.

Brimstone Kiss
Invented in *Brimstone Kiss*

"Sounds like something you'd sip on all night long and I'd knock back in a couple slugs."
—Rick Blaine/Humphrey Bogart CinSim in *Brimstone Kiss*

2 jiggers Inferno Pepper Pot vodka
1 jigger DeKuyper "Hot Damn!" Cinnamon
   Schnapps Liqueur
2 jiggers Alizé Red Passion
Jalapeño pepper slice (optional)
2 ounces champagne (for Version 2)

VERSION 1: POUR all ingredients into a martini shaker with ice. Shake gently. Pour into a martini glass garnished with jalapeño pepper slice. A hell of a drink!

VERSION 2: POUR all ingredients into a tall footed glass filled with ice. Stir well. Top off with champagne. A frothy but potent libation that might lead to pleasant damnation.

Albino Vampire
Invented in *Dancing with Werewolves*

"A sweet, seductive girly drink, but with unsuspected kick."
   —Werewolf mob enforcer Sansouci, in *Brimstone Kiss*

1 ounce white crème de cacao
1½ ounces Stolichnaya Stoli Vanil
1 ounce Godiva White Chocolate Liqueur
½ ounce Chambord raspberry liqueur
(Other brands may be substituted)

POUR VODKA AND liqueurs except the raspberry in the order given and stir gently. Drizzle in the raspberry liqueur. Don't mix or stir. The raspberry liqueur will slowly sink to the bottom, so the white cocktail has a bloodred base (for a final taste sensation with bite).